Praise for *Brentwood's*

"Danger, intrigue, and romance in Regency England... wonderfully appealing London lawman and the beautiful, spoiled heiress he is hired to protect. All served up with Michelle Griep's signature wry humor. Don't miss it!"

—Julie Klassen, bestselling, award-winning author

"Place an unpolished lawman as guardian over a spoiled, pompous beauty and what do you get? Clever dialogue, intrigue, and enough sparks to warm you on a cold night. Add to that a murder mystery, smugglers, and kidnappings and you have a story that keeps you riveted to each page, desperate to know the outcome, and enchanted by every word this author exquisitely pens. One of the few books I've truly enjoyed this year!"

—MaryLu Tyndall, award-winning historical author

"Michelle Griep brings Regency Era London to life as she skillfully weaves together drama, mystery, and romance in her new novel, *Brentwood's Ward*. A dashing hero, intent on helping his ailing sister, must protect a strong-willed young heroine, but who will protect their hearts? Readers who enjoyed *A Heart Deceived* will be delighted when they read this new story from this talented author."

—Carrie Turansky, author of The Edwardian Brides series

"Michelle Griep's latest offering, *Brentwood's Ward*, is a fast-paced, edge-of-your-seat type suspense, with a healthy splash of romance thrown in for good measure. Griep's writing style had me holding my breath through the cleverly twisted tale—until the end, when I let it all out with a long, satisfied sigh."

—Elizabeth Ludwig, author of The Edge of Freedom series

"Pitch perfect! Sherlock Holmes meets Charles Dickens in a story so engaging that you won't put it down until the last page."

—Siri Mitchell, author of *Like a Flower in Bloom*

"In *Brentwood's Ward*, Michelle Griep spins a story of danger and intrigue that lurks at every turn of the page. With her witty play on words and masterful shaping of phrases, the book moves beyond ordinary to delightful. A tightly woven story that will keep readers riveted until the very end."

—Jody Hedlund, bestselling author of *The Preacher's Bride*

"If your idea of a top-notch story is fun characters, sparkling prose, witty dialogue, and a suspenseful, romantic plot, then you'll love Michelle Griep's *Brentwood's Ward*. This engrossing tale is truly a treasure and one for the keeper shelf."

—Margaret Brownley, bestselling author of *Gunpowder Tea* and *Petticoat Detective*

"Deliciously witty and fast paced, *Brentwood's Ward* is a lively yet thoughtful romp with a delightful cast of characters, a unique London setting, and enough romantic twists and turns to keep you on the edge of your Regency chair! Encore, Michelle Griep!"

—Laura Frantz, author of *Love's Fortune*

"*Brentwood's Ward* unfolds like the best British costume drama, full of rich detail, wit, and intrigue. Readers will fall in love with Nicholas Brentwood from the first chapter. This Bow Street Runner has all the qualities a hero needs: integrity, intelligence, and independence; and heroine Emily Payne leads him on a merry chase sure to delight Austen and Conan Doyle fans alike."

— Erica Vetsch, author of *The Cactus Creek Challenge* (July 2015)

BRENTWOOD'S WARD

BRENTWOOD'S WARD

MICHELLE GRIEP

SHILOH RUN PRESS
An Imprint of Barbour Publishing, Inc.

Scripture quotations are from The Holy Bible, English Standard Version®, copyright © 2001 by Crossway Bibles, a publishing ministry of Good News Publishers. Used by permission. All rights reserved.

This book is a work of fiction. Names, characters, places, and incidents are either products of the author's imagination or used fictitiously. Any similarity to actual people, organizations, and/or events is purely coincidental.

Cover design: Müllerhaus Publishing Arts, Inc., www.Mullerhaus.net

Published by Shiloh Run Press, an imprint of Barbour Publishing, Inc., P.O. Box 719, Uhrichsville, Ohio 44683, www.shilohrunpress.com

Our mission is to publish and distribute inspirational products offering exceptional value and biblical encouragement to the masses.

ecpa Member of the
Evangelical Christian
Publishers Association

Printed in the United States of America.

This book dedicated to:

my sweet daughter,
Mariah Joy,
thank you for your unvarnished opinions

my sweet friend,
Stephanie Gustafson,
thank you for your encouragement in so many arenas

and as always for my sweet, sweet Savior,
Jesus Christ
thank You for saving my soul

Chapter 1

London, 1807

"You, sir, are a rogue!" Emily Payne scowled into the black marble gaze fixed on hers, determined to win the deadlock of stares. Horrid beast. Must he always triumph?

Without so much as a blink, the pug angled his head. Sunlight from the front door's transom window streamed over her shoulder, highlighting each of his fuzzy wrinkles. The pup's face squinched into a doggy smile, coaxing a sigh from Emily. Who could remain cross with that scrunched-up muzzle?

"I should've named you Scamp instead of Alf, eh boy?" She smiled then laughed outright when he snuck in a quick kiss on her neck.

Beside her, Mary, her maid, joined in—until Mrs. Hunt, equal parts housekeeper and sergeant major, huffed into the entry hall. Emily glanced at the matron over the pup's head. If the Admiralty were smart, they'd press her into service, and the Royal Navy would learn a new meaning for *shipshape* in no time.

"Sorry, miss. The little beastie got clean away from me." Mrs. Hunt reached for the fugitive, the smell of linseed oil and hard work wafting with the billow of her sleeve. "Hand him over, if you please. It won't happen again."

"Hmm. Don't be so sure." Emily nuzzled his furry head with the top of her chin, well aware he ought not be encouraged, yet completely unable to stop herself.

Mary tsked. "He just can't bear to be parted from you, miss, that's all."

"Which is more than I can say for the males of my own species," she mumbled into the pup's fur. Alf nestled against her shoulder. If only Charles Henley might become so attached, the empty void in her heart would be filled at last. After a last snuggle, she held the pug out to Mrs. Hunt.

But Alf wriggled during the transfer. His back paw caught the lace on her glove, tearing the sheer fabric. Frowning, she inspected the damage. "Oh, bother. Mary, would you—"

"I shall." Her maid turned, but a rap on the front door spun her back around. "Right after I answer the—"

Emily shook her head. "I'll do it. You see to the gloves."

She opened the door to the height of fashion. By faith, the only thing Reginald Sedgewick prized more than his garments was his looking glass. "Uncle Reggie!" She smiled. "A bit early in the day for you, is it not?"

He nodded. Nothing more. Perhaps it was indeed too early for his usual cheerful banter. "Is your father home?" His voice crackled at the edges.

"I've not seen him, though that's not unusual. Come in." She stepped aside, and the scent of bay rum entered with him—or was it? One more sniff and her nose wrinkled. There was nothing bay about it. The man reeked of rum.

He doffed his hat, and she called to her maid, who by now was halfway up the stairs. "Oh Mary, would you be a dear and summon my father before you see to my gloves?"

"Aye, miss." Retracing her steps, Mary scurried past them and disappeared down the same corridor Mrs. Hunt had taken earlier.

Emily turned back to Reggie and swept her hand toward the open sitting-room door. "Please have a—"

The words clogged in her throat as she studied him up close. His cravat knot hung loose. Buttons on his waistcoat did not match the proper holes, and no red carnation adorned his lapel. She shifted her eyes to his. "Is something wrong?"

His jaw clenched, and she suspected his fists might have, too. Then strangely enough, the angry wave subsided. "Nothing a good row with your father won't solve, my dear." A ghost of a smile softened the threat, or was that a grimace?

"How very strange. Usually it is I who am at odds with him." She reached for the bellpull on the wall. "Shall I ring for tea?"

"No need. This shan't take long." He paused, turning the hat in his hands around and around. "Hopefully."

A shiver crept across her shoulders. He was not only disheveled but anxious as well? That didn't bode well, not coming from the jolliest fellow she knew.

Behind her, Mary's footsteps clipped onto the marble flooring. "Mr. Payne is unavailable, sir."

Red crept up Reggie's neck and blossomed onto his cheeks. "Unavailable?"

Mary bypassed them both then halted near the balustrade at the base of the stairs. Did she keep such distance from conservation of steps. . .or fear? She studied the floor as she answered, making it impossible to read her face. "Yes, sir. Detained for the rest of the day. I suggest you call back tomorrow, Mr. Sedgewick."

Reggie breathed out an oath then jammed his hat on top of his head so forcefully his valet would need a shoehorn to pry it off come evening. With a curt nod to them both and a ground-out "Good day," he swooped out the front door. A firm thud accentuated his departure.

Emily slid her gaze to Mary, who returned her wide-eyed stare. "That was. . .interesting. I wonder what Father's done to vex Reggie so?" Would it be business related or something to do with the recently widowed Mrs. Nevens? She suspected the latter, for they'd each been vying for the woman's attention.

Mary merely bobbed her head. "I'll see about those gloves, then."

The girl disappeared up the stairs, and a fresh wave of mourning washed over Emily. Instead of tucking tail and running away in the name of duty, her former maid and confidant, Wren, would have listened to her conspiracy theories. Or likely more than that. . .Wren would have added a few of her own ideas to the mix. Emily sighed, frustrated that even a hundred Wren-would-haves wouldn't bring her favorite maid back. Nothing would—except, perhaps, for a miracle.

"Is Reggie gone?" Her father's bass voice rumbled from the corridor. His head peeked out the study door, fuzzy as a downy-haired tot whose nightgown had just been pulled off.

Emily pursed her lips, shedding one glove after the other. "I thought you were unavailable, Father."

"I am." His big belly and stubby legs appeared. "Leastwise as far as Reginald's concerned."

She set the ripped lace onto the calling card salver then looked up at her father's approach, narrowing her eyes. Something was off kilter. He often avoided her, but never his business partner. "Uncle Reggie was quite put out, you know."

"I do know, but it can't be helped."

She opened her mouth to argue with the absurdity of his statement, but before she could speak, Mary descended the last step and held out a set of white gloves. "Here you are, miss."

"Thank you." She reached for the fresh pair, and a keen scowl slashed across her father's face. "What are you frowning at?"

"You are not going out, I hope. In fact, I quite forbid it."

"Don't be silly." She wiggled her fingers into the cool fabric. "Did I not tell you I've an appointment at the milliner's?"

"You own enough bonnets to cover all the heads of Mayfair proper. No, no, I insist you stay home."

"You do?" Her gaze shot to his. For one glorious moment, she imagined playing the part of papa's little girl—finally—even if she was three and twenty. Regardless of the years, her heart leaped in her chest.

Then stilled when he spoke. "I am expecting someone I require you to meet."

Inside her gloves, perspiration dotted the palms of her hands. The last man he'd brought home for her to meet had nearly been her ruination. Never again. She set her jaw. "Father, you can't be serious. This appointment was confirmed ages ago. Besides which, I need one last fitting for my gown, and if I do not attend to it today, it shan't be ready for the Garveys' ball."

"No more about it, Emily. I will be obeyed in this matter. You are not to leave the house this morning." He lifted his chin and peered down his nose. "Am I understood?"

She took the time to straighten each ruffled hem of her sleeves before returning her gaze to his—a stalling tactic she'd learned from the best. Him. "Quite," she answered.

"Good." He wheeled about and disappeared down the hallway.

Disappointment burned at the back of her throat. Would that he might want to spend a day with her instead of foisting her off on one of his business associates. Swallowing the sour taste, she reached for the doorknob. Her entire future depended upon the upcoming ball—a future that did not include one moment more of pining for her father's love.

Mary's eyes widened. "Miss Emily! Your father said—"

"My father said not to leave the house this morning. But, Mary dearest"—she opened the door and winked over her shoulder—"did you know that right now it's afternoon in India?"

Short of breath and lean on time, Nicholas Brentwood sprinted down Bow Street, dodging hawkers and pedestrians. Though patience was one of his assets, it did not make the top ten of the magistrate's virtues. Nearing the station, he splashed through a pool of waste that leaked into the hole of his right boot, but it was not to be helped. He was late.

Darting through the front door of the magistrate's court, he shoved past milling gawkers waiting to be let into the sentencing chamber. With a "Pardon me," he veered right and bounded up the stairway, two treads at a time. Fatigue stung his eyes, anguish his heart. Though he inhaled deeply the smell of oil lamps, ink, and lives hanging in the balance, the stench of disease yet clung to his nostrils.

He bounded down a narrow corridor, shoulders brushing one wall then another in his haste. Through a crack in the magistrate's door, he slid in sideways and breathless.

Sir Richard Ford stood near the window, regarding the streets of London. Weak sunlight filtered through the soot-dusted glass, highlighting the man's shorn head—a head that did not turn when Nicholas entered. Good. Reining in his heaving chest, Nicholas breathed out a thankful prayer that his less-than-decorous arrival had not been noted. Then he straightened the lapel on his dress coat, covering the rip on his vest beneath. "I'm here, sir. Please excuse—"

The man waved his hand in the air, batting away his gnat of an apology.

Galled that he was the offending insect, Nicholas advanced. "If you would allow me to explain—"

"Permission denied." Ford turned from the window. A frown etched lines on either side of his mouth, deep enough to sink any thoughts of rebuttal.

Nicholas widened his stance and squared his shoulders, taut as a sail in the wind. "Yes, sir."

The man's frown deepened. "Sweet peacock, Brentwood, sit down." Ford strode to the overstuffed chair behind a massive cherry-wood desk and lowered his frame. "You make me nervous."

He made the magistrate nervous? The same man who in mere minutes would don a wig as tall as a small child and sentence countless men to their deaths? Nicholas bit back a smirk and sank into the worn leather seat opposite the desk, grateful to set aside running for the moment. "I can only assume, sir, this is about my recent absences. By your leave, I should like to explain."

The old fellow skewered him with a hard stare, one that might divide flesh from bone by sheer will. "I will have no explanations."

Nicholas clenched his jaw. So, this was to be it, then? His career ended now when he needed money most? Not that he didn't deserve it. God knew he warranted much worse than to be dismissed.

But Jenny surely didn't.

Slowly, feeling every year of hard living and lack of sleep, he nodded and rose. "Very well. I understand. It's been my honor to have served—"

"Reseat your back end, Brentwood. You don't understand a thing."

The chair held his weight, his mind a thousand questions. "Sir?"

Ford leaned forward, the desk becoming one with the man. "You think I don't know about your sister? This is an investigative agency I run, with none but the best in my employ. Every officer knows how you care for her, and none fault you for it." He sat back and lifted his chin. "Neither do I."

The tightness in Nicholas's shoulders eased for the first time in months. Though he hated that all knew his business, it was a relief to be able to stop hiding the burden—a trail he'd done everything in his power to conceal. But apparently not enough. He pierced Ford with one of his own pointed looks. "Did you have me followed?"

"Didn't have to. A certain doctor came here, inquiring after you. Seems the fellow doesn't trust you'll be good for his wages." One of the magistrate's brows rose, a perfect arc on such an austere canvas. "Imagine that."

A smile begged for release, but Nicholas refused the vagrant urge. Not yet. The magistrate didn't often keep a courtroom full of brigands waiting. Something else was brewing. "If this doesn't concern my sister, then why the summons? I don't suppose you're holding up court for tea and crumpets with me."

"I've a task in mind for you, Brentwood." Ford propped his elbows on each arm of the chair, angling his head to the right. One of his favorite bargaining positions. The man eyed him as he might a piece of horseflesh to be bought. "A task that must be tended to immediately, and I'm certain you're the perfect officer for the job. In fact, I will consider no one else."

Unease tickled the nape of his neck, and Nicholas rubbed at the offending sensation. Ford was generally spare with his praise. Why now?

"I appreciate your confidence," he said.

"Bah." The magistrate sniffed. "I'm certain you're the man because you're the one with the greatest need for funding. Am I correct?"

Nicholas shifted in his seat. Exactly how much did his superior know? "Go on."

Ford laced his fingers and placed them on the desktop. "A gentleman of some means approached me with the business of procuring a guardian for his daughter. He's willing to pay a tidy sum to see her well cared for."

Scrubbing a hand over his chin, Nicholas chewed on that information as he might a gummy bit of porridge. Either the man was a reprobate too intent on pleasure to see to his own offspring, or the girl was a hellish handful. A frown pulled at his lips. "Why does he not look after her himself?"

"He sails for the continent on the morrow."

Nicholas snorted. "Seems he ought to have obtained a guardian long before this."

"Yes. . .well. . ." Ford cleared his throat and averted his gaze. "The point is the man is willing to pay a large sum to safeguard his only child, and it's my understanding you could use that money. Yes?"

He tugged at his collar. A marmot in a snare couldn't have felt more trapped. "I think that's already been established."

"Very well." Sliding open a top drawer, Ford produced a folded bit of parchment. "The gentleman, Mr. Alistair Payne, will fill you in on the particulars of the agreement. Officer Moore's got the streets covered and Captain Thatcher the roads, so I shall excuse you from your regular duties until this assignment is complete."

Stabbing the paper with his finger, Ford skimmed it across the desktop toward him. "Here's the address and the agreed upon amount."

Nicholas unfolded the crisp paper. He blinked, then blinked again. Granted, the ink watered into gray at the edges, but even so, a figure stood out sharply against the creamy background. Two hundred fifty pounds—enough to send Jenny to the blessed moon should a cure be available there. He locked stares with Ford. "This is no jest?"

"Really, Brentwood, how often do you see me smile?" His lips didn't so much as twitch. The only movement in the entire room was the pendulum ticking away in the corner clock—that and the rush of blood pulsing in Nicholas's ears.

"Well?" Ford broke the silence. "What do you say?"

The only thing he could. "Yes." He folded the parchment and tucked it into his breast pocket.

"Excellent." Ford pushed back from his desk and stood. "Now if you'll excuse me, I've a few cases to hear."

As the magistrate stalked out the door, Nicholas ignored decorum and sat frozen, too stunned to follow. Amazing, that's what. Did God seriously delight in dropping the jaw of a man such as himself? He rose and glanced at the cracked plaster ceiling, whispering a prayer. "Thank You, Lord. Your bounty never ceases to amaze me."

He crossed the room and stepped into the hallway, hope speeding his steps—and landing him square into the path of a steel-bodied man.

"You're in an awful hurry, Brentwood." A dark gaze bore into his. Though clear of anger, a fearsome enough stare.

"Sorry, Thatcher." Nicholas sidestepped one way, Thatcher the other, an odd sort of dance in the narrow corridor. "On my way to a new assignment. Didn't expect to see you here."

"Surprise to me as well." Samuel Thatcher straightened his riding cloak and planted himself in front of the magistrate's door. "I was summoned for an early meeting with Ford. So early, I neglected to bring up my own inquiries. He still in there?"

Nicholas shook his head. "Not anymore."

"Right." Thatcher blew out a long breath. "Suppose I'll head out, then."

The big man turned the opposite direction, but two steps later, pivoted. "Hold on, Brentwood. New assignment, you say?"

Nicholas nodded. "Guardian position. Ought not be. . .what? Why the grin?"

A smile the size of Parliament slid across Thatcher's face. He backed away, hands up. "Good luck with that one. You'll need it."

Nicholas growled. "What did Ford not tell me?"

Thatcher's grin morphed into a low-throated laugh. He turned and stomped off. "You're just the fellow for the job, Brentwood."

"As are you to haunt the hollows on a horse. That's it, run off like the coward you are." His words didn't stop the man from retreating nor douse the remains of his laughter.

Nicholas wheeled about and strode the other direction. Thatcher was batty, that's what, likely from too much time spent on the byways wrestling with highwaymen. The man probably envied the soft position he'd just landed, holing up in a fine town house, watching over some proper little heiress. For all he knew, she might have a nurse or a governess, and all he'd have to do was recline in the man's study, smoke cheroots, and read the *Times*.

Descending the stairs, he grinned in full at his fortune and entered the foyer. His bootsteps echoed in the wide lobby, empty now that court was in session. He reached for the doorknob then jerked back when it opened of its own accord.

"Ahh, Brentwood." A barrel-chested man entered, not as large as Thatcher but every bit as powerful. All Ford's chosen men were built like bulwarks.

Nicholas nodded a greeting. "Moore. How goes it?"

"Not bad. On my way to testify." Alexander Moore swept past him, shedding his hat and brushing back his wild mane of blond hair. Nearing the courtroom, he called over his shoulder: "And by the smile on your face, I assume you escaped that horrendous assignment ol' Ford was trying to pawn off."

The door slapped shut behind Moore, as soundly as the jaws of Ford's trap snapped down on Nicholas. Replaying the entire interview in his head, the magistrate's throat clearing and his darting gaze stood out as the single tip-off. Apparently the gentleman, Mr. Alistair Payne, had tried to arrange for a guardian long before he set sail, a position both Moore and Thatcher had declined. Nicholas frowned. Ford hadn't chosen him for any special reason other than he was the last resort.

Stepping out into the rank offense of Bow Street, Nicholas flipped up his collar against the chill and cast off any misgivings. After tracking down murderers, gamblers, and whoremongers, how hard could guarding an heiress be?

Chapter 2

Before entering 22 Portman Square, Nicholas stood dangerously close to the carriage ruts in the road and glanced up, studying the place. So many windows would be a problem, as would the servants' entrance below street level to the left of the front door. The roof, three stories up, sat below the neighboring town house—an easy leap down for an intruder bent on topside access. No wonder Mr. Payne felt ill at ease leaving a young daughter home alone in such a burglar's playground.

In four strides, he reached the door, lifted the brass knocker, and rapped. Moments later, the door opened to a flint-faced housekeeper who he might've served next to in the Sixth Regiment of the Black Dragoons. Odd that for such a fancy house, neither butler nor footman answered his call.

Nicholas offered his card. "I'm here to see Mr. Payne."

She didn't just take the thing—she held it up to within inches of her eyes and read the sparse bit of letters as if he'd petitioned to view the crown jewels. "So you're Mr. Brentwood, are ye? What business do you have with Mr. Payne?"

With a doorkeeper such as this, mayhap guarding the place wouldn't be as difficult as he first imagined. "I believe, madam, that if you don't already know, then maybe you ought not."

Her eyes shot to his, gunmetal gray and sparking. "A simple 'imports or exports' would have sufficed. Come in."

She stepped aside, allowing him to pass, then cut him off before he could advance any farther. "Wait here, if you please."

Removing his hat, he studied the grand foyer. Flocked paper lined the walls, graced with enough wall lamps and an overhanging chandelier that the light would likely give him a headache come evening. To his right, a carpeted stairway led upward. At its base, three paces past and to the left, a single door. Closed. Opposite, french doors opened to a sitting room before the rest of the home disappeared down a corridor. It smelled of wealth and lemon wax—

And a faint scent of linseed oil as the housekeeper reappeared from the hallway. "This way, Mr. Brentwood."

He followed her swishing skirt as she retreated once more down the corridor. Stopping in front of the next closed door, she knocked, and a "Just let the man in, Mrs. Hunt," bellowed from behind.

Twisting the knob, she nodded at him. "If you please."

Out of habit, Nicholas scanned the room. Two floor-to-ceiling windows and a large hearth, besides the threshold he'd just crossed, presented four possible points of access. Four. In one room. This could prove a very tedious assignment.

"Mr. Brentwood."

The first thing he noticed at Mr. Payne's approach was the fellow's round belly. Apparently Portman House employed a good cook. At least the eating part of this assignment would be agreeable. His gaze traveled upward then stopped, fixated on Payne's amazingly horrible teeth—chompers any beaver would give a hind leg to own. Nicholas squinted. Were the front two really that big or the rest abnormally small? A man of his standing surely could afford to have them pulled and replaced with porcelain replicas. Or at the very least, could he not have the rascals sanded down and even them out a bit?

Before he breached protocol any further, Nicholas forced his gaze higher and held out his hand. "Mr. Payne."

The fellow clasped his fingers in a firm grip followed by a squeeze. Confident and over so. Quite the contradiction to the man's appearance, for the structure of the rest of his face made him look perpetually surprised. Fuzzy hair, thankfully short and sparse, stood on end, as if he'd just taken a great fright. Dark eyes, brown as dried tobacco, sat below wiry white eyebrows, high set and arched—apparently their normal repose. This man surely made children laugh, perhaps even his daughter.

"Have a seat. I understand you're one of Ford's men, eh?" The freakish teeth punctuated his words.

"I am." Nicholas eyed the furniture to keep from staring. Anchored on an overlarge Persian rug, two library chairs faced a glossy desk. Interesting, though, that no inkwells or papers, ledgers or registers favored the topside. It was bare. Completely. What kind of businessman was this Mr. Payne?

The man sank into a seat behind the desk, cushions whooshing a complaint beneath his weight. "Please excuse the somewhat unconventional greeting at the door. I've given my butler a temporary leave. I hope you weren't too put out by Mrs. Hunt. She can be a bit brash at times."

Nicholas met the fellow's even gaze. "Perhaps you ought to offer her the guardian position."

"I said she's brash, sir, not wily."

After his short encounter with the woman, Nicholas was not convinced. That mobcap hid more than aggression. He tipped his head. "I was not aware that cunning was one of the qualities you desired."

"Yet you are, Brentwood. Cunning, that is. Or you would not be employed as one of Bow Street's finest." Mr. Payne sat back and lifted his chin. "Am I not right?"

Nicholas said nothing.

"Very well, man. I can see you'd like to get down to business. My daughter, Miss Emily, is. . ." His eyes followed his brows upward, and he studied the ceiling as if a description of the girl might be found near the rafters. Silence stretched, revealing more than a score of words could accomplish.

A father speechless about his daughter did not bode well.

After excessive throat clearing, Mr. Payne finally spoke: "Let's just say Emily knows her own mind, or at least she thinks she does.

BRENTWOOD'S WARD

Because of this, I charge you with the oversight of her at all times until I return."

"Which will be?" The thought of safekeeping a prideful girl for days on end—one who may have a beaver bite like her father—sounded as diverting as the time he'd lugged ol' Nat Waggins, escape artist extraordinaire, from York down to Tyburn.

"I expect to be gone a month, give or take and naturally weather permitting, at which point I shall award you 250 pounds. It's very straightforward, Mr. Brentwood. Keep my daughter safe, and the money is yours." Payne leaned sideways and slid open a drawer, procuring a carved wooden box with brass hinges. From his waistcoat pocket, he fished out a tiny key. "Though I suppose you should like an advance, eh?"

"May I ask a few questions?" Not that he'd turn down the payment. Jenny's life hung in the balance without it—and perhaps even with it.

Mr. Payne set the key in the box's lock. A click later, he lifted the lid. "Of course."

Nicholas drew in a breath, girding up for a salvo technique he'd mastered long ago. "I gather you are a merchant, hence the travel, and the import/export mentioned by your housekeeper."

"I am."

"Should the need arise, how do I reach you?"

"You don't."

"Then are there other relations I may contact?"

"None."

"Yet you fear for Miss Payne's safety."

"I do."

"Why?"

That stopped the man but only for the briefest of moments. A pause easily missed, one Nicholas had learned to listen for in the voices of swindlers and cons.

Payne scowled, the effect lightened by the ridiculous teeth

23

peeking through his lips. "You can imagine, Brentwood, that a man in my position garners many enemies. Blood-sucking enemies, no less. Emily is my only heir, hence my one vulnerability."

"What exactly is your position, Mr. Payne?"

The man slammed the box's lid shut with one hand and held out a banknote with the other. "Commerce, Brentwood. The world's wheels turn on the hub of commerce, of which I am the center, leastwise in the shipping industry. Now then, here is your advance."

Nicholas leaned forward and pinched the paper between thumb and forefinger, expecting the man's grip to lessen.

It tightened. "One more thing. There's been a slight change of plans. I expect you to set up quarters here. Now. My ship sails by day's end."

A nerve on the side of his neck jumped. He'd have no time to dash over to the Crown and Horn to let Jenny know of his whereabouts. If she should need him, no one would know where to find him. . . unless he paid a courier to deliver a message. He lifted his gaze to meet Payne's. "Then a change in remuneration should be in order as well, I think."

The man frowned, yet the banknote loosened. He pocketed the sum as Payne withdrew another note.

"Very shrewd, Brentwood. I see why Ford's runners have earned such a reputation."

Runner? Heat burned a trail up Nicholas's spine and lodged at the base of his skull. The man might as well have questioned his parentage. He snatched the added check from the man's pudgy fingers then rose and skewered him with a glance. "I shall give you the benefit of the doubt this time, Mr. Payne, for perhaps you are not aware that *runner* is a derogatory term. One I don't take kindly to being associated with. I am, in your own words, one of Bow Street's finest, not an errand boy or Ford's lackey; I am a detective, sir, an investigator. A sleuth. The kind of man who will stop at nothing to hunt down a criminal and bring him to justice at the end of a rope. Now you are educated. See that it doesn't happen again."

"Well. . .I. . ." Payne's Adam's apple bobbed up and down, his brows ending where his white hairline began. "Of course." He busied himself by tucking away the box then stepped to a velvet cord on the wall and tugged it.

Pocketing the rest of the payment, Nicholas allowed his blood to cool. It'd been a hard battle to become a man of integrity, a fight he'd not see belittled by donning a pejorative title.

"Aye, sir?" The housekeeper's head peeked through the door.

"Summon Miss Emily straightaway, Mrs. Hunt." Payne resumed his seat behind the desk.

Nicholas preferred to remain standing and meet the little heiress with the advantage of height.

"I am sorry, but she is gone out with Miss Mary. Will that be all, sir?"

Color started rising slowly, like mercury up a thermometer, slipping over Payne's ears, diffusing across his cheeks, then inching up his nose. Judging by the rapid spread, his head might pop at any moment—and those teeth would be deadly projectiles. Nicholas retreated a step.

"The devil you say! I specifically forbade her!" Payne sputtered an oath. "Never mind, Mrs. Hunt. That will be all."

As soon as the door shut, Payne retrieved his safe box yet again. He removed a fistful of assorted notes and held them out. "Take it, Brentwood."

Nicholas narrowed his eyes. "You've provided a sufficient advance. What is this for?"

A muscle jumped near the hinge of Payne's jaw before he ground out, "Hazard pay, for indeed, Emily is hazardous on more levels than one."

Emily's shadow arrived at the townhome before she did. Mary's lagged behind, shorter and wider. As her maid caught up, hatboxes draped on each arm like Christmas ornaments, Emily stepped aside and lowered her voice. "Now don't forget—"

"I won't." Mary nodded toward the door, bonnet askew. "Would you mind?"

Emily reached for the knob, grateful that Mrs. Hunt ran a well-oiled household. "Good luck," she whispered as Mary passed then took care to shut the door behind her.

One-one-thousand. Two-one-thousand. Mary ought to have made it to the base of the stairs by now. Three-one-thousand, four. Should have ascended at least a few treads. Five-one-thousand, six and seven-one-thousand. . .

Emily pressed her ear to the cool mahogany, shutting out the *clip-clop*s and grinding wheels of a passing carriage. Eight-one-thousand, nine. She held her breath. *Wait for it. Wait for—*

Mary's shriek, while a bit over the top, trilled from within. The *thumpity-thumps* of dropped boxes were a nice touch. The girl was starting to grow on her, though she'd never replace the spot in Emily's heart for her former maid, Wren. Nevertheless, a smile lifted the corners of her mouth.

And a deep moan leaching through the door wiped it away.

Muffled footsteps pounded across the foyer tiles. Voices, not words, filtered through the wood, but their emotion came through clear enough. Worry. Pain. Fear? La, it sounded as if the entire household congregated just beyond the threshold. She'd never be able to sneak in undetected now.

Slowly she withdrew her ear from the door then turned and leaned against it. What had gone wrong? Ignoring the fading light and passing coaches, she bit the inside of her lower lip and mulled over her plan. All Mary need do was create a diversion by pretending to have seen a mouse. A squeal, perhaps a feigned swoon, something to get the servants—and her father—to set their mind on something other than her late arrival, and she'd slip in unnoticed.

Now that would be impossible.

A gust of wind swooped beneath her bonnet and snagged loose a piece of hair. She flattened her lips and tucked up the stray. Standing on the stoop all evening wasn't an option, and with twilight's growing chill, tarrying much longer wouldn't be pleasant, either.

Emily folded her arms, calculating her next move as she might in a hand of whist. She could waltz in, pretending as if nothing had happened, that she'd not technically disobeyed her father. . .but that wouldn't stop his censure. Mayhap she might play on everyone's sympathy and develop a cough. No, that would only add further restrictions to her comings and goings. Plus she'd have to remember to cough frequently. That wouldn't do at all. Perhaps she ought—

The door flew open. She plunged backward, mimicking Mary's earlier shriek. Strong hands righted her before she bruised her backside and her dignity.

Regaining her balance, she drew in a breath and turned. "I swear I can explain, Father—"

A man, decades younger than her father, studied her with an intense pair of green eyes—eyes that sifted and weighed the content of her heart and soul in one glance. Desire to run and hide from his curious inspection welled in her stomach—and the reaction annoyed her.

She lifted her chin and returned the stranger's stare. A shadow lined his jaw. He'd not taken the time to shave, yet the look favored his rugged style. Dark hair breached his collar's edge, wild and wavy, not quite long enough to pull into a queue. A good pomade would tame it, but she suspected the man would not give in to such folderol, considering the stark cut of his dress coat and plain-colored vest beneath.

He might have stepped off one of her father's merchantmen, but he didn't smell of the sea. . .more like spent gunpowder and boot blacking. She wrinkled her nose. Who was this wild man?

"I should like to hear that explanation, miss, if you please." His arm stretched toward the sitting-room door.

She frowned. Who did this fellow think he was? Hoping to spy Mrs. Hunt or Mary—or at this point, even her father—she rose to her toes, the only way to see past his tall stature and broad shoulders. A single housemaid, Betsy, was all that remained on the stairwell, collecting the last of the hatboxes.

Lowering her heels to the floor, Emily squared her shoulders. "You presume a great deal, sir. I do not answer to you."

"Ahh, exactly what I wish to discuss. Shall we?" He nodded at the open sitting-room doorway.

Emily sucked in a breath. The man was more pompous, and likely as dangerous, as the scoundrel of a captain who'd ruined Wren— and nearly herself—late last summer. She straightened further, posture adding confidence. "I don't know who you think you are Mr.—"

"Brentwood."

"Brentwood." She spit out the name as if it were an olive pit. "This is *my* home. I am no servant to be ordered about within these walls, nor anywhere else for that matter. I owe you no accounting of my personal activities. Furthermore, you may collect your hat and coat, and see yourself out the way you came in."

"Miss Payne"—the man leaned close, his voice intimate and low—"do you really want to have this conversation in the foyer?"

Her eyes followed the slight tip of his head. Gathered atop the stairway landing, Fanny, a lower housemaid with an armful of linens, had joined Betsy, each trying hard not to appear as if they weren't devouring her every word. Had she truly been talking that loud?

She swallowed, her scratchy throat testifying against her. She'd have to concede, or her business would be all the talk of belowstairs.

Still, the smug tilt of Brentwood's jaw was not to be borne. What to do?

Straightening her skirt, she matched his arrogant stance. "Very well, Mr. Brentwood. I shall inquire of you in the sitting room."

Amusement flashed in his eyes. Or was that irritation? Not that she cared, and it piqued her that she'd noticed in the first place. She whirled and strode into the room, the last of day's light blending colors into a monotone. Why had Mrs. Hunt not yet lit the lamps? Where was the woman?

Behind her, boot heels thumped against wood then muted in timbre once Brentwood's feet met the rug. Emily refused to turn. Instead, she peeled off one glove then the other, and laid them on the settee's arm. Tugging loose the bow beneath her chin, she slowly lifted her bonnet and set that aside as well. Behind her, a sigh competed with the ticking of the floor clock, and her mouth curved into a smile. Good. The man, whoever he was, could wait upon her.

"Are you quite finished?"

She cast him a glance over her shoulder. "Momentarily."

"While I've no pressing engagement requiring my attendance," his voice rumbled from behind, "I should not like to spend the entire evening in the sitting room, staring at your back. In short, Miss Payne, your stalling tactics do not amuse."

She spun, the swoosh of her skirts matching the rush of blood through her ears. "How dare you—"

He held up a hand. "I understand your apprehension. It is not so much daring on my part as it is obligation, for currently I am under your father's employ. Had you obeyed the man in the first place, as a dutiful daughter should, this scene would have been avoided."

The sitting-room's shadows suited her mood, dark and growing blacker. "You, sir, are quick to judge. Moreover—"

"Allow me to finish." Challenge thickened his tone, and his words smacked of authority.

MICHELLE GRIEP

When he took a step toward her, she shrank, fear more than compliance dissolving the rebuttal in her throat.

He widened his stance, planting himself but three paces from her. "Your father has recently sailed for business and made you my ward in his absence. You will find me to be fair but firm, and with little patience for antics. Speaking of which, I will have that explanation now for your absence and the subsequent spraining of your abigail's ankle."

Emotions riffled through her faster than she could identify. Her father gone, without so much as a by-your-leave? Not that it surprised her, but did he honestly care that little? Leaving her as the charge of the big man in front of her, a complete stranger? Questions rose like weeds after a spring rain, but only one surfaced. "Mary's hurt?"

He folded his arms. "Is it any wonder? You sent the poor girl up a flight of stairs carrying more boxes than a pack mule."

A slow burn rose from her stomach to her heart. She didn't often own up to remorse—and now she knew why.

She didn't like it.

His green gaze pinned her in place. "Where you went today concerns me less than why. Why would you directly defy your father's wishes?"

"I had an appointment." Her voice sounded small, even in her own ears.

He frowned. "You also had specific instruction from your father to stay home."

"Only for the morning." The petulant quiver in her voice shamed her, and she drew in a breath to mask it.

Twilight's shadows darkened the man's—Brentwood's—face. Or was it her imagination?

"Do you deny you left the house before noon?" His voice boomed.

She threw out her hands, hating the way he exposed her, and worse. . .the sudden desire ripping through her to hide beneath the settee. "How do you know all this?"

30

A rogue grin flashed on his face. "Part of my job."

Blowing out a long breath, she considered an entirely new ploy. Truth. "If you must know, Mr. Brentwood, my father sometimes makes unreasonable requests. I'd scheduled the milliner's appointment long ago—at a most exclusive shop I might add—and I wasn't about to miss it for one of his whims."

"His *whim*, as you put it, Miss Payne, was to be able to say good-bye to his only daughter. He'll be gone nigh on a month, perhaps longer. Was that too much to ask?"

She turned from him, glad now that no lamps had been lit, for he'd surely see the tears burning in her eyes. Her father had wanted to say good-bye to her, after all, and she'd missed it. *Oh God, forgive me.*

"And your abigail, Mary. . . Why did you hide yourself outside the front door and send the girl in to meet with injury?"

His question stabbed a hole in her repentance. She whirled back. "I did no such thing!"

The flinty set of his jaw, the steel in his posture left no room for argument. His gaze heaped coals upon her head.

Once more, he was right. She hadn't felt so afflicted since the mumps. "I didn't mean for her to be hurt. Truly. I merely. . . Wait a minute."

Indignation doused the fire in her belly, and she lifted her face to his. "How would you know I waited outside the front door?"

Instead of answering, he stepped toward her. She sucked in a breath as he neared then slowly let it out when he strode past. Her eyes followed his broad back as he crossed the room and halted at the front window. With a tip of his head, he raised both brows at her.

Narrowing her eyes, she followed his lead and peered out the glass—then swallowed. Why had she never noticed this window gave such a clear view to the front stoop?

She drew back, and when he turned to face her, the air suddenly charged.

"I believe you sent the girl in, instructing her to create a diversion as you waited. In the aftermath, you planned to slip in unnoticed. Am I correct?"

She pressed her lips tight, hiding their trembling, and took sudden interest in the baseboards. Better that than face the all-knowing man scowling at her.

But that didn't stop his lecture. "Servant or not, you owe the girl an apology. Furthermore, while you are in my charge, you will refrain from such devilry. Your father may overlook your schemes, but I assure you, I will not. I am a lawman, Miss Payne. I'll as soon shackle your wrists or lock you up, if that's the way you want to play the game."

She jerked her face up to his. Such arrogance was not to be borne. "We'll just see about that, Mr. Brentwood."

"That we shall, Miss Payne." He angled his jaw. "And so the game begins."

Chapter 3

Sunlight slanted through the sheer window coverings in the dining room, high enough in the sky to reveal that the morning was well spent. Retrieving his pocket watch, Nicholas flipped open the lid, more to rub his thumb over the sketched miniature inside than to confirm the time. *Oh, Adelina.* His gut tensed. His shoulders. His soul. The old familiar ache, one usually stored in a cellar of his heart, rose like a specter—

Until he snapped the lid shut and shoved the watch back into his pocket, banishing memories as if they were lepers. He glanced one more time at the open door. If Miss Emily Payne hadn't shown for breakfast by now, she likely wasn't coming. Not that it surprised him. After yesterday's threat of locking her up, she'd dived into her chamber and never resurfaced. He drained the rest of his coffee, now cold as death, and reset the cup to saucer, then stood—

Just as the woman glided into the room. "Good morning, Mr. Brentwood."

His breathing hitched for the briefest of moments, increasing his frustration. Such a base reaction, however, was not to be helped. Entire battles had been waged and won for lesser beauties than this woman. For truly, Emily Payne was a beauty. Her blond hair was caught up into a pearl coronet, curls thick enough that once loosened would likely fall to her waist. A heart-shaped face framed eyes brown as drinking chocolate, set above lips that would no doubt taste as sweet. Her white day dress, high-waisted and trimmed in pale blue ribbons, clung to the curves that had stolen his breath in the first place. The woman was deadly—on more levels than he'd care to descend.

Donning a face that had won him many a round of faro, Nicholas pulled out a chair for her. "Good morning, Miss Payne, but barely so. Should you have dallied any longer, a good afternoon would be in order, I think."

She tipped her head, studying him, yet took the offered seat, the sweet scent of lily of the valley traveling in her wake. As he settled her chair nearer the table, she glanced up over her shoulder. "Are you always this growly, Mr. Brentwood?"

"No." He sank into the seat adjacent hers. "Your fair presence tends to magnify my starker qualities."

She removed the linen napkin near her plate and shook it out, the snap of the fabric harsh to the ear. A frown shadowed her lips. "Is that a compliment, sir, or a threat?"

Rubbing the back of his neck, he sighed. "Admittedly, Miss Payne, we've gotten off on the wrong foot. I am not the cad you perceive me, and I doubt my first impressions of you are correct, either. I suggest we call a truce and start over."

A slow smile spread, erasing her frown. Dimples appeared on each side of her mouth, indents he'd not noticed in the spare light of last evening. "Very well. . . Good morning, Mr. Brentwood. I am pleased to make your acquaintance."

"Good morning, Miss Payne." He winked. "The pleasure is mine."

Her dimples deepened. "Apparently your charm is every bit as intense as your—"

Claws scrambling across wooden flooring, accompanied by wheezy grunts, echoed in the hallway then burst into the dining room. A fat pug strained at one end of a studded leash, a red-cheeked maid at the other.

"S–sorry, miss! Excuse me, s–sir!"

The maid stuttered—a small flaw but one Nicholas habitually tucked away in his memory for future reference.

The dog yanked the woman to the table, and she bobbed her head at Emily. "Your Alf here will have none of m–me. I d–didn't know what to—"

"You did the right thing, Betsy." Emily bent and unhooked the pup's leash then scooped him up to her lap. "I'll see to my boy."

As Emily nuzzled her chin to the top of the pug's head, Nicholas would swear in front of a grand jury that the dog smirked at the maid.

"Thank you, miss." Betsy dipped a curtsy before retreating.

The dog craned his smug little muzzle toward him, wearing a mien as haughty as his owner's. Nicholas slid his gaze from the pug to Emily. "May I assume the bundle of fur belongs to you?"

"You may." She held the fat pup aloft. "This is Little Lord Alfred the Terror, commonly known as Alf, or Alfie if you feel so inclined."

Her face softened as she rubbed her cheek against the pug's chubby side. Free of guile and without defense flashing in her eyes, Miss Emily Payne quite stole his breath. No wonder her father had reservations about leaving her unattended.

"Pleased to meet you." He spoke to the dog without pulling his gaze from her face.

His voice rang husky in his own ear, nor did she miss the tone, for her eyes widened as she lowered the pug.

Clearing his throat, he gave himself a mental flogging. The woman was entirely too treacherous. "How is your abigail's ankle this morning?"

She settled the dog in her lap, white teeth nibbling her lower lip—and remained silent.

Which was more indicting than a thousand excuses. He'd witnessed the same discomfited silence time and again from the most hardened of criminals. Nicholas cocked his head, knowing the effect to be hawkish. "So, I gather you were remiss on the apology and have not even checked on her as of yet. I suggest this be your first order of business for the day. Other than that, what are your plans? Any pressing appointments of which I should be aware?"

Her nose edged higher in the air as she bypassed the cold toast rack and reached for a biscuit. "None today, but tomorrow I should like to wear one of my new hats when I call upon Lady Westby. She's asked a select few to her home to view her fan collection."

Lest Alf land on the floor, Nicholas passed the jam dish to within Emily's reach. "Well, then, I shall be happy to escort you."

Her biscuit hovered midair, the crystal jam bowl ignored. "Oh no, I really don't think—"

"Your father is paying me very well to attend you, and I never shirk a duty." He leaned back in his seat and folded his arms, enjoying the way her lower lip shot out. "Not to worry, though. I have a way of blending in with the woodwork."

Without a bite, Emily set down her biscuit and met his gaze dead-on. "Am I to understand, sir, that you intend to be stuck to me like a growth?"

Nicholas smiled. He'd been called many things in his day, but this was new. "An amusing way of putting it, but yes."

"There's nothing amusing about the situation, Mr. Brentwood. You can't be serious."

Lifting his chin, he fixed her with a stare. Sometimes silence and one's own thoughts emphasized his position more than a whack over the head with his tipstaff.

"No." She shook her head. "I won't have it. I won't. There is no possible way you fit into my plans. The season is just beginning, and I can't be seen with you at my side. You'll ruin my chances of—"

Her lips straightened to a thin line.

Nicholas leaned forward. "Chances of what?"

She averted her gaze, taking sudden interest in the silver coffee urn at the opposite end of the table.

Apparently he was on to something. "Come now, Miss Payne, I've been direct with you. I expect the same in return. . .unless there's not as much courage beneath that beautiful face as I give you credit for."

She snapped her gaze back to his. So, the little vixen owned a pride as large as her father's wallet.

"I hardly expect you'd understand." Nudging Alf's head up with her forearm, she stroked the sweet spot between his ears. The dog's tongue lolled out in a canine smile. She caressed the animal as if he were the only lover she'd ever—

"Ahh. . ." Nicholas nodded. Of course. He should have known. "Allow me to hazard a guess. You're what. . .two and twenty? Three, perhaps? At any rate, of prime age and social status to shop around for a suitable mate at the marriage mart, eh? I suspect your grand design for this season is to snare a husband. You feel my presence might hinder your efforts." His grin broadened. "And by the way your fair cheeks have turned quite a pretty shade of red, I assume I am correct. Yes?"

Her blush turned murderous. "You are very direct, Mr. Brentwood."

"And entirely accurate?"

Sunshine backlit the bits of her hair not woven in as tightly, creating a golden halo—but the scowl she directed at him was less than heavenly. "Whether I own up to your absurd imaginings is hardly the point." She snipped her words, sharp as scissor blades. "The fact is you, sir, are hardly attired properly to be my escort."

Clothing? This wasn't about marriage but garments? Holding up his sleeves, Nicholas checked each elbow. No rips or tears, and he'd taken great pains to cover the hole in his vest by creasing his lapel just so. His pants, recently purchased and tailored after ruining a pair hunting down old Slim Gant, were too new to even be raveled at the hem. Moving on to inspect his dress coat, he detected only a few frayed threads. Not bad, and indeed far dandier than he'd expected. How could the woman possibly object to his attire when her own was likely plagued with dog hair?

He shrugged. "I surrender. What is wrong with my clothes?"

"They are severe, Mr. Brentwood. Too severe. While quite the match for your personality, if you plan on shadowing me to every function"—her upper lip curled, the same look from eating too much horseradish—"then I insist you invest in more stylish garments."

Though he hated spending money on himself with Jenny so in need, the flare of Emily's nostrils and sharp set of her jaw left no room for debate. Leastwise a debate that wouldn't draw blood. He shifted in his chair, the hard wood of the arm bumping into an ill-healed scar at the base of his ribs—a tangible reminder to choose his battles wisely. "I suppose I could do with a new dress coat, maybe a vest or two. You'll stay put if I go out?"

Alf's fur ruffled with her sigh. She lifted both arms toward Nicholas, jostling the pup, and held out her hands, wrist to wrist. "Bring out your fetters if you wish, though I doubt that is what my father had in mind when he hired you."

Nicholas smiled in full. "Shackles will not suit your fine skin, Miss Payne. Your word will do."

Her hands lowered, but her brows shot up. "My word? Really?"

That she thought him an ogre was not a surprise. That it pricked like a knifepoint did. He softened his tone. "Think of it as a child's game of blocks. You're building trust with me, and I with you. By keeping your word today, you'll lay a foundation upon which to build. Cast the block aside, and I'm not likely to hand you any more until your father returns. The choice, Miss Payne, is yours."

She narrowed her eyes. "Is that not a risk?"

"Yes, considering what I know of you."

A pretty pout twisted her lips. The flash in her eyes was even more beguiling. "You are harsh, Mr. Brentwood."

He curled his hands around the chair arms and stood. Better to gain distance than to reach out and smooth away her sulky frown. "I prefer to think of myself as honest, Miss Payne. A trait you may one day come to value, and one I expect from you in return. Are you up to the challenge?"

Alf snorted at the same time as his mistress. "I never shrink from a challenge, sir."

"No, I suppose you don't." And neither did he. As he bid her leave, though, the real question hammering in his temples was exactly how big of a challenge Miss Emily Payne would be.

Glancing down at Alf, whose squat little body stood at attention at her feet, Emily tried to mimic his compassionate gaze. Why she felt compelled to go through with checking on her maid irked her more than the act itself. Still, it would be satisfying to swipe the superior look off Mr. Brentwood's face next time he asked after her abigail. And honestly, it was her fault Mary lay abed. Before she changed her mind, she lifted her hand and rapped her knuckles on the door adjoining her chamber. "Mary?"

"Come in, miss."

The muted words didn't sound stilted, which would have made this task all the more difficult. Good. Truth be told, she never would have made such a fuss over apologizing to Mary had her horrid guardian not prompted it. Guardian, bah! The thought of the man curdled the tea in her stomach, especially because—though she'd never concede it aloud—she knew his suggestion was the right thing to do.

Emily pushed open the door, Alf tagging at her heels, then stopped short. Across the small chamber, Mary sat in bed, propped atop her counterpane, needlework in her hands. Swaths of linen covered an ankle the size of a small cabbage, so unnaturally fascinating, Emily could not pull her eyes from the sight. The longer she stared, the more grotesque it became. Comfrey and mugwort lay heavy in the air, the words on Emily's tongue even thicker. "Oh, Mary! I am so sorry—"

"La, miss. Think nothing of it." A smile as warm as a hearth fire lit the girl's face. "It doesn't pain me overmuch, as long as I don't stand. Besides, it's a grand excuse for me to loll about all day, leastwise for the next few weeks. Why, I feel like royalty. Please, have a seat. It's nice to have company."

Only one chair graced the room, a rocker, near the coal grate. Emily sank into it and pulled Alf up to her lap. "You're so good, Mary. I envy your charitable heart."

"Go on with you, miss." The girl's laughter bounced from one painted wall to the other—an easy feat in such close quarters. "So much praise is likely to make me ask Mrs. Hunt for a raise in wages, though I daresay your father would have to approve. . .and I hear he's absent."

"That's not the worst of it." Emily rocked forward, careful to keep Alf from toppling off her lap. "My father's gone and hired a guardian for me. A guardian! Can you imagine?"

"Ahh, yes. Mr. Brentwood." Mary's eyes grew as large as her ankle. Sunlight from the single window danced across the girl's cheeks, washing them in a rosy hue. Wait a minute. . . Emily narrowed her eyes. Was that a blush?

"I got a peek at him last night, miss, right after my tumble. 'Twas him who ordered everyone about—even Mrs. Hunt. Rallied the troops, so to speak. Calm yet firm. And if you don't mind me saying, he is quite pleasing to the eye, a real dapper figure, don't you think? All muscle and—" Mary slapped her fingers to her mouth. Apparently whatever tincture the physician had ordered carried a side effect of loose lips.

Emily smiled. Obviously the man had an effect on everyone. "Honestly, Mary, I hardly know what to think. Oh, I'll grant you that he is dashing and all"—her own cheeks grew hot, the traitors—"but underneath is a harsh taskmaster. Do you know he threatened to lock me up?"

Mary's brows shot up, matched by a wicked grin—

A grin her own lips mirrored. "I suppose I did deserve his lecture after causing your accident. Oh, Mary, how will I bear the man's company with you confined?"

"Give him a chance, miss. He can't be all that bad."

Emily blew out a long breath. "He can and he is."

A sharp rap on the door from the hallway cut her off. "Mary? Is Miss Emily—"

"I'm in here, Mrs. Hunt." Shooing Alf off her lap, Emily stood just as the housekeeper entered the room.

"There you are. I've been on quite the search." By the look of her skewed apron and tilted mobcap, Emily didn't doubt her.

"It's about Mr. Sedgewick, miss." She straightened her skirt with one hand while righting her cap with the other. "He's down in the sitting room and refuses to leave until he speaks with your father."

Emily's forehead crumpled, harmonizing with Alf's. "Didn't you tell him Father is away?"

"Of course, but the man won't relent." The housekeeper threw up her hands—a gesture Emily learned long ago to avoid. Pushed beyond her limits, Mrs. Hunt could make a rat-catcher cower. "He asked to speak with you."

"Very well." She glanced down at her pup then back at Mrs. Hunt. "But you shall have to take Alf."

The housekeeper's lips pressed tight for a moment. Then she bent and opened her arms. "Come on, little beastie. Let's go see what Cook has to offer."

Alf shot forward, his stubby legs scrambling across the wood floor. The words *cook* and *walk* produced the same effect.

With Alf cared for, Emily descended to the sitting room and swept through the door. Reginald Sedgewick stood, back to her, with both hands gripping the mantel. The fabric of his waistcoat strained across his shoulders. He looked as if he'd grabbed hold of God's mercy seat.

"Uncle Reggie?"

He wheeled about, the loose cravat of yesterday now flapping completely untied. Only one button secured his vest, the top. Part of a wrinkled shirttail overflowed the waistline of his equally creased pants. Had he slept in his clothes?

"Good day, Miss Emily." His voice was raw.

Emily stepped closer, but not too much. She paused at the tea table by the window. "Are you all right?"

Raking a hand through his hair, he snorted—bullish and bitter. "Hardly. Forgive my abruptness, my dear, but necessity calls for it. I must know. . . Where is your father?"

The question shot through her as effectively as his bloodshot gaze. Had she obeyed yesterday, she might know. "You're his business partner, not I. Have you no idea?"

"Unfortunately, I suspect that I do." With a curse, he spun and slammed his fist onto the mantel, jarring the urn of flowers atop it.

Emily flinched, her breath catching in her throat. She'd seen her father in a rage many a time—overheard heated words from his study—but never had she encountered anger like this from Uncle Reggie.

Silence stretched, like a thread to be snapped—and once broken, it might fray beyond repair. Should she stay or slip out?

She inched back toward the door. Three steps remaining to freedom, her heel sank onto a loosened floorboard. The creak ripped a hole in the stillness, and she froze.

Reggie wheeled about and stalked the length of the room, nostrils flaring.

Fear tasted brassy. She spit out words, attempting to rid her mouth of the sour tang while appeasing the man she thought she knew. "I am sure my father will return within a month's time. He usually does, you know. Then you can clear up whatever is so upsetting to you."

"A month?" He stopped a pace away, his left eyelid quivering. "By then it will be too late."

He shoved past her, leaving behind a trail of upended emotions and a single burning question. . .

Too late for what?

Chapter 4

The grating wheels of a passing dray heaped one more insult atop the din assaulting Nicholas's ears. Lombard Street teemed with barrow men, ragpickers, and not just a few mealy apple sellers. Though people abounded, only one was of interest—one he couldn't see. There was no way to hear the soft footsteps behind him, but all the same he knew they were there, like a rat in a shadow. Edging nearer. Closing in on his coattails. Three, maybe four treads to his one. Timing was everything.

Hold. Hold. And—

Brentwood spun and clamped his hand on a wrist hardly thicker than kindling. Wide eyes stared up at him, the whites of which shone in stark contrast to the girl's soot-smeared face. A swipe of fair skin peeked through dirt beneath her nose, a corresponding smudge on her sleeve where she wiped it. Apparently the girl had a bad habit, though that was likely the least of her problems. Threadbare fabric hung off shoulders so sharp, the sight cut to the marrow, especially since the girl was only eight, possibly nine—though judging by the foul language she spewed, she'd lived a lifetime already.

"Lemme go!" came out amid curses and oaths. She twisted, and her bones ground beneath his grip.

"Surely you know the penalty for thievery, girl."

"I weren't thievin'!" A mackerel on a pike couldn't have wriggled more.

He tightened his grip and squatted, face-to-filthy-face, ignoring the pedestrians flowing past them on either side. "And do you know the penalty for lying?"

"I ain't lyin', you scarpin' cully!"

A frown tugged his lips, and he pierced her with the same stern stare he'd used on Emily. "You can lie to me, girl, but not to God."

"Well. . .maybe. . .maybe I. . ." Her voice blended into the clamor. Beneath his fingers, her muscles relaxed. Her chin, once jutted, now softened to the point of trembling. Angry creases disappeared into the curved shadows of each hollowed cheek. He'd seen that look a thousand times. Despair didn't just weight the soul; it scarred the face.

In the brief space of a blink, Nicholas prayed: *Lord, what am I to do?*

"Don't turn me in, sir." The tear in the girl's eye might be an act. But the appeal in her tone was real enough. "I'm powerful hungry, that's what. I ain't et a morsel since yesterday, and then only a crumb. That's God's truth, sir, it is."

Blowing out a long breath, Nicholas reached with his free hand into a concealed slit inside his waistband. Baring an entire wallet in public was suicide. He pulled out a ha'penny and held it up, both their gazes drawn to the bit of copper. For the street waif, the coin meant life—but would the giving of it hasten Jenny's death?

"What's your name, girl?" he asked.

"Nipper." Her eyes didn't shift from the money.

"Nipper, eh?" He masked a grimace. Beneath that grime lay a girl who ought to be wearing ribbons and twirling about in dresses, not scrounging the streets for marks with fat purses. "Odd name for a girl."

She shot him a glance then zeroed back in on the ha'penny. "Ain't so strange when the one what named me is Maggot."

Nicholas frowned and ran through a mental ledger of criminals in the area. He knew of a Grub and a Fishbait, even a Vermin and a Tick, but no Maggot. "This Maggot, where does he live?"

"Din't say 'twas a he."

"All right. Where does *she* live?"

The girl wriggled, eyes yet fixed on the money. "What for do you want to know?"

He softened his tone yet kept it loud enough to be heard above the street hawkers and coaches. "What do you say, Nipper, if I were to visit ol' Maggot and hire you away from her. Would you like that?"

Her face jerked to his, fire in her eyes. "I might be a cutpurse, but I ain't no bleedin' trollop—"

"No, no. I'm not suggesting anything of the kind." He loosened his grip on her wrist. She yanked back her arm and retreated several steps, but his outstretched coin held her in his orbit. "My sister is in need of care, Nipper, and for the next few weeks, I am not able to attend her. I suspect a small chamber of your own would be a great improvement over some rat hole in a rookery."

Her eyes widened. "How did you know—"

"Do you dispute it?"

She swiped her sleeve across her nose, a nervous reaction that endorsed his earlier guess and sanctioned his new deduction.

Slowly the girl extended her hand, palm up. "All right. Anythin's better than Pig's Quay. I'll take the job. But don't worry 'bout ol' Maggot. She'll let me go, and be glad of it. . .long as I keep her garnished."

Nicholas dropped the coin. She snatched it midair and tucked it away in her shoe.

"You give that to Maggot then scurry back here to the Crown and Horn. There'll be a meal and another penny for you." He stretched to full height and gave a nod down the block.

Her face brightened. Visibly. Like the flame of a match in a darkened cellar. "That I will, sir. You can count on me, or my name's not. . . Hey, what's yer name?"

"Brentwood." He offered his hand.

She inched nearer then snaked out her fingers and shook it, her grip a curious blend of frailty and strength.

And quite the act of faith for a pickpocket. Half a smile lifted his lips. "Besides employment, I should like to give you a new name as well. From now on, I shall call you Hope."

She drew back, mouth agape. "Me? Hope?" Her tongue darted over her lips after she said the name, tasting of it as she might a sugared date. A slow smile brightened her face as effectively as a good scrubbing. "I like it, I do. Hope!"

Then she darted into the traffic and vanished. Speedwise, the little urchin was good at her trade. Hopefully she'd do as well with his sister. He shoved his hands into his pockets and turned, tramping the half street to the Crown and Horn. Had he done the right thing?

Pushing open the tavern door, he shed his hat and threaded his way past men seated in clusters. None looked up. He was as much a part of this pub as the scarred oak tables. The smell of tallow and lard, mutton pasties, and the nutty tang of malt ale curled into his nose and sank to a warm place between belly and heart—home. For the past few years, anyway, and until now.

At this time of day, mostly legal professionals or coach drivers on layover took a draft and a sausage pie, though there might be a random playwright or actor in the bunch. Laborers were too busy toiling the day away, but they'd come later. The cotters, the stave makers, chandlers, and silversmiths, all and more would stop by for a mug on their way home to fishwives and laundry women. Though he didn't envy their lot, he understood the pull of returning to something other than four empty walls and a cold bed each night.

He neared the stairwell entry just as innkeeper Meggy Dawkin barreled through the adjacent kitchen door. In one arm she balanced a platter of cheeses, topped with a loaf of bread. Her other hand gripped a tankard, foam spilling over the rim.

"Good day, Megs. How is she?" Nicholas nodded toward the stairway.

"'Bout time you showed up, Brentwood. I have a pub to run, and I'm no nursemaid." A red curl fell onto her forehead, and she blew upward to knock it back. "Still, I set out your sister's porridge and a mug o' cider early this morn. When I went to pick it up, not a bite or drop was missing. She gets much worse an' you'll have to move her out."

She leaned toward him and lowered her voice. "Can't let it spread that the Crown and Horn houses diseases."

Her words shaved layers off his faith. God forbid Jenny's sickness should spread. But for the moment, this was the best he could afford. In three or four weeks, though, as soon as Payne returned, he'd have the money to move her out to the country.

Oh God, let her make it.

Nicholas scrubbed a hand over his face, feeling a score older than his twenty-seven years. "Has the doctor been here?"

"Like I said, man, I've a tavern to run. He might've slipped in last night when I was dodging pinches and running pints, but he ain't shown his beak today." She whirled to the catcall of a fellow across the room, and a plop of ale foam landed on the floor. "Keep it civil, Bogger!"

Before she set off to topple the fellow—Meggy ran a strict pub—Nicholas called after her. "Oh Megs, I hired a girl to see to Jenny. Small thing. Quite dirty. Goes by the name of Nipper, or possibly Hope. Give her a room and a basin next to my sister's. She'll need to be fed as well."

Meggy frowned at him over her shoulder. "It'll cost you."

"It usually does."

Her lips curved up. "Cheeky devil."

Ignoring her taunt, he turned and tromped up the stairwell, walls closing in like a coffin. Were a fire to break out—no. Better to not think it.

The stairs were steep, and the beam at the landing low. He ducked and veered right. Thin light seeped through a tiny window at the end of the corridor, feeble as the cough leaching through the door where he stopped. He rapped the wood with one hand and reached for the knob with the other. "It's me, Jen. Nicholas."

The hacking increased as he entered the room. Death lived here, crouching in the corner, biding its time. Judging by the rattle of his sister's lungs and gasps for breath, the beast wouldn't wait much longer.

He strode to her bedside and lowered to the mattress. The wooden frame creaked as he cradled Jenny's shoulders and lifted her up. Bones bit into him, sharper since his last visit. "You're worse."

She settled against the pillow he plumped, chest heaving. "Good day. . .to you, too. . .Brother."

"Ahh, Jen. You know I wish you the best of days." He coaxed back the dark sweep of fringe from her brow—hair that should've been pulled up and fastened with pearl combs as any other young lady her age. Her green eyes, dulled almost to gray now, followed the movement. Ahh, such a beauty she'd been before disease came calling. Choking back a sob, he forced a smile for her benefit. "How are you?"

In return, a weak smile quivered across her lips. "Dandy and grand, as always."

He stood, pacing the length of the room—eight steps one way, eight back. That she kept such a sweet spirit attested to God's own grace, but why did it anger him? He spit out a sigh, knowing the answer lay deep in his own wicked heart—a reaction he'd have to face one day. But not this one.

He stopped at the foot of her bed. "When was the doctor here last? What did he say?"

The lines of her mouth softened, and for the briefest of moments, a flash of the sister he knew peered up at him. "You worry too much. At seven and twenty, you ought be fretting over a wife and children, not your sister."

Oh, no. Not that topic again. He folded his arms and widened his stance. "You're stalling, Jenny. The truth."

She pushed herself up farther, the effort expelled in another bout of coughing. "That is the truth, Nicholas. You do worry too much.

Leave me in God's hands, for there am I content. He alone has numbered my days, and try as you might, you can't change that. You are not God, you know."

Though the Brentwood family tenacity served him well in catching thieves and solving cases, it wasn't nearly as agreeable when employed upon himself. "Very well. I shall leave the matter. . .for now." He grabbed the single chair next to a small table and dragged it to her side. "I've got good news and bad. Which would you have first?"

Her gaze darted from one of his eyes to the other, as if she might read the answers without him speaking a word. "Let's get the bad out of the way."

"As you wish." He reached for her hand. "I won't be able to check in with you as often, if at all. I've a job over on the West End, Portman Square. I'll be tied up for three, maybe four weeks."

"That is bad news." She freed her fingers from his and brushed away his own unruly hair from his eyes, her fingertips cool against his skin. "For who will smooth away those lines on your face?"

"Bah. No one even notices, save you." He caught her hand in both of his, ignoring the clammy flesh beneath his touch. "Now, for the good. I've hired a girl to see to your needs while I'm away. She ought be here later today. She's a street waif, but I believe one with a true heart. I think you'll like her. And should you require, you can send her to fetch me."

"But the cost—"

He let go of her hand and pressed a finger to her lips. "Let me finish. By the time I complete this assignment, I'll have enough to see you and the girl moved to the country. Think of it, Jenny, fresh air and lots of it. Sunshine to warm your bones. I am sure God will have you on the mend in no time."

Her brows lifted. "That must be some wage, but for what? Please don't tell me this is dangerous."

"Only for my patience." He smirked. "I'm safeguarding a lady whose father is off on business, though *lady* is hardly a fitting term. Miss Emily Payne is more wily than a brothel madam."

"Nicholas!" Jenny gasped, setting off a spate of coughs and ending with a strained clearing of her throat. "I doubt you're being fair."

He shook his head. How to sum up what he already knew of the woman? "She's everything you're not, Jen. Petulant. Defensive. A rebellious streak as deep as her father's pockets, paling only in size to her pride. One thing she does share, though, is your beauty, in an opposite kind of way. Where your hair is dark, hers is golden. She's got brown eyes to your green. Her skin is pure cream, a shade fairer than yours, and her wit is a bit more prickly."

Jenny's gaze bore into him. "Seems you've observed quite a bit about the lady in your short time with her."

"I'd have to be blind as old Billy Moffitt not to notice her ways. In the space of one day, she disobeyed her father, caused the injury of her maid, and now demands I purchase some gaudier clothing." He threw up his hands and stood. "If she thinks I'll preen about as a pet peacock, all foppish and—"

"She can't be all that bad."

"She can and she is." Bending, he straightened the blanket riding low on her lap. Jenny would defend a bare-fanged badger if given the opportunity.

"Nicholas?" The tilt of her head was their mother's. . .one if not heeded, often earned him the switch. "You asked me to give this street waif of yours a chance. Seems to me you ought do the same for Miss Emily Payne."

Heat filled his gut. Her logic chafed, stinging and raw. Of course, she was right.

But that didn't mean he liked it.

Chapter 5

The sway of the carriage usually made Emily sleepy. Not today. Not with Nicholas Brentwood sitting across from her, the bothersome man. All her nerves stood at attention—an uncomfortable and recently frequent sensation.

While he looked out the carriage window, she jumped on the opportunity to study him undetected—a rare occasion. For the most part, he observed her and her ways, questioning what she did and why she did so. After nearly a week in his presence, she'd discovered very little about him. He, on the other hand, had an irritating way of always turning a conversation around to his benefit.

Streetlamps cast spare light, silhouetting his broad shoulders and pensive face—a face more handsome than she cared to admit. The slope of his nose was straight, the cut of his lips full. His dark good looks gave him an edge, eclipsing thoughts of how much he might be worth, making one wonder for the briefest of moments if it truly mattered anyway.

Faint creases lined the corners of his eyes. Apparently the man laughed, and often, though she'd not witnessed much of his humor. What made Nicholas Brentwood laugh?

A crescent scar curved downward near the apex of his jaw. Not large nor unseemly, but noticeable. When she'd first met him, she'd sensed a certain ferocity held in check, a layer beneath his wit. This arched white line confirmed it. She frowned. Merriment and violence were an odd combination. A swirl of leaves cast about in the wind would be easier to sort through than the character of this man.

"You analyze me as you might a bolt of fabric. Why?"

His gaze remained fixed outside the window. Good thing, for he'd surely notice the fire blazing across her cheeks—and the feeling irked her. Perhaps, as in cribbage, the best defense would be offense.

51

"A few rules, Mr. Brentwood."

He snapped his face toward hers, the green of his eyes deep and searching. "Rules?"

A smile lifted her lips, victory tasting sweet. For once she'd gained the upper hand. "Yes. After our disastrous shopping excursion the other day, I think a few guidelines should be set."

He snorted. "I'd hardly call that a disaster. Still, you make a good point." A flicker of a grin lifted his mouth. "I think a few guidelines are in order."

The carriage wheels bumped and ground over a hump in the road, the springs creaking as he spoke. Had she heard him correctly? Surely he wouldn't give in so easily.

He held up his index finger. "Rule number one, then, is—"

"No, no, no! I meant *I* have a few instructions." Boorish man. Did he honestly think she'd ask for more requirements from him? She shifted on the seat, facing him dead-on. "Rule number one is do not hover about me like an overbearing governess. I would rather you put to use those fade-into-the-woodwork skills you boast of."

Light twinkled in his gaze. "Did I not perform to your satisfaction at Lady Westby's? As I recall, I waited in the carriage."

"Yes, but you called for me to leave far too early."

"An hour was not enough time to view some fans?" He snorted. "Does the lady own the market?"

"Certainly not. I just didn't want to be the first to leave." She cleared her throat, hoping to cover the whiny tone that slipped out.

He rolled his eyes.

Drat. . .he'd noticed.

Nicholas folded his arms, cocking his head at a rakish angle. "What about the day before last, when you insisted on visiting Bond Street? I was a dutiful baggage handler, nothing more."

"Nothing more? It was quite the scene at Mabley's Lace and Glove when you apprehended that shoplifter." Which was an understatement. Who'd have thought that the tiny shop could hold so many gawkers? And she was still hard pressed to decide which horrified her more—the way he manhandled a thief until a constable arrived or that Mrs. Mabley had assumed he was her beau.

"What would you have me do?" His voice rumbled lower than the carriage wheels. "Stand by while the place was robbed?"

Her lips pulled into a pucker. He'd cornered her again. The only correct answer was one she didn't want to voice.

No, better to forge ahead. "Rule number two. You are my cousin Nicholas."

His eyes widened. "Say again?"

"I can't properly be seen with a nonfamily member unchaperoned. What would people think? And worse. . .what would they say? I will not become this season's scandal." She lifted her nose, hopefully mimicking his own commanding posture. "You shall be my cousin Nicholas, visiting from out of town."

He shook his head, sending a dark swath of hair across his brow. "I will not lie for you, Miss Payne, nor anyone, for that matter."

"I'm not asking you to." She sighed. An abigail was so much easier to manipulate than this bully. "Simply don't say anything to the contrary. That's not lying."

"No. It's deception."

His words peppered the air like gunshot, and she flinched. "Must you always be so obstinate?"

"I'm not always. Sometimes I'm cynical and other times downright—"

The carriage pitched to the right, and her head snapped to the side. The pearl comb in her hair slipped, digging sharp ends into the flesh at her temple as her head smashed against the window. Vague shouts from the driver ricocheted inside her skull, as did the bark of Mr. Brentwood's reprimand to the man.

"Emily!"

Her name floated midair, like a puff of dandelion seeds. Something warm wrapped around her shoulders. Something cool pressed against the side of her head. She inhaled sandalwood and strength.

"Just breathe."

Slowly, shapes took on edges. Colors came back. Her cheek rested against a white shirt, which stretched across a solid chest, strong and—

A chest?

Emily pushed away, trying hard to ignore the staccato hammering inside her skull—and the way the sudden loss of Nicholas Brentwood's warmth cut to the quick.

The carriage door flew open and the driver popped in a reddened face. "My apologies, my lady, sir. A blasted crack-brained jarvey cut me off, the half-witted—"

"Mind your tongue and see that it doesn't happen again." Nicholas shifted so that she couldn't see his face, but it must've been a fearsome glower he aimed at the man, for the driver stuttered an "Aye, sir" and resealed the door.

When Nicholas turned back to her, though, nothing but compassion shone in his gaze, warm and strong as when he'd—

"Rule number three, Mr. Brentwood." Her words trembled as much as her body. "Is never, ever hold me like that again."

Nicholas frowned. "You hit your head, Miss Payne, and if you will not have me apply pressure to your wound, then perhaps you ought."

He held out a handkerchief, a red stain in the middle.

Her fingertips flew to her temple, meeting with sticky wetness. "Oh." Her voice was a shiver.

"With your permission?" He lifted a brow.

She nodded then wished she hadn't. Her brain rattled around in her head like dice in a cup.

"Turn a bit, this way." He guided her face aside with a gentle touch. The carriage jerked into motion once again, and even so, he compensated for the abrupt movement, never once applying undue pressure. "It's looking better, though perhaps. . ."

This close, his voice rumbled through her, filling places in her heart that she didn't know were vacant. A tremor ran the length of her spine. This was silly.

"Perhaps we ought return home."

"No, I'll be fine." She inhaled, drawing in determination. She might as well take a gun to her head—though in truth it felt she had—as miss the opening night of *The Venetian Outlaw* at the Theatre Royal. "It's merely a scratch, is it not?"

He leaned closer, his breath feathering against her forehead like the kiss of a summer sun. Smoothing back her hair, he lightly refitted her comb. Why was it so hot in here?

"I've seen worse." He drew back, the tilt of his jaw granite. "And I suppose I'll not hear the end of it if we do turn around. But if you feel nauseous or the slightest bit off center, we shall leave. Immediately and without debate. Is that understood?"

"Yes." Remembering the throbbing from last time, she omitted a nod.

"May I have your word on the matter?"

She nibbled her lip. The man placed far too much value on one's word. "Another building block?"

He answered with half a grin.

"Very well, Mr. Brentwood, you have my word. The second I feel I'm about to swoon, we shall return home." She bit back a smile. She'd never swooned in her life, and she certainly didn't intend to start now.

By the time the carriage eased to a stop, she felt certain she'd arranged her hair to hide her bump. Nicholas descended first then offered his hand. When their fingers touched, even through the fabric of her gloves, a quiver ran up her arm. La. . .she had hit her head harder than she thought.

She shook off the feeling, but once her slippers touched ground, a new one swirled in. Dizziness. She straightened her skirts, concealing a sway, and blamed it on the bright lanterns and commotion of the Theatre Royal. After all, scores of other women must surely be as lightheaded with the prospect of seeing and being seen.

Nicholas offered his arm.

Her stomach tensed. Had he noticed? "I'm fine."

"While I agree there is none finer here tonight than you, Miss Payne, still I insist." He bent, speaking for her alone. "Or shall I heft you over my shoulders as a ragpicker's sack?"

"Have I told you that you're a—"

"Yes. I have duly noted your opinion of me many times over." He settled her hand into the crook of his elbow. "Shall we?"

They swept into the grand foyer, large enough to house the entire population of Grosvenor Square and Mayfair combined, though by now the crowd thinned, most having taken their box seats.

"Your wrap, Miss Payne?" Nicholas stepped behind her and waited as she unfastened her buttons.

While he went to check her pelisse, she darted her gaze from one dress to another, hoping to spy her friend, Bella Grayson. No red curls caught her eye, but a certain blue velvet jacket with golden trim did. Emily pinched her cheeks and tucked up any loose hairs near her injury. Should Charles Henley glance her direction, she'd look her best or die in the trying. With a quick smoothing of her skirt, she took two steps toward him—then a hand on her shoulder pulled her back.

"One moment, if you please."

The loud words traveled on a cloud of rum—hot and sickly sweet. Charles Henley's head turned, and Emily spun before he could identify her. . .hopefully.

Bloodshot eyes stared into hers. Since when did Uncle Reggie imbibe in public? "Good evening, Uncle. I hope this evening finds you in better sorts than our last conversation."

"Any word from your father?"

Her nose wrinkled from the tang of his breath, and she glanced over her shoulder. Charles no longer looked her way. Worse. He engaged in conversation with Millie Barker—the biggest flirt this side of the Thames. "Oh, no." She spoke as much to herself as to Reggie then shifted her body to keep Charles and Millie in the corner of her eye.

"Nothing at all?" Reggie stepped in front of her.

Emily frowned. Her uncle all but blocked her view. "Not a word." She craned her neck one way and the other. No good.

"It's imperative I know the instant you hear anything. Do you understand?" Thunder boomed in her uncle's tone, rolling across the room. Had Charles heard?

Standing tiptoe, she slipped her gaze over Reggie's shoulder while answering. "Mmm-hmm."

Before she could read the expression on Charles's face, her uncle's fingers bit into her upper arms, pinning her in place. The red crawling up his neck matched the lines in his eyes. "Listen to me!" He emphasized each word with a shake.

Her head pounded, centering like a hound to the kill on the tender spot she'd smacked against the carriage window.

"Unhand the lady. Now."

The deadly calm voice of Nicholas Brentwood breached the ringing in her ears—and the glance of Charles Henley her double vision.

If looks could kill, the man scowling at Nicholas would swing from a Tyburn gibbet for manslaughter. Why had Emily spoken to the rogue in the first place? Nicholas had turned his back for what. . . thirty, maybe forty seconds? The woman's magnetism was positively horrifying.

The man looked past Emily to him, smelling like a pirate and looking no better. Granted, his attire was impeccable, but his face twisted into a ruthless mask. Criminals didn't frequent only alleys and shadows. The fellow sniffed, as if he were the one considering something rotten. "Mind your own business."

Nicholas threw back his shoulders. "The lady *is* my business." With one hand, he lifted the edge of his dress coat, just enough for chandelier light to glimmer off the golden spike of his tipstaff.

Slowly, the man's hands lowered. A sneer rose. Emily scooted aside.

"So, you're a runner, eh? Here at the theatre?" The man's voice was a growl. "Should you not be out fetching a call girl for your magistrate or running some other useless errands for the Crown?"

Both Nicholas's hands curled into fists. The spark of fear in Emily's eyes kept them at his sides, but that did nothing to stop the flash of white-hot anger surging through his gut. "May I suggest, sir, that you nick off to Gentleman Jim's if a knuckle bruiser is what you're about. Unless intimidating women is the extent of your courage."

The man's eyes narrowed. "Are you calling me a bully, sir?"

"I don't have to." Nicholas widened his stance. "You've said it for me."

The man swung back his fist. "Why of all the—"

"Uncle, no!" Emily flung herself between them, stopping Nicholas's heart. If the man let loose now, her face would bear the brunt.

He reached for her. "Emily, don't!"

She shrugged off his touch while facing her. . .*uncle*? Nicholas shifted his weight. Something didn't add up. Why would a family member be such a brute? And hadn't Mr. Payne owned that there were no nearby relations?

Emily wrung her hands. "When I hear from my father, I vow I shall let you know. Please, don't do this."

The man's arm lowered—though his fingers did not uncoil.

"Thank you, Uncle. Now if you'll excuse us." She turned to Nicholas, eyes pleading, and laid her fingers on his sleeve. "Shall we?"

His heart pumped, muscles yet tense, fingers still itching to feel the satisfying smash against cartilage and bone.

But then he'd be no better than the sod in front of him. He tipped his head toward Emily. "Very well."

He led her toward the grand staircase, and once out of ear range of the blackguard, he shot her a sideways glance. "Are you all right?"

"Yes." She gazed up at him, lips quirked. "Reggie's interrogation was no worse than one of yours, albeit a bit more. . .physical."

A frown pulled at the corners of his mouth. Likely if he lifted her sleeve, even now he'd see angry red imprints from the man's grip. "Is all your family so harsh?"

"Family?" Her nose wrinkled, and she kept her silence up the first set of stairs. "Oh, he's not really my uncle."

Nicholas shook his head. "Another one of your faux relatives, eh? Tell me, Miss Payne, do you consider all your acquaintances as kinship?"

She pulled her hand from his sleeve and huffed past him. "Don't be silly."

The pout on her face before she turned matched her earlier expression in the carriage. His biceps tightened, the memory of holding her etched indelibly into his arms. As he followed her down the corridor, sconce light slid over each lock of her pinned-up hair, stunning enough to shame the sun. Shadows lingered along curves he ought not notice. A long-forgotten feeling roused deep in his belly. He hadn't looked at a woman like this since Adelina.

No. Better not to go there. Not now.

Or maybe ever.

He increased his pace and caught up to Emily. "So, tell me. What did this Uncle Reggie want?"

She paused in front of a box marked 22A, hand resting on the knob. Her teeth toyed with her lower lip for a moment. "For some odd reason, he's rather put out that my father left town. He's asked me several times to let him know the instant he returns."

She pushed open the door. Venetian accents poured out, the actors already in full boom.

But before her head filled with intrigue and romance, he stalled her with a light touch to her shoulder and a low voice in her ear. "What is the real relationship between Reggie and your father?"

"Something to do with business," she whispered back then stretched her neck to peer into the box. "May we go in? The play's already started."

Nicholas held his ground—and her shoulder. "Is the man always that forceful?"

"No." A glower as dark as the box accompanied her answer. "Not any more than you're being right now."

The truth of her words splayed his fingers. He followed in her lily-scented wake, scoping out the box as they entered. Eight seats, four to a row, and not a one occupied. Either Mr. Payne enjoyed his own private box, or attendance was lacking—not likely on opening night, though. Emily sank onto a velvet-cushioned chair center-front, and he took up the seat next to her on the right. She leaned forward, her face softening as she focused on the stage.

He tensed and swept the auditorium's perimeter to detect any danger. Twice. Finally satisfied, he leaned back and fixed his gaze on the actors, eyes unseeing. Something wasn't right about the exchange between Emily and her. . .*uncle*. A man so heated over the mere absence of a business partner on a routine trip didn't add up.

Unless the trip wasn't so routine after all.

Chapter 6

Reginald Sedgewick loosened his cravat as the hackney he rode in jittered over cobblestones. Breathing had been a forgotten priority for so long that his fingertips tingled. Rage, now spent, left him unhinged—though the rattling his bones suffered could be blamed on the horrid driver. It figured he'd get the broken-springed coach with the one-armed jarvey. Blasted luck.

The cab lurched to a stop. " 'Ere we are then, guv'ner."

A scowl twisted his mouth. Even through the walls of the hack, the driver's voice grated like an off-tune fiddle. Reggie flung open the door and teetered out, one hand clutching the crooked cab for balance. His stomach roiled, and he swallowed back a sour taste.

Now that his feet touched ground, why did the world still tilt?

He paid the driver then paid even more with each painful step to his front door—head throbbing every time his boot met pavement. He should stick to bourbon and leave the rum to pirates and thieves— like Alistair Payne. Fumbling with his fob, he sorted the keys by feel, the slow burn of anger rising once again. The man was a rotten villain.

And what burned him even more was that's exactly how he felt. Twice now—or was it thrice?—he'd treated Emily as if he himself were the rogue. Dastardly behavior. What had gotten into him?

He unlocked the door, stepped inside, then froze. The smell of Burley tobacco curled out from the sitting room, and suddenly he knew the exact cause for his recent ill manners.

Fear.

Drawing in a deep breath, followed by another, he removed his hat, unbuttoned his greatcoat, and hung both on the brass tree. Then he straightened his cravat and while he was at it, brushed out any possible wrinkles in his trousers. He'd known deep in his gut this meeting would come, but that didn't make it any less odious.

Painting a smile on a face as stiff as canvas, he strode into the sitting room. Hand extended, he greeted the lanky fellow puffing on a pipe near the mantle. "Captain Norton, pleased to see you safe and sound. Rather late in the evening for a visit, is it not?"

Norton bent and tapped his spent tobacco into the hearth then stood. Slowly. Like the uncoiling of a king cobra. In three strides he closed the distance between them, his hand snaking out. The captain's grip was no less crushing than the last time they shook, but the flesh more leathery. Calluses were the only calling card the fellow needed to prove his identity. "Aye, it's late, but callin' earlier don't seem to do me no good. You're either out or. . .*unavailable.*"

The man's American accent boxed his ears more severely than the hackney driver's ragged tone. Reggie swept his arm toward a chair. "Please, have a seat. I admit I've been rather occupied as of late. My apologies, Captain."

Norton's eyes followed his arm to the chair then retraced the route back up to his face. "This ain't no social visit, Sedgewick. Pay up what you and Payne owe, and I'll be on my way."

"Yes. . .well. . ." Sweat dampened his palms. Good thing they'd already shook. "Surely you realize that at this time of evening no banks are open. And naturally, I do not keep such an amount on hand." He shrugged. "No, no. Times are too dangerous for that. I suggest you call back, say. . .next week, and I'll have a bank draft written up for you."

"Next week?" A sneer slashed across the captain's face. "My ship's been unloaded nigh on a fortnight, now. Time is money, Mr. Sedgewick. The longer I sit idle, the more it costs. . .if you catch my meaning."

The rum in his belly inched up toward his throat, leaving a burning trail the length of his torso. Brash American. Money grubbers, the lot. The very seed of America's rebellion. Reggie sniffed, hating the captain and all that he stood for. "Of course. I shall include a little extra for your trouble."

"Aye. See that you do." Norton pocketed his pipe and stalked to the door then paused on the threshold. "And see that next time I come to call, the money's a-waitin' for me, for I will have my payment . . .one way or another."

A fine mist collected on the edge of Emily's hood where she stood outside the theatre. The fat droplets hung there, daring her to move. One quiver would loose the floodgates and wash her face. So she stood, still as a Grecian statue, and as thoroughly chilled.

Ahead, Nicholas stepped back from the row of carriages lined up like infantrymen in front of the curb. In the rush of departing patrons, his figure alone commanded her gaze. How could he, without a word, make such demands?

As he strode over to her, greatcoat clinging to the hard lines of his body, she shivered. Water rained down, and she couldn't decide which annoyed her more—that she'd noticed his physique, or the cold rivulets trickling down her cheeks and nose. Retrieving a handkerchief, she dabbed away the moisture on her eyes.

"Are you well?" Nicholas's words hung suspended in the mist, lower in timbre than the chatter of passing theatre patrons.

Fighting a yawn, she made a quick assessment, for a simple yes or no would undoubtedly warrant further questions on the matter. A dull ache loitered at the edge of her hairline—though no more painful than the aftereffects of one of her father's lectures. Cold nipped her toes, and she was slightly thirsty, but other than that, she couldn't complain. Tipping her face up to his, she smiled. "I am fine, though in truth I am looking forward to a good night's sleep and to lounging about on the morrow."

His eyes searched hers, lamplight softening his sharp green gaze. Or—an involuntary tingle ran up her arms—was that concern?

Lips quirking into a wry grin, he cocked his head. "What. . .no shopping or visiting? No running about whatsoever? I fear you hit your head harder than you admit, lady. But I am happy that, for once, you will stay put."

Her smile faded. She'd never said she'd *stay put*.

"Your carriage is tenth in line, Miss Payne," he continued. "Should you like to remain here or walk?"

Tucking her handkerchief back into her reticule, she pulled tight the cords before answering. "It would be faster to walk, I think."

He crooked his arm, and she set her glove atop his sleeve, discounting the muscle beneath—though the memory of his embrace would resurface in an instant if she'd care to reel it in. She sniffed. Such nonsense. The man was a brute, nothing more.

Four carriages ahead, the bob of red curls beneath a royal blue bonnet disappeared into the coach, and a wonderfully wicked idea emerged. Without missing a step, she turned to Nicholas. "I noticed Miss Grayson paid you an inordinate amount of attention during the intermission."

His jaw shifted. No words came out. His stride didn't alter a beat.

"I think Bella finds you quite intriguing, as did several others. With all your observational skills, did you not notice the pretty heads you turned?"

He stared ahead, as if dodging patrons and strolling past the remaining carriages were more valuable than a derby prize. "I have no idea what you mean, Miss Payne."

A slow smile lifted her lips. She was getting to him. "La, Mr. Brentwood. You paid more attention to those in the auditorium than the action onstage. Why. . .I don't think you could sum up the play should I ask you to."

He shot her a sideways glance. "The only way to prevent trouble, Miss Payne, is to identify the danger before it strikes. I am not employed to appreciate performances but to look out for your well-being."

"Danger...here?" She swept out her hand at the merry theatergoers ducking into coaches. The worst offense she could see was an ill-matched Cheshire frock coat paired with sateen breeches that were much too tight. "There's not much threat at the theatre, sir."

"I beg to differ—"

"Miss Payne! Emily! Pray, hold up."

The voice behind crawled up her spine and settled at the base of her neck, raising the finest of hairs. Did Nicholas Brentwood always have to be right? Sure enough, seconds later, danger in taffeta swished up to her side.

Pink-cheeked and slightly breathless, Millie Barker fell into step beside them. "My carriage is just behind yours. Such a coincidence, for I'd meant to speak with you earlier."

Emily choked. The woman had time for no one unless they wore breeches and bathed in money. Coughing into her glove, she hid the snappy retort then forced a pleasant tone to her voice. "By all means, you should join us."

"You remember my aunt, of course." Millie nodded her head over her shoulder.

Emily followed her movement. At least ten paces behind, a dark shape hustled to catch up—a terrifying sight were they in a back alley. A black veil topped off a black cape with black bombazine skirts billowing out like a cloud of death. The woman draped herself in mourning, although her husband had been dead at least a decade.

She turned back to Millie, but before she could respond, Millie looked past her to Nicholas.

"And this is?"

Emily narrowed her eyes. Of course. Nicholas was the bit of breeches Millie had noticed. And what would Miss Barker's face look like when she discovered the man's chilly personality and even emptier wallet? The thought tasted as sweet as one of Cook's pastries. "I am pleased to introduce my cousin Nicholas Brentwood."

Emily studied his face, eager for a reaction. He didn't disappoint, though she doubted whether Millie could see the jump of a muscle along his jaw.

This could be fun. A chance to vex Nicholas and send Millie sniffing down a trail that would take her off the scent of Charles Henley. She didn't have to fake her smile anymore. "Mr. Brentwood, please meet Miss Millicent Barker."

"Miss Barker."

His stiff nod was hardly a cause for the rapture deepening the color on Millie's cheeks. "I am pleased to make your acquaintance, Mr. Brentwood."

He made no further response, but that didn't lessen the blush on Millie's face. She smiled as if the man had just spouted some epic poem about her beauty. Then she turned toward Emily. "Apparently my invitation to you for dinner tomorrow evening was lost, for I have yet to receive your response. Do say you'll come. It's Aunt's birthday celebration."

Emily clenched her teeth. Lost? Hah. She'd never once been invited to the Barker estate. "Oh?" Her voice lilted with just the right amount of we-both-know-you're-not-telling-the-truth in her tone. "Well then. . .I suppose I'll have to check my schedule."

Stopping in front of their carriage, Nicholas turned at the open door and frowned at her. "But you said—"

Millie cut him off. "I'm sure you'll want to rearrange your calendar, dearest. Not only will your friend Bella Grayson be in attendance, but Charles Henley as well."

"Now that I think of it," Emily shifted her gaze from Nicholas's scowl to Millie's hopeful eyes, "yes, I do believe I am free."

"Excellent." Millie beamed. "See you tomorrow evening then, Miss Payne, Mr. Brentwood." His name lingered on her lips, her eyeballs on his form. Then with a huff to her aunt to "please try to keep up," she darted down the row to her own carriage.

Nicholas's chin twitched as if he ground his teeth. "So much for lounging the day away on the morrow, hmm?"

She replied by grasping his offered hand and stepping into the coach. Let him wonder all he wanted. Millie would wind him around her little finger, leaving her free to entice Charles Henley.

She straightened her skirts and smoothed her pelisse as she settled onto the leather seat. As much as she yet again hated to admit Nicholas Brentwood was right, he was. Her goal this season was to snarc a husband, but not just any man.

The prize stag—Charles Henley.

Chapter 7

Wine splashing into goblets, silverware clinking—all sounds receded and time stopped for Nicholas. A fine bead of sweat cooled his brow, and he tugged at his cravat. Four glistening blobs of gray taunted him from their half shells on a gilt-edged plate. Mayhap by loosening his cravat, the oysters would slide down his throat without inducing his gag reflex. This was wrong. Whoever conceived of wrapping one's lips around cold pieces of raw mollusk in the first place? The delight of a warm slab of mutton pie far outweighed this epicurean nightmare. For the tenth time in as many minutes, he thanked God he'd not been born a wealthy man.

Across the table, Emily's eyes laughed at him over the rim of her cup. The little vixen ought to be an officer herself, for her gaze didn't miss much. Three more weeks of this—four if Payne was delayed—and he'd be back to dragging corpses from the Thames or hunting down a murderer bent on a killing jag. And it wouldn't be soon enough. Nothing was more torturous than dressing in garments tighter than a straightjacket while eating fish bait served on fine china.

Picking up her dessertspoon, Emily tapped her wineglass, drawing everyone's attention. "Millie, dear, may I be the first to thank you for your gracious hospitality. How thoughtful it was of you to serve your cook's famous oysters. Don't you agree, Cousin?"

Nine pairs of eyeballs skewered him—Millie's shining, Emily's lit with wicked amusement. He picked up his fork. Very well. Two could play at this game.

"My thanks as well, Miss Barker." He glanced at the pale man beside him. "Though my apologies to you, Mr. Henley. I suspect even the smell of seafood swells your throat."

Emily snapped her face to the fellow, her lips flattening. Indeed, Charles Henley had pushed his chair as far from the table as decorum allowed.

Henley reared back his head and pierced him with a look. "How would you know that, sir?"

Nicholas smiled. "Even now a slight flush creeps up your neck and, though concealed, you scratch the back of your hands as if chafed by wool."

"Very good, Mr. Brentwood! Do tell. . ." Miss Barker leaned forward, one long curl draped over her bare shoulder. A sultry light smoldered in her gaze. "What can you say about me?"

That she was a lioness? A jackal? A leech on the lookout for blood? Without breaking eye contact, he lifted an oyster to his lips and tipped the shell, blocking a retort that ought not be spoken in mixed company—or any other for that matter.

"Come now, sir." Her mouth curved into a feral smile. "Can you detect any secrets simply by observing me?"

She leaned farther, the slant emphasizing her cleavage and the tilt of her lips admitting she knew it. The oyster landed in his gut like a bomb. Once again, the weight of all eyes around the table pressed in on him.

"Why, Miss Barker," he forced a pleasant tone to his voice, "like a fine wine, a woman's secrets are better left to cool in a dark cellar until ready to be served, lest a sour taste remain in the mouth."

"Well said, man!" Beside him, Henley rallied, though it was hard to tell if it was from Nicholas's answer or the fact that a servant had removed his plate of poison. To his left, one man over, a colonel in dress uniform exclaimed, "Hear, hear!" and the fellow next to Henley lifted his glass in a toast.

Millie's eyes narrowed. "I wonder, Mr. Brentwood, what secrets do you harbor?"

"Perhaps you ought ask Miss Payne, for I daresay her eye is as keen as mine."

"Why. . .yes! What a delightful dinner game." Millie flashed a smile at Emily. "Well? What intrigues does Mr. Brentwood hide beneath that cool exterior?"

"My cousin is"—Emily sought his eyes—"orderly to a fault. Demanding as a magistrate. Entirely concerned with honor and justice. Why, I daresay with those traits, he ought be a Bow Street Runner."

Millie's fingers flew to her mouth. "Scandalous!"

Henley snorted. "Imagine."

And the fellow next to him, an Italian named DiMarco, leaned sideways and elbowed him. "You going to sit there and take that, Brentwood?"

"Ahh, but Miss Payne is correct." He threw out the words like a sharp right cross. Blunt truth had ever been his weapon of choice. "With my keen sense of honor and justice, it would hardly serve were I to rebut her in public."

Emily yanked her gaze from him, defeat obviously as desirable to her as a mouthful of oysters to him.

"Judging by that silver tongue of yours, Brentwood," the colonel's voice rumbled louder than the din of chatter that'd slowly resumed, "I'd say you're a lawyer. Tell me, what is your business?"

Nicholas tossed back a swallow of wine. He couldn't very well say he was Emily's nursemaid, though in truth, that was what he'd been reduced to. Replacing the goblet, he paused as the next course was served—a dish of bombarded veal and ragout. His taste buds slowly awoke, and he smiled at the colonel. "I am staying at Portman Square upon Mr. Payne's request."

The colonel nodded. "Completely understandable, given the situation."

The rest of the meal went untasted. Nicholas smiled and parleyed in all the right places, but the colonel's response lodged in his mind like a stone in his boot.

When the women finally departed and the port decanter passed from man to man, Nicholas sat back, glass in hand, drink untouched.

"Looks like you're the prize stallion again this season, Henley." Puffs of cheroot smoke punctuated the colonel's words.

"Yes, and once again I intend to dodge the golden noose of matrimony." Henley downed his port in one large gulp then swiped his hand across his mouth, leaving behind a rogue smile. His hair, the color of a mug of ale, was cropped short and held in check by pomade, stylish, yet not garish—the kind of man who hid behind a carefully constructed mask. "Why purchase the wine cask when sampling grapes from an entire vineyard is so much sweeter?"

"You might get a bit of competition from Brentwood, there." Mr. Barker aimed the red tip of his cheroot across the table. "You seem to have caught my daughter's eye. So? What about it? Which filly will you choose?"

Staring down the barrel of the loaded question, Nicholas tightened his jaw. No good answer could be given without trapping himself. He lifted the glass to his lower lip as if to drink.

"Mr. Henley is correct, no?" DiMarco filled in the silence for him. "These English women are a garden, *molto belle*. Roses to savor in bouquets." The man's eyes twinkled. "It is not the *italiano* way to limit oneself to a single bloom."

Nicholas set down his glass, biting back a grimace. These were the men Miss Payne hoped to snag?

Barker took a long drag on his cigar, the end glowing as bright as his eyes. "Henley might think otherwise when his harem suddenly changes to your tent, Brentwood. Your arrival, I think, is fortunate."

"Oh?" His muscles tensed, desire urging him to jump on that comment and ride it into the ground. Instead, he ran his index finger around the rim of his glass, following the action with his eyes. Better to wait for the quarry to circle back before striking.

"Bully, Mr. Barker, and I vow that Major Hargreave would agree with you." The colonel's bushy eyebrows waggled at Nicholas. "When the old boy catches wind of this, he'll be taut enough in the sails to hear you've jumped on board, especially if it buoys Payne's boat a little higher in the water. Owes him quite a tidy sum, as I understand."

Nicholas tucked the name—Hargreave—along with the remark, into a chest stored deep in his memory.

"I suspect your uncle—was that on your mother's side or your father's?" Barker ground out his cheroot while the truth burned on Nicholas's lips. How to answer that?

"No matter." Barker flicked his fingers, negating a response. "The point is, I suspect Payne is rather in a dither over this whole slave act passing last week. Though it was very insightful of him to expect the passage and summon you to town. At any rate, it's a deuced good thing he's got your fresh blood for a new venue. So tell us, Brentwood, without the slaving industry, what's Payne's game to be now?"

DiMarco, Henley, the colonel, and Barker stared down the table at him. Expectation charged the air.

Lord, please, do not let me shame You with a lie. The prayer barely formed into a coherent thought when a footman swooped into the dining room, small silver tray in hand, and set it on the table in front of him. "My apologies, sir. The messenger said it was urgent and refuses to leave without your answer."

A folded paper sat atop the tray. Nicholas retrieved it, disregarding all the eyes that followed his movement. Sparse words and an ink blot suggested the note had been written in haste:

237 Hancock Lane
Moore

He pursed his lips, inhaling deeply through his nose, then pulled his eyes from the note. He nodded toward the colonel's cigar. "Excuse me, Colonel, might I?"

The man's brows connected, yet he stretched out his cheroot. "Highly irregular, man."

Nicholas connected the tip of the paper to the glowing end,

leaving it there until a wisp of smoke and a red spark grew into a flame. Pulling back his hand, he held the burning note over the tray. When nothing but ash littered the silver, he stood.

"Gentlemen." He strode out the door, a thousand questions piercing the black wool of his dress coat.

❧

Bella's lips pulled into a pout. "I still can't believe you never told me about your cousin. Mr. Brentwood is striking in more than one way. I understand why you kept Millie in the dark, but me? Are we not closer than sisters?"

Emily's mouthful of sherry soured on her tongue. "I suppose I am a horrid person, Bella."

Licking her lips, she averted her gaze. Across the sitting room, Millie sat enthroned on a rosewood wingback, holding court with Catherine, Jane, and Anne. Emily leaned sideways and bumped shoulders with Bella. "But I'm not as bad as Millie."

A wicked smile spread across Bella's face. "You don't know the half of it."

Keeping one eye on the other women, Bella lowered her voice to a whisper. "It seems Mr. Henley took quite a break from his political intrigues to start a scandal of a much more intimate nature. I heard that he and Millie—"

"May I assist you with your wrap, Miss Payne? We are leaving." Nicholas Brentwood swung into the sitting room, his bass tone masking the rest of Bella's words.

Frowning, she glanced up at him. He stood before her, holding out her pelisse like a mandate. Authority surrounded him, magnified by his broad stance and even broader shoulders. The severe cut and dark color of his coat added to his stark manner. Could the man never relent from ruining her fun?

"I am hardly ready to leave now, sir." She turned back to Bella.

"Yet I insist."

Those three simple words pulled her to her feet, though her fingernails dug into the heels of her hands. *Yet I insist* meant an ugly confrontation simmered just below that cool green gaze should she refuse. She'd experienced his strong will often enough in the past week—each time she'd thought to have her own way. The man ought to give up law keeping and apply as tyrant of a small country.

"Is something wrong, Mr. Brentwood?" Millie flew to his side, hands clasped, eyelashes fluttering. The consummate hostess concerned for her guest. Emily choked back a snort. Millie's only concern was that she'd not had time enough to garner the man's attention.

"Not at all, Miss Barker. Simply a matter of business." A small smile softened his explanation. "My apologies for such an abrupt departure."

Millie's lower lip folded, and she turned to Emily. "Men and their business. Entirely too tedious. Why, you and I have had no time to visit at all. I suppose I shall have to call upon you on the morrow, hmm?"

Though phrased as a question, it wasn't. It was a verdict. Or maybe a threat. From the corner of Emily's eye, she caught Bella's raised brow and could feel her own forehead crease. Millie Barker had never once come to call at Portman House.

Emily slid her arms into the sleeves of her pelisse, the heat of Nicholas's hands still warming the shoulders where he'd held the fabric—and then she knew. Millie's call would have nothing to do with herself.

Emily locked eyes with Bella. "You'll stop by as well?"

Bella's gaze strayed to Nicholas. "My pleasure."

"Ladies, I bid you good evening." Nicholas nodded and turned on his heel. "Come along, Miss Payne."

His long, hard lines disappeared through the door. Emily huffed. Was she a dog to trot after him at his command?

Bobbing a thank-you curtsy to Millie and murmuring a "good evening" to the rest, she scurried to catch up with him on the front steps. "You had better have a stunning good reason to pull me from this household at such a breakneck pace, sir."

He glanced at her but didn't answer until he offered his hand at the carriage door. "I'm not entirely sure of the purpose, but not knowing how long I'd be gone, I deemed it best to bring you along."

Emily narrowed her eyes at him on her way up into the coach box. "You don't know where we're going?"

He paused before hefting himself up. "I didn't say that."

Exasperating man. The leather seat creaked as he settled in, his manner as nonchalant as if they were taking a drive in the country. She blew out a breath, long and low. "You don't know *why* we're going?"

"That is correct."

The carriage lurched into motion, as abrupt as his answer, and the jostle triggered a slight headache. Or maybe it was Nicholas who triggered the twinge at her temple. Streetlight reached in through the windows, feathering over the strong planes of his face, sweeping along defined cheekbones and jaw, and resting on the curve of his full lips. A fierce scowl assaulted her own mouth. Oughtn't an ogre look repulsive?

She lifted her chin. "So you're telling me, sir, that you've ruined my chances to charm Mr. Henley, giving Millie free rein to bat her eyelashes at the man for the rest of the evening, and you don't have the slightest idea as to why?"

"Yes, yes, and yes." He cocked his head at her, challenge lighting his eyes. "You ought to thank me, you know. Mr. Henley is a louse."

"Oh, spare me! What would you know of Charles Henley, other than the fact that he has an aversion to seafood, which I think was merely a lucky guess on your part."

"Really?"

She curled her fingers to keep from righting the smug tilt of his face. "You are hardly omniscient, Mr. Brentwood. How would you know the heart of a person?"

"I never claimed to read hearts, just behaviors. Details as well." His eyes held hers, driving home his point. "A person's character is most clearly seen not by what they show, but what they hide."

"Such as?"

The carriage wheels ground over cobbles. A watchman cried the hour. She could even hear Nicholas's body moving inside his greatcoat, the creak of leather as he shifted on the seat, but other than that, silence reigned. Eventually, her gaze strayed out the curtained window, traveling from one passing hackney to the next.

"You will keep what I say in confidence?"

His quiet tone and the implication it carried snapped her gaze back to his. "Do you not trust me, sir?"

The sharp cut of his jaw softened. "I trust in God alone, Miss Payne, and that is enough."

She gaped. "What a lonely way to live!"

"Not at all."

There was a fullness in those words. A kind of naked truth that reached into her own heart and illuminated a hollow shell. If she didn't know better, she'd say that Nicholas Brentwood and God were on speaking terms. No, it was more.

He spoke as if God was his intimate confidant.

The very thought unnerved her, and she ran her tongue over dry lips. "I assure you, Mr. Brentwood, any observations you share shall remain with me. Now. . .what did you see?"

"I assume you mean something besides the hired help palming a pickle fork."

"Seriously?"

His smile reached to his eyes. "No. The Barkers' servants all appeared aboveboard."

She rapped him on the arm as if he were Alf. "Beast."

"It's an offense, you know, to strike an officer of the law." His eyes sparkled as playfully as her pug's. "So. . .this DiMarco fellow, what do you know about him?"

"Not much. He's in town for the season. A family friend of the Barkers. Millie tells me he's on the prowl for a wife."

"He's already had one, you know, or mayhap still does."

She shook her head. This one she knew for certain, and the pleasure of bringing down Brentwood charged through her. "Impossible. Millie says—"

"Millie may parrot what the man has told her, yet the slight indentation on the third finger of his left hand cannot be hidden without gloves, which I noticed he wore until forced to remove them at dinner. And speaking of dinner, did you notice Miss Felton's plate?"

Her attention yanked from DiMarco to Jane. She could do nothing more than repeat his words. "Her plate?"

"Full, or nearly so, at the removal of each course. On the other hand, she drained her cup at least six times before dessert. I've seen sailors keel over with lesser amounts of liquor, yet the lady didn't so much as wobble."

Her jaw dropped. Words stuck in her throat, and it took great effort to coax them out. "Are you saying that Jane Felton. . .tipples?"

Even in the chill evening air, his smile warmed her through. "The woman could drink a Gin Lane sot beneath the table then stand to order another round."

She laughed, the carriage ride suddenly more entertaining than Millie Barker's parlor. "Go on, Mr. Brentwood. Tell me more."

He leaned toward her conspiratorially. "If the colonel should ever regale you with his exploits in the Battle of Trafalgar, don't believe a word of it. I doubt the man's ever set foot in the hull of a skiff, let alone a man-of-war."

"La! Surely you weren't aboard the *Victory*, nor do I believe you to be on speaking terms with Lord Nelson. That being said"—she shifted on the seat, gaining a clearer view of his face—"how would you know?"

"Watch his eyes, Miss Payne. The man's gaze darted about like a caged sparrow, looking anywhere but at me in the telling. And the way he scratched behind his ears, I purposely chose to take a turn about the room lest I caught fleas."

Her eyes widened. "You can tell when people are lying?"

"Frequently."

The carriage pitched to the right, and she flung out her hand for balance, the jolt as unsettling as his words. Not that she lied, but sometimes small falsehoods crossed her lips. Could he detect those as well? Better to change the subject. "Of all those in attendance tonight, surely you couldn't find fault with Mrs. Allen. She is the picture of virtue."

"True. . .but her husband is not."

"Aha! Caught you." She folded her arms, triumph sweet on her tongue. "Her husband was not even present, sir."

"No. I suspect he'd want to keep his swollen knuckles hidden from polite company."

She frowned. How in the world would the man know that?

Before she could ask, Nicholas interrupted her thoughts. "Tell me, is Mrs. Allen proficient with a brush and oils?"

"Quite. But I don't understand how you could know such information."

"Deduction. Besides the cobalt stain inside her wrist, just about even with her sleeve, the lady painted—and quite well I might add—her face."

"You can hardly fault Mrs. Allen or her husband for her cosmetics, sir."

"Of course not. The fault lies in Mr. Allen himself. The coloring around the lady's eye deepened from ivory to beige, with the barest hint of purple, noticeable only when she chanced to pass too near a wall sconce. Had she stepped any closer, I daresay her layers of makeup would've melted to her collar. Mr. Allen bullies his wife quite brutally."

Emily sank back against the carriage seat. "Poor Catherine," she breathed out. "I had no idea."

"My apologies, Miss Payne. Perhaps I ought not have—"

The regret in his voice signaled the ending of the game, a checkmate she wasn't ready to concede.

She sat up straight. "One last thing. You avoided this question at dinner, yet I will ask it again. What have you to say about Millie?"

His eyes darkened, blending into the shadows of the carriage. "I claim Mr. Henley is a louse, yet you don't believe me, so perhaps you ought ask Miss Barker about the content of the man. I suspect she's been jilted in a very. . .personal way."

The wheels jerked to a stop. So did her conceived notions of Charles Henley. Was that what Bella had been about to tell her? Or was this some kind of horrid jest on the part of Mr. Brentwood?

She studied his face every bit as intently as he did hers. If he'd discovered that much information in merely the space of a dinner, what of the entire week spent with her? Had he found out about—no. Her meeting with Wren wasn't even until tomorrow's early hours. Still. . .

"What of me, Mr. Brentwood?" Her voice sounded dry. Crumbly. Like autumn leaves skittering down a graveled road. She swallowed and tried again. "What do you know of my secrets?"

The carriage door swung open. A smile flashed, kind and cunning, illuminating Nicholas Brentwood's face an instant before he vanished into the night, taking his answer with him.

Horrid man.

Gathering her skirts, she ducked her head out the door—then froze.

Why would they leave Millie Barker's dinner party for a visit to Uncle Reggie's?

Chapter 8

Death was in the air. Heavy. Ominous. Nicholas could feel it in his bones. He inhaled a fresh waft of Emily's lily-of-the-valley sweetness, but if his surmise was correct, a stench was soon to come. The only way to know for sure was to keep trailing the grim-faced butler who ushered him and Emily down a short corridor of a three-story townhome.

Men's voices spilled out an open drawing-room door, one in particular lilting with a poorly concealed Midland drawl. Three heads turned at his entrance. Only one broke from the huddle.

"About time you hike your skirts over here, Brentwood." Fellow officer Alexander Moore strode across the room.

Emily drew up beside him, demanding answers, but Nicholas ignored her. "What's this? Smugglers not keeping you busy enough?"

"Later." Moore pulled him away from the door and lowered his voice. He gave an almost imperceptible tilt of his head toward Emily. "She a stable one?"

Nicholas rubbed his jaw, unsure of how to answer. Emily Payne was constant in tongue wagging, steady with frustration, and solid with determination to have her own way, though he doubted any of that was what Moore had in mind. "Come again?"

"Is the woman given to. . .swooning?"

He glanced over his shoulder, more from reflex than actual consideration. As he suspected, Emily stood near the door right where he'd left her, her gaze leveled at him like a well-aimed kidney punch—one that bruised even when he turned back to Moore. "She can hold her own, but what has she to do with—"

"Good. We've no time to waste. Bring Miss Payne."

Moore's brawny frame dwarfed Emily as he swept past her. Nicholas knew that gait. Moore was on a mission and wouldn't stop to explain anything until due time.

With a sigh, Nicholas shepherded Emily forward. "After you."

Her steps dragged, enough that he soon drew abreast of her.

"I don't understand." She slanted him a cool glance. "Who are these men? Where is Uncle Reggie?"

"This is Reggie's house?" Nicholas stopped, paces away from a door guarded by an armed constable—the same door Moore had disappeared through, expecting them to do the same. Blast it! No wonder Moore had questioned Emily's constitution. Squaring his shoulders, he turned to her. "I didn't know. Perhaps you ought to wait back in the sitting room. I'll—"

"It's now or never, Miss Payne." Moore's head popped out the door. The constable didn't flinch, but beside Nicholas, Emily did.

Nicholas frowned. "Listen, Moore, as her guardian I don't think this is a wise—"

"I can think for myself, Mr. Brentwood." In a flash, Emily shot past him and past Moore.

This wouldn't end well. He dashed after her.

The ticktock of a grandfather clock competed with her sharp intake of air. Understandable. Likely the worst crime she'd witnessed in her life was her precious pug stealing a biscuit or two from Cook.

"Uncle!" She rushed ahead and sank to her knees next to the divan, all but shoving a mouse of a physician out of the way.

The doctor scowled at her. "Now see here—"

Moore's hand on the doctor's arm ended his complaint. "You said yourself nothing more could be done. Care to revise that prognosis?"

The doctor's nose wrinkled. "No."

Moore jerked his head toward the threshold. "Then there's the door."

The doctor's lip curled as if he'd bitten into a rotten bit of cheese. Without another word, he snatched a black leather bag off the desk and evil-eyed Moore as he retreated.

Nicholas crossed to Emily's side, all the while cataloging the room in a sweeping glance. The wall safe was open. Curtains marshaled in cold night air. A rat's nest of papers was strewn atop a desk. All in all, the room was as torn up as its master.

Reggie lay ashen faced, still alive but barely. Right of center on the man's chest, a deep stain spread across his open waistcoat. His shirt was ripped apart, blood darkening a poultice left over from the doctor's futile ministrations. Pink foam dribbled out one side of the man's mouth. Indeed, he had minutes left, if that. A pistol ball to the lower lung was a miserable way to go.

Emily took up one of Reggie's hands in both of hers, chafing them as if the fellow were dying of cold instead of a bloody suffocation.

"Thank. . .God. You're not. . .hurt." Reggie's words rasped with fluid, his lips sucking air like a landed fish. His eyes closed with the effort.

"But you. . .oh, Uncle," Emily's voice broke, her own chest heaving. "Why would someone want to hurt you? Or me?"

His eyes reopened, mortality a gray film over each. Hopefully the man knew his Maker, for he'd soon meet Him. "Your. . .father. . ." He wheezed, his fight for air forcing Nicholas to tug at his own cravat.

"I fear for you. . .Emily. . ." Reggie struggled to lift his head. "You must be careful." The words drove him back, flattening him against an overstuffed cushion.

Suddenly, seconds were precious.

Nicholas dropped to his knees next to Emily. He hated to be the one to interrupt what might be her last exchange with the fellow, but prudence was a harsh taskmaster. "Of whom, sir? Be careful of whom?"

Reggie's eyes gripped his. Tight. Pleading. The loneliest moment of a lost one's life was often the last. His lips moved, but no sound came out.

Compassion burned a trail from Nicholas's gut up to his mouth.

"Call on Christ alone for mercy, man. Now is the time."

Maybe Reggie did. Or not. Hard to tell, for an instant later, his wheezing stilled. His gasps ceased. His struggle for life ended in dismal defeat.

For one horrific instant, Jenny's face superimposed over the dead man's, and Nicholas's own heart stopped.

Emily's wail rent the air. She splayed her fingers, dropping Reggie's lifeless hand. Sobs followed. Turning, she buried her face in Nicholas's shirt.

He wrapped his arms around her, one hand patting her back, knowing full well that shock often accounted for the most unlikely of embraces. She trembled, frail and vulnerable, a whole new facet to the fiery woman.

Glancing up, he met Moore's gaze. The set of the officer's jaw confirmed that condolences would have to wait. Even so, Moore stepped outside to give them a minute.

Nicholas pulled Emily to her feet. Sniffling, she retreated a step, a little wobbly but bearing up.

He retrieved a handkerchief from his dress coat and held it out. "Forgive me. Had I known, I never would have brought you here."

"No, don't think it. It's better he had someone he knew with him for the final moments." Her gaze strayed to the dead man on the divan. Color drained from her face. "He. . .he. . .what about my father? What did he mean? Why must I be careful?"

Each word grew shriller, her chest fluttering as if she'd taken the bullet. Nicholas stepped in front of her, blocking her view of the corpse. "Miss Payne—"

"I. . .oh my. . .what if—" She swayed, her eyes dark holes in a face white as cotton. If the woman didn't breathe, and soon, he'd have two bodies on his hands.

Grabbing her upper arms, he forced his face into hers. "Emily!"

Startled, she met his gaze. A faint bluish line rimmed her lips.

"There is nothing to fear. I'm here, and no one will take you from me. Do you understand?" He measured his words, doling out each one like a lifeline, willing her to grasp onto the strength in his voice. "Upon my word, I'll keep you safe. I vow it, on pain of death."

Her throat moved with a swallow. A lost little girl couldn't have looked more exposed. Slowly, color crept back into her cheeks. The trembling beneath his fingers stopped.

"Good." Half a smile tipped his mouth. "You're doing better already."

"Thank you." Her voice was a whisper. A shell. Hardly more than a piece of chaff on the wind.

But it was a voice, nonetheless.

He smiled in full.

Officer Moore, maid in tow, cleared his throat as he entered the room, cuing an end to consolation. Nicholas released Emily's arms, pleased that she remained straight and tall. "Now then, you shall return to the drawing room. Mr. Moore and I have a bit of work to do in here."

Her eyes widened. The lovely pink in her face fled once more. "But—"

"None of it. You're a strong one, you are." Lifting his chin, he looked down his nose at her. "Unless my assessment of Emily Payne is incorrect. Do you hide a yellow streak beneath those skirts?"

She set her jaw, a blue spark of anger lighting her eyes. "You, sir, are a—"

"Rogue. I know." He nodded toward the maid while turning Emily to face her. "Go."

"This way, miss." The maid spun, apron strings fluttering behind her. Clearly, sharing a room with her deceased employer didn't top her list of favorite duties.

When he felt sure they were beyond hearing range, Nicholas lifted his eyes to Moore's. "So, what have we got?"

Moore stalked to the open window, a hunter on the trail. His long legs stretched with the grace of a lion. His dark blond hair, longer than decorum allowed, blew back with the breeze, adding a mane-ish effect. "As you see. Point of entry."

"Don't you mean exit?"

"That, too. I queried the servants. No one was admitted by the front door. In truth, no one suspected anything other than that Reginald Sedgewick was alone in this study."

Nicholas rubbed at the tension in his neck. "Then what?"

"Some kind of heated debate, I suppose. One which Mr. Sedgewick lost." Moore swept his hand toward the mess on the desk and the overturned chair behind it.

The clock in the corner kept a steady beat as Nicholas studied the room. He fingered through the documents. Correspondence mostly, notes inquiring about shipment arrivals or departures. A few invoices, all headed with Sedgewick & Payne. Stepping around the desk, he righted the chair then peered into an open wall safe. Empty. He frowned. "But why lose a heated debate when he obviously handed over all his valuables? Unless. . ."

Nicholas squinted and ran his fingertips over the locking mechanism. A Bramah, without so much as a scratch. No surprise, though. As far as he knew, no one had yet collected the two hundred guineas promised by the manufacturer for picking one of their locks. He turned to Moore. "No sign of force."

Moore rubbed the back of his head. "Unless he was shot first then told to—"

"Unlikely. If that were the case, Reggie there would be sporting a blown kneecap, not a hole in the chest. Why comply when death is imminent?"

"True." Folding his arms, Moore nodded. "It could be the vault was empty when he opened it, hence the argument, leading to rage and eventually murder."

"And if the suspect left here unsatisfied, monetarily speaking, then that would explain Sedgewick's warning." A growl rumbled in his throat. "Which is clear enough on Emily's part, but what of her father? Were Reggie's last words a warning *for* her father or *from* him?"

Moore shrugged. "What exactly is Mr. Sedgewick's tie-in with your ward? Why spend his last moments on earth to see that not only Bow Street was summoned but Miss Payne in particular?"

"Exactly." Nicholas ran his hand through his hair. "That's what concerns me most."

And it did. More than he cared to admit.

Chapter 9

After hours of tossing and turning, recounting ghastly images of her uncle's lifeless eyes, Emily was glad to focus on something else—even if that something else taxed her in ways that were every bit as nerve-racking. Slipping out of the town house an hour before dawn for a clandestine meeting with her former maid had seemed like good idea at the time she'd arranged it. But now. . .

Clutching her package to her chest, Emily glanced over her shoulder. A dark, empty street stretched behind, made all the more ominous by a fine mist suspended midair. Her footsteps alone echoed off the brick townhomes. At this hour, only an occasional carriage or a dray bent on an early delivery run traveled the lanes of Portman Square. So why the breath-stealing impression that eyes followed her every move?

She resettled the pack over her shoulder and tugged her hood forward. Nerves. That's what. Barely six hours ago Uncle Reggie had died right in front of her. No wonder jitters marked her every step. If Wren weren't counting on her, she'd still be curled up under her counterpane, sleeping off the dreadful experience. Leaving the safety of her bed had taken more courage than she'd realized.

And what would Nicholas Brentwood say were he to find her chamber empty?

She quickened her pace. She'd just have to make sure he didn't. Two blocks down, she turned right. Ahead, near a cabstand that wouldn't house a hack for at least another hour, a lone figure lingered beneath a sputtering lamppost. The shape was slight, short, and entirely Wren-sized. Emily shot forward.

Her former maid met her halfway. "Oh, miss! So good to see you."

Emily slung the bag down to the wet cobbles and folded Wren's hands into her own. Cold flesh chilled through the fabric of her gloves. "It's always good to see you, Wren. How are you holding up?"

"I'm well, miss, as is the babe." Wren pulled back her hands and rested them on the swell of her belly. For a brief moment, half a smile lit her face. "Thanks to you, that is. Without you. . .why, I don't know what I'd do."

"None of it. You're a strong one, you are." The same words Nicholas used for her tasted sturdy and warm in her own mouth and hopefully lent similar courage to Wren. "Please tell me you've found a place to stay."

"I have. I've got four walls and a bed of my own, which is more than I can say for other girls in my. . .condition." Wren's gaze lowered.

Anger lifted Emily's chin. "It's not fair, Wren. None of this is. That scoundrel of a captain ought to be scratching out his existence in the streets instead of you. And my father"—she sucked in a sharp breath, mourning afresh her mounting loss of respect for the man—"why I'm still so furious he let you go without references, I can hardly stand it."

"Don't fret. It's all right. Truly. I've found peace." She reached out one hand and squeezed Emily's. The sharp angles of her cheekbones softened, and through the mist and dark, light sparkled in her eyes. "I know it's strange to hear me say so, but I forgive them both, your father and Captain Daggett."

"Wren!" *Forgive them?* The words boxed her ears, foreign and completely abhorrent. Emily yanked back her hand. "How can you? They ruined your life!"

"No, miss. It's not like that, not at all. I see it different now." The peaceful look in Wren's eyes spread to lighten her whole face, or was that simply streetlight reflecting off the mist on her cheeks? "Only by losing everything could I gain the one thing I would've overlooked."

"What's that?"

"Need."

Emily frowned. "You're telling me that need, want, the lack of shelter, food, and clothing, is a *good* thing?"

"Didn't call it good, miss, but it is a blessing." Wren's smile would shame the sun, and mayhap did, for along with it the hint of dawn barely bleached the sky. "Aye, miss. I know it don't make sense, but I've found that God is more than enough, even in the direst of situations."

Emily couldn't help but shake her head. "You're starting to sound like Mr. Brentwood."

"Mr. who?"

She sighed, for truly. . .how to put into words her conflicting emotions about the man? One minute a bully, exacting and demanding, the next consoling her as a dear friend. Even now, if she closed her eyes and thought of it, she could feel his solid arms circling her, breathe in his peppery shaving tonic, lean into his strength.

A fresh waft of morning fires being stoked banished the memory. Nearby, households awakened. She bent to retrieve the oilskin bag and held it out to Wren. "Here is an old dress of mine I've let out in the front. It ought hold you over until—when did you say?"

Wren hugged the pack to her chest. "Nigh but two more months now, near as I can figure."

Emily lifted her chin, a gesture she'd seen Mrs. Hunt use to rally the servants a hundred times. "Well then, there's some tincture in the bag from the apothecary, good for you and the babe. A spoonful at night and one in the morning. I've included a spoon."

"Ahh, miss. You're always thinking."

The warmth in Wren's voice burned a trail to her heart. How she missed the girl and her sweet ways. "Tucked deepest inside is a coin purse. There's enough to hold you over in food until we meet again next month. Same time and place?"

"If you don't mind. Thank you. One last thing, though I hardly deserve more. My mother, does she. . ." This time there was no mistaking mist for the single tear sliding down the girl's face. "Does she ask after me?"

Emily's lips pressed into a tight line. Must it be her lot to break the girl's heart afresh? "In truth, Wren, I've not told her yet that I've been meeting with you. I've meant to, but the time's never been quite right. Oh, I've hinted around and such, but your mother's as adamant as ever when I bring up your name. I feel sure, though, that once the babe is born, once she sees the sweet little one, she shall change her mind."

"Aye. Mayhap." Wren's voice was hollow. She settled the pack over her shoulder and dipped a small curtsy. "Good day, miss."

Emily nodded, for truly there was nothing more to say. Watching Wren retreat spent the small account of optimism she held for the girl. To what part of town would Wren's feet take her? Who would be there for her should something go wrong? Except for Wren's growing belly, she was so small, so vulnerable.

Shivering, Emily turned her back to the desolate figure. Dampness soaked into the leather of her shoes while she retraced her steps. As she neared the corner, a quiver shimmied along her shoulders—but not from cold. The distinct thud of boots pounded dully in the mist behind her.

She increased her pace and refused the urge to look over her shoulder, denial lending some confidence. *Please God, may it be one of those coal heavers on an early delivery.*

But the boot thuds upped their tempo as well.

Fear settled low in her stomach, making her feel as if she might vomit. The ghastly memory of Uncle Reggie lying waxen and gray added to the nausea. She'd made a huge mistake coming here by herself. The realization burned white hot, like the pretty red coal in the grate she'd touched as a tot. She'd discovered its danger too late ...just like now.

Still, maybe the fellow behind her was simply in a hurry. After all, she—

The world spun. Her back slammed against a brick wall. Every nerve shrieked a warning, but she couldn't scream.

A glove covered her mouth.

Hot breath blazed across her forehead. "I'll remove my hand, but upon my word, you scream and this will go all the worse for you. Do you understand?"

Emily's head moved beneath Nicholas's fingers. A stingy nod, but an acknowledgement nonetheless. Her hood had fallen back. Lengths of blond hair cascaded over his sleeve. He lowered his hand, bypassing the pretty neck he'd love to wring, and clamped his fingers onto her upper arm instead. "You little fool. What are you doing out here alone?"

"You frightened half my life away!" Her voice shook, as did the slim arms beneath his grasp. "I was meeting a friend. Nothing more."

But he would not be moved. Not yet. "Only criminals meet by shadow of night."

"Wren is a friend! One who needs my help. How dare you infer anything other." Her body writhed with each word. "Now let me go."

"Not until I've had the whole story."

"I told you—"

Was the woman truly that daft? "Blast it! You saw what happened to Reggie." He clenched his jaw instead of shaking her like the empty-headed rag doll she playacted. "How am I to keep you safe with a handful of half-truths?"

Instantly she stilled. The whites of her eyes glistened abnormally white. "Surely what happened last night has nothing to do with me."

"Honestly, Miss Payne. This is not a child's game we're playing. Why do you think your father hired me in the first place?" He jerked his head toward the spot where she'd been standing only minutes before. "I suppose you didn't take the time to notice the cutthroat across the road from the cabstand."

Her gaze slide past his shoulder. "Don't be ridiculous. I don't see any. . .oh my. . ."

"And I'll wager you also didn't see the blackguard trailing you on your way here, either. What sorry state do you think you'd currently find yourself in had the flash of my pistol muzzle not guarded your steps?"

Her eyes widened. "You mean you—"

"I mean you can thank God for waking me when I heard the floorboard squeak outside your chamber door!"

Her face blanched, gray as the dawning daylight. She tipped her head back until it rested against the brick wall. Moments passed, as did an early morning carriage behind him, the ground-level fog muffling the grind of the wheels. Perhaps it was a bit much for her to take in, but finally—mayhap—she understood the gravity of her situation. A small victory. Nonetheless, every successful battle, no matter how slight, led to winning the war.

With a sigh, he released his hold on her and stepped back. "Who is this Wren that so desperately needs your help, enough so that you'd endanger your own life?"

Once again her gaze darted toward the cabstand, as if by looking the woman might magically reappear. "Wren—*Lauren*—Hunt was my abigail before Mary. I've known her for years. Wren and I practically grew up together." Her voice softened. Apparently she was very fond of the girl. Then quick as a spring cloudburst, a shadow crossed her face. "She was forced to leave several months ago."

"Why?"

"She is. . ." Emily's gaze shot to the ground. "Wren is with child. Because of me."

"You?" He snorted. "Hardly possible, and is in fact an impossibility altogether."

She snapped her face back to his. "Do not think to school me in the specifics of nature, Mr. Brentwood. Would you have the story or not?"

He raised both hands. The woman could change emotions faster than a cutpurse in a crowd. "Go on."

She took her time gathering the loose ends of her hair, tucking them behind her head, and reseating her hood before she continued. "It was late last summer. We'd just settled at Abingdon, our country home. Father had a guest in for an early season hunt. The weather was hot, oppressively so. I'd ventured out late one evening, seeking air, and Father's guest, Captain Daggett, chanced upon me—though now I realize it likely wasn't chance."

She paused, her face hardening into a brittle mask. "I managed to fight the man off, but Wren, well. . .when she came looking for me, Daggett took her instead."

Nicholas rubbed his jaw. How much of this was true? He didn't doubt Emily could scare off a baited bear with her tongue, and the figure she'd met at the stand was with child, as stated. But was Payne such a rogue as to throw out a long-standing servant into the street? "Surely your father—"

"Father chose to believe Daggett's pack of lies." Her tone took on a hard edge—one he hadn't heard before. "And I suspect were it me instead of Wren, he'd still have sided with the man." She nodded toward the stand. "That could just as easily be me."

The woman ought to be onstage. Drama was in her blood. He shook his head. "You must be mistaken. There's got to be more to it, reasons your father chose not to share with you."

Her gaze locked on to his, resolute and slightly unnerving.

What he read there chilled him to the marrow. These were no theatrics.

"Business is my father's life, Mr. Brentwood. Without money, I daresay he'd stop breathing. Once set on a deal, he'll allow nothing or no one to alter his plans, whether that means banishing a dear family servant. . .or his only daughter. Fortunately for me, it didn't come to that. But sweet Wren—"

Her voice cracked along the edges, and if the tears shining in her eyes spilled over, he'd rip off his gloves and wipe them away.

Instead, he simply said, "Thank you."

Her brow crumpled. "For what?"

"Your honesty. Truth is a gem to be admired and very pretty when it comes from your lips."

Were the sunrise not obscured by clouds, it would be chastened by the blush rising on her cheeks. This was no pretend pleasure. It was real. Fresh. And entirely alluring. A charge passed between them. He could see it in her eyes, feel it in his gut.

"Yes...well..." The fine lines of her neck moved as she swallowed. "I'm not usually so candid. Do you have this same effect on criminals?"

"What effect is that, I wonder?" He tucked his chin and purposely lifted one eyebrow, knowing the result it would have.

She leaned forward, a breath away. He heard the small sound of her lips parting, but he daren't lower his gaze to them. Danger didn't issue only from the barrel of a gun.

For the good of them both, he retreated a step and pivoted. "We should return."

Before she could answer, he set a brisk pace, feeding off her protests to slow up and using her indignation to cool the warmer feelings he ought not entertain. Caring *about* a client was one thing. Caring *for* a client was quite another animal altogether.

Still, she had shown an extra amount of compassion for her former maid. Quite in contradiction to her sometimes shrewish demeanor. Perhaps, underneath it all, she hid more heart than he suspected. Unique thought—one he'd mull over later.

By the time they reached the townhome door, they both were breathless. She from the insane pace he'd set. He because of the figure stepping from the sheltered nook leading down to the servants' entrance.

Perhaps Hope hadn't been the best choice to name the little urchin, for her appearance meant anything but.

Chapter 10

*P*lease, God. . .grant that I get there in time. Nicholas spent the entire carriage ride from Portman Square to Lombard Street alternating between silent prayer and peppering Hope with questions.

It was the longest ride of his life.

Before the hackney wheels stopped turning, Nicholas bounded out the door. Hope's feet hit the ground behind him. Though still early morning, Lombard Street was in full bloom, which for some odd reason irritated him. The hawkers were too loud. The horse droppings too foul. The world had turned brash and harsh and entirely too precarious. He flipped a coin to the driver without missing a step.

Ducking into the Crown and Horn, he strode the length of the pub, avoiding eye contact with Meggy Dawkin as she delivered a plate of mutton hash to a customer. Nevertheless, he felt her stare. She wouldn't condemn him for all to hear. She didn't have to. The way she thunked the plate onto the table voiced her opinion in no uncertain terms. Mistress Dawkin wanted his sister out of there, and so did he.

But not in a wooden box.

He took the stairs two at a time, crediting Hope for the deft way her footsteps tapped behind his. By the time he reached the second-floor corridor, the doctor was already stepping from Jenny's room. He was a tall man, angular in an almost grotesque way. His black greatcoat shrouded his length like a shadow, an eerie image of the grim reaper.

Nicholas closed the distance in a heartbeat. "Is she—"

Dr. Kirby held up a hand. "She's resting, for now, but she won't stand another attack. I suggest you say your good-byes."

The incendiary words scalded his ears then burned deeper, branding his soul. How exactly did one let go of their last family member? He met Kirby's even stare. "Is there nothing you can do?"

Hope hovered at his back, but Nicholas felt his own optimism dwindling as Kirby shook his head.

"I told you from the start, Brentwood, I'm no miracle worker. Better you bring your requests to God, if you think He's listening." The doctor sidestepped him with a nod of his head and an added "good day."

Nicholas stood stunned. Of course God was listening—but that didn't mean God would answer in an agreeable fashion. Sucking in a shaky breath, he twisted the knob and eased open the door. No sense waking Jen if she'd just gotten settled.

His care was wasted. Her eyelids raised the instant his boot crossed the threshold. Overlarge eyes, framed by gaunt cheekbones, gazed into his. The slow move of her pale fingers drawing up the bedclothes spoke of weariness. The downward slope to her brow, resignation. His chest tightened. He'd seen that look many times on the battlefield and more recently on Reggie.

He knelt on the cold wooden floor and lifted one of her hands in both of his. His posture mimicked Emily's from the night before, but hopefully this prayer would see a different result.

He forced a smile, though likely it looked more like a grimace. "Ahh, my sweet Jen. How are you today, hmm?"

"Dandy and grand. . ." She winced. "As always."

Her voice was a thread. Thin. Fragile. Instinct urged him to buoy his own with enough strength for the both of them. "I suspect, then, that there shall be no end of the balls I must take you to or the dinners you should like to attend. And the suitors. Well, I suppose I'll have to beat them away with my tipstaff."

Her frail smile disintegrated. "Dear Brother. When shall we stop this masquerade?"

He swallowed, but it did nothing to relieve the lump in his throat. "Never."

The word came out harsher than he intended. Carefully, he tucked her hand beneath the blanket then stood and raked his fingers through his hair. "Two weeks, Jen. Only two, and my employer shall return. I'll have the money to see you off to the country. You'll breathe easier there—I know it—and you'll find that this isn't a charade after all."

He knew he was rambling, but it couldn't be helped. "You'll be dandy and grand—" His voice cracked, the following words nothing but a whisper. "As always."

Her gaze pierced his soul. "For one who values truth, Brother, you employ a lie with ease."

"Jen, I—"

"Don't make excuses." Morning light streamed through the single window, a bright contrast to this deathly conversation. The lone sunbeam slid along her skin-wrapped bones like a knife, cutting and severe. Already she looked like a cadaver.

"Allow me this moment to speak my heart, for I may not have many more. I shall miss you, dearly, but please understand, I am going to a better place. A place I want to be." She paused, her chest riffling the blanket with her quickened breaths. "Let me go, Nicholas."

He clenched his hands into rock-hard fists. God help the next criminal that crossed his path, for this depth of emotion could not be contained for long. It wasn't fair. None of it. He should've died a hundred times over for his wicked ways, not her.

"I should like to rest now." Her voice was a fragment of a whisper, barely pulling him from his thoughts. Slowly, her eyelids closed.

"Of course." He bent, kissing her brow as a benediction, unable to keep from wondering if it would be the last time. "Sleep sweet."

Straightening, he lingered, casting a long look at the shell housing his sister.

Then he turned and stalked out.

Hope stood exactly where he'd left her, leaning against the

corridor wall. She looked up at his appearance. "Is Miss Jenny dea—"

He scowled at her. "Don't say it."

The girl's decorum was nonexistent. Not surprising. Death played alongside the street children, ever present in their games, ready to steal another one of their companions when they weren't looking. 'Twas a gruesome round of hide-and-seek.

Nicholas shook off the morbid thought. "My sister is resting. Have some broth ready when she wakes. I'll return as soon as I can, but don't hesitate to fetch me once more if she. . .no. That won't do."

Jenny ought not be left alone. He scrubbed his jaw, stubble pricking his fingertips. The late night and early morning hours he'd kept slowed his mind. *Think. Think.*

Digging out another precious coin from his pocket, he handed it to Hope. "If my sister needs me, hire a cab, just like I did this morning, and tell the driver to deliver the message. Can you do that?"

Hope bobbed her head. "Aye, sir."

"Good." He tromped down the hall and flipped up his collar as he descended the stairs. A small barricade to hide behind, but he had no stomach to argue with Meggy about moving his sister now. As his foot left the last tread, he scanned the public room. The last swish of her skirt hem, followed by streaming apron strings, disappeared through the kitchen door. He hustled past the diners finishing their breakfasts and slipped out the front.

Relief lasted only until a brawny man in a dun-colored greatcoat rounded the corner and plowed through the pedestrians, straight toward him.

Nicholas frowned. "I don't suppose you're frequenting the Crown and Horn for the hash, eh, Moore?"

Alexander Moore's hat sat low on his brow, making Nicholas aware he'd neglected to don his own. "You've given me quite the rundown this morning, Brentwood."

Nicholas fell into step beside him. If Moore had taken the time to track him, something was up. "You know me. I like to keep on the move. Where are we going?"

Moore shouldered past a knife grinder blocking their way, barking about the quality of his sharpening services. "There's someone you ought to see down at the dead house."

Nicholas shot him a sideways glance. "Who's that?"

"That's exactly what I'm hoping you can tell me."

❧

Emily stifled a yawn, the third in as many minutes. She straightened her back, but the settee cushions beneath her felt softer with every tick of the clock. If she sat here any longer, she'd curl up next to the little pug snoring at her side.

"Really, Emily, I've far overstayed my visit. In truth, I may have set a record." Across the sitting room, Bella turned from the window. The sheer curtain shimmied into place. Displaced daylight backlit her red hair, creating a radiant halo. "There's no sign of Millie. Do you think she'll really call?"

Standing, Emily wiggled life back into her feet. Alf jerked up his head then must've decided the effort wasn't worth abandoning his comfy bed. His scrunchy face flopped back down onto his paws. Emily sighed—better that than another yawn. "You're right. And you're a dear. I owe you for frittering away your morning with me."

"Pah! You saved me from having to shop with Mother. You know how much I abhor traipsing from one merchant to another."

Ringing the bell for the maid, Emily smiled. What woman in her right mind wouldn't want to browse for new shoes or a bonnet? "Remind me again why we are friends?"

"Opposites attract, or so I'm told." Bella returned the grin then stooped to pat Alf between his ears. "Good thing, for you shouldn't like to be compared favorably to your wrinkly pup now, would you?"

"Not if I'm to attract Mr. Henley this season."

Bella straightened, humor draining from her face. "Have you listened to a word I've said? After all I've told you about him and Millie, why would you even want to interest that man?"

Emily stepped forward and placed a light touch on her friend's arm. "Not that I doubt you, but honestly, I don't feel I have a choice. Father won't put up with me forever. You know it's only for my mother's sake—God rest her soul—he's been gracious thus far. Besides," she continued, squeezing Bella's arm, "if only half what you shared is true, don't you think Millie is the one to blame every bit as much as Mr. Henley? For goodness' sake, Bella, you've seen the woman in action. She's nothing but a lace-covered tart."

Bella's lips twitched. No wonder. She was probably battling over whether she should gasp or giggle. "True, but that hardly means Mr. Henley should have, well. . .you know. Once word of this gets out, which shan't be long if you and I already know, Millie will be ruined, and Henley will merely get a pat on the back."

Emily frowned, the double standard grating her sensibilities as a tooth gone bad. It was as ludicrous as Wren's situation and about as just. No doubt Millie deserved whatever she had coming, but Wren didn't. Why should she have to live in a hovel while the lecherous captain sailed the high seas, free to prey on the next ruffle and bow? Her frown deepened into a scowl. "Whoever came up with such ridiculous societal rules is a bird-witted cod's head."

"Emily!"

A wicked grin erased her glower. "Sorry. I didn't mean to say that aloud."

The maid pattered into the room, holding Bella's pelisse aloft. Turning from Emily, Bella shrugged into her wrap—but not fast enough for Emily to miss the twist of her lips. "Please, Em, rethink your options. Mr. Henley isn't the only available man in London."

"But he is the richest. And at three and twenty, I find my options get more limited with the passing of each season."

"Just. . .be careful." Bella's eyes sought hers. "I'd hate to see anything happen to you."

"Have you ever known me to act without thinking it through first?"

Her friend's pretty lips parted, but Emily beat her to it. "Go on with you. I'll see you tomorrow at church, hmm?"

"Do yourself a favor and pay attention to the sermon for once. Who knows, perhaps God will change your mind about Henley. You're obviously not listening to me." Her tone softened as she headed toward the door. "And give that yummy Mr. Brentwood my regards whenever he returns, in a discreet fashion, of course. Until later, Em."

Bella's departure left a void, one that fatigue quickly filled. Emily arched her back then snapped her fingers, rousing the pug. "Come along, Alf. A cozy counterpane is calling our names."

She crossed the room and hall. Doggy toenails tip-tapped double-time to her pace. Each step up the staircase required effort, hers because she was weary, his from stubby legs. Perhaps she ought not have spent the entire morning waiting around for Millie. At least that's the premise she'd hide behind for now—for if she cared to peek around the sides of that flimsy excuse, she was afraid of what she'd see.

Nicholas Brentwood. Horrid man. Why should she give a fig about where he'd disappeared to with that waif of a girl? Yet it bothered her to no end. Not that it was her business. She ought to be reveling in the freedom she'd enjoyed from breakfast until now.

So why wasn't she?

Another yawn stretched her jaw as she padded down the second-floor corridor to her room. Passing by Mary's door, she slowed, and Alf bumped into her hem. One of Mrs. Hunt's stern reprimands leached through the paneling. What in the world had her abigail done to warrant such a scolding? Though she was still unable to walk, Mary had worked wonders with her needle, stitching fine designs upon nearly every one of Emily's day dresses.

With a shush to Alf, Emily leaned her ear to the door, removing the muffle from the housekeeper's words. "Your last warning. One more slipup like this and you'll be out the door with nary a reference. And don't you think I won't. Why I—"

"M–miss?"

Emily jerked upright and spun, biting back an unladylike oath. Alf didn't hold back though—he yipped. Emily shushed him then turned to the maid. "Betsy! For heaven's sake, don't sneak up on me like that."

The maid's head dipped, scarlet darkening her cheeks. "S–sorry. There's a c–caller for you. Shall I turn her away?"

"Yes." Emily inhaled deeply, calming her racing heart. Was this entire day to be fraught with one startling moment after another?

Mrs. Hunt's tirade continued without pause, and as Betsy turned to leave, Emily once again leaned toward the door—then immediately straightened.

"Betsy, wait." She turned to the departing maid. "Did you say the caller is a woman?"

Near the top of the stairway, the girl paused. "Aye. A Miss Barker."

Drat. Should she socialize, eavesdrop, or cave in to her fatigue and snuggle up with Alf?

"Mind the dog, Betsy. I'll attend to my guest." She swooped past Betsy, tucking up loose bits of hair as she descended the steps. No sense handing Millie a reason to judge her appearance.

Emily swept into the sitting room, sizing up Millie in a glance. She wore a periwinkle gown, which peeked out from a matching pelisse and was topped off with a bonnet so lacy and ruffled and large, that if taken apart, the thing might clothe several little girls. Emily frowned, calculating when she could scoot over to the milliner's and have her latest purchase redone to such a standard, then greeted her guest. "Miss Barker, how kind of you to call."

Retreating back to the door, Emily reached for the bellpull. "My apologies. I am mortified Betsy didn't take your wrap."

"No need. I shan't be staying long, unless. . ." Millie ran a gloved finger along the length of the mantel as she strolled the room. "I am disappointed you feel the need to address me as Miss Barker. Are we not on a first-name basis by now, dearest?" She circled back. "For I feel sure, Emily, we shall be the best of friends."

Emily pressed her lips together, remembering the warning Nicholas had spouted days ago. *The only way to prevent trouble. . .is to identify the danger before it strikes.*

Oh, yes. A close friendship with Millie would be quite the hazard.

Pasting on a smile, she crossed toward the settee. "Shall we sit, Millie?" The name left a tart taste in her mouth.

Millie stopped near a framed silverpoint study. Either she took a deep interest in such artwork, or she was snubbing the offer on purpose. "That was quite an abrupt departure you made from dinner last night." Millie spoke without facing her. "I hope your cousin's business was profitable, whatever it was."

Unbidden, the awful gray face of Uncle Reggie surfaced. Emily shifted on the cushion. "Not really."

Millie turned then, a feline smile curving her lips. "Too bad. Mr. Henley asked after you."

"He did?" A secret thrill raced through her. Perhaps she was making progress, after all.

"Did Mr. Brentwood happen to make mention of me?"

Only that he suspected she'd been jilted—in an intimate way. Emily bit her lip. She couldn't very well spout that, so she said a simple, "Yes."

A tiny squeal squeaked out of Millie, not unlike Alf when a bone was involved. She abandoned the silverpoint and sank into the chair adjacent the settee. "You must tell me about your cousin, dearest. His likes. His dislikes. He will be accompanying you to the Garveys' ball next week, will he not?"

"Hopefully not."

Millie's eyebrows nearly lifted her elaborate bonnet off her head.

Though it was God's honest truth—Mr. Brentwood would be proud—still. . .she couldn't let it stand without revealing to Millie her reasons why. "I mean to say hopefully he will not decline, though I don't suppose he will."

"I see. Well," Millie leaned forward, "you know how I adore games. Why don't we play one?"

Emily tilted her head. "Such as?"

"For every secret you tell me about your cousin, I shall give you one of Mr. Henley's. Would you like to play?"

Millie seemed relaxed, but in that one drawn-out moment while Emily debated an answer, she could see by the thin set of Millie's lips and the slight tic along her jaw just how eager the woman really was.

And so was Emily.

Chapter 11

The east side of the Thames, though geographically not far from Portman Square, was a world away from the pretty ladies and their dandier counterparts on the western edge of town. Even on the brightest spring days, sunshine didn't stretch to warm these streets. Nicholas tugged his coat tighter as he kept pace with Officer Moore. On each side of the narrow lane, buildings stooped like rheumy old men, hunched at the shoulders. Snuff-colored laundry hung overhead, laced from window to window. Nicholas eyed the patched fabric on a pair of frayed trousers and shook his head. Why bother to wash such a drab garment in the first place?

"Something doesn't meet with your approval?"

Moore's question cut into his thoughts—and his conscience. "I think my time spent at Portman Square is making me into a snob."

"You always were a bit priggish, if you ask me."

Nicholas frowned over at him. "I didn't."

"Fair enough." Moore spoke without slowing a step. "Oh, I nearly forgot. It seems Ol' Georgie isn't the only one on the list of 'who Americans love to hate.' "

His frown deepened. Moore liked nothing better than to toss out his nuggets of information, one crumb at a time—an annoying tendency. "What's your point?"

"Apparently your 'Uncle Reggie' isn't a favorite with the Yanks."

They parted momentarily, a mound of horse droppings splitting them as effectively as a rock in a streambed.

"After you left last night," Moore continued, "Sedgewick's valet remembered a caller about a week ago. The man left no card, yet the valet recalled not only the man's drawl but his name—Captain Norton."

Nicholas grunted. "I shouldn't think that would be unusual.

Sedgewick & Payne are a shipping company, after all."

"This one, however, left with a threat. Said he'd return in a week."

"Sure fits the time frame. Perhaps we ought make a call on this Captain Norton."

Moore grunted. "We?"

"If you've the time."

They rounded a corner, which channeled them into an even narrower lane surrounded by soot-blackened tenements. How a corpse cart heaped with a body or two could fit through this lane without scraping its sides was a wonder. Moore took the lead, in silence. He remained quiet for so long, Nicholas redirected his wondering away from the carts to if the man would ever answer.

"I suppose I've the time to hunt down this captain," Moore finally said.

Above them, a woman draped over a windowsill whistled for his attention. She pulled aside a tattered shawl, revealing skin the color and texture of porridge.

Nicholas averted his eyes, ignoring her ribald comments. He had to take two quick steps to catch back up with Moore.

"Scurvy smugglers. Blackjack and Charlie aren't cooperating with my investigation. You'd think they'd packed up and moved shop. Though I shouldn't be surprised if they heard it was me, the infamous Officer Moore, who's the one looking for them."

Nicholas rolled his eyes. "Your pride never ceases to amaze me."

Moore shrugged. "I'm an amazing type of fellow."

Moore stopped in front of a gloomy building, known simply as the Plank Street Dead House. The brick walls wept chunks of mortar to the ground. In the resulting pits, black mold grew in cancerous welts. High-set windows near the eaves, open for ventilation, added a noxious stench to the fetid air wafting in from the nearby muckyard. Add a few flames, and truly, the place could be hell on earth.

Moore shoved open the door. "After you."

Nicholas swept past him into an office barely larger than a casket.

Randall, the clerk, smiled at their entrance. He sat behind a tall, narrow-legged desk, ink smudges marring his thin cheeks. Minus the smears, he'd be the same color as the bodies he housed. "G'day, guv'ners. Come to visit my little lovelies, 'ave you?"

"That we have." Nicholas took the offered pen from the clerk. He dipped the nib in the ink and signed his name onto the ledger.

Moore sketched his name after him then lifted his sleeve to his nose. "How you stand the stench is beyond me."

Randall inhaled deeply, his chest straining the single remaining button on his waistcoat. "Ahh. Why that's a sweet perfume, it is. As long as you can smell it, you know yer still a-kickin'."

Nicholas elbowed Moore. "He makes a good point, you know."

Moore planted his coat sleeve against his nostrils ever tighter.

"Righty, then." Randall slammed the ledger shut and pulled out a key ring from the top drawer of his desk. "This way."

He jingled over to the door, and as he fumbled with the lock, Nicholas asked, "I've often wondered, Randall, is that really necessary? Are you keeping your '*lovelies*' in or the body snatchers out? Seems a bit pointless with you at the guard."

"Policies, mostly. You know, big-wigged rules and all. We may be a dead house, but we ain't no fleetin' fly-by-night kind of joint. And don't forget the effects. Sometimes a swell or two comes my way and you never know what's in their pockets. Pays to keep it locked up." With a final jiggle of his key, the bolt finally clicked. " 'Ere you go then."

The door swung open to a dimly lit room, chilled by a row of ice blocks lining two of the walls. Nicholas took care crossing the threshold. The stone floor slanted toward the farthest wall, the side facing the muckyard. At that end, melted ice and runoff funneled into a great drain. He frowned, resisting the urge to wipe his hands over his waistcoat.

"Identify as many as you can. Wouldn't mind cleaning house a bit." Randall's voice was dull in the big space.

Moore lowered his sleeve, but only long enough to get out a rush of words. "I got a tip-off from one of my regulars that you took in a bloater day before yesterday. Come in from one of the Skerry warehouses down by the Wapping Wharves. Said the fellow was picked over pretty good. Stripped, actually. Likely was one of those swells you mentioned, but scavengers got to him before you. This ringing any bells?"

"I may not know my lovelies' names, but I knows 'em intimate well, I do. Come along." Randall darted forward, trotting down a long line of marble slabs. Apparently he didn't house the same qualms about slipping.

Nicholas trailed behind Moore. Rarely did death make him flinch. Bodies were part of his job. Even the stench of putrefaction, while not pleasant, didn't trigger his gag reflex. No. . .something deeper unsettled him. Something pregnant with hideous possibility. As Nicholas passed by sheet-covered corpses, he wondered where each soul had gone. It was here in this gallery of decay that he felt the enormity of eternity—and it stole his breath.

God should so bless everyone with a visit to the dead house.

" 'Ere's the one." Randall stopped halfway down the row and peeled back the cloth. Though he professed great affection for his wards, Nicholas noticed the man took care not to let his sleeve come in contact with the sheet.

"This the chap yer lookin' for?"

Moore stepped aside and inclined his head toward Nicholas, never once removing his arm from his nose. "You tell me."

Nicholas closed in.

It was a man, distended to eye-popping proportions, though he'd probably not been a reed of a fellow to begin with. He wore the marbled color of one who'd died a fortnight ago, except for his legs.

From midthigh on down, the skin was tar colored. The top half of his head was ragged, chewed to bits, probably by rats, judging from the bite sizes.

Bending, Nicholas studied the cadaver's neck. A ligature mark cut deep, and if he cared to look closer—which he didn't—he'd likely find a sliver or two of hemp. He glanced up at Randall. "Does the impression go all the way around, or is there a gap?"

"Gap at the back, guv'ner. Weren't no strangulation. He were hanged."

Nicholas nodded. "Then the only question that remains is was it self-imposed or not? Though I'm not quite sure why you needed me to confirm what you already knew."

Randall shrugged, and Moore mumbled something. Hard to tell with a sleeve blocking his mouth. Nicholas cut him a lethal glance.

Slowly, Moore pulled his arm from his nose. "Fine. Have it your way. But if I lose my stomach all over your shoes, don't complain."

Nicholas frowned. "Go on."

"About a fortnight ago," Moore began, "one of my informants—goes by the name of Badger—bumped into this fellow down near the wharves. Badger's always on the lookout for me, let's me know when something's out of place. Like this fellow." He nodded toward the body. "Said the man looked nervous, and well he should. Dandy clothes ought not be worn in that nest, as you know. A week later, he found the fellow's body hanging in an abandoned warehouse two piers south. He let me know about it early this morning as I left my flat."

"Why didn't he come to you right away?" Nicholas interrupted. "Why wait to tell you about it?"

"Badger feared he was being watched. That mob I'm hunting suspects his loose lips. Rightly so. Badger waited till it was safe. By then, the body was taken down, gone over by ragpickers and street waifs, and delivered here to Randall."

Nicholas studied the body one more time. A fat dead man who may or may not have committed suicide. A mystery, but one he didn't have time for at the moment. He shifted his gaze back to Moore. "I fail to see what this has to do with me."

"Badger told me he caught the fellow's name. Badger's that good. Got a way about him that loosens—"

Moore continued talking, but Nicholas didn't hear him anymore. His heart beat too loud in his ears. He snatched the soiled sheet from Randall's hands and used a corner of it to shove aside the swelled tongue protruding from the corpse's lips. Teeth stared back at him.

Large.

Overlarge.

Nicholas scowled, holding back the base response that rose to his lips. He'd been right. There wasn't anything even remotely routine about the business trip Payne had taken.

Emily jerked awake then reached to massage the resulting kink in her neck from having dozed off on the settee. Her arm prickled as well, a sudden rush of blood stinging the sleeping flesh.

She frowned, realizing she was in the drawing room. Had she dozed off? La, she'd much rather have stayed in dreamland. Leaning her head back, she closed her eyes. If she concentrated on the soothing tick-tock of the corner clock, maybe she could pick up where she'd left off. Mr. Henley was sweeping her around a ballroom, eyes fixed only on her, whispering sweet—

"Hie yourself off!"

Mrs. Hunt's outburst carried in from the front foyer, shattering her fantasy once and for all. Straightening, she turned an ear toward the open drawing-room door and caught another round of Mrs. Hunt's warning volleys. What in the world?

Emily stood, wobbling momentarily on stiff legs, then crossed the room. An involuntary cringe tightened her shoulders as more of Mrs. Hunt's words sliced through the air. A butcher's cleaver couldn't cut to the bone as deftly as her sharp tongue. The last hapless peddler that'd ventured upon their front stoop had lost his hat when he'd fled from her scolding.

And he'd never returned to reclaim it.

With a quick pat of her hair to tuck up any strays, Emily slipped into the foyer. "Is there a problem, Mrs.—"

The door burst wide open. The housekeeper stumbled backward, tripped on her skirt hem, and crashed to the floor.

A brute of a man shoved his way in. His oilskin cloak smelled of whiskey and salt and danger. Emily held her breath when, for one heart-stopping moment, he shoved his face into hers.

"There's no problem as long as I see Payne." His voice was low and discordant, like an unresined bow skidding across a cello string. "Where is he?"

Emily stiffened, fear clouding her thoughts. She couldn't piece two words together if her life depended on it—which it might.

"Stupid English wench." The man's greatcoat whapped against her as he wheeled about. He stalked over to the sitting room, stuck his head in the door, then stomped down the corridor and repeated the process at each room he passed.

Emily spun to Mrs. Hunt. By now she'd propped herself up against the entry table, face pale as washed parchment.

"Quick," Emily ordered, "go get Mr. Brentwood."

"He's not returned yet." Mrs. Hunt nodded toward the open front door. "Run! Get yourself to safety."

Emily hoisted her skirts, eyeing the door. She took two steps then hesitated. This was her home. Before she could form another thought, boot heels thumped back into the foyer behind her.

She turned, straightening her shoulders, and willed courage into her voice. "As you've seen, my father is not here. Now leave."

The man tramped toward her, a dark light in his gaze. Cold perspiration dotted the tender skin between her shoulder blades. This was entirely too much like what happened to her and Wren last summer. . .but in a different way.

A murderous way.

"Where is he?" The man stepped so close that his breath coated her forehead and slid over cheeks. If she inhaled, he'd be part of her.

"Gone. On business." Each word was a chore.

A muscle jumped in the man's jaw. His eyes bore down hard, the blue-black color of rage. "His business was with me."

Emily lifted her chin, hoping confidence would follow.

It didn't.

He pressed closer, his cloak rustling the muslin of her day dress. "Maybe I should switch who I do business with, hmm?"

She ought say something, anything, but her mouth had dried to dead leaves. Could he feel her body trembling?

Mrs. Hunt sprang forward, heaving her shoulder against the stranger's arm. "Leave her be!"

Only the fabric of his sleeve moved.

Emily's heart thumped in her chest, pulsing a sickening beat in her temples. "My father will return in a fortnight. I suggest you call back then."

The man's lips pulled into a hard-edged smile. Mouse-colored teeth flashed beneath his moustache. "Perhaps I'll stay and wait for him here."

"Perhaps you won't." Behind him, Mrs. Hunt advanced, a brass candlestick wielded high over her head.

He turned. She swung. Metal cracked against bone.

The man staggered, the growl of a wounded bear ripping from his throat. The candlestick clattered to the tiles.

Without missing a step, Mrs. Hunt shoved him in the chest with both hands. As he toppled backward out the open door, the housekeeper grabbed Emily's arm and yanked her aside then slammed shut the door and drove home the bolt.

They both stood motionless, breathing hard, blinking. The maid Betsy gaped from the stairway landing. Even Mary had hobbled to join her side. Cook tromped down the corridor, rolling pin in hand. "What's the ruckus?"

Though surrounded by familiar faces, Emily felt eerily isolated.

"I'll be back!" The man shouted through the door. "You hear me! I'm coming back!"

His curses leached through the front door, pinning her in place. But only for a moment. Hiking her skirts, she bolted up the stairs, shoving past Betsy and bumping into Mary. She ought to stop and apologize for Mary's grunt of pain, but her steps didn't slow. She ran to her room and slammed the door shut, turning the lock into place.

Across the room, the looking glass reflected her image. Pale. Shaken. And the longer she stared, the more she saw Wren's face overlaying hers. Last summer's wretched scene replayed in her head until she leaned back against the door and closed her eyes to escape.

But that didn't stop her from seeing the stranger's savage smile—a leer that would visit her in nightmares and linger even in daylight.

Suddenly she longed for the safety of Brentwood's strong arms.

Chapter 12

Are you out of your mind?"

Nicholas focused on the remaining daylight pooling on the floor in the magistrate's office. He ought lift his head, show a measure of respect, but the cold wooden planks were preferable to the fire in Ford's eyes. He sucked in a breath and held it, the tightness in his chest matching his taut nerves. Would this day never end? Keeping a foolish woman from harm, comforting his failing sister, finding his employer dead, and now this. Not that he'd never been dressed down by the magistrate before, but with fatigue fraying his tightly woven resolve, the man's censure nipped particularly deep.

"Bah! I'd expect such an appeal from a simkin like Flannery, not from a seasoned officer such as yourself." The scrape of Ford's chair and the accompanying footsteps pulled Nicholas's face up.

The magistrate leaned back against the front of his desk, arms folded.

Nicholas worked his jaw. He knew exactly what was coming—and he deserved every bit of it. It'd been a foolish request to begin with. No. . .worse. A cowardly one.

"The fact that your employer is dead is neither here nor there, and well you know it." Ford's tone scolded harsher than a fishwife's. "You are committed, now more than ever, to remain with this case until it is solved."

It wasn't often he argued with Ford, but this time, with his sister's life on the line, he matched the magistrate's even gaze. "For all I know, it could've been suicide. Case closed."

Ford scowled. "Merely conjecture, and you know it."

"For now, it's all I have." The words were ashes in his mouth. He shifted, the creak of the chair's worn leather complaining with his every movement. Of course the magistrate was right. It was nothing

114

but desperation that prodded him to ask to be relieved of the case in the first place. But unless he received another offer for hire—and soon—Jenny's life would be forfeit.

"Have you given thought to Miss Payne?" Ford's question pierced, sharp and precise.

Nicholas deflated with a long breath. How to tell Ford that other than his sister, Emily Payne invaded more of his thoughts than any woman since Adelina?

Slowly, he reached into his pocket and retrieved his watch. Flipping it open, he ignored the time and instead rested his gaze upon the small image pressed inside the cover. The ink on the portrait's dark curls had bleached to gray. The eyes, the nose, the crescent lips—barely distinguishable. When had the likeness faded so much? Why, when he tried to recall Adelina's voice, could he only hear Emily's?

Re-pocketing the watch, he lifted his eyes to Ford's. "Of course I've given her thought. Either way, murder or suicide, Miss Payne will have scandal attached to her name."

And her hopes to marry well—her future—would be dashed. The image of Emily's friend, the pathetic figure clothed in fog and a thin cloak, rose like a specter. Without money, Emily could become that figure.

Nicholas swallowed the chalky taste in his mouth. "She'll be ruined."

Ford's gaze bore down. Hard. "You sound as if you care."

For a snippet of a pampered girl who ran headlong into trouble? Did he? He shifted in the chair.

Should he?

He snorted. "What I care about is the rest of my payment for this assignment. How am I to collect from a dead man?"

A shadow crossed Ford's face. "Avarice? From you? I expected better."

Nicholas clenched his teeth and looked away. Ford was right. And if he looked deeper—which he wouldn't—he suspected the roots of his anguish went far beyond the lack of money for Jen.

But for now, he'd cling to that buoy. "My sister worsens, sir. If I don't get some funding soon—"

"Payne promised you a total of 250 pounds," Ford interrupted. "How much have you received?"

He snapped his face back to the magistrate. "Half, roughly."

"And the second half was to be yours upon his return, yes?"

Nicholas cocked his head. "That was the arrangement."

"I'd say, Brentwood, that Payne has returned." Ford unfolded his arms and strolled back to his seat. "Though not quite in the state you expected, eh?"

He pondered that for a moment. Was Ford seriously suggesting...? "What are you getting at?"

"I know that, second only to your precious pocket watch, is your lock-picking kit. I daresay it's even now in your breast pocket, am I right? I merely propose you employ your skills and retrieve the balance of that payment for your sister's sake. Then remain on the case until it is solved for Miss Payne's benefit."

The idea lodged in his mind like a stone in a stream. Everything else circled around it in a silent whirlpool. Payne's lockbox was in the bottom drawer of his desk. It would be easy enough to take what was owed him then bundle Jenny off to the seaside—and also free him to pursue unhindered some kind of justice for Emily.

Nodding, he stood.

"And, Brentwood," Ford matched his stance, "I think it best if you keep Miss Payne in the dark about her father's demise, for now, at any rate. I understand your hesitation about labeling Payne's means of death, but it is undeniable his partner was murdered. If the two are related, you ought keep a sharp eye on her. For reasons we may not know, she might be next. Hearing of her father's demise will be hard enough. Heaping fear for her own life atop that would be worse.

Needless to say, the sooner you solve this, the better."

Ford's ominous deductions shadowed Nicholas as he stalked out of the room, clung to him when he stepped into the twilight of Bow Street, and haunted him for the entire cab ride to Portman Square. Emily's future was as precarious as Jenny's—and both depended upon him. His heart missed a beat with the weight of it. As the hackney rolled to a stop, he swiped his tired eyes with the back of his hand and breathed out a prayer: "God, do not let me fail them as I did Adelina."

He smacked open the door with his fist and landed heavy feet onto the cobbles. After paying off the jarvey, he retrieved his key and unlocked the Payne's front door.

Two steps past the threshold, he froze.

Only a small vigil lantern on the sideboard lit the foyer. No chandelier glowed overhead. To his left, nothing but shadows gathered in the sitting room. He squinted down the corridor. The dining room was dark as well. If not for the subdued dong of the study's clock chiming half past seven, he'd swear it was well past midnight.

Nicholas frowned. Emily never turned in this early.

A sharp intake of breath spun him around. There, in the single highback gracing the entryway's corner, Mrs. Hunt jerked awake.

"I beg your pardon, Mr. Brentwood." The housekeeper shot to her feet, face flushing deep enough to be seen even in the spare light. Straightening her skewed mobcap, she bobbed a hasty greeting then wrinkled her nose.

Immediately, he retreated a step. Though he was immune to the dead-house stench that had woven itself into the fibers of his clothing, apparently Mrs. Hunt's nose was not. "My apologies for the odor, Mrs. Hunt. I shall change garments straightaway and send these off for a good cleaning. Now, please explain what the deuce is going on."

Her lips puckered, as if she were deciding whether to continue the conversation while inhaling such a stink. "Miss Payne asked me to keep watch by the door until you returned, and I regret to say I must've dozed off. It's been a rather trying afternoon."

His frown cinched tighter. Trying afternoon, indeed. Had the pug escaped? Or the milk curdled before teatime? He shrugged out of his greatcoat and reached to hang the garment on the coat tree, nearly stumbling on an upturned corner at the edge of the rug hidden in shadow. Straightening it with the toe of his boot, he turned to Mrs. Hunt. "Did Miss Payne bid you douse the lights as well?"

"That she did."

He spread his hands wide. "What on earth for?"

"She wanted to give the impression she'd gone out for the evening." Despite his smell, the housekeeper took a step closer and lowered her voice. "In case the man returned."

He froze. "What man?"

"Around four o'clock, a blackguard came to call. Refused to give his name, merely insisted he see Mr. Payne. I informed him that Mr. Payne was gone on business, but he would have none of it. Pushed his way right in and searched the whole of this level. He took liberties with Miss Emily"—she nodded toward the candlestick on the side table—"so I cracked him a good one on the skull to get him out."

Nicholas's fingers curled into fists. "What kind of liberties?"

"Pressed her flat up against the doorjamb, the filthy scoundrel. Then he fingered her hair, plain as you please!"

Heat surged through his veins, but he kept his tone cool. "A description, Mrs. Hunt. Distinguishing marks. Manner of speech. Anything you can remember."

The dull lantern light traced a grimace on the housekeeper's face—which suddenly paled. If a simple memory of the man had such an effect on this bulwark, the fellow must be fearsome indeed.

The housekeeper closed her eyes, the white of her apron whiffling with a shiver. "Dark eyes, ruddy complexion. What I could see of it, that is. His head was bald as a babe's, with a birthmark the color of port spilled down the back. He were short, as far as men go, but stocky. Solid. Like he were no stranger to work. An outdoor fellow, if you ask me. I shouldn't wonder if he were one of Mr. Payne's captains, though I've never seen the likes of him before. But of one thing I am sure."

Her eyes popped open. "Miss Emily has every right to be anxious. He'll be back, and no doubt about it."

Filing away Mrs. Hunt's prediction along with the rest of the information, he carefully kept out one word to explore further. "A *captain*, you say? Did the man have an American accent?"

The housekeeper curled her upper lip, more pronounced than when she'd first detected the dead-house odor on him. "I pride myself on keeping as far from those filthy beasts as possible, Mr. Brentwood. Still. . .I suppose he could have been, now that you mention it. He called Miss Emily an *English* wench."

"Thank you, Mrs. Hunt. You've been most helpful." He turned and took the stairs two at a time. It was either that or punch a hole into the plaster for the slur to Emily's character.

Ignoring convention—and the clipped steps of Mrs. Hunt ascending the stairway behind him—he stopped in front of Emily's chamber and rapped. A single wall sconce flickered in the corridor, the resulting shadow a monster against her door. "Miss Payne, are you all right?"

Mrs. Hunt kept watch, but at a distance. Smart woman.

No sound came from Emily's chamber. Not even one of Alf's yips.

He pounded harder. "Miss Payne?"

Nothing. Not an indignant "coming" nor a "by your leave, sir." Just quiet.

This time the wood rattled in the frame against his fist. "Emily!"

More silence—except for his own pounding heart and the gasp of the housekeeper down the hall.

Blood rushed to his head, heat to his gut. Gads! What if the man had breached the wall to her window? Or lowered himself from the roof? Was he too late already?

Nicholas reared back, preparing to kick the spot just below the knob. Sweat soaked his shirt. One. . .two. . .

The door opened several inches, and a sleepy-eyed Emily peered out—eyes that popped wide when she took in his stance. "Mr. Brentwood! This is highly irregular."

Should he gather her in his arms or scold her for nearly getting a boot to the belly?

He opted for stomping toward her. Bracing his hand against the frame, he leaned inches from her face. "Why did you not answer immediately?"

The question came out harsher than he intended, no surprise with the way his nerves jittered on edge.

Her lips flattened. "Really, sir, besides the fact that your stench preceded you, would you have had me open the door in my nightgown?"

Involuntarily, his eyes strayed lower, past the hollow of her throat, to the ribbon tied below her collarbone. The wall sconce brushed a warm glow over skin that was likely even warmer. And softer. Here was a woman that angels would envy.

A tremor ran through him, and suddenly breathing took entirely too much concentration.

"Did Mrs. Hunt not explain to you the situation?" she asked.

Her question snapped his gaze back to her face. What had gotten into him? Slowly, he let his hand fall and edged back, straightening his shoulders. "Mrs. Hunt is not at fault. I merely came to see that you are all right."

A strange glint flickered in her eyes. Was it simply the spare light, or something more?

"I am whole, if not a bit shaken." Her teeth worried her lower lip. Either the woman was coaxing out the rest of what she had to say. . . or hindering the words.

"I am happy to hear it." A small smile tugged his own lips, especially when she sulked at his faux pas. "What I mean to say is that I am happy to hear you are whole. It does not please me that you are shaken."

"Of course, and. . ." She inhaled. Deeply. A curious act with the stench he wore.

"And?" He prodded.

"Merely. . ." Her pert little nose lifted an inch. "Thank you for inquiring."

He nodded. "It is my—"

"Yes, I know. It is your duty." An unreadable shadow snuffed out the gleam in her gaze.

It was an unaccountable loss—one he'd dearly love to replace. He reached toward her, but at the last minute curled his fingers to his palm instead. "Miss Payne, I—"

"No matter." She shook her head. "Suffice it to say I appreciate now that my father hired you. I am indebted to you for your service until he returns."

"Yes. . .well. . ." A kidney punch would have been less stunning. His short nails dug grooves into his palms—into flesh that was clammy and moist and sickening. How to explain to this wide-eyed young woman that her father wouldn't be returning home?

Ever.

❧

Emily narrowed her gaze. Was that a tic in the corner of Brentwood's right eye? Hard to tell, but she'd swear the strong lines of his throat tightened. Was she imagining it, or did her words affect him as deeply as they moved her? They were sincere—which was slightly shocking and a whole new sensation. But indeed. . .she *was* indebted to the man for her safekeeping. Something about Brentwood, knowing he was here now, housed beneath the same roof, made her feel protected.

Sheltered. A feeling she'd not experienced since before last summer, and especially not earlier today.

Her gaze returned to his—and she froze.

He stood silent. Statuesque. Nicholas Brentwood's sudden stillness spread from the hallway, wound through the gap in the door, and wrapped around her shoulders. Filling her. Quieting her. Quenching the hundreds of questions that burned on her tongue while igniting thousands more in her head.

Tension heightened with each breath, until breathing was out of the question.

Nicholas broke the spell first. He retreated several steps, shadows blurring the black outline of his frock coat. Dark hair spilled over his brow as he nodded. "Now that I see you are safe, Miss Payne, I bid you good night."

His deep voice caressed her an instant before he turned. Darkness bathed his body as he stalked down the corridor until he was submerged, leaving behind nothing but a shiver.

"Good night," she whispered then pressed the door shut and leaned her forehead against the cool oak.

What was that all about? The air between them had been more charged than a lightning storm—and as unsettling.

"Is all well, miss?"

Mary's voice spun her around, heart racing. Across the room, propped against their adjoining door and clutching a makeshift crutch in her free hand, her maid cocked her head. "I heard the knocking and got here soon as I could."

Emily frowned. Two, nearly three weeks, and still the girl couldn't serve properly. A trifling injury never would've slowed Wren to such an extent. Still. . .her gaze lowered to the maid's misshapen ankle. She'd never asked Wren to. . .what was it Mr. Brentwood had called it? Be her personal pack mule?

"No need to fret, Mary." Emily padded across the carpet and sat on the edge of her bed. "All's well."

"Are you certain, miss?"

The way her pulse fluttered? Or with the fine bead of perspiration dotting her brow? Emily sank against the propped-up pillows, losing herself in linen and lavender.

No. She wasn't certain at all.

Chapter 13

Morning rain pelted the window that reached from the floor to the ceiling of Mr. Payne's study. The fat drops sounded like grapeshot to Nicholas, who paced the floorboards. Should he go through with this, or not?

The gray light filtering inside the chamber suited his mood. The night before he'd wrestled with more than the bedcovers; he'd spent hours struggling with Ford's suggestion to *"retrieve the balance of that payment for your sister's sake. Then remain on the case until it is solved for Miss Payne's benefit."* It seemed fair. It wasn't like he was stealing. He'd work for it, after all. And in truth, by the time he'd figured out the identity of Reggie's killer, he'd likely be owed a great deal more than what was in Payne's strongbox. The fee he'd been promised was for a simple guardianship, not the solving of a murder.

Slowly, he pressed the door shut then turned and surveyed the room before he crossed it. Two framed pictures of a fox hunt adorned one wall, a stag's head mounted between. To his right, a row of hip-high bookcases supported a bust of Plato and a large cigar box. Neither sported a speck of dust, nor did the clock in the corner or the potted fern by the window. As he neared the big desk, he suspected that if he cared to bend over it, he'd likely see his stubbled jaw and bleary eyes reflected quite clearly.

Pausing, he sniffed. Linseed oil and cherry tobacco. Yes, indeed. The Portman House staff did a fine job of keeping Payne's sanctuary preserved.

Scooting behind the desk, he slid out the right bottom drawer, just as he'd seen Payne do when they first met. It was empty. He shoved the drawer back in place and moved on to the next. And the next. Odd. No parchment. No blotters. No ledgers, quills, or sealing wax. The desk was completely cleaned out. Either the man had something to hide, or he'd never intended to return—

Or someone had been here before Nicholas.

He sank back in the chair, lacing his fingers behind his head and mentally ticking off everything he knew for certain. The list was short. "Painfully short, my friend," he whispered to the stag head, whose glass eyes stared into his from across the room. "You saw everything that happened in this study. What, I wonder. . . ."

He shot to his feet and closed in on the trophy. Cleanliness was one thing, but the odd-colored paneling below the stag's right shoulder was quite another. No wonder he'd not found the strongbox in the drawer.

Grabbing hold of the twelve-point buck, he lifted, twisted slightly, then slowly retreated a step. He stifled a grunt as he lowered the heavy head to the floor. By the time he straightened, his biceps burned—and so did his curiosity.

Unstained by cigar smoke, hearth fumes, or daylight, the outline of the trophy preserved not only the wood but also the sanctity of a small door. Nicholas patted the buck's head in thanks before pulling a leather kit from his breast pocket.

With ease, he opened the panel, revealing another door. This one was outfitted with an ornate circular lock cover inlaid with brass. A slow smile slid across his lips. Good. Looked like a lever tumbler, one that would require a bit of time and skill, but entirely doable.

Retrieving a short pick and a counterweighted lever arm, he re-pocketed his pouch and inserted the lever into the keyhole. It took several tries, but eventually he found the right balance, applying a gentle yet firm pressure to the lock inside. With his other hand, he inserted the pick.

Now came the thorny part.

Using minute movements, he fished around for the tumbler giving the most resistance, while at the same time, keeping his other hand deadly still. When the pick's tip sent the barest tremor up his finger, he lifted, slowly, and. . .victory. The tumbler's slot caught on the bolt's post.

He inhaled deeply. Halfway there.

The fingers on his other hand tingled from inactivity, but he held them steady. One slip now and he'd have to start over.

Footsteps clipped from the other side of the study door. Nicholas froze. Judging by the timbre and speed, Mrs. Hunt was on a mission—hopefully not one involving the dusting of a stag's head or the polishing of a desk.

Was it right to ask God to keep him from being detected?

As the steps faded, he slowly let out a breath. Gathering his scattered concentration, he jiggled the pick half a hair's width to the left. Two wiggles later, the second lever lifted. With both bars trapped in the slot, he shot the bolt and swung open the door.

His shoulders sagged, and he sighed. The box inside had a lock as well.

Jamming his tools between his teeth, he slid out the chest and padded over to the desk. This time he'd repeat the process sitting down.

He used the steady thrum of the rain against the windows to fall into a deliberate trance. The tumblers in this one were worn—all the easier to skim the pick's tip from lever to lever, yet trickier to get them to stay in the slot. Mrs. Hunt's footfall returned in the corridor, but this time he dismissed the threat. She'd not enter the room. She'd send Betsy.

When finally all the levers were wedged, he slid the bolt, opened the lid partway, then once again froze.

Tapping steps echoed in the corridor and stopped just outside the study door. He slipped off the chair so fast, a muscle pulled in the back of his thigh. A bolt he didn't want to hear clear a metal plate sounded from across the room, followed by the barest grind of hinges.

How would he explain to a maid why he crouched like an overgrown bird behind his employer's desk while clutching the man's strongbox?

"Betsy?"

Mrs. Hunt's voice carried from the back of the house. Yes! *Go, Betsy. Go see what your—*

The hinges ground slightly more. One footstep crossed the threshold. Nicholas's heart stopped. Did the girl have a hearing problem as well as a speech impediment?

"Betsy!"

This time the housekeeper's tone was steel. The door clicked shut. Tapping steps retreated.

And a single drop of sweat trickled down Nicholas's temple. Briefly, he closed his eyes. *Thank You, Lord. I can only assume that Your protection thus far means something.*

Swiping his brow on his sleeve, he regained the chair. He grasped the lid, opened the chest. . .and frowned. Disappointment—and dare he admit relief?—drained the last of his fine motor skills. He reached in and pulled out the single item gracing the velvet-lined box.

At least the decision to take what was owed him had been made.

Lifting a fat chunk of wax to within a hand span of his eyes, he squinted then flipped the piece over and inspected the other side. It was a key mold, and judging by the telltale starburst-shaped end, it was designed for a Bramah lock—

Like the one he'd seen in Reggie's study.

He lowered the template and scrubbed a hand over his jaw. Why would Payne want to empty out his business partner's store of money? Wouldn't that be like robbing oneself? He pondered that, until one of his earlier thoughts reared its head for the second time this gray morning.

Unless Payne had never intended to come back. But why—

Sharp yips bounded down the corridor and stopped at the study door. Nicholas slammed shut the box's lid. No time for further pondering.

Pocketing the mold and his pick set, he dashed across the room and slid the chest into the safe. He eased the door shut—while little paws scratched at the other—then bent and hefted the trophy back to its perch.

Thankfully, the barking subsided as he straightened the stag's head, and by the time he finished, the scratching had stopped as well. Glancing at the ceiling as he headed for the door, he shot up a quick prayer.

Thank You, God.

Then he reached for the knob, swung open the door—and came face-to-face with a fuzzy muzzle held by a frowning young lady.

"What on earth are you doing in my father's study?"

Alf squirmed in her arms, and Emily bent, relegating the pug to the floor. His paws hit the ground running—in the direction of the kitchen. Fickle pup. Just as well, though. She straightened and studied the man in front of her unhindered. Nicholas Brentwood's face was shadowed by stubble and possibly fatigue, creased somewhat at the brow—and completely unreadable. If she'd surprised him, he sure didn't show it.

"The more pertinent question, Miss Payne"—his green eyes searched her face like waves lapping against a shore, wearing away the sand grain by grain—"is why you suspected I was here in the first place?"

She frowned, hating the uncanny way he had of always making her feel like a half-wit. "You don't corner the market on deductive reasoning, sir."

"Oh?"

She lifted her chin, a more ladylike gesture than lifting her palm and slapping the smirk off his face—though not nearly as satisfying. "First, you were not at table in the dining room. Second, Betsy said your chamber was empty when I asked if you were up and about.

And third. . ." She paused. Should she admit that she really hadn't known he was in here? No. Better to let him think she was as keen an investigator as he.

"Alf and I"—she nodded down the corridor where the pup had disappeared—"are an unbeatable pair."

"No doubt." His gaze bore into hers, and he advanced a step, crossing the threshold and pulling the door shut behind him.

Everything about the man was intense, and standing this close, the urge to run pounded with each heartbeat. She drew back, but only two paces—enough distance so she could breathe easier yet not enough to show retreat. He smelled of risk and possibility—faintly spicy and very masculine. With a definite hint of sandalwood soap. Interesting, though he'd not taken the time to shave yet this morn, he'd apparently washed off the sickening smell that had clung to him last evening.

"Now that I've answered your question, Mr. Brentwood. . ." she matched his stare, daring him to be the first to look away, "it's only fair you answer mine. So I repeat, what were you doing in my father's study?"

His gaze darted down the corridor, followed by a sweep of his arm. "Shall I explain on our way to breakfast?"

A small smile curved her mouth, victory tasting as sweet as one of Cook's raisin cakes that she hoped waited for her on the dining-room sideboard. "Very well," she conceded then turned and headed down the hall.

Nicholas fell into step beside her. "Your. . .visitor, shall we call him? Obviously the man who barged in so rudely yesterday afternoon was looking for something, some key bit of information only your father could supply. Other than the study or your father's bedchamber, where else might that information be?"

She felt his eyes upon her as they walked, but no, she'd not get sucked into that green whirlpool again. "My father's affairs are as foreign to me as they are to you, sir."

"Are you really so surprised, then, that I investigated the room?" He stopped, allowing her to pass him by and enter the dining room.

Did he always have to be so logical? Ignoring his question, she crossed to the sideboard and selected the largest piece of raisin cake on the platter. Apparently Cook had been reading her mind—and good thing, too, for she would've requested the treat had it been absent.

She waited for Nicholas to pull out her chair. Then she sat and lobbed another question. "Did you find anything in Father's study?"

He sank into the seat adjacent hers and reached for the coffee urn. At her nod, he filled her cup first then his own. By the time she stirred in a spoonful of sugar and a dollop of cream, he'd drunk his, refilled once more, and retreated behind the crisp sheets of the *Chronicle*.

Emily frowned. Her father often escaped in such a manner. Why was her guardian trying to avoid her?

"Well?" she prodded. "*Did* you find anything?"

His eyes peeked over the top of the paper. "Yes."

The paper shot up, hiding his face and ending his side of the conversation.

But not hers. She leaned forward, reached out her butter knife, and slit the paper right down the center. The noise masked the rain buffeting the windows, but not his growl.

"Miss Payne, do you honestly think such antics—"

"You can't possibly expect that I'll let you get away with that snippet of an answer. Tell me, here and now. What did you discover?"

He sighed and folded what was left of the paper into a mound at the side of his saucer. For a moment, she wondered if he'd still refuse to reply. What recourse would surpass slicing his newspaper in half? Her eyes slid to the crystal pitcher next to the coffee urn, and a half smile begged to be released. Perhaps a cold bit of water over the head—

"What I discovered was a curious woman and her nosier pup."

She sank back in her seat. Had she really fallen for that bait? "Droll, Mr. Brentwood. Very droll. Should Bow Street ever dismiss you, I daresay you've a career on Drury Lane writing dramatic dialogue."

A rogue grin lightened his features and, as much as she hated to admit it, lightened the dreary gray morning, as well.

"I'll take your advice under consideration, Miss Payne. So tell me, why was it you—and Alf, I suppose—were seeking me out?"

She speared a piece of raisin cake with her fork and savored the sweet bite before responding. "I did have other callers yesterday besides that blackguard that barged in. Miss Barker in particular." She eyed the man across from her, but the mention of Millie's name didn't so much as twitch his eye. Hmm, that could be a problem, considering the deal she'd cut with Millie.

After one more bite for fortification, she continued: "Miss Barker reminded me that the Garveys' ball is but a week away. Naturally, I've already got my gown, but I should like to add a few accessories—"

"No."

She blinked. Was he objecting to the ball, the gown—though he'd not seen it—or her desire to purchase a new hair coronet and matching earbobs? "What do you mean, no?"

"Are you about to ask me to follow you about town while you shop for said accessories?"

Pleased that he understood her the first go-around, she loaded her fork with one more bite of breakfast cake. "Yes."

"No," he answered.

Her fork hovered midair. "Mr. Brentwood, you can't expect me to stop my life just because some misguided fellow pushed past Mrs. Hunt and entered our home. I admit it was a frightening event, but—"

"Have you forgotten about Mr. Sedgewick's murder?"

She set down her fork. Eating now was out of the question.

Outside, a gust of wind rattled the dining-room windowpanes like bones in a grave. She shivered. Horrid thought, as bad as the image of Reggie's final breath. "Of course I've not forgotten, but I find it hard to believe that his situation has anything to do with me. I am not now, nor ever have been, associated with business intrigues."

"Are you really so self-centered, Miss Payne?" Brentwood's voice lowered in timbre and gained in strength. "Did you ever consider it might have something to do with me?"

Her gaze shot to his. "What are you talking about?"

He sighed, giving her the distinct impression he chose his words as carefully as for a tot. "Let's review. I'm charged with your safety, yes?"

"Yes."

"Your father's partner is murdered, a stranger breaks into your home, and your father turns up—"

He stopped. Suddenly. His eyes grew distant and hard. Either his coffee didn't sit well on an empty stomach—for he had yet to fill a plate—or he'd been about to say something he ought not.

She leaned forward. "Turns up what?"

He reached for the coffee urn yet again. Three cups?

"Turns up unable to be reached, Miss Payne." He took a sip before he continued. "Though he prepared us for that much before he left."

The beginnings of a headache lurked behind her eyes, ready to spring out if this conversation became any more complicated. She reached for her own cup in hopes of drowning the pain. "I fail to understand what that has to do with shopping."

"I need you to stay put for the day while I make a few calls of my own."

Behind her, the rain thrummed against the glass. No one would call on her in such weather. The day would stretch unbearably long. Surely she could think of something to change his mind. And if that beastly fellow happened to return—*aha*!

She straightened in her seat. "I wasn't safe here alone yesterday, Mr. Brentwood. What makes you think today will be any different? Perhaps if I accompanied you—"

"Don't worry. I've already sent for a colleague to watch the place. You see, Miss Payne, I generally try to think two moves ahead of the game." He bit into his bread and chewed, deliberately holding her gaze.

Drat. As much as she hated to admit it, he really did think of everything. She pushed back her chair, appetite completely gone, and cocked her head at the same angle she'd seen her father employ time and again before he sealed a bargain. "I'll make a deal with you, Mr. Brentwood."

"Really?" He finished off his bread and wiped his mouth with the napkin. "Why do I sense that wagering with you just may involve the selling of my soul?"

She tipped her head farther. "Is it for sale?"

"No."

"Then you've nothing to worry about, hmm?"

She waited, holding, as if they played at nothing but a simple card game instead of the possible fate of her future.

At last, Nicholas broke the stalemate. "I suspect I may regret asking this, but what do you propose, Miss Payne?"

She flashed him a smile that had earned her many a dance with an unsuspecting beau. "As a reward for my best behavior today, you shall take me to Bond Street tomorrow."

What went on behind those eyes of his, dark as a forest and with depths she could only guess at? If he'd not agree to this. . .then what?

"Your *best* behavior?" he finally asked.

Her smile widened, and she tilted her chin. Millie wasn't the only one with an arsenal of flirtatious moves.

His eyes narrowed, clouding to rival the storm outside. "That tactic might work with Mr. Henley, but it does not with me."

Her shoulders sagged. Rotten man. She bit her lip to keep it from quivering.

"Nevertheless. . ." he leaned back in his seat and folded his arms, "I suppose I can't expect to keep you under lock and key. You're hardly a criminal, are you?"

She bit harder. The only criminal in the room was him. Big bully.

"If I accomplish all I hope to today, I shall be at your disposal on the morrow."

Her mouth dropped, quivering lip discarded along the way. "My complete disposal?"

A shadow crossed his face. "What have you in mind?"

She sniffed, going for a blend of proud vexation. "What makes you think I have anything other than shopping in mind?"

"Let's just say I have my suspicions."

She mimicked his smirk. He could suspect all he liked—for he had a right to. With him absent for the day, she'd have all the time she'd need to dream up and put a few newly formed schemes of her own into motion.

Chapter 14

Nicholas left behind the Payne townhome and crossed the street, sidestepping a mound of horse manure, then flipped up his collar against the rain. The shower was steady enough to drench any exposed skin. Annoying, but not enough to make him turn back for an umbrella. One more encounter with Emily, and she just might try a new tack to get him to escort her shopping. He'd rather take a bullet to the head than traipse around Bond Street today.

Or any day.

Entering the arched opening to the Portman Square garden—at the center of all the homes on Portman Lane—he cut an immediate right. Ten paces off, a tree trunk appeared to divide as a figure, dressed in deep brown, stepped out from behind it.

"Sure and it be a fine day to have me put on surveillance, Brentwood." While Flannery spoke, he swiped his thumb and forefingers along the front brim of his hat, sending a spray of droplets off to the side. His red beard dripped with the excess. "I hope yer doublin' what yer payin'."

Nicholas smirked. "I wouldn't complain if I was you, nor ask for further compensation. Ford doesn't take kindly to mewling harpies."

Flannery threw back his shoulders. "Watch it, or I've a mind to keep to meself the scrap Moore asked me to pass along."

"Let's have it." Nicholas held out his hand.

Flannery reached inside his oilskin coat and produced a folded parchment. "What is it I'm watchin' for, if I may be so bold?"

The question bounced around in Nicholas's head as he opened the paper and read Moore's scrawl:

Captain Norton. Billingsgate dock. Best I can do.
Watch your back, for I can't. Off to Dover.

"Well?"

Nicholas refolded the paper before answering. "Keep a sharp eye for anything out of the ordinary. Though this"—he held up the note—"might lead me to the fellow you're guarding against."

Grant that it may be so, Lord. Pocketing the slip, he savored the first tang of hope he'd tasted in a long time. If Norton was the murderer, there'd be a fat chest of money somewhere on board his ship. He'd haul the captain down to Bow Street, collect his share from that chest, deposit the rest with Miss Payne, then see his sister off to better health. He closed his eyes. *Yes, Lord, grant that it may be so.*

He opened his eyes and fixed his gaze on Flannery's sharp blues. "One more thing. On the off chance Miss Payne exits, follow her. She's not to escape your sight. Understood?"

"Aye." Flannery nodded then cocked his head. "But if she slips out the rear, I can hardly be held—"

"Drago's covering the back. Any other questions?"

A sweep of wind howled in from the west, shaking the overhead branches. Even with his hat pulled low, Flannery took the brunt of the wet onslaught. He rubbed his face and flicked the water from his fingertips. "Ye'll be puttin' in a good word for me, then, with the magistrate?"

"Keep my ward safe, and. . ." Nicholas shrugged and stalked off.

"And what?" Flannery's voice trailed him. "What, Brentwood?! Ye can't be leaving me without knowin'—"

"Mind what I said about mewling," he called over his shoulder. Better the man should be vigilant, prepared for dangers unknown, than slack about his mission. He winced as that thought hit him head-on. Did God ever use the same tactic with him?

After hoofing it past Seymour Street to Duke and another half mile down Oxford, he finally found a hack available for hire. The rain shield was missing and the springs were gone on the left, giving the cab a perpetual list to the side, but at least it had a roof.

By the time he reached Billingsgate, though, he wondered if a soaking walk mightn't have been a sounder choice, for the driver had bumped through every rise and dip in the road. His teeth rattled even when his feet hit solid ground.

Thames Street, rain or not, bustled with people. Nicholas shoved past fruit sellers and fishmongers and veered into the nearest lane. Soot-smudged warehouse walls towered on each side of the narrow avenue leading to the river. The overpowering stench of mackerel and bloaters smacked him in the nose. Why on earth would an American merchant choose to dock at the largest fish port in London? Granted, a fair amount of other goods passed from deck to dock in this area, as evidenced by the added odor of Spanish onions, but a Yankee merchant. . .here?

He set his jaw, chewing that one over. Something wasn't right.

All manner of vessels lined the river on this side of the bank. Many were small, wherries and skiffs, a single Gravesend shuttle sitting among them. This early in the day, most of the fishing rigs were still out to sea.

But directly to his left, a two-masted merchantman hunkered low in the water, no doubt ready to soon set sail. On deck, a few hands stowed ropes and tightened riggings. A leather-cheeked sailor descended from the gangplank. He was so raw-boned and angular, it hurt to look at him.

Nicholas increased his pace. "You there."

The man lifted his face toward him. "Aye?"

Up close, the wrinkles in the fellow's skin were as deep as a peer's pockets. Nicholas slid his gaze to the man's eyes. "I'm looking for Captain Norton. This his ship?"

"Who's askin'?"

Nicholas shifted, allowing the bulge of his tipstaff to peek from beneath the flap of his coat. "The name's Brentwood, on business from the Bow Street magistrate."

"If this has anything to do with the papers, you best hurry over to Customs." He lifted his chin, indicating the ungainly building that crouched like a beast on the waterway. "Too late."

Nicholas frowned. "Too late for—"

"Is there a problem, Skully?" A raspy voice came from behind, heavy with an American accent and followed by the woodsy scent of Burley tobacco.

Nicolas turned and offered his hand to the captain—or was he a killer? "No problem, Captain Norton. Just a few questions. My name is Nicholas Brentwood, Bow Street officer."

The captain's gaze darted from his, to Skully's, then back again before he reached out and gripped Nicholas's hand. His fingers were strong enough to right a keeling ship on a raging sea, steady enough to train a pistol barrel at a man's chest, and firm enough to shove past a housekeeper—

But his face was nothing like Mrs. Hunt's description. Disappointment added to his weariness.

"So tell me, Brentwood," Norton drew back his hand, "why should I answer to you?"

Nicholas hitched his thumb over his shoulder. "Like I was telling your friend here—"

"First mate." Pride sharpened Skully's tone—the same wounded egotism Nicholas used when someone labeled him a runner.

"Fair enough. As I was telling your first mate, I'm on business from the Crown." Once again, Nicholas parted his greatcoat at the hip, making the tipstaff as clear to Norton as he had to Skully. "Shall we?" He tipped his head toward the boat.

The captain folded his arms. "Here will do."

Nicholas studied Norton's face, set as granite. The man's gaze didn't waver. No hint of a smile played on his lips. Apparently this was more about power than evasion.

"Very well," Nicholas conceded. "I understand you had some

business with a Mr. Reginald Sedgewick."

"Sedgewick!" A storm darkened the man's eyes. On the side of his neck, an earthworm of a vein emerged. "Rotten scoundrel!"

And then, spent as quickly as the fury of the spring tempest, a smile dawned on Norton's face. He grabbed Nicholas's shoulders. "You've righted things for me? Have you my money?" He looked past Nicholas to his first mate. "Hear that Skully? We're not taking it on the chin, after all!"

Shrugging off the man's grip, Nicholas scrambled to make sense of the abrupt change. Either the captain was playing him like a well-tuned violin, or this was a dead end. "Where were you two nights ago, Monday, April 6?"

Norton's grin faded. "What's that to do with—"

"I'm the one asking the questions here."

The granite look returned, colder. Harder than before. "Then you should snippin' well be asking Sedgewick, not me. He's the criminal. Filthy thief."

"Sedgewick's dead, Captain, and unless you satisfy me, I'll haul you in as the number one suspect." Behind him, a whiff of air sounded. Nicholas spun. He caught Skully's forearm before the man's fist dented his skull, then he snapped the sailor's arm around his back. If he yanked upward any harder, Skully's shoulder would dislocate.

Which would be quite the nasty sight should the wiry man's bone decide to pop out as well.

"This is exactly why America rebelled," Norton sneered.

"I'm waiting, Captain. So's Skully." He nudged the man's arm. Skully grunted.

And several guns cocked behind him from aboard deck.

Facing death wasn't new, but it never failed to ramp up his heart rate. Nicholas skewered Norton with a stare. "Call them off, or prove yourself to be worse than Sedgewick."

The captain's jaw contracted. Tension twanged the air as real as the four warning bells off London Bridge.

Finally, Norton lifted his eyes to the men aboard his ship. Without a word, hammers eased back.

Nicholas released a breath and tightened his grip on Skully, lest the man think Norton's gesture would slacken his resolve.

The captain scowled. "Monday night I was at the Bull's Head, meeting with a merchant, Thomas Gilroy, of Mandrake and Gilroy. He paid for Sedgewick's shipment, at half rate of course, and cut me a deal for a new trade. Square it with Mr. Gilroy if you don't believe me."

Norton stepped forward, leaving no room to doubt his claim. "My papers are cleared, and I'm sailing today."

That the captain hated Reginald Sedgewick was plain enough— but his alibi was easily confirmed. Mandrake's office was just down the block. Nicholas could confer with Gilroy before the captain's spyglass caught sight of the estuary.

"I suppose you'll need your first mate, then." Nicholas released his hold and stepped back, giving Skully plenty of swing room should he feel the need for retribution.

The first mate didn't disappoint, but the captain stayed the man's arm with a curse. "We don't need more trouble, Skully!"

Nicholas sidestepped them both. "Good day, gentlemen."

Ignoring the foul barrage of name-calling as he stomped down the dock, he wondered how much money one must lose to instill such a passion. Exactly how much the captain had lost was anybody's guess, but gold was nothing in comparison to how much Emily or Jenny would lose if he didn't find the real culprit.

And soon.

Beeswax rained onto the envelope, each drip puddling into a melted pool. If Emily squinted so that her eyelids were just about closed, everything blurred, making it look like a splotch of molten gold—

a far brighter hue than the colorless gray outside her bedroom window. Before the wax hardened, she picked up the brass seal and pressed the Payne family crest into the center. There. Signed and sealed. Now to deliver. She hoped Millie was home—and that Nicholas Brentwood hadn't instructed the man across the street to stop her from paying a call.

A slow smile curved her lips as she peeked out the lace sheer at the miserable-looking fellow. Standing under a tree for the better part of the morning, soaking up drizzle like a giant fungus, surely he couldn't be enjoying himself. Her smile grew. She could remedy that. With a few bats of her lashes and maybe a giggle or two, she'd gain an escort to Millie's.

She stood and crossed to a wardrobe solely committed to hats. Just opening the doors sent a thrill racing through her tummy and wafted the fresh scent of lavender into the room. Her friend Bella collected shoes, Millie men, but bonnets? Ahh. She'd take a new bonnet any day and every day had she enough space to store them.

Placing a finger to her lower lip, she scanned the shelves of hatboxes. Her eyes caressed each one like a lover returned from sea. Most were tall, some short, several fairly wide, but finally she settled on a pale pink box with gray stripes and freed it from its wardrobe prison. She padded over to her bed, anticipating the moment when the lid lifted and a brilliant flash of a puffed red crown would—

"I've a mind to dismiss you now!"

Mrs. Hunt's voice slid through a crack in the door adjoining Emily's room to Mary's. Emily paused, hatbox in hand. What could the maid have possibly done wrong? Her ankle, considerably shrunken but yet painful, certainly kept her out of the way.

But perhaps that was the issue.

Setting the box on the end of her bed, Emily turned and crept to the door between her chamber and Mary's. She missed most of Mary's reply, except for a few sniffles that punctuated her last words.

"You can't blame me for being laid up."

"I don't." The housekeeper's tone, though quieter, was still terse. Emily imagined the accompanying scowl etched onto Mrs. Hunt's face.

"But that doesn't get your work done," she continued. "Betty and I are doing double-time what with your chores and ours. I should think that you could at least get through that pile of mending in a timely fashion."

"I was hired as a lady's maid, Mrs. Hunt, not a seamstress for the entire household. That my sewing skills don't meet your approval is as much out of my control as healing my own ankle."

Emily stifled a gasp then leaned closer. Even without a visual, this was as entertaining as a night at the theater.

"That sort of cheek will send you packing," Mrs. Hunt's voice hardened. "And without a reference, I might add."

The threat jerked Emily ramrod straight. She knew that tone. She knew those words. Mrs. Hunt hadn't spared her own daughter—Mary wouldn't stand a chance if she pushed her situation any further. Though she wouldn't miss Mary to such a degree as losing Wren, she had grown accustomed to the girl. The thought of breaking in yet another lady's maid was tiresome.

Emily shoved open the door and sashayed in. "Mary, dear, would you mind reading to me today? Everyone else is too busy, and I feel a headache coming on. I'm so glad you're available like this. Oh!" She fluttered her hand to her chest and widened her eyes at Mrs. Hunt. "I didn't realize. . . Did I interrupt something?"

The housekeeper's face was pinched so tight, even Emily flinched.

Smoothing her hands on her apron, Mrs. Hunt darted a glance at Mary before she answered. "I suppose I'm finished here, miss. I am late for a meeting with John as is."

"Oh? He is returned?" *Thank the Lord!* Casting off her plan to sweet-talk Mr. Red Beard, Emily swooped over to Mrs. Hunt, letter outstretched. "Would you see that this is delivered to Millie Barker as soon as possible?"

If the woman's face scrunched any more, her eyeballs would be lost. "I'll have John see to it." But before she disappeared out the door, she volleyed a parting shot at Mary. "At least the butler has resumed his post."

Mary sagged in her seat near the hearth, a heap of garments draped over the rim of a basket at her side. "Thank you, miss. You'll never know—"

As the girl sat there, eyes shining with tears about to spill over, Emily couldn't help but be reminded of the day Wren had sat in the very same spot, telling her the ugly truth of a fate that could have easily been hers.

She swallowed the sour memory and forced a smile that belied her words. "I know more than you ever should."

Chapter 15

The following morn, Emily opened the door and finally—*finally*—escaped the house. Intent on a shopping spree as triumphant as Trafalgar, she had to discipline herself not to skip to the carriage.

Hours later, fingering a pair of amethyst drop earrings, she wasn't so sure about a victory. After three stores, not one package sat in the carriage. She'd been uninspired at Dalton's Lace and Glove. The clerk at Fairmont's outright ignored her, and it still vexed her as to why Rollins Slipper & Shoe had suddenly instituted a new policy of pound-notes-up-front.

She set the earbobs onto the glass counter and heaved a sigh. Posted near the front door, Nicholas mimicked her. The sound satisfied. The earrings did not. Purple, though her favorite color, wouldn't give her the dazzle she hoped for with her golden ball gown.

"These aren't quite right," she told the clerk behind the counter—who promptly sighed as well.

As the narrow-nosed fellow replaced the jewels, she sidestepped down a ways, her gaze traveling from stringed pearls to emerald pendants. Leaning in for a closer look, she blinked. A glimmer flashed at the corner of her eye. She turned her head to look, and her jaw dropped.

There, beneath the glass, a universe of tiny stars sparkled, lit by a ray of sun reaching through the front window. Her breath caught as she eyed a tiara sprinkled with diamond chips. Whoever wore that crown would be the queen of the ball—and she'd long since felt she was royalty.

Noting her interest, the clerk pulled out the magnificent piece and held it aloft. Brilliant glitters of light dotted her vision, so stunning her lips parted and thirst parched her throat. For a second, she was speechless.

He lifted it higher and looked down his thin nose at her. "Should you like to try it on?"

To her right, a green skirt swished into view. Emily glanced over. Eyes wider than a beggar's ogled the sparkles on the tiara. And next to the gaping girl, an older woman—presumably her mother according to the droop of her jowls—stepped forward. The pair looked like bloodhounds on the hunt.

And her tiara was the prey.

Emily jerked her face back to the clerk. "No need. Package it, if you will, please." She upped her volume. "I shall take it with me."

Boot steps thumped across the floor. Nicholas Brentwood drew up alongside her, blocking the sunshine and snuffing out some of the glitter of her new headpiece. "Do you really think that's wise, Miss Payne? A fine jeweler such as Asprey's will send an armed delivery—"

"Don't be silly." She pasted on a pleasant smile, all the while keeping track of the duo on the trail.

"Excuse me," said the clerk. "I shall return shortly." He took his long nose and the tiara with him, backtracking down the counter. Either he sensed the coming battle, or he simply went to box up her piece.

Emily watched until he disappeared through a side door then turned on Nicholas. "I see no need for delay. You are armed, are you not?"

The creases of an impending—and by the looks of it, quite magnificent—scowl started at the corners of his mouth. "I was hired to protect you, not a frivolous piece of jewelry."

"It's not frivolous!" She stamped her foot. An infantile reaction, but gratifying in every respect save for one.

It made the bloodhound in the green pelisse step closer with a look of hope in her eyes.

Emily lowered her tone. "That tiara is necessary, not that I expect you to understand. What would you know about a woman's accessories?"

He folded his arms, a common lecture stance her father often employed. "If you can't catch the eye of a man without the aid of trinkets, then I suggest the man's not worth catching at all."

"It doesn't hurt to embellish the package."

"I beg to differ. For you see, Miss Payne—" he bent toward her, so close his breath warmed her ear—"your *package* needs no further embellishment."

The quiet words sunk deep, sending ripples out to her fingers and toes. A compliment? From him. . .for her? Now that was as stunning as the tiara—

Or was it his unwavering gaze that suddenly seized her heart?

She turned and faced the glass case before he noticed his effect and was rewarded by the return of the clerk. Immediately, her brow puckered. Why did he carry her sparkles unwrapped? And who was the buttoned and bowed man next to him?

"Miss Payne?" The other man's shiny black eyes fixed on her. His dark frock coat clung tight, leaving a wide opening in front where a white starched shirt stretched over his belly. A snowy cravat looped into circles at his neck. All in all, he looked like an illustration she'd once seen of a penguin.

"Yes, I—excuse me." She snapped her gaze back to the long-nosed clerk. With one hand he straightened the velvet bedding beneath the glass, and with the other, replaced the tiara. What a dolt. "Perhaps I was not clear. I should like that boxed up."

The clerk's lips parted, but the other fellow spoke. "Miss Payne, unless you can produce a banknote for five thousand pounds, I'm afraid you'll have to wait. There is an unpaid balance on your account."

The man's words rattled around in her head like rocks in a tin can. She had to wait? What did that even mean? She returned her gaze to him. "I'm sorry. Who are you?"

"Mr. Davitt." He lifted his chin, and if his chest puffed out any farther, one of those buttons would pop. "Manager of Asprey's."

"Well, Mr. Davitt," she matched the pretentious tilt of his head. "There must be some misunderstanding. Whatever the balance is, rest assured my father will see to it as soon as he returns to town."

"Miss Payne," Nicholas's voice curled into her ear from behind, "we should leave."

She cut him a sharp glance over her shoulder. "You, sir, promised to shop all day."

Then she forced a smile she didn't feel and dazzled it on Mr. Davitt. "Now then, please deliver the tiara—"

"I'm afraid that is out of the question."

His refusal pulled her gloved fingers into fists, but popping a penguin in the chest just didn't seem right. Poking at his pride, however, was altogether fair game. "Apparently you don't understand, sir, so I'll speak slowly and clearly that you may follow along. My father, Mr. Alistair Payne—that's p-a-y-n-e—is a name to be trusted, and when he hears of this insult, you'll be lucky to find yourself the manager of the thimble store in Cheapside."

If the man's nose lifted any higher, a nosebleed would follow. "Allow me to be plain. Until the account is cleared, there will be no further deliveries or purchases from Asprey's. I bid you and the gentleman a good day."

"But—"

Mr. Davitt spun, the tails of his frock coat whapping the counter. The clerk merely sniffed. And a combined gasp—both female—came from the left.

Ignoring them all, Emily traced the outline of the headpiece with one finger on the glass. The tiara sat so near yet was trapped beyond her reach. Her whole head ached, knowing the snug feel of those diamonds nested in her hair would never be a reality, leastwise not in time for the Garveys' ball. And if she didn't land Mr. Henley this season. . .moisture welled in her eyes, blurring the glittery little universe into washed-out gray. What was to become of her? Live as a spinster in her father's house until death? If he allowed her, that is.

To her side, the horrid girl stifled a giggle—a girl who might very well purchase that crown and live happily ever after.

Unlike her.

"Emily."

She spun. Had Brentwood seriously used her Christian name? In public?

"I suspected that might grab your attention." Half a smile tipped his mouth. "Let's go."

He offered his arm. Walking out of here would admit defeat. But honestly. . .what choice did she have?

The solid muscle beneath his sleeve lent her strength, enough to straighten her shoulders and force her eyes dead ahead as they crossed to the door. The burn of the girl's stare scorched her back.

Outside, as Nicholas led her down the block to their carriage, other shoppers bustled by, each trailed by servants carrying packages and parcels. She flexed the fingers of her free hand. Why did emptiness weigh so much? What was going on? She'd never been refused service. She'd never tasted the hot green sting of humiliation quite so bitterly.

Deep in thought, she slowed her steps. Nicholas gave her a sideways glance.

"Don't fret. It's for the better that you didn't purchase that gaudy bit of frippery. Your smile's brighter than any tiara." He nudged her. "Come on, let's see it."

She lifted her face to him. "Are you trying to be kind, sir?"

A grin slid across his face. "Is it working?"

Her lips twitched, but she pursed them. "Not yet."

"Well then, I shall have to try harder." He stopped in front of their carriage and waved off the driver then reached for the door himself. Once opened, he turned to her, his smile fading. "I meant what I said, you know."

Her brow crumpled. "What. . .that the tiara was too frivolous a trinket or too gaudy?"

"No." He locked eyes with her. "I meant that you don't need diamonds to attract a man."

The sincerity of his words shivered through her. She'd heard flattery before. Enough to distinguish counterfeit from real. For all his bluster, Nicholas was genuine in a way she'd never experienced—a way that drew her in and wrapped around her shoulders.

He broke the spell with a nod toward the open carriage door. "Shall we?"

When she clasped his offered hand, a queer shot of heat raced up her arm. She smoothed her palm along her skirt as she seated herself—a vain attempt at wiping away his touch, for to admit his effect would be scandalous. But the action did nothing to remove the sound of his voice directing the driver outside.

Immediately, she popped her head back out the door. "Stop first at the Chapter Coffee House, if you please."

Nicholas looked up at her from the street. One of his brows rose—only one. . .his I-know-something's-up look. "Since when are you interested in political or literary debate, Miss Payne?"

She slunk back inside the safety of the carriage and busied her hands with pressing the wrinkles from her skirts. Just because shopping had been a dismal failure, didn't mean the rest of the day must be a loss.

She had larger battles to win than Trafalgar.

Chapter 16

The carriage lurched to a stop in front of the Chapter, but the thousand swirling thoughts in Nicholas's mind kept right on rolling, even as he opened the door and delivered Emily to the threshold of the coffee and chocolate drinking establishment. Was he doing the right thing? A woman of Emily's caliber ought not deign a visit to a coffee shop, so something unique was obviously pulling her in. Not that she'd admit to it. Her pretty lips had remained sealed the entire ride, and she'd taken great interest in staring out the carriage window, humming a little tune.

Among those *how come*s and *wonder why*s, he was preoccupied as well with their shopping experience. Either the merchants' aversion to offering Emily service meant that Payne's debts had finally caught up to him, or word of her father's death had leaked out. And if common shopkeepers knew, it was only a matter of time before Emily discovered it—

A truth, he determined, she should hear from his lips and none other's. He'd never overridden a directive from the magistrate before, but this time, he just might have to.

Not now, though. He clenched his jaw and pushed open the shop door. The scent of cigar smoke floated above the earthy tones of coffee and chocolate. For a brief moment, he allowed the aroma to work its magic and loosen the tight muscles in his shoulders; then he handed over their penny entrance fee.

Emily touched her fingers to her nose. Apparently the smell didn't appeal, which made her request even more curious than the silence he experienced on the ride over. The refusal at Asprey's had shaken her in a way he didn't understand.

Nor could he grasp her sudden urge to risk her reputation for the sake of a cup of hot chocolate or mug of coffee. Each morning he'd taken breakfast with her, Emily barely sipped half a cup of either. Something else was afoot—something she'd not own up to—so he'd have to let it play out. He doubted very much, though, that it had anything to do with an education in politics or bookselling, which was most often the case with these patrons. He studied her as she scanned the room then lowered her hand to reveal a small smile.

Ahh, that explained it. Intrigue had everything to do with this stop.

He chased her skirt as she wove past small tables and paused at one midway across the room. Horrendous position to defend, but all the perimeter seats were filled. Worse, every eye was drawn to the arrival of a female—one of only three in the room, unless servers were counted.

Charles Henley rose from his chair and leaned toward Emily, closer than decorum dictated. He snatched her hand, brought it to his mouth, and pressed his lips against her glove longer than customary.

Stepping up behind her, Nicholas scowled at the man. "Henley."

The man's gaze lifted. Slowly, he released his hold on Emily's fingers. "Brentwood. . .I didn't expect to see you here."

"Funny. You don't seem a bit amazed to see Miss Payne."

Adjacent him, and still seated, Millie Barker beamed. "Oh, Mr. Brentwood, Emily, what a surprise!"

"Isn't it?" Emily flashed him a smile over her shoulder. "What luck!"

A groan surfaced at the back of Nicholas's throat. This explained the flurry of couriers Flannery reported going in and out of Portman Square yesterday. How many missives had it taken to arrange this meeting?

Henley was quick to pull out the empty chair to his right and offer it to Emily. The only seat left to him, then, was between Millie and her aunt, who dozed, chin to chest. The drone of a dozen conversations took the edge off the woman's snores; still, each inhale was thick and snorty. Some chaperone. He slid out a chair of his own, giving credence to the rumors he'd heard of Millie's exploits. Mr. Barker ought to invest in a guardian of his own for the woman.

Gritting his teeth, he ordered chocolate for Emily and something stronger for himself. He'd never frequented this particular shop but hoped their coffee was a kick in the head. He'd need it to survive this little tryst. Narrowing his eyes at Emily, he frowned. He never should've given in to coming here in the first place.

Millie bent toward him, eyelashes aflutter. "What a delight to see you, Mr. Brentwood."

He leaned back, better to view Emily and Henley but with the added bonus of evading Millie. "I didn't realize literature or politics was your game, Miss Barker."

"Hmm?" Her smile grew, the slight movement of her lips setting the feather atop her hat bobbing slightly.

"A coffee shop is the least likely place I'd expect to find a woman for it is most often visited by those interested in partisan discourse or the bantering of philosophical ideas." He cocked his head. "And you don't strike me as one with such interests. . .unless there's something you're not telling me."

She leaned closer. "Oh, Mr. Brentwood, I'd tell you anything."

It took every muscle in his body to keep from rolling his eyes.

"Though I must say it's nothing like that." She giggled then nodded at her snoozing chaperone without varying her gaze from his face. "Aunt here was positively in need of refreshment, for as you can see, she tires easily, poor dear. Our carriage happened to be passing by, and so I thought we should stop. Kind of a novelty experience, you see. Imagine my surprise when Mr. Henley hailed us to his table."

"Happened by, eh?" he asked Millie but kept his focus entirely on Emily and Henley. Millie's flirtatious conduct paled in comparison to Emily's, for she employed hers in a more subtle way. The tilt of her head, the parted lips, a coy smile—he sucked in a breath. Why she felt she'd needed that gewgaw at Asprey's to make herself more appealing was a mystery. If Henley's lips weren't shut, his tongue would loll out of his mouth like the dog he was.

"Truth be told, I've never actually been to a coffee shop, Mr. Brentwood." Millie's voice was a gnat in his ear.

"But you have, am I correct, Mr. Henley?" His question pulled the man's gaze off Emily and landed it squarely on him. A cheap victory but worth every cent.

"Of course. During the day I frequent the usual haunts, but at night. . ." A slow grin bared Henley's teeth.

"Wherever you go, sir, I am sure you add much to the conversation." Emily's words puffed out the man's chest a full two inches before he turned his face to her.

Henley leaned in so close, his breath ruffled the fine hairs at her temples. "I excel in conversation, among other things."

A sudden urge to deliver a right uppercut tingled through Nicholas's fingers. Though he understood Emily's precarious social standing—more so now than ever—that didn't mean he had to like it.

Or Henley.

Next to him, Millie tucked up a curl of stray hair then trailed her hand down the curve of her neck, around to her collarbone, where her fingers settled on the bodice of her gown—a move that couldn't have been carried out better by a strumpet in an East End brothel.

"Oh!" Her fingertips fluttered at the crest of her bosom. "My brooch. . .it's gone!"

"How horrible. Do you think it was stolen?" Emily's sentiment was true enough. Her timing and tone, questionable. Henley said nothing.

"Yes! Oh, it's so clear to me now." Millie answered after a perfect pause—too perfect. "I believe my brooch was stolen. It must've happened back on Oxford Street when Aunt and I encountered a street beggar. Mr. Brentwood. . ."

Her hand flew to his sleeve. He stared her down.

"Emily's told me of your strong sense of justice. I daresay you could right this in an instant. Would you accompany me? I'm certain Mr. Henley and Emily wouldn't mind our absence. Nor would Aunt."

If he didn't stop this now, Millie's dramatics and Henley's advances would steal any pleasure he might find in the mug of coffee headed his way. He removed Millie's hand from his arm. "No need, Miss Barker."

"No need?" Her brow wrinkled, causing the feather on her hat to startle. "Whatever do you mean?"

At long last, the serving girl delivered a cup first to Emily then to him. He downed a big swallow before answering Millie, singeing his tongue in the process and glad for the pain. "If indeed your brooch was stolen, the thief would have already hocked it down at St. Gile's, though I doubt very much it was pinched in the first place. Unless you happened to embrace said beggar, I should think you'd notice so close an encounter."

Millie's lips tightened into a line, not nearly as pretty as one of Emily's pouting poses—and for some reason, that pleased him.

He nodded toward the door. "I suggest you search your carriage floor, Miss Barker. Most likely it fell during the process of getting in or out."

Millie exchanged a glance with Emily. A storm raged in her blue eyes then just as suddenly, calmed, and she tipped her face back to his. "Why, you're a genius, Mr. Brentwood. I feel sure with your sharp eye helping me, we'll find my brooch in no time. My carriage is just outside."

This time when she leaned toward him, she twisted in such a way that the fabric parted, giving him a most advantageous view of her bosom.

"Shall we?" She rose slightly, leveling her chest even with his eyes. Sighing, he set down his mug, coffee sloshing over the rim. "Do sit down, Miss Barker, and describe for me your brooch."

For a moment, her lips pursed, and then she sank. Slowly. He fixed his gaze on her face instead of her provocative movements, all the while keeping Henley within his line of sight. If the rogue nudged his chair any closer to Emily's, he'd acquaint the man's skull with the metal end of his tipstaff.

"My brooch is gold, naturally, about a finger span in width. There's a flower at center, a ruby in its middle. Two turquoise-studded flowers sit on each side. It's really very pretty. Scrolled leaves cover the entire piece like this." She traced a loopy pattern in the air with her finger.

She needn't have. Her words confirmed his suspicion without further embellishment. He lifted his cup and swallowed a few good gulps before answering. "Your description has revised my opinion of the matter."

Millie's brow crumpled, and Emily cut in: "Really, Mr. Brentwood. The chivalrous thing to do would be to help, not simply change your mind."

"Chivalrous, yes, but necessary?" He turned to Emily. "No."

"Here, here!" Henley said, raising his cup. "Chivalry is overrated."

"Not my meaning at all, Henley, though I don't suppose you know the definition of the word in the first place."

Emily gasped.

Henley merely smirked, the action narrowing his eyes. . .or did he do that purposely? "You're not so scrupulous yourself."

Nicholas stiffened. What dirt did this snake in the grass think he'd make public? But ladies first. He turned to Millie. "Lest you think I'm heartless, Miss Barker, I believe your brooch is at home. A piece of that magnitude would leave quite a visible pinhole in the tight weave of your dress. I see no such evidence. It may be that you intended to wear it but simply forgot and left it on your nightstand."

Her cheeks flamed as he nodded toward her chest. Were it anyone but Millie Barker, he'd suspect embarrassment as the cause. In her case, it was probably because her plans had been thwarted.

Shifting his attention, he sliced a deadly gaze at Henley, sharpening each word like a blade's edge on a whetstone. "Now then, Mr. Henley, what would *you* know about morals, mine or otherwise?"

Millie's head reared back, eyes wide, ears likely wider. Emily babbled about weather and carriage traffic, throwing out one trivial bone after another.

But a dog's fangs, once bared, were not easily diverted from a bite. From her angle, Emily couldn't see the tightening of Henley's jaw, but Nicholas didn't miss it.

Henley faced him squarely across the table. "I'm not the buffoon you think I am, Brentwood. I've studied you with as much finesse as you track my every move. I'd wager your sudden appearance while Payne is gone is no accident. I don't believe for a minute you're here to lift the prospects of the man's business."

Henley leaned forward, his voice low and even, meant for him alone. "You're here to lift the skirts of the man's daughter."

Nicholas seized Henley's collar and hauled the man to his feet. The table tipped sideways. Their chairs crashed. And then. . .silence.

All eyes trained on them. Whispers rustled in the corners of the room, like dead leaves skittering across cobbles. Aunt, coffee in her lap, was wide-awake now.

Henley's face turned purple. His fingers clawed at Nicholas's grip. He'd pass out soon if Nicholas didn't loosen his hold—not that he wasn't tempted. Whether Millie had asked for it or not, Charles Henley had already ruined her. Emily would not be his next conquest, if he had any say in the matter.

But not if he ended the man's life here and now.

Henley's body started to sag.

God, help me.

"Let him go!" Millie shrieked and slapped at his arm.

Nicholas shoved the man away. Henley toppled backward, landing with a satisfying thud on his backside. Twisting on the floorboards, he turned aside and coughed until he retched. Nicholas brushed his hands, content with his work.

But satisfaction vanished the instant Emily turned on him.

The clear brown of her eyes changed to the angry, muddied waters of the Thames. Her disgust tore at him, her rage drowned the last breath from his lungs.

"How dare you!" Her voice was as dark as night.

He clutched his hands into fists, helpless against the sudden realization that thunked low in his gut. No, this couldn't be happening. Not here.

Not now.

"Out! Get out!" A knife-wielding shopkeeper burst from a back doorway. "Take your fighting to Gentleman Jim's or I'll call a constable!"

Irony tasted bitter in Nicholas's mouth as he tipped his hat in compliance. He was a lawman.

And he was in love with the woman who gaped at him with hatred.

Chapter 17

Bracing both feet against the sides of the carriage door, Emily gripped the handle with a death hold. If Nicholas Brentwood thought she'd allow him a cushy ride home after ruining her life, the insufferable man could just think again. Crouching inside the carriage in a most unladylike fashion, she pulled so hard her fingers were beyond aching—they were numb.

Outside, Nicholas bellowed, "For the last time, open this door, or I'll—"

"You'll what? Choke me like you did Mr. Henley? You can walk. Drive on, Mr. Wilkes!"

The carriage didn't move. Hadn't Wilkes heard her orders? Maybe her guardian had him writhing on the ground as well.

"Do you have any idea how much attention this is attracting?" Nicholas's voice was a growl, low, threatening. . . .

And likely correct. Horrid man. She could only imagine the onlookers gaping in a semicircle outside the carriage. Theatrics attracted more crowds than a hat sale.

But just as in netting a bargain, timing was everything. She tightened her grip. The muscles in her arms quivered with the strain.

"So be it." Nicholas's voice was lethal—as would be his next tug on the door.

Listening with her whole body, Emily heard him shift his weight, plant his feet, and then—

She let go.

The door flew open. Nicholas stumbled backward, plowing into the spectators.

For the first time since her life ended moments ago at the Chapter Coffee House, Emily smiled. Then she turned and scooted to the farthest side of the carriage. Smoothing her skirts, she sank into the

158

seat and gazed out the window, pretending she was alone. Perhaps, if she tried hard enough, she could even pretend Millie wouldn't gossip and Henley would overlook the entire incident.

The carriage tilted to the side as Nicholas climbed in. The wheeze of the seat across from her suggested he'd sat. A latch clicked, and her head jerked as the wheels began to eat ground.

"Emily, I—"

"Do not presume to call me by my Christian name, sir."

His coat rustled as he shifted. "I merely want to—"

"I'd prefer not to discuss it." She clipped out each word, like scissors snipping holes in a paper.

Nicholas's sigh filled the carriage, expanding to envelop all of London by its enormity. The seat creaked, and she couldn't be sure, but it sounded like he turned his head to look out the opposite window, completely dismissing her.

Which annoyed her even more. Giving up the silent treatment, she turned to him. "I don't know how you can sit there so calmly, knowing you nearly killed a man and ruined my life, all within the space of an instant."

"Your life is hardly ruined, *Miss Payne*."

"Then allow me to make things plain to you, Mr. Brentwood." She spit out his name as prickly as he'd stabbed the air with hers.

He didn't even blink.

By faith, he was bold! How dare he look so unperturbed—and handsome, which pushed her anger to a whole new level.

"Millie will spread this from Mayfair to St. Martin's before we get to Portman Square. Mr. Henley won't give me a second look at the Garveys' ball next week, nor will any other man if he's to expect a sound beating from you as the result. Why, I've never been so mortified in all my life. And when my father gets home—"

"I thought you said you didn't want to talk about it!"

She narrowed her eyes. "Your smugness is rivaled only by your callousness. I don't expect you to understand my situation, but you could at least show a little compassion."

He ran his hand through his hair, his gaze holding hers. It took him a full minute to speak. "Truly, I am sorry for the embarrassment I caused you. I let my anger get the best of me—a foe I've not completely mastered. Thankfully, God is patient. I pray you will be, as well."

His apology chipped away the sharp edges of her resolve. His soft, green gaze sanded it smoother. She straightened each finger of her gloves before answering. No sense letting him think he'd won so easily. "Fine. Apology accepted. Still. . ." She matched his earlier sigh. "Mr. Henley may never approach me now, not after this."

A muscle moved on his jaw. "One can hope."

"He is my best prospect!"

"But he's not your only prospect." Nicholas leaned forward, as if by proximity he might drive home his words. "Marriage is a lifelong commitment. Do not run headlong through a door that will lock tight behind you, without first discovering what's on the other side."

The truth was loud in the space between them. His words echoed what Bella had warned her against. A queer jolt ran from shoulder to shoulder. Was that really what she was doing? What did she know of Henley, now that she thought upon it? What if he really was as lecherous as Captain Daggett?

Thunder shook the carriage, and she grabbed the seat's edge for support. Impossible. Sunlight yet streamed through the window. Had they collided with another carriage?

Nicholas banged on the carriage wall. "Wilkes, is there a problem?"

Outside, a man's cry answered—followed by a rough "Hyah" and crack of a whip. The carriage picked up speed, much too fast for a London street. Had highwaymen now taken to attacking city folk?

Emily scooted down her seat, bumping her bottom along the leather bench. As much as she hated to admit it, the closer she drew to Nicholas, the safer she felt.

He didn't give her a second look as he jiggled the door handle.

"What are you doing?" Her thoughts rattled along with the carriage wheels. "Shouldn't we wait for Wilkes to stop the carriage before you open the door?"

"Get back," Nicholas ordered.

"What's going on?"

He threw his shoulder against the door. The thing didn't budge. Emily frowned. "Stop it!"

The carriage lurched, and the wheels rumbled faster. What was Wilkes thinking to drive so insanely?

And why would Nicholas want to get out now?

He turned to her, danger flashing in his eyes. She'd seen him look at her sternly before, but never like this. Coldness gripped her heart.

"Move!"

In the space of a breath, his back was to her, blocking her view. He shoved his hand inside his greatcoat and withdrew a gun.

Not needing to be told twice, she scrambled into the farthest corner of her seat.

Sparks flashed. A gunshot snapped, sharp and brittle as a broken bone. The acrid stench of gunpowder filled the coach, burning the inside of her nose. Outside the door, a man's deep cry competed with the horses' pounding hooves.

Nicholas jammed his free hand into his coat and pulled out a pouch. He worked so fast, his muscles flexed and rippled beneath the taut fabric of his coat. The tension in him was magnificent—and completely horrifying.

A scream stuck to the roof of Emily's mouth, barely letting words escape. "What's happening?"

"Quiet!"

There was no question of disobeying that voice, even if she wanted to. Something was wrong—very wrong. Fear thudded deep in her chest. More than anything she'd ever wanted—even the tiara—she suddenly longed for a faith the size of Nicholas's. Would God hear a desperate cry from her?

She squeezed her eyes shut. If nothing else, she'd meet death without gazing upon its face. *Please God, don't let me die. Don't let Nicholas die. Help!*

The world shifted. Her eyes flew open. She flailed as the carriage careened around a corner. Wheels skidded. Horses screamed their protest. And then—

She was tossed forward as the carriage stopped. The sudden lack of movement was as jolting as the wild ride. Before she could think, Nicholas shoved open the door. On her other side, glass exploded over her.

A wooden club flashed in front of her face then disappeared. Emily stared at the sparkly shards in her lap, her thoughts as hard to piece together as the awful jagged edges.

"Emily!" Nicholas's voice broke as sharply as the window.

She turned her face to him, but her body jerked the opposite direction. Pain grabbed her arm, sliding a sharp line from wrist to elbow. Someone pulled her from outside the window, forcing her up and out. Her skin screamed over spikes of broken glass. Fire shot from elbow to armpit. She'd never fit, not through that hole.

Not in one piece.

From inside the carriage, a warm grip wrapped around her waist. With a grunt and a heave, Nicholas yanked her back.

"Switch places." His voice was a growl in her ear as he shoved past her, using his body as a barrier between her and the window.

For a second, she breathed easier.

Then fingers bit into her arms from behind and hauled her backward. Downward. Outside.

A scream ripped up her throat and ended as a man's gloved hand smashed against her mouth.

"Don't fight this, pretty lady." Hot breath burned into her ear.

"It'll all be over soon."

A rag was shoved into her mouth before everything flipped. A man's hard shoulder cut into her belly, and her face smacked against his back. He carried her as casually as a sack of yesterday's bread. Her head pounded with a rush of blood, her heart with panic. Would Nicholas even notice she was gone? And when he did, would it be too late? Tears slipped past her lashes.

Either God hadn't heard her prayer—or He didn't intend to answer.

As soon as Emily was safely behind him, Nicholas ripped off his greatcoat and shoved it over the windowsill then leaned forward and scanned the situation. Bricks walled his sight, hardly two feet from the carriage. Either they'd stopped perilously close to a building, or they were in an alley.

From above, arms shot down. One pair. Good. He could deal with a single man on the roof. Nicholas snagged one of the arms, dug his fingers into flesh, and yanked downward.

Then let go.

A head, followed by a body, plummeted past the gaping hole that had been the window. Bone cracked against wheel rim. Curses ended with a grunt. Breathing hard, Nicholas turned. Surely Emily would have plenty to say about this.

But she wasn't there.

Before the realization fully sank in, darkness filled the doorway, taking on the shape of a demon. Or was it a cloak-covered thug? Nicholas leaned back and kicked. His boot heel smacked against bone and flesh, sending a man sprawling into a wall hardly three feet from the carriage.

So, this was an alley.

And that was a thug.

Nicholas snatched his gun off the seat and vaulted out the door.

Like a lightning bolt, a knife blade flashed toward him. He jumped back and cocked the gun with his thumb. Dark eyes peered into his, twin pools of depravity—and something more. Was that a memory skimming across the man's face, recognition flaring his nostrils? No time to decipher it now. Nicholas lifted his gun.

The brigand turned and ran.

Edging sideways, past horses pawing in their harnesses, Nicholas tore after him. "Stop!"

The thug glanced over his shoulder. Big mistake. His foot shot out on an oily patch of God-knew-what, and he fell. The knife flew from his hand. Before he slid to a stop, Nicholas towered over him.

And fired.

A bullet at close range was never pretty. Neither was the man's scream ricocheting off the bricks.

Nicholas dropped to one knee and grabbed the man's face, forcing his mouth shut. "Get to a surgeon. You might lose the leg, but you'll have your life as a prize. Thank God for that, for I'd as soon have killed you."

Bolting up, he tucked the gun in his belt and shot forward, following blood splats in the gravel. Maybe one day he'd be thankful for the gruesome trail that would lead him to Emily.

But not now. Not with visions of what he might find. Two paces later, he stopped dead.

His heart twisted like a groan.

Ahead, clearing a corner in the T-shaped alley, a Sampson-sized brute carried Emily over one shoulder. She bounced like a plaything gripped in a dog's teeth as he pinned her with one arm. His other hand held a gun, the muzzle aimed at Nicholas's chest.

Nicholas pulled his own gun and lifted a prayer. The screams of the man behind him foreshadowed that this might not end well—especially since he hadn't the time to reload. Schooling his face, he bluffed. "Drop the girl, or you're a dead man!"

The man stopped, twenty paces off. "Son of a jackanapes! If it isn't the mighty Brentwood. Come to aid the damsel in distress, eh?"

Nicholas squinted, the voice dragging a memory from a pit of nightmares he'd long since banished. "Nash!" He spit out the name like a rancid bite of meat. "I should've finished you off when I had the chance."

Emily struggled on the man's shoulder, her elbow catching him hard in the back of the skull. His head jerked forward, but that did nothing to stop Nash's grin. "Aye, ye should've."

"Not to worry." Nicholas lifted his gun higher, eyeing along the muzzle as if about to shoot. "Now's as good a time as any."

"You wouldn't take the chance of hitting a lady." Nash's face tightened into sharp angles. "Drop the gun."

"Drop the girl!" Nicholas countered.

Nash threw her to the ground, her backside grinding into the broken bits of glass and other splinters of refuse that made up the alley floor. The cruel blackguard! Apparently happy with his deed, a smile slashed across Nash's face. "Your turn."

Nicholas's heart pounded in his head. What to do? Think...think! *Lord, a little wisdom here—now—would be appreciated.* Immediately, a scripture came to mind. The speed wasn't unusual. The passage was.

"And the great dragon was thrown down."

"Drop it!" Nash hollered.

The rest of the passage drowned out Nash's voice. . ."*He was thrown down to the earth, and his angels were thrown down with him.*"

Nicholas gritted his teeth. *Is that really what You want, Lord?*

"Last warning, Brentwood, if you want to live."

The scripture condensed into three solid words. *Throw. It. Down.*

His gaze shot to Emily, who scrambled backward like a crab on sand. As soon as she cleared just enough space to keep her safe, Nicholas splayed his fingers. The gun crunched against gravel. Was this it, then? His life ended here in an alley? Not that he wasn't ready, but what would become of Emily?

And then he saw it.

Nash pulled the trigger. Sparks flew. Metal clicked. Then—

Nothing. No bullet. No searing pain.

The gun did not go off.

Nash's jaw worked as his thumb reset the cock. Stupid move. The action wouldn't help him—and it gave Nicholas time to snatch up the other thug's dropped knife.

Stooping, he grabbed the handle, flipped the knife up into the air, and snatched the blade. Then he whipped it back and snapped a release. The blade sailed true, gouging into the fleshy part of Nash's gun arm. The weapon dropped against the cobbles and went off with a roar.

The bullet ripped through flesh, muscles, tendons, bone, and shot out the other side of Nash's lower leg.

Nicholas took off at a dead run. Passing by Nash, who now howled on the alley floor, he pumped his feet in time to his racing heart. Once again, Emily was out of sight. Surely God hadn't brought him this far to lose her now.

Did You, Lord?

He flew around the corner, chest tight, lungs burning, his muscles flexed to face who knew how many more men.

Then he slowed.

Emily was alone in the passage, pounding on the only door in the dead-end part of the T. Her hair ravaged over her shoulders and down her back, her hat long since lost. The sleeves of her pelisse and the gown beneath hung in shreds. Blood dripped off one elbow.

In four strides, he swept her up and cradled her in his arms. *Thank You, God. Thank You.*

Her tears dampened his shirt. Her blood warmed his skin. A fierce protective instinct stole his breath as she choked on sobs.

"You're safe now," he comforted.

Her body shuddered against his. "I was so. . .afraid!"

"Shh. It's done." He bent his face to her ear, breathing in her lily-of-the-valley scent. "I've got you, and nothing will take you from me. You hear?"

The tightness in her body slackened, though her weeping continued. Perhaps it was what she needed.

"Go ahead," he whispered. "Cry it out."

He turned, fighting against a rising desire to return to Nash and kick him in his bloody leg for the fear he'd caused her. No doubt Nash was the ringleader of this little escapade. . .but why? Maybe a few kicks more would loosen the scoundrel's tongue—and if not, all the better, for he'd be forced to utilize other, less pleasant techniques.

Clearing the corner of the brick wall, Nicholas stopped. He set Emily's feet onto the ground and stepped in front of her.

The alley was empty.

Chapter 18

Ambrose de Villet rubbed a hand over his skull. Stubble pricked his palm. Was a decent shave in this godforsaken rat hole of a country too much to ask? And now this. He slugged back a shot of bourbon, relishing the burn as it sank to his gut, then carefully set his glass next to the crystal decanter on the desk.

Turning, he nodded at Skarritt and Weaver, the two men who flanked the makeshift office door. Neither said a word as he strode past them. Their footsteps simply thumped in rhythm to his as they fell in line, echoing from floor to rafter in the abandoned warehouse. Daylight streamed in through cracks in the walls and holes in the roof. The place was a sieve of rot. Half a smile twisted his lips. Funny how all the rays of light pointed accusing fingers at the battered man propped against an empty crate.

Nash. Stupid dog. He should've known better than to hire such a buffoon.

Ambrose halted five paces from him. Nash grimaced in his shirt-sleeves, one of which was torn and slick with blood. His coat was wrapped like a growth around the bottom half of his leg, the fabric wet and dark. Drip by drip, Nash's life wept onto the warehouse floor.

Ambrose cocked his head as he studied the man. A mere girl couldn't have done that much damage.

Glancing over his shoulder, he locked eyes with Skarritt, who in turn looked at Weaver. Both men stalked forward, until Nash stood in the center of their triangle.

"So, my friend." Ambrose folded his arms. "Where is the girl?"

"Wasn't—" Nash gasped. A spasm clenched his jaw then slowly faded before more words flowed. "Wasn't as easy as you said."

Ambrose sniffed, unimpressed with the English dog's pain. "What happened?"

"Brentwood happened!" Nash's voice was as angry as a bruise.

What was this? A code word? Some local jargon? A vein throbbed on the side of his neck, pulsing his skin against his starched collar. "Brentwood?"

"He's a runner. One of the best." Nash turned aside and spit then pushed away from the crate. "I'm done with this job, and I'm done with you, Mr. Dee. I came to collect what's owed me."

Ambrose slid his gaze to Skarritt and lifted his chin. A slight movement, but economy most often produced wealth.

Skarritt shot forward. Two quick jabs sent Nash to his knees, bone crunching against oak. His howl screeched as off pitch as bootnails sliding down a slate roof.

Ambrose paced forward, stopping inches from the man. "Before we discuss your. . .resignation, tell me of this man. This Brentwood."

Nash's chest heaved. Curses were as thick as his breaths. A fresh trickle of blood leaked from his shoulder. What a pathetic fool.

Ambrose circled him, planting one foot after the other, counting his steps. Counting the last of Nash's heartbeats. At full circle, he stopped. "I'm a businessman, Mr. Nash. Your lack of decorum is somewhat unsettling. If you hope to walk out of here alive—and I hold that phrase loosely, considering your leg—then I suggest you cooperate."

Nash lifted his face. Hatred poured off him, vile as his sweaty stench. "Have it yer way, then. Brentwood is ex-military. Keenest eye I've ever seen, with a wit to match. Trained Portuguese gunners in '01."

. The beginning of a smile lifted Ambrose's lips. "We all know how that one turned out. Oranges for Queen Maria. Disgrace for England. Perhaps the man's not as invincible as you say."

Nash shook his head and squinted, a shard of sunlight piercing his eyes. "You don't understand. The Portuguese would've beat back the scarpin' Frogs had Brentwood stayed on to help fight. You can be sure of that. It took Lord Nelson to finally clean up that mess, didn't it?"

Ambrose stooped, eye level with the man. His shadow shut out the daylight on Nash's face. In a measured tone, quiet, firm—deadly—his mother tongue slipped past his lips. *"Le sang français traverse mes veines."*

Nash's eyes widened. His lips moved, though it took quite a while before sound came out. "You. . .you're. . ." His head swiveled, wrenching a glance from Skerritt to Weaver. "He's a Frenchie!"

Ambrose smiled in full, mirroring the grins on the other men. Nash's jaw dropped like an unhinged skeleton's.

"My full name is Ambrose de Villet, though Mr. Dee suits me better in situations such as these." Stepping back, Ambrose once again folded his arms. Let the dog think on that for the last few moments of his life. Looking past Nash, he met the gazes of Skerritt and Weaver. "We've a few things to work out, then. Not only has Payne vanished, but his daughter appears to be unreachable so long as this Brentwood is in her attendance. Yet appearances often deceive, hmm?"

Skerritt shifted his weight. Weaver lifted a brow. Neither said a word.

Ambrose continued. "I will not return to Sombra without the money. One way or another, I will have it. For the moment, Brentwood or no, I think a ransom is still our best option. Men?"

Skerritt and Weaver nodded.

Nash scowled. "You're crazy. Brentwood will kill you."

Laughter tasted sweet, and for one long, intense minute, Ambrose savored the humor of Nash's words. Unfolding his arms, he fisted his hands on his hips. "You think I care about dying?"

"Like I said. . ." Breath by ragged breath, Nash pushed up to stand. The blood drained from his face—what little he had left. "I want out. I'm done."

"Oui, mon ami." The smile slipped from Ambrose's lips. His eyes shot to Skerritt's.

And his next words were as sharp as the knife sticking out from Nash's back. "You are done...and so is Brentwood."

Chapter 19

Ahh, miss, you're an absolute vision! You'll turn every head at the Garveys' ball."

Mary straightened in front of her, and Emily glanced down at the yards of silk settling in a golden shimmer around her legs, landing a whisper's length above the carpet in her chamber. Hand-sewn pearls embellished the gilt embroidery at the hem, catching the lamplight like tiny beacons afloat a sea of richness. The skirting rose to just below the bust, where it drew in tight. Appliquéd embellishments wove an intricate pattern around her ribs. More pearls, more gold, crisscrossed at the center of the bodice and cinched together at the top then fanned into a lacy ruffle that feathered across a low neckline. A modest amount of flesh peeked out to entice the eyes of any man.

As Emily crossed the length of her room and sat in front of the vanity, she frowned. Why wasn't she sure anymore of which man she wanted to attract?

Mary's skirt swished behind her, a soothing rustle though slightly offset by the lingering limp in her gait. "I beg your pardon, miss, if I were too forward."

Emily waved her off. "No, Mary. Nothing of the sort."

Closing her eyes, she gave in to her maid's tugs with the hairbrush. How to explain that for the past week, ever since the attack on their carriage, she couldn't shake the feel of Nicholas's strong arms holding her? Or the way he'd taken down every last man to get to her in spite of the threat to his own life? Would Mr. Henley have done the same? A sigh slipped past her lips. Henley couldn't even take on one man in a coffee house.

"Are you well, miss?"

Her eyes popped open, and she blinked at herself in the mirror. Her skin was a shade paler, her cheeks a little sharper. Or mayhap the lamplight simply painted odd shadows and leeched her rosy color. "I am well. Why do you ask?"

"You've been a mite quiet, as of late. Not that I think you're a great talebearer to begin with. Still. . ." Mary's hands twisted lengths of hair as she spoke. "You've hardly been out of the house."

"Mr. Brentwood's been too preoccupied to escort me."

"He has been in and out a lot, hmm?" Two hairpins stuck out at the corner of Mary's lips, adding a lispy quality to her voice. "But you've not taken any callers, either."

"Mr. Brentwood thinks it's wise if I don't receive anyone unless he's in attendance." She tilted her head to the right, allowing Mary to gather up some stray wisps.

"Yes, well, it's certainly not the preball flurry I expected." Mary removed the last of the pins from her mouth and secured the bulk of Emily's hair on top of her head. "No packages, appointments, or fittings. If I may be so bold, is something else amiss?"

Emily grimaced, though if she was honest, it wasn't only caused by Mary's use of the curling iron too near her ear. Something was amiss. If she could verbalize it, she'd likely feel better, but slippery emotions she could barely hang on to—let alone name—dangled just beyond her reach. "I suppose that attack left a mark on me. A shadow, so to speak."

"It were dreadful, miss, that's what." Lowering the curling iron, Mary bent closer. "You don't think that tonight, I mean. . .surely nothing more will happen. . . ."

Mary's voice died out, yet the words floated in the air like unmoored phantoms. Emily shivered.

In the looking glass, Mary's gaze bored into hers. "Are you sure you're up to this ball, miss?"

Was she? What *was* wrong with her?

Lifting her chin, she forced a smile. "I am confident Mr. Brentwood will have everything under control. He usually does."

Mary lifted a brow. "You speak of Mr. Brentwood as freely as you mention Mr. Henley."

"Which is none of your concern." The harsh words slipped out before she could snatch them back.

Mary straightened, lips pinched, and silently resumed curling loose tendrils of hair.

Emily sighed. Truly, she'd not meant to be so severe. Mary's observation simply rankled her in a way that rippled unease clear to her fingertips. Since the moment she'd met the man, her world had flipped topsy-turvy. Nicholas Brentwood vexed her to no end. He invaded her home, her time, her thoughts. No wonder she spoke of him as much as Mr. Henley.

Mary's fingers tugged a little harder than normal, prickling her scalp—and conscience. Just because she was unsettled didn't mean she must snap at her maid.

"Nice work, Mary." She offered the girl a half smile as a peace offering. "Lovely work, truly. You are a magician when it comes to hair."

The tight lines around Mary's mouth softened. She pulled on a spiral of hair, and a single stylish curl draped from the crown of Emily's head, past her bare neck, and onto her shoulder. "There, miss. I shouldn't be surprised if by tomorrow morning you don't have several offers."

Emily reached for her perfume bottle. Mary's expectation was a very real possibility—one she'd hoped for, planned for, anticipated as reality.

So why did her stomach suddenly twist as tightly as the bun on her head?

Dabbing on some lily-of-the-valley-scented oil, she tilted her head and listened. Doggie claws scratched at her chamber door. Poor pug. She'd neglected him as much as her callers. Once again, she met Mary's eyes in the mirror. "Will you let in Alf?"

As Mary disappeared from the glass, Emily leaned closer. Her hair gleamed golden, done up in a simple pearl coronet. Nothing like the tiara, but. . . She turned her face slightly. Yes, some pink glowed on her cheeks, and the chocolate brown of her eyes, if not as stunning a color as Bella's blues, were at least shiny and bright. Perhaps an offer or two would roll in tomorrow morning. What would Nicholas say to that?

What would she?

After a few yips and scurry of paws, Alf jumped up on her lap. She scooped him aloft, rescuing herself from questions she couldn't answer and saving her skirt from his toenails. "Little scamp!"

Tongue lolling, Alf cocked his wrinkly face at her, and she smiled. "But I can never stay cross with you."

"I'm waiting, Miss Payne." Nicholas's voice bellowed up from downstairs and through the open door.

"You're as ready as you'll ever be, miss." Mary held out her hands for the pup.

After transferring Alf, Emily stood and tugged up her gloves as high as the fabric would stretch then lifted her arms. "Nothing's showing?"

Mary pitched her head right then left. "Not that I can see, miss. No one but Mr. Brentwood will know of your scratches."

Emily rolled her eyes. "They're hardly scratches, Mary. More like ugly gouges."

"Yet they are completely hidden."

"Miss Payne!" Nicholas sounded as if he ordered a squad of soldiers to battle.

Emily lowered her arms and gave one last pat to the wrinkles on her skirt Alf's paws had inflicted. "I suppose I'd better hurry along. I'm sure Mr. Brentwood's mood is foul enough from having to wear new evening clothes."

Mary smiled. "That were a fine battle, I hear tell."

Emily returned a grin. "I suppose it wasn't fair to force the issue with Mrs. Hunt in the room to back me up, hmm?"

"It worked, didn't it?"

Emily nodded. Though Mary wasn't a thing like Wren, she'd earned a place in her heart all the same.

"Miss Payne!"

"Oh, bother." Emily scooted to the door then paused and looked over her shoulder. "Don't wait up on my account, Mary. I'll wake you when I return."

"As you wish. Enjoy the evening, miss."

Emily rushed down the hallway and, as she neared the landing, heard the distinct sound of footsteps pacing a route at the bottom of the stairs. From the sitting room, the last chimes of the hour vibrated through the air. La, was it already nine o'clock? Had it really taken her that long to get ready?

She lifted her skirts and hastened down the stairs.

At the last step, she paused, her jaw agape. Who was this man in her foyer? In her life? Suddenly she wasn't so sure she had the courage to take the arm of such an imposing gentleman and head out into the night.

For a gentleman he was. Nicholas Brentwood's severe appearance had been subdued into that of an aristocrat. Not that he was foppish. In fact, he could hardly be accused of frill or fanciness at all. Rather, an aura of elegant power cloaked him as neatly as the plain black tailcoat stretching across his shoulders. Beneath, he wore a dark waistcoat, highlighted with fine silver embroidery—his one concession to extravagance. A white shirt contrasted in stark defiance, made all the more stunning by the silk neck cloth he'd secured around his neck with a single pearl pin. His fitted trousers—black, of course—ran the length of his long legs down to plain but shined leather shoes. Though he'd shunned the traditional light-colored pantaloons and stockings preferred by most men, the way his clothing rode the lines of his body, convention be hanged.

His gaze traveled over her, softer than a summer breeze skimming past leaves, and when his green eyes finally settled on hers, she caught her breath. Stillness spread out from him. Time slowed. Space and air and life—everything stopped for the briefest of moments. Silence breathed with him, as did she, for he commanded it without a word.

Then just as suddenly, all shifted back into a normal cadence.

Her mouth curved into a smile. Whatever had passed between them was intoxicating. Forbidden. Impossible, really. . .yet wholly and completely heady.

As she descended the last step, she mulled over Mary's parting admonition and decided to take her advice. No matter the outcome of what the morrow may bring, she would enjoy this evening.

Very much.

Nicholas snapped shut his watch and tucked it back into his pocket. He needn't have looked. The chiming of the sitting-room clock verified what he already knew. They were late. Not that he cared a fig about some silly ball, but regardless of the occasion, tardiness grated on him like skidding bare-fleshed on gravel.

And he had the scars to prove it.

Finally, silk swished behind him. The pad of slippers on tread turned him around. High time she quit her dilly-dallying and—

He froze. A jolt of heat hit him square in the chest. The only words that came to mind were *fear not*.

For an angel stood in front of him.

Emily paused on the last step, wide-eyed, lips parted. Lamplight brushed a soft glow over her shape. Warmth radiated from her, golden and brilliant—as if all the stars in the universe met and mingled in one focused point, igniting the space between them with risky possibility.

His gaze traveled the length of her, memorizing every line and curve, each delicate fold and shimmer of her gown. Then slowly, like a man gazing at a lover as he's led to a noose, he lifted his eyes to her face, for indeed, she held his heart in her hands. She could snuff the life from him if she knew.

Her cheeks wore the first blush of a spring rose. Her eyes gleamed with amber fire. His fingers longed to reach out and discover if her skin was as soft as it promised.

She descended the last step, her sweet lily scent pulling him toward her. The sweeping arc of her lips mesmerized. . .so full, so red. His heart beat a primal rhythm, wild and deep. Three paces, that's all, just three and he could wrap his arms around her slim waist, lower his mouth to hers, and—

A shudder ran through him, settling low in his belly. If he didn't contain this here, now, the evening would end with regret.

He scowled and wheeled around. "About time you deigned to make an appearance, Miss Payne. I've been waiting the better part of an hour. Does it really take that long to make yourself presentable?"

"Well!" She huffed behind him. "Good evening to you, too, Mr. Brentwood."

He grabbed her pelisse from the coat tree near the door and held it out. "We're late, thanks to you. Don't expect me to be pleasant about it." He suppressed a cringe as his own harsh tone boxed his ears, but better to anger her. Better she keep her distance.

Better he keep his. *Oh God, help me, please.*

She frowned up at him. "A real gentleman would have first remarked on my gown or my hair before laying blame, if indeed he blamed at all."

Turning, she allowed him to guide in one arm after the other into the sleeves of her wrap. Her movement enticed. Her nearness stole his breath more effectively than the ridiculous neck cloth choking his throat. He stepped back and wrenched open the door with more force than necessary, welcoming the slap of cool night air against his face.

"A true lady would value punctuality, and furthermore"—he

BRENTWOOD'S WARD

offered his arm—"whatever gave you the idea that I was a gentleman?"

"My mistake." She lifted her chin and bypassed him without a look.

Good. At such a rate, hopefully she wouldn't notice the absence of Wilkes—her usual driver. The man now gripping the reins sported a shock of red hair beneath a felt hat. His jacket bulged with a brace of loaded pistols. And a seasoned driver would've set the wheel brake instead of allowing the horses to jitter the carriage back and forth.

Nicholas locked eyes with Flannery, sitting in the driver's seat, a second before assisting Emily into the coach, then he swung up behind her.

Emily sat center on the seat, the farthest point from either window. Smart girl. He sat opposite her, his back covering the fine line in the seat cushion where he'd modified a small hidey-hole to store extra firearms.

Her hands gripped the seat's edge as the carriage lurched into motion, and she turned her face from him. He bit back a smile. Her anger was a useful tool. Freed of the burden of conversation, he listened for the rush of feet, hooves, wheels, anything that suggested an imminent attack.

The ride, however, was uneventful—and that set his teeth on edge. It'd been nearly a week since Nash's ambush. Why nothing more? Nicholas's jaw ached from clenching it, and he rubbed his chin. Even bribing his best informants, he'd gained no new knowledge about Nash nor uncovered anything about her father's death. Though at first he'd been reluctant to follow Ford's advice to keep Emily in the dark about the man's demise, the magistrate's wisdom had finally sunk in. Grief was hard enough borne without the closure of all the whys, whens, and hows. And so he'd pursued every possible lead, wearing down precious boot leather in the process. The only certainty he'd gained was further confirmation that his sister hadn't much longer to live.

179

And that chilled him more thoroughly than Emily's silence. If he didn't conclude this case soon and obtain the rest of his payment from Payne's estate, he'd never move Jenny to the country in time. Tucking his chin, he breathed out another "God, please."

The carriage stopped. He descended. This time when he offered his hand, Emily's fingers rested atop his. Music spilled out the open foyer door, growing louder as they gained the marble stairs facing a towering estate on the western edge of London. So many torches and outdoor lanterns burned on the front lawn, the sun need never make an appearance on this street.

Two footmen in crushed velvet livery flanked the entrance. One held out a white glove for the engraved invitation Emily produced from her beaded reticule. With his free hand, the dandy servant extracted a monocle tethered to a golden chain and lifted it to his eye. Either the Garveys were particularly discriminating, or they simply wanted to make a show of their highly trained, man-sized monkeys.

Once inside, Nicholas paused. His gaze darted from the crowd on the stairway, to the people clogging the corridors, to the sitting room on the right filled with giggling girls and their matrons, then beyond to the open veranda doors. He let out a long, slow breath. No wonder Nash had bided his time. Guarding Emily in this throng would be impossible. If he was going to strike, this would be the perfect place.

Especially when she loosed her fingers from his arm and shot forward, vanishing into a swirl of taffetas and satins and shiny brass buttons.

Nicholas slipped sideways through the crowd after her. A search of the first floor earned him nothing but a few sneers from uppity fops afraid he was closing in on their territory, and several unabashed ogles from ill-chaperoned women. What kind of looks was Emily attracting without him at her side? He took the stairs two at a time, dodging couples and servants alike.

By the time he spotted her laughing with Bella near a punch table on the far side of a dance floor, he couldn't decide if he should throttle her or blend into the crowd undetected to watch the beguiling way her dimples deepened when she smiled.

Across the room, her gaze shot to his.

He wove past spectators, keeping a wide berth from the dancers at center, until he closed in on Emily and her friend. "Good evening, Miss Grayson." He tipped his head to the pert little redhead then turned on Emily. "Miss Payne, I'll thank you to consider that I am not as familiar with this household as you appear to be."

"Ah yes, my apologies." She dazzled a grin at him. "I forgot that a gentleman would've known his way about."

"Touché." He quirked half a grin in return. "Shall we start over? Completely, that is."

He bent at the waist, first to her then to her friend. "Good evening, Miss Payne. Good evening, Miss Grayson."

Bella's brow crinkled. "But you already—"

Emily cut her off with a sweep of her hand. "Don't mind him. My cousin is in a rather ill humor tonight."

"As will you soon be." Bella set down her punch glass and leaned toward Emily. "Don't look now, but here comes Mr. Shadwell."

A ripple teased the fabric of Emily's skirt from bodice to floor. Either she'd just clenched every muscle or she'd repositioned her feet for a good sprint. Nicholas snuck a glance over his shoulder and suddenly understood why.

Plowing through the last square of a cotillion, a red-nosed man, with a belly that further attested to his love of spirits, headed straight for them. Mr. Shadwell gave a cursory nod at Nicholas and Bella then bowed low before Emily, grabbed her hand, and planted a kiss upon her glove.

Nicholas smirked. She'd had the nerve to suggest *he* didn't behave in a gentleman-like fashion?

"Miss Payne, how delightful!" Shadwell straightened, wobbling slightly—as would anyone so off center with a belly like his. "I've been waiting with bated breath for a glimpse of your beauty tonight."

Baited was right. A distinct waft of anchovy pate filled the air. Nicholas cocked his head, curious to see how Emily would handle this affront.

She edged closer to him, away from Shadwell, though she did greet the man. "Mr. Shadwell."

Shadwell smiled. "I insist that the next dance belong to no one but me, my dear."

Emily grabbed Nicholas's arm. "So sorry. I'm afraid I've already promised the next dance. Am I not right, Mr. Brentwood?"

Her eyes sought his, her brown gaze pleading. He studied her closely. Was she holding her breath?

He opened his mouth, but the yes that came out wasn't his.

Behind him, a voice curled over his shoulder like smoke. "The lady is right."

Nicholas turned.

Henley peeled her hand off his arm and tucked it into the crook of his own. "Miss Payne's next dance is spoken for by me."

Chapter 20

Emily licked her lips, her mouth dry as bleached bones, though she'd just drunk a full glass of punch. In the midst of the dozens of dress coats filling the ballroom, only two interested her. Her eyes shot from Mr. Henley, to Nicholas, then back again. Both set their jaws, but Nicholas's held a sharper edge, his challenge loud, though he said nothing. He simply stood, shoulders back, stance wide. She'd never been to a cockfight before, but she now understood the desire to wager, for she'd bet all her money on Nicholas were a scuffle to break out.

Which is exactly why she pressed her fingers into Mr. Henley's sleeve and smiled up into his face. "The music has already started. Shall we?"

"I protest!" Mr. Shadwell whined like a tot who'd been told no. "Clearly, I was here first."

Nicholas glowered at the man. Shadwell blanched and took a full step back. Why had the ninny dared approach her so boldly?

"You are mistaken, sir, for I accompanied Miss Payne to this ball in the first place." Nicholas cocked his head, studying Shadwell as he might a bit of manure on his shoe. "Furthermore, I defend the lady's prerogative to dance with whomever she wishes."

He turned to her then. So direct was his gaze, she might very well be the only other person in the room. He lifted his brow, and once again the strange sensation of time stilling wrapped over her bare shoulders like a whisper.

She swallowed.

Next to her, Mr. Henley opened his mouth, but Nicholas held up a hand. Could he command a storm to stop as well? "Miss Payne, is it your wish to dance with Mr. Henley?"

Moisture prickled across her forehead, her palms, the crease behind her knees. It was a simple enough question, but the implications were legion.

She cleared her throat, looking—hoping—for words. Was he trying to bully her into defying him? Or killing her with kindness?

"Yes." It was the only logical reply. The right answer. One to which she shouldn't give a second thought.

So why did her voice sound empty? Her heart turn cold?

Fighting back a shiver, she coerced her lips into a smile then turned and allowed Mr. Henley to lead her across the room to the end of the dance line. Her guardian's eyes burned into her back with every step. She wasn't sure how to feel about that, other than acknowledge the little flip in her stomach that she couldn't control—and try to ignore how lifeless her hand felt on Henley's arm instead of resting on Nicholas's warm sleeve.

With her free hand, she massaged her temple. This was insufferable. Finally, her chance to sway Mr. Henley into pursuing her, and she brooded like a moon-eyed schoolgirl over Nicholas Brentwood, Bow Street Runner. What was wrong with her?

Mr. Henley patted her hand and shot her a sideways smile. "I've been waiting for this moment."

"You have?" She gazed up at him, searching his eyes. Nothing inside her tingled or zinged or. . .anything, really.

And when had she started to prefer green over blue?

She forced her smile to deepen. "What I mean to say, sir, is that I, too, have been waiting for this moment. I am honored you sought me out."

But her smile faded as they swept past the dancers and out the door, leaving the ballroom behind. Mr. Henley's pat on her hand turned into a strong-fingered grip.

Her brow puckered. "Have the Garveys added on a new ballroom elsewhere?"

"Not that I know of." He led her down the stairway, slipping her a glance from the corner of his eye. "I merely wanted to have a word with you. Alone. Without your guard dog."

"Mr. Brentwood is not my. . ." The rebuttal lay like a heap of ashes on her tongue. Wasn't that exactly what her father paid him for? What kind of dolt was she to have feelings for a man who was little better than a servant, if indeed the odd sensations were anything other than some tea that didn't set well in her stomach?

As they sped along, she stole glances at Mr. Henley. Centuries of money echoed in his steps. Aristocracy fit him as neatly as his imported Italian shoes and fine silk shirt. The spicy scent of costly cedar aftershave tweaked her nose. Here was a true gentleman, one with wealth, connections, poise. A future.

Her slippers patted double-time to his long strides. Faces blurred past. Conversations blended into a dull roar, and her lungs started to burn. "I object, sir! Must we go this fast?"

"Sorry." Yet his pace belied his apology. He strode out the open french doors, across the veranda, and descended the steps into the garden.

"Mr. Henley, really!" She yanked her hand from the crook of his elbow and pressed it to her chest, gasping. "I can barely breathe."

Behind them, torches twinkled. Ahead, nothing but hedgerows stood black against the night sky, soaking up the moonlight between them. Clearly the party ended at the veranda.

Henley stretched out his hand. "Come along, my dear. There's a seat, not much farther."

The queasiness in her stomach increased, not unlike the sensation when she'd escaped the captain's advances late last summer. Surely, though, this was different.

Wasn't it?

Slowly, she smoothed her hands along her skirt, shoving down memories. "I don't think I should—"

"Honestly, Miss Payne. I've seen you alone countless times with

Mr. Brentwood." Mr. Henley's teeth glinted in the faint torch glow reaching this far from the festivities. "Surely you won't hesitate to sit with me."

Emily frowned. "You forget, sir, that Mr. Brentwood is my cousin."

"Is he?"

A chill leeched up through her slippers. "What is that supposed to mean?"

His upper lip quirked. His gaze cut to his offered hand then back to her.

Should she? Wasn't this what she'd hoped for all along? So why did her slippers drag as she stepped forward?

Bella's warnings, Nicholas's concerns, her own gut feelings screamed an alarm, but Mr. Henley's grip engulfed her glove, pulling her along. His grin flashed white in the darkness, skeleton-like. He led her deeper into the garden, along a path lined on one side with boxwoods as tall as her head.

Ten more paces and he stopped. Letting go of her hand, he inclined his head to an alcove cut into the hedge. A small wrought-iron bench nestled in the recess. Torchlight didn't stretch this far. Music and voices and laughter lapped at the far edges of the night.

"Please, have a seat." Henley's tone was mild, his gesture non-offensive.

Still, her heartbeat pulsed through her veins and throbbed in her wrists. Clearly he had much to say, for her ears alone, or he never would have brought her here. Something as important as a proposal, perhaps? But if it weren't, was the risk to her reputation worth otherwise?

What to do?

She lowered to the cold metal and lifted her face to where he stood. Shadows hid his expression, making it impossible to guess at his emotions. La, she could barely name her own.

But she could guess. "Are you cross about the coffee-shop

incident? I assure you—"

"On the contrary." His words ended with a small laugh. He sank next to her, his outer thigh pressing against hers. "I am delighted it happened."

She scooted away from him until the arm of the bench cut into her side. "Why would you say such a thing? Mr. Brentwood embarrassed you in no small way, sir."

"Ahh." He nodded, and a swath of his hair fell forward on his brow. "But you see, Miss Payne, it made me realize just how much I want you."

In one swift movement, he closed the distance between them, bringing with him the smell of pomade and desire. His breath fanned over her cheeks as he pulled her into his arms. "Emily, there is something I should like to ask you."

She bit her lip. This was it, exactly what she'd wanted. What she'd been waiting for. Working toward. Counted on as the very beginning of her new life.

Or was it?

His lips crushed against hers, forceful, seeking. Bruising. She wrenched from him, wriggling to free one hand.

Then she slapped him for all she was worth.

"Please, Mr. Brentwood?"

Though it was hardly more than a whisper, Miss Bella Grayson's request piggybacked on the vibrato of a cello string, pulling Nicholas's scrutiny from the dance floor. Next to him, the pleading eyes of Emily's redheaded friend sought his as Mr. Shadwell reached for her hand.

"I know 'tis a great honor I bestow upon you, Miss Grayson." Shadwell's head bobbed, as did the flap of skin beneath his chin. "I understand your hesitance to dance with a proficient light-foot such as myself. But don't let it overwhelm you, my dear. I often have that effect."

"It's simply not possible for me to say yes, Mr. Shadwell." Bella Grayson slipped to Nicholas's other side, putting him smack between her and Shadwell's big belly.

Casting a last glance over his shoulder—and seeing no flash of Emily's golden dress nor Henley's blue suit among the dancers—Nicholas flexed his jaw. Perhaps he could save a damsel in distress and gain a better view of Emily at the same time. He turned and offered his arm to Miss Grayson while speaking to Shadwell. "What the lady is so graciously trying to say, sir, is that she's dancing with me."

Bella's fingers clung to the curve of his forearm like a drowning woman clutching a life preserver. Nicholas led her to the end of the dance line, leaving Shadwell blustering a few *I never*s and a distinct *who'd have thought*.

As Miss Grayson took her place, she smiled. "Thank you, Mr. Brentwood. You saved my life."

"Happy to be of service, but in all honesty, I must admit ulterior motives." He stood opposite her and scanned the row of merrymakers as the lead couple skipped down the center. Not Emily or Henley, but a flash of gold at the other end of the line blazed for a moment like a shooting star.

As he and Bella sidestepped, moving up the line, Bella leaned toward him. "I can't help but notice your preoccupation with Emily. Why did you let Mr. Henley sweep her away from you?"

"You heard her. She wished it." He bowed as the next couple skipped down the middle, hating the frivolous steps. Whoever invented such a ridiculous custom in the first place? Still, Magistrate Ford's requirement of logging hours with a dancing master came in handy for assignments such as this—he'd give the man that.

"Pardon me for my boldness, Mr. Brentwood, but you don't strike me as one who easily gives in to a woman's whims." Bella arched a perfectly curved brow as she circled him then stepped back to face him. "And by now you've surely discovered that Emily is often whimsical."

He suppressed a snort. That put it more than mildly. "You are perceptive, Miss Grayson."

Dipping right then left, he held the position a second longer than decorum allowed, gaining another glimpse of gold from the far end—and a glower from the woman next to him.

"So, why did you?" Bella's question circled around him, and then she paused, once more standing in front of him. "Allow Emily to dance with Mr. Henley, I mean."

"Not only perceptive but determined, hmm?" He retreated two steps, as did she, allowing yet another couple to hop-skip down the inner aisle.

"And your answer is?" Bella smiled sweetly as they sidestepped up another rank.

Nicholas couldn't help but grin back. Bow Street could use as dogged a pursuer as this one. Flannery could even learn a thing or two from her. "I meant to keep Miss Payne occupied and somewhat corralled. Mr. Henley was simply a means to that end."

A flash sparked at the edge of his sight. He craned his neck forward then back, straining to see past the other dancers for a glimpse of Emily's golden skirt—but even without looking, the tightening of his chest confirmed what he already knew.

She was gone.

Nicholas broke the line, calling to Bella as he swept past her. "Excuse me, Miss Grayson."

A sharp tug on his sleeve turned him around.

"Hear me out, Mr. Brentwood." Bella stood tiptoe, garnering raised brows for her bold behavior. She leaned nearer, ensuring his ears alone would hear. "I'm not sure what Emily means to you, but I speak with a certain knowledge that she means nothing to Mr. Henley. Pray do not let her be alone with the man. Ever. He is not to be trusted."

He nodded, her words echoing in time to his heartbeat as he wheeled about. Of course, he couldn't be certain it was Henley who'd led Emily away, but for now, he must assume. He descended the stairs two at a time and scanned the reception hall before his shoe hit the last tread. No gold. No Henley.

His search of the sitting room ended with giggling girls and several wagging fingers from their matrons, but no Emily.

A huge buffet had been set up in the ground-floor promenade. Tables of food, ices, punch fountains, and ornate pastry towers stretched the length of an entire wall, but not one gilt-threaded skirt swayed among the rainbow of colors. Suddenly his cravat didn't just smother. It choked. Tugging it loose, he reentered the reception hall and shot down a different corridor. Pianoforte music poured out an open door at the far end, followed by applause. A swarm of heads began to enter the hallway—tricky to dissect at eye level.

But not atop a chair.

Backtracking, Nicholas dashed down the hall and swung into a small sitting area, sporting a table, two side chairs—

And Millie Barker.

"I thought I saw you pass this way." She stepped toward him, laying a hand on his shoulder. "You're just the man I was looking for."

"It will have to wait, Miss Barker." He sidestepped her and grabbed one of the chairs.

"Such theatrics, sir. Planning on taming a lion, are you?"

Behind him, laughter and footsteps grew louder. He strained his ears. Did any voice carry Emily's light tone?

Nothing about Millie's tone, however, could be construed as light. "Put down the chair, Mr. Brentwood."

"I've not the time!" He turned. If he didn't get out there now, he'd miss his chance.

Millie shot around him. "Not so fast, sir. I have some information you might like to hear."

Beyond her, couples began to stroll past the double-wide doorway. Nicholas frowned down at her. "Not now!"

"La, I should think you'd like to hear this now." She batted her eyelashes, though her attempt at innocence merely annoyed him further.

She mumbled something, but he shoved past her. Only when he cleared the threshold of the sitting area did her words strike home. He pivoted back around. "What did you say?"

Sconce light sharpened the bones of Millie's cheeks, the skin nearest her eyes creasing as she smiled. "I said, Mr. Brentwood, that I know what happened to Emily's father." Her smile widened with her nod. "I know *exactly* what happened to Mr. Payne."

Chapter 21

How dare you!" Emily drew back her fingers, palm stinging. Her anger pooled on Mr. Henley's cheek in the shape of a small handprint, visible even in the spare moonlight. She shot to her feet, swallowing the lump in her throat, unsure if it tasted like fear or relief.

She'd never doubt Bella or Nicholas again.

Fire sparked in Henley's eyes. Before she could run to the sanctuary of the Garveys' ballroom, his arm snaked out. Strong fingers dug into her forearm, trapping her in place. Shadows hid half his face, the other half lit with a grin. A feral cat could have produced none better.

"I wager Brentwood has dared more than a simple kiss, my dear." His tone was sensuous. The way his eyes skimmed over her, defiling.

"Beast!" She yanked her arm, but his grasp tightened. "Let me go!"

"So quickly? I think not. . .not when it's taken me this long to get you alone. It is my understanding, Miss Payne, that you've wished for this all along."

"Wished for what? Brutality? Humiliation? You are mistaken." She tugged, yet his fingers bit deeper, drilling into the barely healed wounds beneath her glove.

Suppressing a wince, she glowered down at him. "Millie may have given in to your charms, sir, but I am not Millie. And you are no gentleman!"

With one swift yank, he twisted and pulled. Her bottom hit the metal bench so hard her teeth juddered, and for an instant, tiny dots of light danced like fireflies in the night.

"Must you insist upon such drama?" His fingers slid up her arm then clamped onto the back of her neck, holding her in place. "Should we not talk this over like civilized human beings?"

"There's nothing civil about you." She arched away from his

nearness—but was blocked by the arm of steel at her back. "And I have nothing to say, other than to repeat, let me go!"

Her voice bounced from boxwood to boxwood, the effect muffled and impotent. The alcove they sat in closed in on her, as stifling as the heat from Henley's body as he pulled her closer—oppressive as the captain who'd done the same last summer.

He reached up and caressed her cheek with the back of his knuckles. "I have it on good account that it is your intent to marry this season."

She jerked her face aside. "Are you daft? So it is for half the women in London."

"I've also heard..." He leaned in, nuzzling her neck. His voice was a hot whisper. "That I am your intended prey."

She froze. Only Bella, Millie, and Nicholas were privy to that information—and she was pretty sure which one had told.

"I entertained such a notion...once." She sharpened her voice to a razor's edge. "But no longer. And I'll thank you to remove your hands."

Wriggling in Henley's arms, she gained a tiny amount of space as his head drew back. Why had she ever thought him handsome? Worse, why had she ever thought him the only one who could make her happy? As much as she hated to admit it, Bella and Nicholas had been right, and the truth slapped her with as much force as the mark she'd left on Henley's cheek. The perfectly fitted suit in front of her housed nothing but the bones of a rake. His gaze violated to a depth that sank low in her stomach, and she shivered.

Slowly, a grin slashed across his face. "Ah, my dear, it pains me, this sudden coldness you own. Perhaps I ought to warm you up."

A queer glimmer shone in his eyes. Either the moon had finally risen to such a slant as to drop in a spare glow of light into the alcove—or an intent she'd rather deny simmered within him.

She shoved him with both hands. Still, his grip would not lessen.

"I will have none of it. And I will have none of you! If you don't let me go, I shall scream."

"Such a feisty kitten!" His grin widened. "But hear me out. Millie did, and to her benefit, I might add."

Not that she'd completely doubted the rumor of a tryst between Millie and Henley, but what had any of this to do with her? Emily scowled. "I don't understand."

"You see, my sweet, there's a reason I've avoided the matrimonial noose thus far." Henley's free hand lowered to his pantaloons.

Emily's heart stopped. Surely this wasn't happening.

"I find that women long for financial security much more ardently than a simple band on their third finger. A lifetime pension need not be restricted by fidelity. I intend to make you my mistress. You'll be well cared for. Is that clear enough?"

"No!" She sucked in a breath then yelled even louder. "Stop!"

"Don't bother playing the innocent. The secret is out about your *cousin*. What you see in Brentwood baffles me to no end." The moon's light broke over the top of the hedges in full, lighting Henley's skin to a deadly gray. "I don't understand the ruse, my dear, but I should like a turn at the game you play so deftly with Brentwood."

Her heart was loud in her ears, each beat dredging up memories she thought she'd drowned. Panic choked her, blocking out all but a ragged whisper. "What game?"

"This one."

The back of her head smashed onto the cold bench seat. And then he was atop her, his body a sword, all edges and violence.

"No!" She screamed a dark, throaty roar.

Henley merely laughed. "Holler all you like. I rather like it. Besides, your runner's not around to defend your reputation this time. I believe Millie has him occupied."

As her skirt slipped up, her panic sunk deeper. Fabric ripped. So did her last remaining hope.

And she suddenly understood exactly how Wren had felt last summer.

～

Nicholas held the chair aloft, gripping the back so tight his fingers turned numb. Behind him, chatter from passing couples filtered into the small sitting area, each female giggle a reminder that Emily was out there. Somewhere. He narrowed his eyes at the raven-headed tart in front of him. "If this is a ruse, Miss Barker, I swear I'll—"

"Do you really think I'd trifle with an officer of the law?" She lobbed the question like a grenade then stepped toward him, eyes glimmering. Her red lips pulled into a pout—but not sullen or innocent. It was a sultry pucker, one only a trollop could perfect.

For the moment, he dropped the chair. Wooden legs thudded onto carpet, wobbled, then stilled. Though the timing wasn't his choosing, he discarded the guise of being Emily's cousin with as much relief as stepping out of a pair of leg shackles. "What do you know?"

"Ahh, so I finally have your attention, do I, Mr. Brentwood. . .Bow Street *Runner*?" Her lips flattened into a sneer. "You're less than a commoner. I can't believe I was ever interested in you."

"And I am not interested in your opinion." He sidestepped the chair and stalked toward her. Grabbing her shoulders, he barely restrained the urge to shake her. "I care only for the facts, and so I repeat, what is it you know?"

"Such violence, sir." Her eyes slid from one of his hands to the other, then she lifted her face and smiled in full. "I rather like it."

He dropped his hands, but not without curling them into fists at his side. This woman was more vexing—and dangerous—than Emily.

Millie craned her neck past his shoulder then crooked a finger at him. "Come. Why don't you pull up that chair, and I'll tell you a little story."

Running a hand through his hair, he sighed. He didn't have time for this. Emily still needed to be accounted for, though as long as she was with Mr. Henley, he supposed she was likely protected from abduction by Nash. Somewhat, at any rate. And Millie's eyes did gleam with a knowledge she ought not possess.

"As I've said, I think you'll want to hear this." Millie's voice cut into his mental debate. "Unless Emily's father is of no importance to you."

He grabbed the chair and set it opposite the table where Millie sat like a queen about to behead a subject. Her jasmine perfume, overdone to the point of irritating his nose, disgusted him to the same extent Emily's lily scent pleased him.

"Make this quick, if you please." He sat so forcefully, the table jittered, rattling a crystal vase and sending ripples through the rose petals.

Slowly, Millie ran a manicured nail across her lips. "No small talk, no sweet nothings, no. . .soft words before the act, hmm?"

On the streets, he frequently encountered women such as this. The only thing that made Millie different was the grand trappings with which she operated. A scowl was his only response.

"Hmm, I daresay you're as puritanical as Aunt." She toyed with a loose curl near the nape of her neck. "You've already met my father, but I don't believe you've had the pleasure of meeting my grandfather . . .on my mother's side, that is. His name is Lowick. Mr. George Lowick."

Lowick? The name landed like a handful of rocks thrown into a pond, agitating a hundred memories, until at last one single ripple lapped up to shore.

"The newspaper mogul?" he asked.

"The very same." When she nodded, sconce light brushed over her face in such a way that the angle of her nose, the tilt of her brow, agreed with her claim. She did, indeed, resemble a much younger and feminine version of Lowick.

"Go on," he said.

"Apparently there's quite the story soon to print. Something about a certain body found hanging from the rafters over on the Wapping Wharves. One of Grandfather's newsmen took an interest in it." While she spoke, she wrapped then rewrapped the coil of black hair around her finger. A nervous reaction, but not enough to indicate lying.

Yet.

He cocked his head. "Bodies in that part of town are tuppence a dozen. Why would a newsman take note of some bloated cadaver?"

"Mr. Nibbens, or Nibbs as Grandfather calls him, has been investigating a ring of resurrection men. I suppose a man in your profession would be familiar with that trade. At any rate, these body snatchers operate near the old Skerry warehouses, and so it was strange that a fine, fresh body hadn't been sold when all it would've taken was a swipe of a knife to the rope." She shrugged, as if the import of her words had nothing to do with a man who'd lived and breathed and loved. "The corpse ended up over at the Plank Street Dead House, all parts attached and intact. . .even the teeth. Kind of you to identify the fellow."

He narrowed his eyes, the merry sounds of the Garveys' ball receding.

"It's too bad, really. Your intelligence intrigues me, your skill at subterfuge, as well. And your strength. . ." She leaned forward, reaching across the small table to trace little loop-de-loops on his arm. "Positively delicious. I suppose I could lower my standards for one night."

He shot to his feet. Emily was light and air compared to this death trap in a dress. "You've not told me anything I don't already know, Miss Barker. Now if you'll excuse me, I have—"

"Oh, sit down. I'm not going to bite you." She leaned back in her chair and shook her head, her ringlet dangling like a noose. "La, such a man of business. I haven't finished my story yet. I should think you would want to hear the rest."

Duty weighed heavy on his shoulders, pressing down, smothering. But where exactly did his duty lie? With the deceased Mr. Payne or the out-of-sight Emily? He folded his arms and planted his feet.

"Quite the warrior stance, sir." Millie's eyes raked over him. "Ah well, it's to be expected, I suppose, from a man like you."

"Just finish your tale, Miss Barker."

"Very well," she sniffed. "Besides a cultivated relationship with all the mortuary clerks in the city, Nibbs has ties to the underworld. Acquaintances that a lawman such as yourself couldn't make. Too risky. Smugglers tend to shy away from men with tipstaffs." Her eyes slipped to his waist then returned to his face. "Though I don't see any bulges on you tonight. Pity."

Nicholas frowned. "You know an inordinate amount of seamy information for a lady."

"One of my specialties. . .among others."

Beauty, wealth, and corrupt to the core. He swallowed back scorn and measured out his words. "Miss Barker, either you get to your point, or I'm leaving."

"Very well." She sighed. "Nibbs is tied up with his resurrection story, but Grandfather tells me an investigation will be made into the possibility of Mr. Payne's dalliance with smugglers."

Unfolding his arms, Nicholas rubbed the back of his neck. It was a small bone she'd thrown—one easily verified by Moore. Her tidbit didn't surprise him nearly as much as the source. "Why would your grandfather tell you that?"

"He didn't. Not outright." Her smile grew. "Nibbs isn't the only one with connections. I intend on marrying well, Mr. Brentwood, and knowledge is power. I gather it where and when I can, and I use it as efficiently as you might wield a pistol."

He thinned his lips into a sharp-edged grimace. "Women like you sicken me."

Her smile vanished. She rose and stepped toward him like a black cloud about to burst. Anger flashed in her eyes. "And women like your simpering Emily Payne sicken me. The more fools like her that I crush on my upward path, the better. The nerve of her leading me to believe you were her cousin. Her father is dead, and I can't wait to see her face when I tell her!"

Millie's words spread like a cancer in his bones. He should've told Emily, despite Ford's urgings. He should've borne her grief, lent his shoulders to her tears. He clenched his jaw so tight, it crackled. What had he done? If Emily heard of her father's death from Millie, the blow would not be kind.

It would be deadly.

The victory in Millie's tipped chin and bright eyes was too much to bear. Rage boiled deep in his gut. He flexed his fingers, keeping them from curling tight. He should count before he spoke. . .one to keep it civil, two to keep from wringing Millie's neck, three to—

Forget it. He stepped toward her. "If you breathe one word about this to Emily, I swear to God it will be your last."

Millie lifted her face to his, standing so close her skirt hem brushed against his legs. No fear lit her violet eyes. Only guile. "You don't strike me as the type to seriously harm a woman, Mr. Brentwood. You've not got it in you." She shook her head. "Too gallant."

With a growl, he shoved her back, pinning her against the wall. Sconce glasses chattered like teeth. "Grand thoughts toward someone who's less than a commoner, wouldn't you say?" He kept his voice low and hard. "You're right, though. I wouldn't hurt you, not personally. I'd have you locked up. I hear hell's a kinder home than the bowels of Newgate Prison."

Her throat bobbed, and finally—*finally*—a shadow of terror snuffed out the gleam in her eyes. "Let me go!"

Funny how the pleasure he expected to feel withered into shame. He dropped his hands and retreated then wheeled about before leaving. "Tell me, Miss Barker, for I am curious. What did you hope to gain by informing me of all this?"

She stood where he'd left her. But slowly, as she stepped from the wall, an interesting transformation took place. Her smile returned. The tilt of her head, the lift of her shoulders, all spoke of renewed confidence. And if he looked closely enough, he thought he detected a bounce in her step.

Her pretty lips opened like a grave and issued a single word. "Time."

Time? What was that supposed to mean? Her answer echoed through his head like the slamming of a door in an empty house. She'd hoped to gain nothing but—

His blood ran cold. He'd been duped.

Nicholas fled the room and tore down the corridor, ignoring the huffs he left in his wake. How many precious minutes had he wasted? A quick sweep of the first level turned up no golden gown. He took the stairs three at a time and burst into the ballroom. Those nearest the door gaped at him upon his entrance; those farther when he skirted the room. He was a beast, circling in a cage of preening birds, none of which wore the bright gilt of Emily's skirts.

"Mr. Brentwood?"

Bella's voice halted him. He paused long enough to ask, "Have you seen Miss Payne or Mr. Henley?"

"No." A fine gathering of lines troubled the skin on her brow. "You don't think—"

Her voice faded as he dashed out the door and down the stairs, darted through the sitting room, and sprinted onto the veranda. Everything in him wanted to cry out Emily's name, hear her answer, but he stopped and stood dead still. The few couples dotting the terrace already slanted curious glances his way.

To his right, along the side of the mansion, was a vast courtyard, unlit and uninhabited. Directly ahead, paths stretched into blackness.

Every nerve on edge, he blocked out the party chatter and listened to the sounds of the night, staring into the darkness, and—

Nothing.

No sinister shadows crept about in the dark. No screams of panic rent the air above the music filtering out from the Garveys' mansion. His shoulders sagged, as did his spirits. She wasn't here. Emily was gone. And if she'd been taken out the front, off the property, only God knew where she was. He lifted his face to a sky spread with stars and a moon that saw all.

But God, You see more. Show me where she is. Wisdom, Lord. I ask for Your wisdom.

He hoped that wisdom would come on the fly, for he had no further time to remain idle. Sighing, he pivoted toward the open veranda door and—stopped, inhaling deeply. A faint scent of lily of the valley wafted on the night air.

A flower whose blooms had already withered for the season.

Chapter 22

Nicholas spun and sprinted to the edge of the veranda, not caring what the other couples on the terrace thought of his bizarre behavior. Three main paths, like spokes on a wheel, branched off the rounded platform, each leading into a different maze of hedges. All were unlit, rife with sinister possibilities. Which one to choose?

"Emily!"

Her name scraped out his throat in a voice barely recognizable as his own. Behind him, drifting out the open windows, the vibrato of violas and cellos skipped from string to string. To his side, a few murmurs of "poor man" or "what's he about?" added to the noise. All masked any cry that Emily might have issued.

He leaped down the few stairs, chose a trail at random—the closest—and bent to study the walkway. It was pea gravel, lined by bricks set in a sawtooth pattern. Indents troubled the surface at regular intervals, wide set and deep. A man, or a very tall, heavyset woman had last traversed this path, neither of which described Emily.

Unless the man had carried her.

Filing away the possibility, he dashed to the center path and stooped yet again. Footprints pitted the pebbles in a similar pattern. Yet next to those depressions, the gravel blurred into two scattered ruts, a curious combination of dragging and scampering.

And not nearly so deep.

His shoes kicked up a spray of rock as he launched down the center trail.

He left behind torchlight and safety. Ahead, a light-colored flash peeked out from the hedges a little below waist level and then disappeared just as quickly. Was it a signal? A warning? A discreet plea for help?

Slowing, he blended into the backdrop of boxwood. Millie had been right about one thing. He carried no tipstaff tonight. Stepping onto the brick edging to eliminate the crunch of gravel beneath his shoes, he pulled out a dagger tucked inside his waistcoat.

As he crept, the sound of labored breathing traveled on the air. A man's grunts. A woman's whimpers. His fingers wrapped tight around the hilt. Whether he surprised a young couple in the throes of passion or had indeed discovered his missing ward, the act he was about to interrupt would not end well.

When he finally gained a view into the moonlit alcove, he paused. A dark dress coat lay discarded on the ground, a sateen waistcoat pooled upon it. Bare legs, likely what he'd seen kick out, were now trapped beneath a man—a sandy-haired man who straddled a wriggling woman. One of his hands covered her mouth. The other tugged at his unbuttoned trousers. Golden fabric bunched around the woman's hips below him.

Rage quivered along each of Nicholas's nerves. This would not end well at all.

Shoving his knife back inside his vest, he then stowed his anger as well. If either remained in his grasp, he'd kill Henley—not that he couldn't be certain he wouldn't anyway.

God, help me.

He sprung from the shadows and grabbed Henley's shoulders from behind. In one swift move, he whumped Henley to the ground and threw all his weight atop him. Shock widened Henley's eyes an instant before Nicholas smashed his fist into his face. Never had the crunch of bone and snap of cartilage sounded sweeter. Slick warmth coated his knuckles as he pounded him again. Henley's body slackened. The assault didn't. The filthy cully deserved every bit of a sound beating and—

"Nicholas!"

Emily's voice shattered his concentration like a rock through a window, jolting him to awareness. Lungs heaving, he stood and staggered back. Retrieving the man's cast-off waistcoat, he wiped the blood from his swollen fingers then threw the fabric down and turned to Emily.

She stood, arms wrapped tight around her waist, huddled to the side of the alcove. One sleeve hung loose, ripped at the shoulder seams, the other was gone completely. Her pearl coronet was missing as well, and her golden hair hung wild to her elbows. Moonlight glistened on the single teardrop sliding down her cheek.

His breath caught.

So vulnerable, so out-of-sorts, she'd never been more beautiful.

"Are you all right?" He stepped toward her, shoving down a swell of resurging rage that made him want to turn back and kick Henley in the head. "Senseless question, I realize, but I must know, did I get here in time? Did he. . ." He stopped inches from her and studied her face, hoping, wishing. . .praying. "Did he hurt you?"

Her lips pressed tight. Though spent tears streaked her face, the slight shake of her head uncoiled every muscle he'd been clenching. Closing his eyes, he breathed out a thank-you to the One who'd guided and hastened his steps.

"I've been so wrong." Her voice was wobbly and small, yet strong enough to snap open his eyes.

"You and Bella. . .you were both right," she continued. "Henley wasn't the man I thought he was, hoped he was. He's. . .he's not like you." Her eyes shimmered with fresh tears. "There's no one like you."

He sucked in a breath. Women looked at him all the time, but never the way Emily did in that moment. Never this unguarded. Not even Adelina had, the girl he'd loved so long ago. The admiration shining in Emily's gaze was so intense, so pure, the pressure of it slammed his heart against his rib cage. If he gathered her in his arms now, he'd never let go. So he retreated a step and ran a hand through his hair—anything to keep from reaching out to her. "I'm not the paragon of virtue you think I am, Miss Payne. In truth, you may revise your opinion when

I say what I must."

He paused, memorizing the look of esteem softening the lines of her face, for it would likely be the last time he saw it. Yet if he didn't speak now, Millie surely would. "There's something I've kept from you. Something you should know. This is the worst possible time to tell you," he swung out a hand toward Henley's body. "But I must."

Her nose crinkled in the funny little rabbity way he'd come to cherish. "What is it?"

Absently, he rubbed his smarting knuckles. He'd told countless people of the demise of their loved ones, but this was different. This was entirely too...personal. How to tell the woman he'd come to treasure that her father's body lay in a holding crypt until the investigation into his death ran its course? That the man she depended upon was gone forever? Whether suicide or murder, the scandal would be such that she'd never again hope to make an advantageous marriage match.

As if she could hear the course of his thoughts, she shivered and ran her hands over her upper arms.

"You're chilled. Allow me." He shrugged out of his dress coat and wrapped it around her shoulders. The silk of her loose hair caressed his fingertips in the process. The warmth in her "thank you" weakened his resolve. She'd never let him this near her once she learned of his deception.

He breathed in so deeply, his chest strained against his shirt. Beating a man senseless was easier than this. Retreating to arm's length, he planted his feet into a fighting stance, though it didn't provide nearly the amount of confidence he'd hoped for. "Your father ...well, you see, he's...gone."

She cocked her head like a robin, alert to a possible danger. "Gone?"

Behind him, a deep groan rumbled in Henley's chest—a moan teetering on the edge of consciousness.

"I'll explain, but come along." He stretched out his hand to her.

"Or we'll be attached to more scandal than either of us will care to admit to."

⁓

Emily slipped her arms into the long sleeves of Nicholas's dress coat. The fabric yet carried the heat from his body, and she shivered in response. As she pulled the coat tight around her, it felt like an embrace. His embrace. Safe. Warm and protected. The cloth smelled somewhat metallic and sweaty, just like the man, but she didn't care. She couldn't. The breakneck speed of her emotions—fear, despair, relief, longing—dazed her in a way she'd have to sort through later.

She lifted her hand to his. As his fingers wrapped around hers, her lips parted. Strength flowed up her arm. Despite the degradation of the evening, she had no doubt that from now on, everything would be set to rights.

He led her through the garden maze, the dark hedgerows not nearly as suffocating as when Henley had dragged her out here. Though Nicholas had rescued her in time, the touch of Henley's hands, the bruise of his lips against hers, sullied her in a way that had crawled under her skin and taken up residence.

Oh, how Wren must suffer.

Light from the mansion flickered into view. As they neared the veranda, Nicholas paused and turned to her. "You've been through enough this evening. If you like, we can avoid putting our bedraggled selves on display and cut through the side yard instead of exiting via the house."

A genuine smile tugged her lips. For all his rugged bluntness, inside beat the heart of a true gentleman. "Yes. I'd like that very much."

"Stay close, then. I'm poor concealment, but I'm afraid I'm all you've got. We'll move fast. Ready?"

She nodded.

He wasn't jesting.

Gravel nipped the thin heels of her kidskin slippers as she raced to keep up. Nicholas sprinted from shadow to shadow, never resting in a dark hollow long enough for her to catch her breath. It was an odd dance, replete with ghostly bars of a quadrille hovering on the night air from the gala inside. From shrub to shrub, they skirted the open grounds nearest the mansion, avoiding the attention of the couples on the veranda. Thanks to Henley, this was by far the most unorthodox exit she'd ever made from a ball.

Nicholas didn't stop until they reached a twelve-foot-high wrought-iron fence—a fence with no gate in sight.

Emily threw a hand to her chest, panting. "Now what?"

Nicholas dropped her other hand, a low groan in his throat. Hopefully he was forming some kind of solution. She was too busy breathing.

"Take off the jacket." Nicholas's voice cut into her apprehension.

She lifted her face to his. Had he really just told her to remove his coat? "I beg your pardon?"

"Do you trust me?"

Her heart answered before she could dissect the question. "Completely."

"Then hand it over." He held out his hand.

She peeled off his dress coat and shivered from the chill that immediately gripped her arms. Nicholas threw the coat to the ground, missing her scowl as he bent and laced his fingers together.

"Whatever are you doing?" she asked.

Shadow masked half his face as he looked up at her. "Step into my hands."

"But—"

"Ah, ah, ah," he shook his head. "You said you trusted me completely."

She scowled, her own words tasting like soured milk. Slowly, she lifted her foot. As soon as her heel rested in the palms of his hands, the world rushed down in a blur. Instinctively, she stretched out her hands and grabbed the rail at the top of the fence, using the momentum to pull herself atop it. Her already ruined skirt snagged on a jagged edge and ripped further, but she held on and threw one leg over the fence, teetering astraddle like a ropewalker she'd once seen at a carnival.

Clutching the top rail like a saddle horn, she gaped down at Nicholas then gasped. He looked so small. So far away.

And there was no one to boost him. Unless he possessed superhuman qualities she'd not yet seen, there was no way he'd be able to follow her.

"Catch my coat," Nicholas shouted up at her.

Before she could ask what in the world he was talking about, a swish of fabric hit her dangling leg. Holding tight to the fence with one hand, she swiped down the other and barely snagged the hem of his coat before it fell away.

"Tie the sleeve around your wrist, tight as you can, then dangle the rest of it down to me."

Clearly the stress of the situation had skewed his thinking. Merely the weight of his jacket balled in her hands made her wobble. " But... I can't pull you up."

"Just do as I say and remember what you said about trusting me."

The man was a dog with a bone. She'd have to live to her nineties to outlast her hasty plea of trust in the fellow. She fumbled with the fabric, but tying a knot one-handed was hard. Doing it while clinging to the top of a fence, impossible.

"How's it coming?"

"Slowly, especially if I have to keep answering you." Eventually, though, she managed to secure it around her wrist and cast the rest of it downward, dangling the fabric just above his head.

He grabbed the sleeve. "Now jump."

"What?"

"Trust, Miss Payne. Trust."

Anger pushed her over the edge. Literally. She leaped into a free fall, but not for long. Her arm yanked, and for a single stunning moment, she hung suspended. Then plummeted. The sudden jerk on her arm made his plan clear. He'd never intended for her to pull him up with her own frail strength. By soaring downward, her body acted as a counterweight to boost him skyward.

Though none of that mattered when her feet hit the ground. Her knees buckled, and she crashed, jarring through every bone. A *whoompf* landed somewhere beside her.

"Let's go." Nicholas's voice breathed into her ear. His grasp hefted her to her feet. Was she on her feet? Hard to tell. The world tilted one way then another. A strong arm wrapped about her shoulders, straightening out sky from ground.

Nicholas ushered her to the line of carriages snaked along the drive, taking care to keep to the shadows. Not that he had to, really. Coach drivers were either too preoccupied in passing small flasks among themselves or too unaware as they snored on their benches. Normally, if she'd caught Wilkes so engaged, she'd have censured him. This time, just to have him present and able to get them out of there quickly, she might kiss his cheek.

By the time she reached the family coach, however, she lacked the energy to even care. Nicholas swung open the door and hoisted her up. The familiar smell of leather and axle grease eased her nerves a bit as she sank onto the seat. Soon all this would be over. . .ended with as much finality as her dream of marrying Henley. A dream that was better cataloged as a nightmare, now. Why had she never noticed the rotten content of the man's character before tonight?

Leaning her head back, she closed her eyes. The answer pained her as much as the throb in her shoulder. She'd been far too busy looking at Henley's bank account to notice.

Outside, Nicholas's deep rumble conferred with another man's, one bearing a distinct brogue. Either Wilkes had some Irish blood in him that she'd never recognized, or she was way beyond tired.

The carriage tilted. The door shut. The cushion she sat on jiggled, and her eyes popped open. Moonlight seeped in the windows, pooling on the broad shoulders next to hers.

Nicholas sat a breath away, on her side of the carriage, wearing a mantle of silver light.

"You all right?" Concern warmed his voice as he reached for her hand. She'd not even noticed his coat was yet shackled to her wrist.

"I hardly know." She watched his fingers tug at the knot. One of his sleeves flapped open, revealing a forearm just as knotted with muscle. He freed the ruined coat then flung it onto the empty seat across from them.

Yet he did not move away.

"It's been quite the eventful evening." His murmured words blended with the turn of the coach's wheels. He lifted her wrist to eye level, examining it. In the space of a heartbeat, a frown darkened his face. "I'm afraid you'll have a bruise here come the morning."

"Then it shall match the rest of my body, I suppose."

She ought pull her hand back. She ought move away. Indeed, a lady would protest at his nearness. But the little circles his thumb whispered over her inner wrist held her in place.

"For that I am sorry indeed." His eyes slid from her wrist to meet her gaze. Compassion, genuine and intense, caressed her more gently than his touch.

Without a word, she leaned closer, pulled like a flower toward the sun.

He bent nearer.

Then immediately released her hand and looked past her, out the window.

An odd sense of loss shivered through her. Following his line of sight, she turned and peered out the glass into the night. This far from

210

town, no streetlamps lit their route. Fear that had never really packed its bags and departed knocked against her ribs. She turned her face back to his. "Do you think we'll be followed?"

"It's happened before." He returned his gaze to her, though a smirk lightened the intensity. "But don't fret. Flannery's more skilled in evasion than your Wilkes."

"Flannery?"

"The fellow who's driving. I'd have told you," he shrugged, "but I didn't want you to worry."

His words in the garden barreled back with astonishing speed. He'd been about to tell her something when Henley groaned. Something she wasn't entirely sure she wanted to hear, for whatever it was couldn't be good.

But she had to know.

She shifted on the seat, allowing the fullest measure of moonlight to fall upon his face, intent on listening with more than just her ears. "There's more you've kept from me. You said so yourself."

A muscle rippled at the apex of his jawline, as if words he didn't want to speak were shouldering their way to break an escape.

Emily swallowed. Suddenly she didn't want to know why. Not really.

But words tumbled out her lips before she could catch them. "What did you mean when you said my father was gone?"

A shadow darkened his face, though hard to tell if it came from without or within.

"I'm afraid I've sorely underestimated you. You show a rare courage, the caliber of which I don't see in half the officers of Bow Street. So bear up. What I'm about to tell you will no doubt hit you broadside." He paused long enough to reclaim her hands and cradle them both within his. "Your father is dead, Emily."

Dead? The word exploded into a thousand pieces. There was no way to gather in all the implications, for they traveled too fast and too far. She wrapped her fingers tight around Nicholas's and held on.

He squeezed back. "You have suffered much. It's all right to weep."

She gasped. No, it wasn't all right. It was impossible. Unspent sobs clogged her throat and a wealth of tears burned her eyes, but she could no more cry than speak. So she stared into the black wall of the carriage opposite her, refusing to look at the light in Nicholas's eyes or the glimmer of moon outside the window. Either would be her undoing. For now, darkness was her friend.

How long she sat, she could only guess to be an eternity, but at last, Nicholas spoke.

"Emily?" Worry poked holes into his voice. "I vow before God I'll find out what happened to your father. Justice will be served. You have my word on it."

She turned her face to his. Lines creased his brow. Lines put there by her. After all he'd been through on her behalf, she owed him. At least a little. Especially truth, for dearly did he value it.

"He. . ." Was that squeak her voice? She cleared her throat and tried again. "He wasn't my father."

Chapter 23

What the deuce are you talking about!" As soon as the heated words spewed out his mouth, Nicholas clenched every muscle in his body. Control. That's what he needed. Breathe in, breathe out, subdue the tremor running along every nerve. Anger led to mistakes. And it was no mistake he'd lived through war on two continents or survived the thugs terrorizing London's streets for this long. Not that he hadn't gained scars, but how big of a jagged red mark would this woman leave on him?

Emily flinched and edged away from him, stopping only when her back hit the carriage wall. "You've no right to be so cross. You've not been straightforward with me, either."

Unlocking his jaw, he forced a calm to his voice he didn't feel. "Do not think to play me like a flash game of wicket. If I am to help you, I must be told everything."

Spare starlight from the clear night streamed in through the window, casting a ghostly glow upon half her face. Her eyes were wide. A loose curl trembled over her brow, begging to be brushed aside. Besides a darkened smudge of dirt on her cheek, her skin was the pale hue of exhaustion.

She'd been through a lot this evening. He'd grant her that. Blowing out a long, slow breath, he softened his tone further. "I will have the truth, and I will have it now. All of it. Am I clear?"

Her hands clenched together in her lap, bunching the fabric of her already ruined skirt. "All?"

He nodded. "If we're to sort through this mess, then yes. Indeed."

Fine, white teeth nibbled her lower lip before she answered. "Very well. Go on. Tell me if you're keeping back any more information from me."

His first thought was to smile. The second, to throw her over his knee and supply the sound thrashing she deserved for such cheek. He went with his third impulse and merely eyed her with a growing admiration. "A gentleman always allows a lady to go first."

"A gentleman also keeps a lady's secrets, and so I ask. . ." Her eyes sought his, looking deeply into one then the other. "I know I said I trust you, leastwise I did in the heat of the moment, but can I? Really?"

He cocked his head and studied her in return. "If I am to continue to protect you, then I'm afraid you must."

Her lips, yet swollen from Henley's abuse, curved downward. "And I am afraid you're right."

Though she'd agreed with him, she fell silent. A faraway glaze shone in her eyes. Only God knew what thoughts she chewed on, though judging by a poorly concealed wince, none were sweet. As he waited for her to continue, he took to counting the seconds then moved on to tallying how many times the rolled-up window shade banged against the top of the glass. Still, he waited. Sometimes truth ripened at a rate slower than the plodding horses Flannery guided.

The grit of wheel upon gravel changed to the smoother grind of cobblestone as they drew closer to the inner city, and at last, Emily's lips parted. His every sense heightened to full alert, a skill honed to a sharp edge by countless interrogations—as both the examiner and the examinee.

"Quite honestly. . ." She started slow, her words picking up speed as she spoke. "I have no idea who my real father is. I was raised as Mr. Payne's daughter, for he dearly loved my mother, so much that no one suspected she'd carried anyone's child but his own. Oh, he loved her all right, but the truth is—" Her lips flattened into a straight line. "He never loved me."

"How can you say that?" He raked a hand through his hair, though the action did nothing to reconcile her twisted logic. "The man hired me, for more than a fair amount, to see to your safety. That hardly sounds like the action of a man who doesn't care."

"He wasn't protecting me. He was protecting his name." She flourished her fingers through the air. "The grand Payne family legacy."

"Come again?" Leaning back, he watched her, closely, grateful for the streetlamps now adding an extra measure of brightness through the coach windows. From the flash of light to shadow and back again, he searched for any hesitation, the slightest bit of nervousness—a twitch or tic. Any movement out of character that would brand her a liar.

She swept away the loose curl with one hand, but before she spoke, it sprang back again. Was everything about the woman wild and defiant? "The world knows me as Emily Payne, daughter of the illustrious and wealthy merchant Alistair Payne. I am his only heir, albeit counterfeit, so how would it look if he didn't show some responsibility toward me? Though I suspected all that would change soon enough should the recently widowed Mrs. Nevens have returned his ardor and conceived him a son. Only Uncle Reggie hindered that plan. He and my father may have been business partners, but they were rivals concerning that woman."

"If what you say is true—" He held up a hand, stopping her rebuttal. "I'm not saying it isn't, but if you are not the man's offspring, then I don't understand why he claimed you in the first place. You once told me all he cared about was business."

A sad smile—or was it a grimace?—pulled at the edges of her mouth. "As I've said, because of my mother. She was the one thing he cherished above money. On her deathbed, she made him promise to look after me as his own. And he did. . .materialistically. Nothing more. So forgive me if I do not cry a thousand tears of grief for a man who was little more than the business manager of my life. And believe me—" Glistening eyes belied her brave words. Her voice lowered to a whisper. "It wasn't for lack of trying to make him care. He was the only father I'd ever known, and I dearly wanted him to love me."

He saw her clearly, then. Like the air cleared of soot by a fresh rain. The confident woman sitting before him, the feisty Emily Payne, was nothing more than a little girl looking for affection. Nicholas sucked in a breath, so stunning was the revelation. Indeed, she'd spoken more than truth. She'd bared a glimpse into her soul.

To him.

He reached for her, every inch of his skin yearning to pull her close. Shelter her. Show her that despite her father, she was worthy of love—and indeed, had garnered all he had to give.

But he pulled back his hand. After what she'd been through with Henley, he'd be a rogue to act in the same manner. So he simply said, "I'm sorry."

And he was. Sorry that the most important man in her life had shunned her. Sorry her future teetered on a precipice. Sorry that the thought of kissing her overruled common sense and decency.

"Don't be." She looked out the window with a sigh. "It's the way of the world."

Her voice wore all the starkness of bones left to bleach in the sun. Abandoned. Dead. His heart broke at the sound.

"No one escapes this life without scars, Miss Payne. Not even God." He kept his tone even and soft. Not that he could heal her hurts, but he knew the One who could. How would she receive it, though?

Slowly, she turned her face to his, one fine brow arched.

It was all the permission he needed to continue. "How you grew up, the coldness of the only father you ever knew, it wasn't right. And it didn't go unseen. You will face your Father one day, your true Father. And I can promise you this: He will welcome you with open arms if you but turn to Him now."

Her eyes narrowed. "You speak as if I am nothing more than an upset child."

"Is that not what you are?"

Though she didn't think it possible, a flood of new tears burned Emily's eyes. Her heart beat loud in her ears. Nicholas's question pinned her in place, every part of her, like a butterfly skewered onto a display board. The turn of this conversation required a toll she wasn't entirely sure she could pay, and by this point, she had no more reserve from which to draw.

He was right of course. Mostly. Upset was too small a word to cover the broad river of emotions flowing through her. But one thing was for sure—

She'd never felt more of a child than now.

Her gaze lowered from his eyes to the strong cut of his jaw, traveled past his broad expanse of shoulders, and rested upon his chest. His black waistcoat, once so becoming and stylish, was unbuttoned and torn. The shirt beneath, splattered with blood. Truly, it ought repulse her, yet there was nowhere on earth she'd rather rest her cheek right now. If she could lay her head there, for only a few minutes, would everything be made right?

And if she did as he said and turned to God, would heavenly arms wrap around her?

The carriage jolted out of a rut, flopping the runaway piece of hair back into her eyes. Gathering the loose curls together with one hand, she pulled it all back from her brow and looked him full in the face. She'd think on all he'd said. . .but not now. "We are not speaking of me, but of my father. So now it's your turn, Mr. Brentwood. Tell me what happened. How did he die?"

He cocked his head. "You still refer to him as father, though I know the truth?"

She did. She would. For always. She owed him that, at least. "The man may not have loved me, but he did provide for me. I will honor that as much in his death as I did while he yet breathed. What. . .why are you smiling?"

The gleam of Nicholas's teeth brightened the dark. "You are an enigma. You know that, don't you?"

She frowned. "And you are evading my question."

"If nothing else, you are determined. I'll give you that." Nicholas scrubbed a hand over his face then sighed. "I am still trying to piece together all the snippets of facts concerning your father's death, which is why Chief Magistrate Ford suggested I not inform you in the first place. Suffice it to say, you may take heart in knowing that your father's end was relatively swift."

"That doesn't tell me much."

"No, it does not." His eyes glimmered with knowledge—much more than he spoke—yet his lips pressed tight. Was he trying to safeguard her. . .or himself?

"I was honest with you, sir. The least you can do is the same." A fishwife couldn't have sounded more bitter. How on earth did he evoke such extremes in her?

He lifted his chin and looked down his nose. A fine, strong nose. It annoyed her that he could sit there and look so confident, so. . . handsome. And it annoyed her further that she noticed.

"I assure you," his voice lowered, "I am being quite forthright."

She threw up her hands. "But you've not told me any details!"

A smile spread across his face, and he leaned toward her. "Did you know that your nostrils flare quite prettily when you're angry?"

"And your eyes flash a brilliant green when you're resolved to keep information to yourself." The carriage slowed. Her heart rate didn't. Frustrating man! "If you think you can charm your way out of this, sir, then you don't know me half as well as you credit your powers of observation."

"I never laid claim to charm, but I assure you, my observations are as keen as ever. Did you also know you've an enchanting dimple when you realize you're not going to get your way?" His grin grew. "Yes, there it is." He lifted his hand and his thumb brushed against the side of her cheek.

A trail of fire burned where he touched. This was ridiculous. She'd slapped men for lesser infractions. But now. . .her hands lay limp and motionless in her lap. Traitors.

"And just before your lips pull into a pout, there's a tiny quiver here." His fingers slid lower, tracing her jaw. Then, gentler than a whisper, slid back up and cupped her cheek.

She leaned into his touch, pressing into his warmth. "You. . ." Swallowing back the tremor in her voice, she tried again. "You notice my chin?"

His features softened, and he slid across the seat, moving closer. So close, his breath feathered over her skin as he spoke. "I notice everything about you and have since the day we met."

The carriage stopped—or mayhap the world did. Her gaze fixed on his mouth. She'd breathe if she could remember how. Deep in her stomach, a quiver shimmied upward, and the sensation frightened.

But mostly delighted.

Without thinking, she closed her eyes, inhaling his scent of spice and passion and possibility. A faint groan rumbled out from him, primal and altogether enticing. He wanted this, then, every bit as much as the desire pulsing through her veins. She lifted her face to the heat of him.

And the carriage door opened. "Here we are, safe as ever. And I'll be thanking ye to mention that to ol' Ford, aye Brentwood?"

Chapter 24

Nicholas froze, his ardor cooling to the same temperature as the hard leather carriage seat. A musket ball to the head would've been as welcome as Flannery's voice. Emily's eyes shot open and peered into his, blinking. It couldn't have been for more than a second, but what he read in those brown depths embedded into his heart for an eternity. Loss, pure and raw, gaping like an open wound. But loss of what? Discretion? Restraint?

Or the loss of his kiss?

She shoved past him as he whispered her name, the only word able to slip past the guilt closing his throat. He never should have taken advantage of her jumbled emotions. Not tonight. Not ever. What a wretch. He was no better than Henley.

He tried again. "Emily, wait."

But it was too late. She clasped Flannery's upstretched hand and fled out the carriage door before he could turn her around.

A groan rumbled deep in his chest. Leaping to the cobbles, he scowled at Flannery. "Your timing leaves much to be desired."

"What are ye goin' on about?" Flannery lifted his cap and scratched his head. The spare moonlight, more than half hidden now by a cloud, muddied his usual red locks to an earthy tone. "Did I not do a fine job of seein' ye here in one piece?"

The slam of the town-house door jerked Flannery's gaze away. When he looked back at Nicholas, his brows raced to his hairline. "Don't tell me you and the lass were. . .why, stars and thunder! That was a handy move. To be sure, what a grand way to guard a lady."

Nicholas ducked aside, narrowly escaping a sound clap on the back, then froze. Something more than the unwelcome praise grated on his nerves. . .but what?

He scanned the area. No suspicious figures skulked about. No riders or coaches approached the Payne household. In truth, the street was completely empty, leastwise as far as he could see, which in the dark wasn't too far. Pivoting, he studied the townhome's facade for anything unusual—a gutter pipe askew, perhaps, or a rope dangling from a chimney.

Flannery followed his lead, his head craning back and forth. "Something amiss?"

Nicholas grunted, for truly, nothing else could be said. Narrowing his eyes, he strained for one more look into the black shadows draped over the townhome like a shroud. Not one thing was out of place besides him and Flannery, standing on a curb in the dead of night, gawking up at the house in the dark as if they might purchase the thing.

And then he knew.

He broke into a run and flung open the front door, holding hard to the knob to prevent it from banging against the wall. Surprise was a weapon he'd learned long ago to heft with precision. Flannery's footsteps trailed close behind. Glancing over his shoulder, he touched a finger to his lips then turned and raced up the stairs, two at a time.

When he reached the landing, his heart skipped a beat. Emily stood halfway down the hall, hand poised to push open her chamber door. If he called out to stop her, the noise would alert the intruder he suspected, who in turn would escape. Clue lost. Dead end. But if he didn't and she walked into that room, a knife might be pressed to her throat before he could reach her.

"Emily, no!" He raced down the hall before half a question passed her lips. When he reached her, he grabbed her shoulders and steered her to the opposite wall. The action widened her eyes.

"What is happen—"

"No time. Stay put." He wheeled about and drew his knife in one movement then nodded at Flannery to flank him. Flinging wide the door, he listened. A *thwunk* sounded out, brass hitting plaster, not flesh. No one behind the door, then.

Nicholas edged to the left, jerking his head for Flannery to go right. There were plenty of potential hiding places in a woman's bedchamber. Inside the wardrobe. Beneath the bedskirt. Behind an overstuffed wingback in the corner. But he sheathed his blade and stalked past all to the sheers swinging in front of a half-open window. He bent and leaned over the sill. In the narrow courtyard between the two townhomes, footsteps pounded into the night.

Flannery joined him. "Shall I make chase?"

Though he'd like nothing better than to serve the scoundrel justice, preferably at the end of a rope, Nicholas shook his head. "By the time you catch your balance, he'll be long gone."

Flannery scooped off his cap and slapped it against his thigh, uttering a curse. Two sharp gasps—Emily's and another's—sounded behind them at the door.

"Mind your tongue, man." Stepping back from the window, Nicholas turned. A pale-faced Emily and a scowling Mrs. Hunt peered in from the hallway. "Ladies, a moment, if you please."

Emily's gaze darted from the window to him. "Where are we to be safe, if even my own chamber can be breached?"

He scowled. It wasn't right that such an ugly fear had crawled into a corner of her heart—and even worse that he was helpless to remove it, for truly, she was correct. There was no safe place for her now. "As you can see, no one remains. Await me in the sitting room, and I'll attend you shortly."

The housekeeper murmured something into Emily's ear as she took her arm and ushered her away. Their skirts barely swished from view before Flannery threw up his hands. "What tipped ye off? I didn't see a blasted thing out of the ordinary."

"Nor did I." Nicholas turned and pulled down the window. When he faced Flannery once again, the man's mouth had twisted into quite the question mark.

"Ye make about as much sense as a ravin' bedlamite."

"Think on it. When was the last time we passed a carriage?"

"Maybe two or three crossroads back." Flannery's eyes studied the ceiling corner, far left, but Nicholas doubted the man saw plaster from molding. Flannery was back on the road, driving a carriage in his mind. Seconds later, his gaze shot back to Nicholas. "Aye, 'twas two. I remember a dray aside the road on Wigmore and Duke."

"A dray? In this neighborhood? At this time of night?" He doled out the questions like bread crumbs, leading Flannery to draw his own conclusion instead of cramming it down his throat. If the man didn't learn to think for himself, Ford would never hire him on as an officer.

Flannery cocked his head. "What are ye getting at?"

"Whoever was here had point men out there. Granted, this is a residential area and the hour is admittedly late, but did you not think it odd we were the only two on the street? Those men allowed us to pass, but none others."

"But why? Why not attack at that point?"

"Remember when I signaled you to quiet your steps?" He waited for Flannery's nod before continuing. "Silence is a weapon often more dangerous than outright attack. It's easier to haul off a wriggling bit of a woman if no one's around to call an alarm or even knows she's been taken in the first place, and it would give them the advantage of lead time, cooling their trail."

Flannery's eyes widened as those seeds of information took root. "And so you'd not have me give chase for I'd be outnumbered, eh?"

He nodded. "As I said, your timing leaves much to be desired. By the time you dropped, rolled, righted yourself, and reached the blackguard, he'd have a few strong-arms with him to put an end to your evening and possibly your life."

With a last deep inhale of the leftover lily of the valley permeating the room, Nicholas strode to the door and, without pausing, called over his shoulder. "Come along."

"I've a feeling this is going to be a long night," Flannery grumbled from behind.

Mrs. Hunt and Emily rose as they swung into the sitting room, both overflowing with questions.

Nicholas held up a hand. "Ladies, answers are in short supply for the moment, and I fear what I am about to say next will merely add more confusion. But there's nothing to be done for it, I'm afraid."

Reaching into the half-torn pocket of his waistcoat, he retrieved his pocket watch and flipped it open. "You have five minutes, Miss Payne, to change into the drabbest gown you own and tuck whatever necessaries you need into a small satchel."

She recoiled as if she'd been slapped. "Whatever for?"

"We're leaving. Now."

"You can't be serious!" Mrs. Hunt stormed up to him like a thunderhead. Flannery retreated a step.

Nicholas held his ground. "I've never been more serious."

"Taking my lady into the night? Whoever was in her room is lurking about out there." Light from the single lantern sparked off her flinty eyes. "This is madness! You might as well be leading her into a lion's den."

He sidestepped her, lining up for a clear view of Emily. "And now you've got four and a half minutes."

"You can't possibly expect me to—"

"I can, and I do. . .four minutes fifteen seconds."

He watched her closely. Color crept up her neck and flushed her cheeks. Good. Anger would serve her better than fear, for if she suspected where he was taking her, she'd dig in her heels.

As if she'd read his mind, her shoulders stiffened. "Where is it that we're going? Where are you taking me?"

"Better that you don't know." Turning on his heel and crossing to the door, he breathed out a prayer. Was he doing the right thing? *God, please, let it be so.*

Emily tensed and cast one last glance at her chamber window. If a man's face popped up against the glass, she'd scream. Or faint. Possibly both. What a horrid nightmare this evening had turned into—the night that was supposed to have been a dream come true.

Outside her door, boots thumped down the carpet runner, growing louder with each step. Time was running out.

"Hurry, miss," Mary said behind her.

To her left, Mrs. Hunt rattled about at the vanity, clearly as upset as she. The normally pragmatic housekeeper ransacked through hairpins and cosmetics as if Emily were packing for a Midland holiday instead of escaping to who-knew-where.

Spinning on her heels, Emily turned to the wardrobe and bent. She reached deep into a corner then yanked out an old bonnet from the top of a box she'd meant to set out for the ragpickers. The half-starched head covering was a macabre substitute for the tiara at Asprey's. With one hand, she twisted her hair and piled it atop her crown. With the other, she pulled the worn fabric over her head, capturing most, but not all of her curls.

A sharp tap at her door shattered her already broken nerves, and she flinched. Mary gasped.

"It's time." Nicholas's deep voice seeped through the wood.

Mrs. Hunt laid a hand on her arm. "Don't you think you ought to stay here, miss? Going out with Mr. Brentwood, not knowin' where he's taking ye? It's scandalous, that's what."

Emily licked her lips, her gaze darting from the housekeeper to the window, then back. "No more scandalous than what would've happened had Mr. Brentwood not stopped me from entering my chamber when he did. Extraordinary situations call for extraordinary measures, is that not what you always say?"

Mrs. Hunt's mouth pinched as tight as a spinster's corset. "Fine time to start listening to me now."

Nicholas shoved open the door and stepped aside without a word.

Mrs. Hunt squeezed Emily's arm then gave it a pat and let go. Turning, she faced a somber-jawed Nicholas. "See that you take care of Miss Payne, or I'll rain down brimstone upon your head. And don't you think I won't."

"I don't doubt it for a moment, Mrs. Hunt." He held out his hand for the small satchel in the housekeeper's grip. "Nevertheless, you have my word. I shall return in the morning. Until then, Flannery's keeping a lookout, so rest easy."

Then he cocked his head at her. "Shall we?"

Emily let her gaze linger for a moment on the white counterpane spread atop her bed. Every muscle in her cried out to snuggle beneath the quilt and draw it up over her head, shutting out the evening's insane turn of events.

But instead she inhaled and stepped toward the only man remaining whom she could trust.

"I'll be praying for you, miss." Mrs. Hunt's words followed her down the hall, as did Mary's uneven footsteps.

Nicholas wheeled about. "I'm sorry, Mary, but you'll have to stay. I take Miss Payne alone."

"But—" Emily's and Mary's voices swelled into one big objection.

Which was promptly cut off by the raising of his hand. "It will be difficult enough for me to bring one lady where I intend. Two, impossible. I will be trusted in this matter completely, or not at all. What is it to be?"

Mary opened her mouth, but Emily shook her head with a sigh. "I'm afraid he will not be persuaded, Mary, so save your breath."

"Are you sure, miss?"

Was she? Thus far, she had found her judgment of a man's character sorely lacking. Was she wrong about Nicholas, as well? Her stomach tightened, but even so, she nodded. "Yes. But I would covet your prayers as much as Mrs. Hunt's."

Mary's eyes glistened. Were those tears? For her?

"Of course, miss. Godspeed."

Emily pulled her gaze from her maid back to the man beside her, hoping she'd made the right choice. "Satisfied?"

What went on in that head of his, she could only guess at, but the grim set of his jaw did not bode well. "Come along, Miss Payne."

As Nicholas led her toward the back of the house and down the servants' stairs, she noticed his fine silk trousers were replaced with the serviceable woolens he'd worn when she'd first met him. The ruined dress coat and embroidered waistcoat had been exchanged for a heavy greatcoat—the one that smelled of bootblacking and gunpowder. His dark hair was loose, no longer tamed for a gala ball. A black hat hid most of it. And it truly had been bootsteps she'd heard, for the shiny leather shoes he'd donned for the dance were probably now lying on the floor in his chamber. What a far different picture the two of them presented, slipping out of the rear of the townhome, than that of a few hours earlier when they'd strolled out the front.

Nicholas paused at the gate to the back alleyway and turned to her, his eyes moss green and hooded. "It's quite a hike I'm expecting of you. Are you up to it?"

She swept her hand toward the carriage house, the building so close that if she cared to sidestep a few paces, her palm would slap against the wood. "We have a small gig."

He shook his head. "Afraid not."

She narrowed her eyes. "Then why ask?"

Just then the moon escaped its half cloak of a cloud, lighting a wicked grin on his face. "I could heft you over my shoulder if you like."

She scowled, which was more of a response than he deserved.

"Right, then." He pushed open the gate. "Onward."

He wasn't jesting. Though she'd worn her most serviceable shoes, they were meant for a promenade through town, not a hike down rough cobbled passageways. Before long, pains crept up her shins, and she faltered over the hem of her skirt to keep up with his long-legged strides. When her big toe hit an upcropped bit of stone and she lurched forward, Nicholas reached back and grabbed hold of her forearm.

"The offer still stands." His face was shadowed, his gaze unreadable beneath the brim of his hat.

She sniffed then wished she hadn't. The closer to the city's innards they drew, the worse the stench. "I will not be toted about like a sack of puppies, if that's what you're hinting at."

Was that a smile that flashed in his gaze?

"At least take my hand," he offered.

His fingers wrapped around hers, and though at first she kept up, the longer they walked, the more her steps lagged. He led her down one dark alley to another, the buildings progressively closing in the farther they went. The effect was smothering. Cobbles gave way to gravel then eventually thinned out into nothing but worn dirt, littered with broken gin bottles and piles of refuse. Occasionally the whites of eyeballs flashed in dark recesses as they passed, and more than once Nicholas growled out a "shove off" to a bawdy suggestion or an outright threat.

Emily sped up. Viewing the greatcoat stretched across his shoulders from behind wasn't nearly as comforting as feeling the muscle of his arm brush against hers when she managed to remain by his side. There was safety in the heat of his body, shelter in his strength. And the fact that she trusted him so completely was as frightening as the dreadful neighborhoods they passed through.

When the alley narrowed so much that soon single file would be their only option, he pulled her out into a street. They skirted the sprawled body of drunkard who smelled overly ripe for the grave, and for a moment she feared the man actually was dead, until a snore erupted from his open mouth.

A few steps later, a woman emerged from the side of a building, her bosom spilling out of a bodice two sizes too small. Bolder than a king's man, she swung her hips over to Nicholas's side and slipped her arm around his. " 'Ave a go at it, mate? Yer li'l princess there could learn a trick or two from me. For a spare coin, she can watch, if ye like."

A slow burn worked its way up Emily's neck and spread onto her cheeks as the woman's words began to make sense. Why had he brought her here? Had she misplaced her trust?

"Not interested." Nicholas shrugged off the woman and looked down at Emily without slowing his pace. "Sorry. You've seen and heard more this evening than a lady ever should."

Her lips twisted into a wry grin, surprising herself that any shred of humor yet remained. "In truth, I wonder if this evening shall ever end."

His eyes held hers a moment more before he faced forward. "We're almost there."

Tired buildings stood elbow-to-elbow, leaning against one another for support. The windows were so sooted over, it was hard to tell what kind of merchants or craftsmen inhabited the bottom levels.

Without warning, Nicholas led her into an alcove and produced a key from his pocket. After two locks clicked their release, he turned to her. "It's tight quarters, so you'll have to follow me. Make sure to slide the bolt on the door once it shuts. I'm afraid it will be dark until I can light a lantern, so you should locate the bolt before you close the door completely. Can you do that?"

She could feel her brow wrinkle with trying to keep back the many questions flitting about in her head. Still, she nodded.

He swung wide the door. There was no threshold, merely the tread of the first stair leading up into blackness. What kind of place was this? He ascended the staircase, narrow as a coffin, and quickly disappeared from view. No wonder he'd asked her to lock the door. For him to even turn around in such a tight space would require an acrobat's skill.

Locating a steel bar as thick as two fingers and long as a child's foot, she rested her fingertips against the cool metal and pulled shut the door with her other hand then slid the bolt over until it caught home. Though she could yet hear the rhythmic thud of Nicholas's boots somewhere above her, the ensuing darkness reached in deep, stealing what was left of her composure.

"Nicholas?" Her voice was a kitten's mew, but it was not to be helped.

"Wait there if you like."

Another bolt clicked above, likely at the top of the stairs. Hinges complained. Floorboards creaked. Several sharp strikes of a flint carried surprisingly loud in the darkness, and then—

Light, blessed and brilliant. Nicholas stood at the top of the staircase like an avenging angel, banishing the darkness back to the netherworlds.

Relieved, she started upward. The steps rose sharply, each one adding more of a burn to her thighs. A lifetime of handprints darkened each side of the walls, and she was glad her arms didn't brush against the filth. She clutched her skirts tighter, keeping the fabric from contact, and pushed away thoughts of what might cause the underlying smell of sweat and toil and desperation.

Nicholas stepped aside when she reached the top, allowing her to pass in front of him.

But she didn't. She stopped and faced him. Better to hear straight up his intentions than give in to wild imaginings. "What's to become of me?"

His jaw locked.

She held her breath.

"For now. . ." he said slowly. The muscles in his neck gleamed in the lantern light as he looked down at her. "A warm bed and some much needed sleep."

"And then?" she pressed.

A shadow crossed his face, darkening his eyes to haunted green pools. Then he tipped his mouth into a smirk. "Do not borrow trouble from the morrow when tonight's given you a fair enough wage, hmm?"

She frowned. Not exactly the comforting words she'd hoped for, but in light of the situation, they would have to do. She turned and crossed the threshold into a desolate room. On one wall, a table and a single chair kept company. A small hearth graced another wall, with a coal bucket and a tinderbox to its side. Nicholas entered behind her, shedding light onto a wooden-framed bed pushed against a third wall. At its foot, a large chest with a huge padlock sat like a bulldog. Only one window graced the small chamber, barren of curtain and smudged by lantern smoke. This was no Portman Square townhome.

She turned to Nicholas. "What is this place?"

He shrugged off his greatcoat and draped it over the chair then turned to her with folded arms. "It's my home."

Chapter 25

With a last glance at Emily, her lashes feathered against her cheeks as she slept on his bed, Nicholas pulled shut his door and locked it. He padded down the stairwell and took care sliding open the bolt on the outer door so it didn't screech. Such a measure likely wasn't necessary, for she slept sounder than a babe in arms, but he'd not risk waking her now. It'd taken too much convincing to get her to surrender to sleep in the first place. Not that he blamed her. She'd never shared a bedchamber with a man before, and it hadn't been easy to persuade her to do so.

Stepping into the street, he rolled his right shoulder and winced from a kink that refused to loosen. A fitful few hours of rest had done him no good. Perhaps the floorboards in front of the hearth would've been a kinder mattress than the chair.

In the early morning light, Eastcheap wasn't nearly as formidable as when trekking it in the dark. Directly across the street, a one-legged man with more gums than teeth sat on a stool, selling rags from a basket. Two washerwomen darted past, scurrying to collect their loads for the day. A smudge-faced chimney sweep trudged after a larger fellow carrying an assorted load of brushes on his back. None were as fancy or tidy as those strolling about the West End of London, but neither were they the vermin that arose when the sun set.

After a quick check-in on his sister—who grew weaker with each passing breath—and a thorough going-over of instructions with Hope, he hailed a hackney. He begrudged the spent coin, but it was not to be helped if he intended to return before Emily awoke.

Yawning as the coach rolled along, he reviewed once again the details of an idea he'd hatched in the predawn hours. By the time the hackney turned onto Bow Street—clogged with traffic, as usual—he'd patched up the last remaining holes in his plan. If Ford didn't go for this, well. . .he rubbed his tired eyes. Would that his charm influenced the magistrate as soundly as it had Emily.

He paid off the jarvey several blocks from the station and hoofed it the rest of the way, increasing his pace when he glanced at his pocket watch. Men buzzed around the front door, and he darted through the swarm. Inside, he shouldered past an overflow of people spilling into the foyer then veered left and pounded up to the second floor. Halfway down the corridor, Emmanuel Whinnet was just pulling shut the magistrate's door.

Nicholas eyed the thin clerk as he strode toward him. Even as a twig, the man would be a poor piece of kindling. "Ford in there?"

Whinnet blinked at him. "Aye, but be forewarned. The Baggley boys are on the docket this morning, and he's in the hanging mood. Perhaps you ought come back later."

Nicholas frowned. "Not an option."

Whinnet tugged at his collar. "Watch your neck then, Brentwood."

He smiled at the outspoken clerk, though truth be told, were the man not blunt as a bludgeon, he would not have lasted long at Bow Street.

Nicholas raised his knuckles and rapped on the magistrate's door.

"Whinnet!" Ford's voice boomed from behind the oak. "I clearly told you fifteen minutes and not a second less. If you wish to swing next to the Baggleys, then keep it up."

Nicholas leaned toward the wood and lowered his voice. "Whinnet's tucked his tail and run, sir. It's me, Brentwood."

The door flew open. Ford's mouth twisted into a glower darker than sin. Nicholas straightened his shoulders to full attention.

The magistrate had not yet donned his tall wig, and as he spoke, a sheen of perspiration glistened atop his shorn head. Whinnet was right. Ford was steamed up this morn.

He skewered Nicholas with an evil eye. "I can only assume that things are wrapped up on the Payne case?"

Nicholas cleared his throat. This wouldn't be easy. "May I come in, sir?"

Ford's brows drew together, as if the solid line might block him from entering. "Make it quick."

Nicholas strode into the room and planted his feet next to the chair in front of the magistrate's desk. A queer odor assaulted his nose, and he sniffed, trying to pinpoint the stink. Curiously, the acrid smell was strongest when he faced forward, where Ford took up residence behind his desk.

"I see the question on your face." The magistrate reached down and pulled up his judicial wig. Normally a dulled ivory color, it now bore a blackened ringlet of singed curls on one side. "Whinnet was heavy handed with the iron this morning."

Nicholas suppressed a smirk. The Baggley boys had no idea what kind of wrath they'd be facing today.

Ford dropped the hairpiece like a dead cat. "Now that that's been cleared up, perhaps you can make it quick, as I requested."

Nicholas lifted his chin and widened his stance. "Miss Payne has suffered two abduction attempts. I won't allow a third."

Ford sank into his chair. The whoosh of leather matched his sigh. "Let's have it then. What do you need?"

"Moore."

The magistrate shook his head. "He's not yet returned from Dover. If he doesn't sort out that smuggling mess and soon, our patrons are likely not to be so. . .patronizing."

"Must be pretty bad if the revenue men and Moore are getting the runaround."

"Quite." Ford drummed his fingers on the desk, the *tat-tat-tat* like a cascade of grapeshot. "Why the sudden yearning for Moore? Is Flannery not working out?"

"No, it's not that. I'll use him. It's just. . ." Shifting his weight, he debated how much information to feed Ford. Judging by the creases on each side of the man's mouth, he ought serve it all up—on a platter. And quickly. "I intend to lure out whoever's responsible for the abduction attempts, Sedgewick's murder, and likely Payne's demise as well. For that, I need someone with me I can trust. Someone who's proven."

Ford cocked a brow. "Your plan?"

"I'll escort a Miss Payne decoy into a compromising situation, allow the capture of said decoy, then follow the culleys back to whatever rat hole they're hiding in."

"Where you'll go in with guns ablaze, I suppose, assuming of course that you're still in one piece after. . .*her* abduction."

His mouth quirked. "You know my style."

Ford shook his head, frowning. "Who would be daft or desperate enough to don a dress and play the part of a helpless lady, knowing that if he's found out, his throat will be slit?"

Reaching up, Nicholas rubbed the back of his neck. If only the action would loosen some persuasive words from his tongue. "That's the part I need to talk to you about, sir."

Ford's fingers immediately stilled. "What is this going to cost me, Brentwood?"

"An officer's commission, nothing more." *Hopefully.*

Ford leaned forward in his chair. "Let me guess. Flannery."

Nicholas said nothing. To flatter the magistrate by congratulating his intuitiveness would only stoke the man's ire.

The corner clock's ticking replaced Ford's tapping, each tock chipping nicks into Nicholas's strategy. If Ford wouldn't agree to this, he'd have no choice but to use a real woman. But who?

At last the magistrate planted his hands on his desktop and pushed up to stand. "I can think of nothing better at the moment. Very well, then. I shall offer Flannery a commission on the condition you vouchsafe his service brings no shame to Bow Street."

A muscle tightened at the side of his neck. Was the man worth such a wager? Should he allow Flannery to hold his reputation in his hands? Hard to say, but of one thing he was certain—the woman on the run and holed up in his room was worth every risk.

"If he lives through this assignment," Nicholas measured out each word, "then yes, I think I can heartily recommend him."

"Well, if he's foolish enough to give it a go. . .I daresay you ought have him shave first." Ford scooped up his wig, wafting a fresh wave of burnt-hair stink through the room. He scowled as he jammed it atop his head. "And what of Miss Payne, while you're racing about town chasing down villains?"

"Not to worry." In his mind's eye, he could yet see her sleeping like an angel beneath his bland woolen blanket. "She's safely tucked away where no one will find her."

❧

A kaleidoscope of images flashed against the back of Emily's eyelids— her standing like a princess in a golden gown, the twist of Henley's lips before he'd wrestled her down to the bench. Nicholas's green gaze gently holding hers when he'd hovered so near her in the carriage. White curtains billowing into her chamber like ghosts from the grave. A tremble spidered across her shoulders, and she was unable to decide if the skin on her neck was clammy from fever or fright.

Her eyes fluttered open, focusing on a plaster wall inches from her face. For a few moments, her gaze traced hairline cracks from nick to ding as she tried to pretend the pattern was the tiny yellow-flowered print that papered her room. It might have worked, were fatigue still fogging her brain. But the longer her eyes remained open, the more reality seeped in, hard and angular as the lump in the mattress biting into her hip. Still, there was a slight amount of comfort when she inhaled, the thin pillow smelling of Nicholas's musky scent. Stretching, she rolled over, intending to ask him what the day would bring.

Instead, she gasped.

Fathomless blue-gray eyes stared into hers, half of one hidden by a swath of straight, dark hair. Emily clutched the blanket to her neck in reflex, though it was naught but a slip of a girl staring at her, perched on a chair next to the bed—the chair she'd last seen occupied by Nicholas. The girl couldn't have been more than eight or nine, but judging by the tilt of her head and sober pucker to her mouth, she'd already lived a lifetime.

"Who are you?" Emily asked.

"Hope's me name, m'um. Better than Nipper." The girl leaned closer. "Don't you think?"

Slowly, Emily lowered the blanket and rose up to settle on the edge of the bed frame. She'd slept fully clothed, so no need to worry about indiscretion, though she did methodically smooth out wrinkles from her skirt. As she did so, she simultaneously scanned the small room for Nicholas's muscular form. A study in futility, for she would've noticed him right off.

Not even his greatcoat remained.

"Yer pretty."

The squeaky little voice pulled her attention back to the girl on the chair. "Oh. . .thank you. I vow I must look a fright, though I suppose that doesn't matter now. Could you tell me where Nic—" Emily bit her lip. Why did the man's Christian name rise so easily to her tongue? Was this what came of sharing a bedchamber with him? She cleared her throat and tried again. "Where is Mr. Brentwood?"

"Dunno. Din't tell me." Hope hopped off the chair and walked the few paces over to the table. What a cryptic little mouse.

The fabric of the girl's dress scraped over sharp shoulder blades as she reached forward. She pulled a drab square of cloth off a basket then uncorked a squat, green bottle. Apparently finished with her task, she turned and leaned back against the tabletop, crossing one ankle over the other. The pose added years to her small body. "Mr. B sent me to see to your needs. I brought ye some water to freshen up a bit, and a loaf of bread with some jam."

"Thank you." Emily stood and arched her back, wondering which of the hundreds of questions she should ask first. "May I inquire as to how you know him? Mr. B, that is, as you call him."

A smile spread across Hope's face, and for the first time, Emily noticed the girl scrunched up her nose much like she did. She couldn't help but return the girl's smile. Hope unearthed and partially filled a long-forgotten space deep down in her heart for a little sister.

"Why. . .ye're as kind as Miss Jenny, I can tell. Miss Jenny's been teachin' me to speak real proper like." Hope bounced on the balls of her feet. "How'm I doin'?"

The girl's zigzaggy line of conversation was hard to follow, but the way she rose higher on her toes, Emily sensed it was important for her to try. In the depths of the girl's gray-blue eyes, a yearning for approval glistened like sunlight off glass. Was this how she'd looked at her own father?

"You're doing very well, Hope." Emily crossed over to the girl and bent to eye level. "But as for Mr. Brentwood?"

"Tha's right. Got sidetracked, I did. Now, let's see. . ." Her teeth worked her lower lip, and she looked down. The index finger of one hand tapped over the fingers of her other before she finally lifted her gaze. "I reckon 'tis been 'bout three, mebbe four weeks now since he plucked me from the streets."

"Plucked?" She frowned.

Hope laughed. "Ain't as awful as all that, m'um. I guess I shoulda said saved, for so he did. Weren't no better day than that morn I tried to poach Mr. B's purse."

Saying nothing, Emily straightened. What was there to say? Hope's quirky statements made as much sense as the mess she currently found herself in. Bypassing the girl, she retrieved a crust of bread from the basket and took a bite without bothering to spread any jam atop it, though a small jar peeked out from the basket.

Hope watched her for several chews. "If ye don' mind, miss, I bin waiting a long while for ye to wake. I ought be off to see to Miss Jenny. She's real sick, and I fear to leave her alone for so long. Is there aught I can do for ye afore I go?"

Emily returned the bread to the basket and brushed her hands together. Other than wave a magic wand and rid the world of whoever it was that sought her life, there was truly nothing more the girl could do. "Did Mr. Brentwood say anything at all about when he'd return?"

Hope shook her head, the action swinging the swath of hair to cover half her face instead of just one eye. "No m'um."

"Very well. Thank you for the provisions. I suspect your Miss Jenny is missing you as well, so run along." She retreated once again to the bed and sank to the frame. What was she to do here? Alone. Sitting in a man's room, afraid to stay and more afraid to leave? Sighing, she rested her elbows on her knees and rubbed out the lines in her forehead.

A light touch on her shoulder lifted up her face. The girl moved as quietly as Nicholas.

"Don't look so sad, m'um. If Mr. Brentwood's carin' for ye, ye got nothin' to fret about. He's a good man, he is. I knows it, and now so do you."

Little fingers patted her sleeve, earnest as a grandmother's. Emily couldn't help but smile at the girl.

"Tha's more like it." Hope's mouth curved, revealing a dimple on her right cheek. "Hey! I know. Whyn't you come with me to visit Miss Jenny?"

The girl looked at her with such an imploring tilt to her chin, it would be difficult not to promise her a pony had she asked for one. But this request? Probably not the best idea for her to traipse around town with only a pixie of a girl at her side. Emily reached up and smoothed back the floppy bit of hair covering Hope's face before answering. "I don't think that's wise. Mr. Brentwood might get angry were I to be gone when he returns."

Hope shook her head, her bottom lip pooching out in defiance. "I don't think he'll mind a bit."

"You're a very confident young lady, Hope. What makes you so certain?"

She shrugged, her thin shoulders raising little hills at the tops of her sleeves. "Only makes sense he'd search for ye o'er at Miss Jenny's if he doesn't find ye here."

"Really?" She tried, but there was no unraveling of the girl's logic. "Why is that?"

"Pish! Why, she's his sister, m'um."

Emily could feel her brow wrinkle. Nicholas had a sister? Why on earth had he never spoken of her?

Chapter 26

Emily stood behind Hope as the girl jiggled a key in the lock to Miss Jenny Brentwood's room. She'd debated long and hard about coming here, but in the end, curiosity won out. That, and the wish to escape the suffocating jail cell of Nicholas's chamber. In comparison to his place, even the corridor of the inn she now stood in was large—though just as shabby. A carpet runner lined the hallway, threadbare in spots and dulled to an allover shade of dirt. Overhead, the plaster was darkened by burnt lamp oil, collecting in black pools above each wall sconce. Mrs. Hunt would have spasms just thinking about the cleanup required were this building left in her charge.

Nabbing a stray lock of hair, Emily worked it into the loose braid at the back of her head and patted it into place. They'd walked quickly to the inn, much like last evening's jaunt, but it was shorter and not nearly as frightening. If anything, with her knack for melding into crowds, Hope led her more invisibly than Nicholas.

Hope pushed open the door and called out in a singsong voice, "Look, Miss Jenny! I've brought you a new friend."

Emily stopped just inside the threshold. Weak daylight spread like a disease from the single window, coloring the small chamber with a gray pallor. The woman lying on the bed matched the colorless hue. Suppressing the urge to turn and run, Emily held her breath. Death lived here. She could smell it.

Maybe this had been a mistake.

Hope rushed over and knelt beside the bed, taking up the hand of the raven-haired wraith lying there. She'd likely been a beauty, once, with her oval face and pert little nose. Now her skin stretched over bones so sharp, it cut to the heart. Sickness was indeed a cruel thief. Jenny's resemblance to Nicholas was striking—and entirely too startling. What if that were him abed and dying?

Sadness, cavernous and cold, wrapped around her shoulders, and she shivered.

Jenny's lips moved, murmuring something to Hope, but her words were too delicate to travel the length of the room.

"Her name is. . ." Hope glanced over her shoulder. Her mouth twisted from one side to the other as if she swished around salt water for a rinse. "Why, I just been callin' you m'um, ain't I? Mr. B told me yer name, but I weren't payin' him no mind at the time." She turned back to Jenny and lowered her voice. "I guess I shoulda asked her name, eh?"

Emily stepped forward. The awkward moment had dragged on long enough. "I am—"

"Miss Emily Payne."

She froze.

Jenny's voice was parchment, frail and thin, yet bolstered with confidence—the same tenor she often heard in Nicholas's words. Emily suppressed a gasp. How could Jenny Brentwood possibly know who she was?

"Have we met?" she asked.

Green eyes stared up at her, paler than Nicholas's, but lit with similar intelligence. "Only through my brother's vivid descriptions. You're every bit as lovely as he said. How I've longed to meet you face-to-face." Shifting on her bed, she lifted a hand. "Hope, would you—"

A deep cough rattled up from Jenny's chest, cutting off her words and her breath.

Emily reached toward her, but what to do? Prop her up and risk breaking her? Offer a handkerchief to cough into or a glass of water to quench the rattle, neither of which she had? Illness was a stranger she'd never dined with nor had the slightest idea of how to serve. Helpless, she turned to Hope.

The girl merely flitted to the table and dragged over a chair, setting it next to the woman who possibly rasped out her last breaths. "Have a seat, Miss Emily, though I think I shall call you Miss Em. Goes nice with Mr. B. . .Mr. B and Miss Em." Her face brightened. "I like it."

"Shouldn't you. . .shouldn't we. . ." Emily threw out her hands toward Jenny. "She can't breathe!"

"Not to worry. Give 'er a moment, miss. She always does this." Ignoring the struggling Jenny, Hope skipped back to a small bench on the other side of the room and picked up two rag figures no bigger than her hands.

The insanity of it made Emily want to scream. Unsure of what else to do, she sat and clenched her hands in her lap, riding out the wretched eternity until Jenny finally relaxed against her pillow.

Emily leaned forward. "Is there nothing to be done for you? Is there anything I can—"

"Don't fret." Blue rimmed Jenny's lips, where a hint of a smile struggled to rise. "I'm dandy and grand, as always. But there is one thing. . ."

Such a shadow darkened her face, Emily bent closer, unsure if words would pass the lump in her throat. "Be at peace. I am listening. I'm not in the best of situations currently, but I vow I'll do whatever I can to help you."

Jenny nodded, the movement as slight as the breaths lifting her chest. "You are very kind. I feel as if we're sisters already. I ask only that you take a care for my brother, would you? My passing, it's. . .it's going to be hard on him, I fear."

Hard? Emily pressed her lips into a thin line. It would be all that and more, judging by the short moments she'd spent in Jenny's presence. The woman had no doubt been a gem. Her death would rip through Nicholas in ways that would leave an ugly scar. Her own heart dried to dust at the thought of the anguish he'd suffer.

Skimming the white counterpane, Jenny slid her hand slowly toward hers. Her touch was as cool as the last gasp of an autumn breeze. "You've done him much good, you know. You've taken his mind off me. It's God's plan. I am sure of it."

Emily snorted. "Some plan. I've brought him nothing but trouble."

"You've given him purpose."

A frown etched her lips. Purpose for what? Risking his own life?

"Nicholas has always taken care of me." The play of shadow and light filtering in from the window warmed Jenny's face—or perhaps it wasn't light at all, but adoration. "Always, from the time our parents died. I was five. He, no older than Hope."

Emily sat still, afraid that if she moved, Jenny might stop. The rare glimpse into her guardian's life was a great treasure, one she intended to hoard.

"We managed by God's grace, he and I, though sometimes it's hard for him to see that. Don't get me wrong. His faith is solid, it's just that sometimes. . .well. . . ." Jenny smiled in full then, and for one spare moment, her true beauty escaped the shroud of sickness. Kings would fight for a woman such as this.

"Sometimes Nicholas forgets that he's not the one in control." Jenny's fingers patted the top of her hand. "You need to remind him."

Emily pulled away. "I hardly think he'd listen to me on such matters. Besides which, I don't expect he's signed on as my guardian for life."

Jenny's green gaze bore into hers, and this time Emily couldn't stop her gasp. She'd swear before a magistrate it was Nicholas looking out.

"You may be wrong about that," Jenny said at last. "He loves you, though after Adelina, he swore never to love again. You've changed him, Emily, in ways you'll never know."

In her mind, she quickly searched every conversation she'd ever held with Nicholas. Not only had he never mentioned a sister, he'd never mentioned any woman. She leaned closer to Jenny, keen on learning about the man she'd trusted. "Adelina?"

"You ask as though he's not spoken of her. Though in truth, I'd be surprised if he had. Years ago, ahh. . .he was so young. As was the Portuguese girl, Adelina. He met her while on assignment training gunners in Guarda. He's quite the shot, you know. He'd intended to marry her, until he was wounded, and. . ." A shudder rippled across Jenny's shoulders. "Adelina was killed by a Spanish invasion. My brother, he. . .well, he never forgave himself."

Emily sank back in the chair. All the times Nicholas overreacted about her safety suddenly made sense. What a horrific burden he carried. "But surely it wasn't his fault!"

"No." A faint smile lifted Jenny's lips. "Of course not, but such is the commitment of my brother once his heart is given. And make no mistake about it. . .he's given his heart to you."

Emily's pulse faltered as Jenny's words sank deep into her soul. How could the woman speak with such certainty when everything else about her was frail?

"And so I repeat, please. . .take a care for him, would you?" A cough broke out, gargling her words. "Take. . .a. . .care."

Jenny's eyes widened, and a slow trickle of blood leaked out her right nostril. Her hands flew to her chest, her fingers squeezing the fabric of her shift as if the movement might force air into her lungs.

Emily shot to her feet. "Hope! Does she always do this as well? Is she going to be all right?"

The girl dropped her dolls, one rolling on the floor as she ran to Jenny's side. She pulled the woman up to a sitting position, but still Jenny's breaths fluttered out like a bird with broken wings. One by one, stark red drips mottled the blanket.

Hope's eyes pooled with a well of tears. "No, miss. She ain't never been like this. I don't know what to do!"

❧

Nicholas's gaze ricocheted around his room. Chair, empty. Table, littered with a half-eaten crust of bread, a bottle, and a basket.

Obviously Hope had been here. The bed was rumpled, a blanket thrown back atop it. At its foot, his campaign chest was untouched with padlock in place. His gaze skipped from there to the window, and he narrowed his eyes. The thread seal he'd attached from sill to glass was still in place—no one had slipped in uninvited. He rubbed at the knot embedded in his shoulder.

So. . .where was Emily?

Relocking the door behind him, he trotted down the steps and examined the bolt on the street-level door. No sign of forced entry marred the wood or the metal. Had she been lured out?

Ignoring the panic welling in his gut, he scanned the street. Afternoon light painted different angles and shadows, but nothing looked out of the ordinary. The barking tune of the fellow hawking rags directly across the road from him added kindling to a newly sparked headache.

"Rags a binny, rags a bone, buy yer rags an' take 'em 'ome."

Nicholas pressed two fingers against his temple. More like the rag seller ought go home and stuff one of his rags in his own mouth, so tatty was his voice. The man had been there since morning. Hadn't he sold enough by now?

Wait a minute. . .he'd been there all day? Nicholas crossed the road at a brisk pace, dodging a passing bandy wagon.

"Rags a binny, rags a—" The one-legged fellow cocked his head like a robin spying a fat worm. "Need a rag, sir? I got the finest 'ere."

Nicholas stopped an arm's length from the fellow. Any closer and he'd gag from the rag seller's sour body odor. If the man smelled that bad, how putrid were his rags?

Nicholas shook his head. "What I need is information."

"All I gots is rags." With perfect balance, Ragpicker kept his seat as he kicked his single boot against the tall basket on the ground. "Ye want one or not?"

Must everything cost him? Reaching into a concealed pocket

in his greatcoat, he pulled out a ha'penny and held it up. "Did you happen to see a young lady, very pretty, exit that door over there?" He pointed toward his own lodging.

Dirty fingers snatched the coin from his. "Mebbe. Memory's not so good, y'see."

Nicholas sighed and held out another offering.

The coin vanished as fast as the gummy smile splitting the man's face. "Aye. She were a looker, that one."

"Which way did she go, and was anyone with her?"

The man opened his mouth, but all that came out was, "Rags a binny, rags a bone, buy yer rags an'—"

With a flick of his arm, Nicholas grabbed the man's throat and squeezed. "You've been paid a fair amount already." He let go, giving the fellow just enough time to cough and curse. "Now answer my question."

"North," he hacked. "With a girl."

"That wasn't so hard, hmm?" Retrieving a last penny, Nicholas handed it over then wheeled about and strode down Sherborne Lane.

First he'd chew out Hope for bringing Emily to his sister's, then he'd have a word with Emily for—

His steps slowed, and he squinted. Surely he wasn't seeing this.

Down a block, Emily strolled toward him, alone. Undefended. Unaware. Above her, one story up, a fat woman with a large bucket leaned out a window, about to drop her slops. Behind her, a black-bearded sailor—considering his golden-ringed ear and bowed legs—followed close enough to reach out and reel her in. To her side, a dray passed in the street, heaped so high with barrels, the slightest dip in the road would send one toppling her way. She'd be crushed. And in front of her, two men swaggered out of an alley, each carrying half-empty bottles of gin.

Nicholas shot forward, ignoring her gasp when he grabbed her by the shoulders. In five long strides, he guided her into a sheltered alcove of a nearby glassery, out of the pedestrian flow and away from public scrutiny. His heartbeat pounded in his ears. "You'll be the death of me! How am I to keep you safe?"

Overly large brown eyes stared into his. Her drab bonnet only served to magnify the golden shimmer of the hair beneath. How could she be so beautiful that it tore into his soul?

Blinking, she drew in a breath. "I didn't think—"

"Of course you didn't think!"

She flinched.

He closed his eyes and counted to ten—then reversed from ten to one before opening them again. Sighing, he lowered his voice. "Where were you?"

"I was with your sister, waiting until the doctor settled her with some laudanum." Emily frowned up into his face. "She almost died! Why did you never tell me of her?"

"There was no reason."

"There was every reason! Had I known sooner, before I got into this dreadful situation, I could have helped."

"You?" He stepped up to her, forcing her back against the brick wall. A smirk begged for release, yet he fought it. "Think on it. When I first met you, your world consisted of pampering a pug, hat shopping, and snagging that scoundrel Henley. Would you honestly have wanted to help my sister?"

The longer she remained silent, the more her bottom lip quivered.

"Maybe not at first." Her voice was small.

But true.

Curious, he leaned in, inches from her face, and studied the depths of her luminous eyes. Gilt flecks floated atop brown, shimmering like candlelight against dark velvet, but no guile, no deception, swam in those pools. Never had he seen her so open, so unguarded.

The effect stole his breath, making it impossible to speak. Clearing his throat, he demanded an answer he feared. "What's come over you?

Tell me what changed."

Saying nothing, she lifted her hand and reached toward him like a lost lover who'd finally returned home. When her fingertips grazed his brow, he turned to granite. The contact was white hot. One by one, she smoothed away every crease, every line that tightened his forehead. Her gaze tracked the motion.

His heart followed her touch.

When she pulled her hand away, he was lost.

"Everything changed," she said.

Simple words, but the huskiness of her voice kicked off a complex reaction in his body. Blood pumped. A pang shot into his belly and sank. Low. Heat poured off him in waves. The thin space between them was a chasm too painful to bear. Pulling her close, he wrapped her in his arms, a groan rumbling somewhere in his chest.

She quivered against him—but did not protest.

Her name surfaced on his lips an instant before he pressed them against hers. She tasted of light, cinnamon, promise. . .all that was right and good. Her mouth moved against his with an intensity that surprised him, burning like the summer sun.

Closing his eyes, he breathed her in, and wondered if he'd ever truly breathed before. Her hands slid up his back, her fingers curling into the hair at the nape of his neck. He slipped his hands lower, locking them into place at the small of her back. Bending farther, he trailed kisses down her neck and pulled her closer, drawing her hips against his.

"Emily," he mouthed her name against skin so soft, he wanted to weep. When she arched into him, he knew he must have her.

And the thought turned his blood to ice.

He released her and backed away. Time stopped. How long they stood there, he could only guess. He gaped, frozen in place by the host of feelings drifting around him like ghosts in a graveyard, each one howling from the separation. The memory of her body fused against his seared into his bones. God. . .what had he done?

She stared at him, drawing the fingers of one hand to her mouth. Slowly, she traced her lower lip, touching the swell. Her gaze was intense, the color in her cheeks deepening with each of his heartbeats. Was she reliving the kiss?

Or regretting?

"Emily—" His voice broke. What kind of guardian was he? "I'm sorry. I'm so sorry."

Behind them, the usual sounds of London's streets continued on as if nothing had happened. What a lie. Something had happened, leastwise for him. He could only guess what he'd done to her.

"Don't be." Lowering her hand, she smoothed the wrinkles from her dress then lifted her chin, proud and defiant as ever. "I'm not."

Her words were as easy to grasp as feathers in the wind, but when they settled, a slow smile curved his mouth. Shaking his head, he grunted. "As I've said, you will be the death of me, woman. Come along. Let's get you off the street."

She fell into step beside him, the bustle of Eastcheap filling the silence until she spoke: "I am worried for your sister. She ought be moved to a nicer place. Somewhere warmer, or cozier, someplace"— she shrugged—"healthier."

He arched a brow down at her, amazed at her shift from passion to empathy. "Why do you think I took your father's offer in the first place?"

Her eyes widened, as if she'd discovered for the first time that he wasn't an ogre. "But, my father, I mean. . .what will you do now?"

"In your case, I have a plan. As for my sister, well. . ." He looked forward, and instead of seeing the busy street in front of him, Jenny's drawn face filled his vision. "I had a plan, once, but it's not so clear anymore."

"Nicholas?"

His Christian name on Emily's tongue jerked his face toward hers. "Aye?"

"She asked me to remind you that God's the One in control, not you."

Once again he directed his gaze forward. The words ought be comforting, for indeed they were solid and true.

So why did he feel as if he were just about to jump off a cliff?

Chapter 27

"Here you go." Nicholas threw a blue dress across the Portman House sitting room. With the seams let out and a panel added onto the back, it looked like a crippled heron as it flew through the early evening light. Draped across Flannery's shoulders, the bird would come to life in a spectacular way—one that would be talked about down at Bow Street for months to come. Truly, he ought not smile.

Flannery snatched the material with one hand and held the gown up. His scowl grew in size and depth the longer he looked at it.

Before the man could complain, Nicholas retrieved two precious oranges from a bowl on the tea trolley and rolled them across the floor. "And don't forget these."

"What're those for?"

Without a word, Nicholas brought his hands up and cupped them to his chest.

Flannery glowered. "Sweet flying peacock!"

Nicholas dodged the fruit missiles, choosing to ignore the *thwunk* of them smacking the wall behind him.

"No! I won't do it!" Flannery balled up the dress and chucked it to the carpet. "This goes beyond what ye asked in the first place."

Nicholas rubbed his jaw with one hand. Negotiating with Emily for a spot to sleep on the floor in front of the hearth had been child's play compared to this. "Think on it, Flannery. You know as well as I the past few days have produced nothing. Occupying her chamber overnight with the window cracked open. Me spending the bulk of my time absent from the house. Even you donning a bonnet and tooling about town in the carriage didn't attract anything but some lewd remarks from a near-sighted drunkard. So unless you've a better idea, we give this a shot. Besides, who's going to recognize you in a dress?"

Flannery folded his arms, his scowl softening at the corners. Progress.

Nicholas lifted his chin. "Need I remind you there's a commission in this? We catch the villain; you become a full-fledged officer."

His lips leveled to a straight line. Advancement.

"Sometimes duty calls for extreme measures. If you're not up for it, perhaps this isn't your line of work."

Flannery narrowed his eyes. "Did you ever have to wear a dress?"

"No." He paused long enough to let Flannery think he held the winning hand, then played his trump card. "But I did have to pose as a harlot in a molly house to snag a suspected parliament member with immoral tastes. I barely got out of there with my breeches intact. All I'm asking you to do is wear a dress and sway your hips as we walk down a few streets."

"Pah!" Flannery swiped up the gown.

Victory.

Nicholas gestured toward the door. "Go change in the study. I'll see you're not disturbed."

Flannery stomped past him, mumbling all the way. Waiting until the grumbling faded then finally quieted behind the slamming of a door, Nicholas sank onto the settee and tipped back his head.

"Thank You, God, for small triumphs," he whispered and closed his eyes. The past several days had been grueling, to say the least: keeping Emily occupied in a room hardly bigger than a cell at Newgate, keeping his own emotions in check while spending so much time with her—hard to do with the memory of her kiss forever etched onto his lips. It was a tight balancing act between that and despair over Jenny's failing condition.

Failure weighted his shoulders as well, and he rolled them against the cushion. Why had the abductors not made another attempt? Did they know about Payne's death? Was it safe to take Emily home?

A gruff throat clearing and heavy footsteps hauled him to his feet, and when Flannery swung through the door, Nicholas's jaw dropped. Somewhere deep, laughter ignited, but if he let it explode, the game would be off—not that the knowing stopped an openmouthed grin from stretching his cheeks.

Flannery's hand shot up. "Don't be sayin' anything. Don't be sayin' anything at all!"

Nicholas closed his mouth, every muscle in his gut quivering with the strain to keep from hooting. Flannery stood in front of him, for all the world looking like a dog-faced spinster. And an angry one at that. The long sleeves, poofy and opaque, hid his muscles—but not the hairy knuckles he bunched into fists.

"Don't even think it. I'm warning ye, Brentwood!"

It took several deep breaths to assure he wouldn't lose his composure when he spoke. "Fine. Let's get to work then."

Flannery stalked toward the door.

Nicholas snagged his skirt and pulled him back. "Not so fast. We start right here."

"I thought the point of this was struttin' about on the streets, not in some nimbly parlor. Hard to catch a fish when yer bait isn't in the water."

"After seeing you stomp across the room like an overgrown strumpet bent on a mark, trust me, we've got work to do here. With a gait like that, the only thing you'd catch is the pox from a burly wharf ape."

Red crept up Flannery's neck. "Are ye sayin'—"

"I'm saying let's work on your deportment."

"My...what?"

"Your poise. Your posture." Nicholas threw out his hands. "Call it what you will, man, but you must learn to walk without losing your oranges."

Flannery's gaze shot to his chest. One fruit migrated south. The other had slid nearly under his armpit. He grabbed them both and resettled them front and center.

"Good." Nicholas strolled to the door, allowing plenty of space for Flannery to practice. "Now then, chin up. Shoulders back. And with a slight sway of your hips, glide."

In an instant, Flannery's eyes changed from seaside blue to the dark gray of a tempest. Good thing the man was armed with nothing more than citrus.

"I will not—"

"Flannery," he growled the name, "if this is to be believable—"

"Who's to be believin' I'm Miss Payne when I nearly equal your height, am wider in the shoulders, narrower in the hips, and a flamin' carrot top to boot?"

Lifting a finger, Nicholas pointed to the window, where even now shadows blotted out the last bits of daylight. "Which is why we'll take our stroll in the dark."

"Oh, bloody—"

"Tut, tut." He wagged his finger in Flannery's face. "A lady never utters vulgarities."

"Fie!" Flannery spit out. "This better be worth it. Chin, shoulders, hips, glide. I got it."

"Then let's see it."

Muttering, Flannery kicked into motion. He tilted his head, shimmied his shoulders, and shifted his behind one way then another. The oranges slipped, the blue skirt swished, and the redhead went down. Hard.

Nicholas bent, riding out a wave of laughter that wouldn't be stopped, until his lungs hurt and his eyes watered. Flannery let loose a barrage of foul oaths, which only made it funnier to see an Irishman in a dress cursing like a gambler on a losing spree.

"I never!"

Behind them, Mrs. Hunt's voice sobered Nicholas enough to straighten and turn. She held out a note with his name penned on the front. As soon as he pinched it between thumb and forefinger, she whirled and whisked off down the corridor.

Flannery hollered after her. "I never did either!"

Nicholas wheeled back to the dour-faced man. "Go on and practice some more. I'll leave you to it for a while."

He retreated to the study and sank into the chair where he'd first met Payne. With the back of his hand, he wiped the moisture from his eyes then broke the seal on the parchment. Perfect timing for a diversion.

His gaze settled on the words, and as he read it twice over, he wondered how one could understand that which didn't make sense:

Come at once. Your sister draws her last breaths.
                                                    —*Dr. Kirby*

For at least the tenth time, Emily flung open the door of Nicholas's chamber and looked out. Once again, her shoulders slumped, tiring of the game. Nothing but darkness stalked up the stairs. Where was he? He'd not left her alone for these many hours since the day he'd first brought her here, which was not only unusual, but undesirable as well.

And entirely unfortunate.

She tugged her cape snug against her shoulders, wishing it was Nicholas's embrace instead of thin wool, then stepped out and shut the door behind her. What else could she do? If she waited any longer, she'd miss Wren. As it was, even with speedy steps, she'd have to meet Wren first to tell her to wait, then retrieve some supplies from the house. Or maybe Wren could follow her back and hide in the shadows. If only Mrs. Hunt would simply relent and listen to reason—and to her heart.

She tripped on the last stair and flung out her free hand, slapping it hard against the wall. The resulting sting assaulted her palm every bit as much as the realization smacking her own heart. Who was she to judge Mrs. Hunt, when unforgiveness toward her father hid like a spider in a crevice of her soul? Sooner or later, she'd have to deal with that. Setting down the lantern, she took a deep breath and made up her mind.

Later. Definitely later. Making it safely back to Portman Square took priority.

She slid the bolt, opened the door, and blew out the lamp. Better to blend into the shadows than blaze like a beacon. Drawing on every trick she'd gleaned from Hope, she stepped out into the street and merged with the night. If Nicholas knew she was out here, he'd kill her.

Unless the footsteps behind got to her first.

Chapter 28

Nicholas crashed open the door of the Crown and Horn and tore through the taproom. Cutting too close to a table, he slipped in a pool of spilled ale. His foot shot out, and he flailed, but quickly righted himself. The teetering table didn't. Wood and grog flew, along with the patron's insults and Meggy's threats. Ignoring all, he bolted ahead and took the stairs three at a time.

God, please. God, please. Not much of a prayer, but it was all he had left.

He sprinted down the hall, his pounding feet rattling the sconce glasses in their holders. The sound mocked like skeleton's bones, an eerie portent he'd rather not acknowledge. What if he was too late?

Two paces from Jenny's room, he stopped.

So did his heart.

Hope sat on the floor in the hall, her back to the closed door. Fresh tears slid down tracks already worn on her cheeks. Her mouth opened, but no words came out. They didn't have to.

He knew.

She shot to her feet and plowed into him. In reflex, he wrapped his arms around her. She sobbed, but he didn't feel his shirt dampen or the shaking of her shoulders. He didn't feel anything. He wouldn't let himself. Not yet.

"Hush, child." His voice sounded far away. Lost. Just like Jenny was to him.

Guiding the girl over to the wall, he peeled her slim arms from his waist. "Sit. Wait. I'll be. . .a moment."

She sank to the floor and buried her face in her hands. Surely the waif had seen death many times over—but such was the effect of losing Jenny. And if it moved a hardened street child who'd known his sister not quite a month, what would it do to him?

Turning, he sucked in a breath and crossed to the door. Each step took a force of will, his boots weighted as if his feet were ten stone apiece. But it wasn't just his feet. Everything felt heavy. His lungs. His hope. His faith.

Inside, a single lamp burned on the table. Light brushed a last glow of luminescence over Jenny's pallid skin. Crazy laughter tightened his chest. What need did the dead have of light?

The closer he drew, the more his steps dragged, the habit of walking quickly becoming forgotten. He dropped to his knees beside the bed, and for a moment, he closed his eyes, reliving a nightmare he'd hoped never to have to repeat in real life.

He hadn't been there for Adelina, either. An ambush ending in a firefight between the Portuguese and Spanish had laid him up for months and kept him from her as she lay dying. The Spaniards attacking her village spared no one, caring nothing for women and their screams.

He should have been there.

He should have been here.

"Nooo!" His fists smashed into the bed frame, bruising his hands and jostling Jenny's body, reanimating her if only for a second.

The movement sobered him.

Reaching out, he brushed back the matted hair from her brow. How much had she struggled? How great was the pain?

"Ahh, Jen—" Sobs choked out his words. No matter. What was the use?

Silently, he pulled out of his memory each time she'd answered *"dandy and grand, as always."* Every *"you worry too much."* And shook his head at the *"you are not God, you know."*

A groan escaped him. Oh, how well he knew that.

He drew his hand back and held his breath. Still. Silent. Mayhap, if he listened hard enough, he might hear her sweet voice one last time, faint as the distant sound of chimes in the wind. What would she say? What would her last words have been?

The sniffle of the crying girl in the hall and the muffled whoops of late-night revelers in the taproom quickly ended such musing.

Rising, he grasped the blanket's edge and drew it up—slowly—his gaze reluctant to let his sweet sister go. She looked peaceful. He'd give her that. And why not? She was now with the One she loved most.

With a last long look, he pulled the blanket higher, covering her face.

But not his shame.

He stepped back and shuddered. He'd failed her, every bit as much as he'd failed Adelina. If only he'd gotten her moved to a better place, been able to pay for better care.

Been a better man himself and come home to her instead of traipsing around foreign battlefields in a search of fortune and fame.

"Good-bye, Jen." The words came out rough and jagged, though truth be told, he was surprised they came at all. Her name hung in the air like a phantom then dissipated into the dark.

He pivoted and stalked out to the hall. Hope sat balled up exactly where he'd left her.

He reached for her. Inches away from patting her head, his fingers recoiled. "Go to bed. We'll talk tomorrow."

Without waiting to see if she obeyed, he turned and stomped off. Meggy said something as he crossed the taproom. Hard to say what, since all he could hear was the rushing in his ears. He ought arrange a time with her for the body to be removed—but thinking of his sister as a body was too foreign an idea to entertain. Too fragile. If he weren't careful, all his thoughts would splinter into sharp points. Maybe if he walked awhile, fast enough and far enough, the fog in his head would lighten.

He stormed out of the Crown and Horn and turned left, hoping with the desperation of a starving man that someone—anyone—would throw him a crumb of interference, for he dearly wanted a fight. The need to pummel and be pummeled quivered in his muscles and ached in his soul.

In a mood blacker than the streets, he wandered up one and down another, through alleys, along the wharves. In defiance of the chill air, sweat made his shirt stick to him like a second skin. No one stopped him. None so much as commented, in spite of the challenge he glowered into the nameless faces he passed.

Long past midnight, he turned toward Eastcheap. Sleep wouldn't come, but morning would. Emily must be told. Life must continue. All the musts he should attend to echoed in his head, far off but real.

Exhausted and empty, he pulled out his key. No resistance dragged against the bolt when he turned it. Recalling when he'd left—a lifetime ago now—he retraced mentally each step of locking the door. Yes. He definitely had secured it. He was too careful not to. He was always careful. *Oh God, why hadn't I been more careful with Jenny?* A sob rose to his tongue, and he bit down hard, savoring the coppery taste.

Then he yanked open the door and frowned at the lantern on the lower stair. A tremor rolled over his shoulders, traveled the length of his spine, and lodged deep and low.

"Emily!"

Heart racing—surprising, really, to know that it still worked—he flew up the stairs and, on a hunch, shoved the other door without trying the lock. It swung wide, hinges complaining at the force. His gut tightened. Hope plummeted. Entering the room would likely only add to the nightmare, yet it was one more must that couldn't be denied.

God, please. God, please.

Not much of a prayer, but it was all he had left.

⁂

Ambrose de Villet stood in the dark, feeding off the blackness, soaking in its sanctification. His mother had died birthing him during the witching hour, and he'd spent each successive minute of his life anticipating the night. It was home, breath. . .sustenance. As satisfying as the rigid stance of the pregnant Englishwoman twenty paces from him. She feared him. He could smell it.

And it was good.

Reaching into his pocket, he pulled out a lump the size of a severed fingertip. Harder, though, and much more sweet in a bitter sort of way. Saliva rained at the back of his throat. He popped the horehound candy into his mouth, savoring the first tang sliding over his tongue. But the best, the most enjoyable, part was the cool trail that crawled up high and sank in roots just behind his nostrils. When he inhaled, the chill magnified a hundredfold. The shiver running through his bones was delicious.

Too bad it didn't last long enough. Not as long as he'd stood here, waiting for the Payne woman to meet her friend. Stupid girl. Stupid English. Four weeks on their *rosbif* soil had sullied him to the point of scrubbing his hands raw. By this time tomorrow evening, though, the darkness of a ship a'sea would wash clean the entire month of blunder and mishap.

Biting down, again and again, he ground the candy until it was nothing but a sticky memory in the hollows of his teeth.

Footsteps cornered the end of the block, beating a fast clip against the cobbles. Light enough for a female, determined enough that this was no wanderer. He flattened against the brick.

"Wren!" The Payne woman's voice was breathy as she closed in on the big-bellied sow. "I'm so glad you're still here. Sorry I'm late. Things have been. . .difficult."

"Not to worry, miss."

Ambrose relished the quiver in her tone. It vibrated on the air, terrible and sweet, reminding him to reach into his pocket and pull out another candy.

"I haven't had the time to gather some things for you, Wren. Wait here, and I'll—"

"No. You must come with me. I. . .I have something to show you."

"What are you talking about? Where? What?"

The muscles in his neck tightened. He'd been forced to walk a rope lashed between two roofs once. One misstep, one untrue placement of the foot, and failure would rise up from the ground. He liked heights about as much as the turn of the women's conversation.

"Not far. Not far at all, miss. Please! It's important."

"I don't understand. What's going on?"

"Will you. . .will you trust me, miss?"

"Wren, what's wrong?"

Ambrose swallowed the candy whole and stopped breathing. This could all fall apart and fast. Not that he'd mind killing the stupid English whore. A slow smile tugged at his lips. Ending two English lives with one snap of the neck would be satisfying indeed.

His eyes widened. What was the senseless cow doing? She leaned in close, far too close to the Payne woman. This was not part of the plan. Was she whispering a warning? Steeling his muscles, he was about to step from the wall, when the large one turned toward him and began walking. He froze.

"Wren. . .wait! I know something's wrong. What is it?" The Payne woman raced after her.

Ahh. His smile grew. The English whore was smarter than he credited. Whatever she'd said into Emily Payne's ear had apparently worked. She stopped two paces from him, close enough that the pain on her face sent a jolt through his belly. This was going to be far more exciting than he'd expected.

Emily Payne's hasty steps suffered a quick death, ending when her eyes locked onto his. She jerked her face toward the woman with the ridiculous bird name. "Why did you—"

"I'm sorry, miss. I didn't have a choice."

Like a worm yanked out of a fish's jaw, the pregnant woman turned and fled down the street, leaving the Payne woman gaping.

Chapter 29

By the time Nicholas reached Portman Square, the first hints of dawn soaked through the fabric of his greatcoat. The air was damper, chillier, and smelled like a musty cellar. The sky had yet to lighten, but that would come soon enough. God's handiwork never failed.

Unlike him.

Drawing in a deep breath, he swallowed a rising tide of despair and unlatched the front door. Surely he'd find Emily here. Mayhap she'd merely had enough of the oppressive walls in his small chamber and yearned for the spaciousness of her own. Maybe she simply missed her little pug. Whatever reason, he'd praise God to see her safe and sound in her own home—then he'd deal her a sound reprimand. Of all nights to vanish without taking his leave, she had to choose this one?

He closed the door behind him and padded up the stairs. No sense waking the entire house, especially if Emily was curled up beneath her counterpane. Of course she would be. She had to be.

Oh God, make it so.

After two quick raps with his knuckles, he leaned close to her chamber door. "Emily?"

Silence.

He pounded harder. "Emily!"

Nothing.

The knob twisted easily—hadn't he warned her to always lock a door? The same intuition that broadsided him as he stood outside Jenny's room hit him anew. He swung the door wide and looked into the dark chamber. The scent of lilies taunted him on the inhale. So did the shadows reclining on the covers of Emily's empty bed.

If she wasn't here, then where?

Scrubbing his face with one hand, he retreated down the corridor, the stubble on his jaw as prickly as the possibilities of where Emily might be. The prospects were endless, most sinister, and a few he'd not entertain for a king's ransom. He clung to the one innocent hunch left him and descended the back staircase to the lowest level.

As housekeeper, Mrs. Hunt's room was the first on the right at the bottom of the stairs. This time he didn't bother to temper his volume.

"Mrs. Hunt!" The door rattled in the frame. "Mrs.—"

"Coming!"

The bang of a wardrobe, some swooshes, and a whole lot of muttering preceded the slit-eyed, night-capped woman.

"Mr. Brentwood!" The candle in her hand lit half her face, the other was shrouded in darkness. Never had she looked so weary. "Why. . .what—"

"Is Miss Payne here?" He nodded toward her chamber. "Has she sought your company for the night?"

The housekeeper's eyes popped wide open. "Why, I thought she were with you, sir."

He wheeled about, raising both fists. Then at the last moment, he flattened his palms to the opposite wall and leaned his forehead against the cool plaster.

His thoughts leaked out into prayer. "God, now what? Where is she?"

He listened hard, straining to hear or feel anything. A nudge. A direction. A lightning bolt with a note skewered onto the end telling of Emily's location.

"What is it?" Behind him, Mrs. Hunt's voice was as small as Hope's. "What's gone wrong?"

His shoulders slumped as he turned to face her. "I'll tell you what's gone. Emily."

A knock, not as loud but just as urgent, crept down the hallway from the servants' entrance. His eyes met Mrs. Hunt's. "Expecting anyone?"

"No, sir."

He shot down the corridor, the housekeeper's nightgown and wrap rustling behind. Judging by the tap of her slippers, she matched his pace step for step. By the time he opened the door to a very small, very pregnant woman, Mrs. Hunt had gained his side. She swayed then grabbed his forearm.

"What are ye doing here?" The housekeeper's voice was a shiver in the dark.

Nicholas looked from the unexpected visitor to Mrs. Hunt. Apparently this was no stranger.

Without warning, a snippet of memory clicked into place, as deftly as he might pick open a lock—following Emily in the darkest hour before dawn, hiding in the shadows as she delivered a small bag . . .to the woman who now stood before him. Lauren "Wren" Hunt. That was it.

No wonder Mrs. Hunt's fingers dug into his arm.

"Please," Wren said, "just listen."

Behind them, the slap of sensible shoes hit the tiles, preceding the baritone voice of Cook. Should she ever choose to trade professions, there was likely a lighthouse in need of a foghorn somewhere. "What's all this? Half the house awake and I've not even had a chance to boil water yet. Why—" A gasp punctuated her tirade as she drew near. "Look who's come back."

Cook's proclamation prodded Mrs. Hunt like a cattle brand. Loosing her hold on his arm, she instead grabbed Wren's and pulled her inside. She swept past the gaping cook, calling out as she scurried along, "We'll take tea in my sitting room. Mr. Brentwood, don't dawdle."

Nicholas glanced up at the sky as he shut the back door. *Quite an interesting answer, Lord.* Then he turned and hustled to catch up.

Eyeing the small room, he took a position near the hearth. Banked for the night, it offered no heat, not that it needed to. The housekeeper generated enough warmth as she bustled about lighting lamps.

Across from him, a table with an inkwell and a stack of papers sat in front of a window. In the corner, Wren perched on one of two wingback chairs. No pictures graced the walls. No knickknacks adorned any whatnot shelves. Mrs. Hunt obviously kept the maintenance of her own rooms down to a minimum.

While Mrs. Hunt flitted about lighting lamps, he studied the girl. "Have you seen Miss Payne? Has she met with you? Have you any information?"

Wren's eyes glistened a moment before she buried her face in her hands.

"La, Mr. Brentwood. Give the girl a moment." Mrs. Hunt scowled at him then plopped into the seat adjacent Wren. The stern lines of her face masked any emotion. The housekeeper would not only make a great sergeant but a piquet player, as well. "As soon as you're able, Lauren, we'll have the truth, and all of it."

Swiping her eyes, the girl straightened in her chair. After a final sniff, she faced her mother. "As much as you'd like to believe otherwise, I have only, ever, given you the truth. And this time, I beg you hear me out for Miss Emily's sake."

For an instant, the housekeeper's reserve cracked. Her brows connected in an angry line then just as quickly returned as if they'd never met. "You two have always been thick as thieves. It's not right. Not between a lady and a servant."

"Miss Emily's shown me more kindness than—"

"I suggest we leave the past behind, ladies." He upped his volume, redirecting the conversation. "What news have you of Miss Payne?"

Wide-eyed, Wren reached into a pocket and pulled out a slip of paper. "I am to deliver a note to Mr. Payne."

Nicholas crossed the room in three steps. "Mr. Payne is unavailable. I act in his stead."

Wren's gaze moved from his outstretched palm to his face. A hundred questions shone in her gaze. "Who are you?"

"Mr. Brentwood is a law keeper. He can be fully trusted, and in fact may be Miss Emily's best hope." Mrs. Hunt nodded toward the girl. "Go on."

The paper passed easily from her fingers but once fully resting in his palm, weighed heavier than a brick. So much depended on what this note might say. Odors of horehound and fish wafted upward as he unfolded the ripped segment of yesterday's *Chronicle* and read words written with a heavy hand in grease pencil:

Old Saproot Warehouse, Pig's Quay Wharf
8:00 p.m. unarmed and alone
500 pounds

Emily's throat burned. If Alf's water dish were available, she'd shove the pup out of the way and lap it up—were it not for the gag in her mouth. Her eyes were plenty moist, though. Not that crying helped, but she simply couldn't stop, and what else was there to do? She sat on a precarious stack of crates, terrified the act of breathing might be enough to topple her over. There'd be no way catch herself. Ropes cut into her wrists, pinioning her like one of Cook's poultry. If she fell, she'd crack her head against the warehouse floor and kill herself.

But as horrifying as it was to sit here and wonder if she might plummet to her death—or what would become of her even if she didn't—far worse was the stabbing pain in her back. From Wren. Why? She closed her eyes. *God, why?* Betrayal chafed her heart more painfully than the rag biting into her mouth. Finally she understood the black unforgiveness running through Mrs. Hunt's veins, for it pumped through her own, heavy and thick.

On the far side of the warehouse, three sharp bangs rapped against wood. Behind her, heels thudded on planks. The bald brute who'd dragged her here passed beneath her, hollering over his shoulder, "Take her down."

Daylight streamed through cracks in the walls. If they hauled her out of here now, she might have a chance to attract attention and get some help. She clutched tightly to that hope. It was the only one she had.

A freestanding ladder on wheels rolled over to her tower, but climbing up was no prince to her rescue. The stink of sour ale and mutton reached her an instant before his rough hands. He lugged her over his shoulder like a sack of kittens to be drowned. She winced at the horrid thought then complied by going limp. Better to save her fighting strength until she stood a better chance.

"Right, then. Let's see her."

The words barely registered before the world flipped and she stood on her own. A man-shaped shadow stepped out from a row of crates. When a shaft of light flooded his face and his gaze met hers, her heart stopped.

She knew those eyes. The coldness of them washed over her like seawater, leaving behind a wake of panic, exactly as it had late last summer.

Captain Daggett.

Her stomach heaved, and she doubled over. Nausea wasn't an option with a bound mouth. She focused on her skirt hem and counted the embroidered scallops one by one—anything to ignore the convulsing of her belly.

Daggett's laughter rang out, grating as knife against bone. "How much ye askin' for her?"

"Five hundred pounds."

"Gads! I could buy the Queen Mother for that."

At the snap of some fingers, she was jerked upright, her back pressed against the bully behind her, his arm across her chest.

The bald thug opposite her smiled at Daggett. "Ahh, but this one is—"

"I know what this one is." The captain drew so near, his hot breath hit her forehead. She flinched.

Reaching up, he twisted a loose curl of her hair and rubbed it between his fingers. "I know exactly what this one is."

"She'll bring a fine price," the bald man continued. "You'll make your money back and more, if sold to the right buyer. And I have it on good authority you are a man with many connections."

Daggett leaned closer and bent, his breathing loud in her ear. "He has no idea, hmm?"

Then he wheeled about and offered his hand to the bald man. "Yes, I believe she will bring a good price. I'll take her."

His words spun in her head. Or was that the room? Hard to say. Nothing was solid anymore—except for the fear driven deep into her soul.

Chapter 30

Nicholas strode down the narrow lane, his gaze scouring the shadows more thoroughly than a street sweep intent on a coin. Not many figures inhabited this condemned stretch of riverfront. Those who did were cutthroats and thugs. Though plans for a new dock were in the works, as far as he and the river wardens were concerned, it wouldn't be built soon enough. This boneyard of warehouse skeletons needed to be buried. Deep.

At intervals, dark clouds blotted out the moonlight, adding a sporadic inky depth to the night, which had its benefits—and detriments. Tightening his grip on his end of the heavy chest toted by him and Flannery, he could only pray the darkness would work to his advantage and not for the men who'd taken Emily. Filthy scoundrels. If they'd harmed her, violated her. . .

His gut twisted into a sodden, knotted rope, strengthening his resolve.

Anger had its pros and cons, as well.

Beside him, holding up the other end of the wooden box, Flannery cleared his throat. "Not that I be needin' a hand-holding." He slanted a glance at Nicholas. "But I wouldn't mind ye running over those instructions again."

Nicholas snorted. "You nervous?"

A string of mumbled curses unraveled past Flannery's lips. "More than a strumpet in church!"

Nicholas smirked at him. "Good."

"Ye're a cold one, Brentwood."

"A certain amount of fear keeps you careful. It's too much or too little that can be deadly."

Flannery's end of the chest sagged. "Could you refrain from using that word?"

"Your part in this isn't too difficult. You'll be fine."

"Easy for you to say. Ye're not the one whose head might be blown clean off."

Nicholas nodded left. Flannery followed his lead. They entered an alley and stopped halfway down. Moonlight glinted off the perspiration dotting Flannery's brow as they eased the chest to the ground. The Irishman was right about one thing. He very well might lose his head.

But Nicholas's position wouldn't be any less dangerous.

Straightening, they retreated several steps. Nicholas bit back a smirk. As if the added distance of a few paces would save their lives should the chest explode now.

He faced Flannery and kept his tone low. Who knew what ears the wooden walls towering above them held. "All you do is open the lid. Remove the cloth from around the gun hammer, then make sure it's pulled back and locked into position."

"On the inside front, aye?"

Nicholas nodded, choosing to ignore the quiver in Flannery's voice. "Once that's done, pour plenty of gunpowder onto the pan and lower the frizzen. This isn't the time to be stingy nor tidy. Cover it good. You've got the extra powder?"

The question was unnecessary, but he threw it out there anyway. Sometimes confidence had to be touched to be felt.

Flannery patted the bulge at his hip, his hand shaky as a drunkard's. "Right here."

"Then all that's left is to take the string attached to the trigger and fasten it onto the lid. Make sure to close the cover nearly shut before you put the loop on the hook. Close it—gently—and wait, looking as if you're guarding a great treasure. Run toward the river as soon as you see the vermin coming for their payment. I'll meet you there with Miss Payne. Got it?"

"Lock the hammer. Liberal powder. Lower frizzen. Hook the

loop. Er. . .loop the hoop. I mean—"

Nicholas grabbed him by the shoulders, shoving his face inches from Flannery's. He knew that look—the glassy eyes, the pinched lips—and it didn't bode well. "Focus, man. You can do this."

Flannery sucked in a breath so big, his Adam's apple rode the current down. His eyes darted everywhere except to look straight at Nicholas. "I'm not so sure I'm cut out for this." The words were a ragged whisper.

Nicholas clenched his jaw. There was no way he could do this alone. "Flannery, I'm counting on you." He measured out each syllable, slow and dangerous, compelling the man to meet his gaze. *"Ni neart go cur le cheile."*

Though he'd butchered the brogue, apparently he'd pulled it off. The icy blue of Flannery's eyes thawed immediately.

"Ye've a bit o' the Irish in ye, eh?" Flannery's chin lifted, slight but noticeable. "But ye're right. There is no strength without unity, and to be sure, I won't let a brother down. Ye can count on me."

Nicholas released him and retreated a step, refraining from telling the man he was about as Irish as King George. "Then let's be about it. There's a damsel waiting to be saved, aye?"

A half smile quirked Flannery's mouth. "For the lady."

"For the lady, indeed." Nicholas wheeled about and retraced his route then turned left when he cleared the alley's mouth. The closer he drew to the warehouse door, the harder his heart thumped.

He knew exactly how Flannery felt.

Pausing before the thin piece of wood blocking him from Emily, he glanced heavenward. "Go before me, God. Nothing more. Nothing less."

Then he kicked open the door. The force vibrated up his leg, lifting half his mouth into a smirk. Even he needed confidence once in a while.

He entered what might've been a front room at one time. Two

strides in, the cold metal of a gun muzzle pressed into the back of his head.

Excellent. At least he knew where the weapon was.

"Stop right there. Hands up, Mr. Payne."

So far, so good. They'd bought the grayed hair and painted-on wrinkles. *Thank You, Lord.*

With a smooth movement, he complied, cataloging information at breakneck speed. The click-drag-click of the hammer meant his skull hosted a breech-loaded flintlock. Judging by the angle and pressure, the man holding it was an inch or so shorter than himself, but his build more than made up for his height. His accent labeled him a Bristol boy, born and raised. The man's accomplice, the one patting his hands down each of Nicholas's legs, was a slighter fellow—but that didn't make him any less dangerous. And neither the news of Payne's death nor his bankruptcy had reached these scoundrels, for they thought him to be the man.

Behind him, the flare of a flint sparked a lantern into life, creating monstrous shadows. He was a meager David amid Goliaths.

"Follow the light, and don't try anything."

The muzzle shoved his head forward, emphasizing the gunman's words. The other man passed him, and Nicholas fell into step as directed.

A bead of sweat trickled down between his shoulder blades. It didn't matter how many times death handed him its calling card, the familiar physical reaction always sent a jolt through him.

They wound their way past a half wall of rotted shipping crates. The moldering stench triggered a tingle in his nose, and he fought to hold in a sneeze. Any quick movements would be a death warrant. If this was his night to die, so be it. But God help him, it had better not be Emily's.

He counted each step. Memorized every twist and turn. Most matched up to what Hope had told him. But not all—and his whole plan hinged on what the girl remembered of this particular warehouse.

They stopped near the back of the empty space. To his left, nothing but rotted floorboards and a broken-glassed window facing the alley where Flannery waited outside. If he listened hard enough, he just might hear the Irishman's ragged breaths. To his right, crates had been gathered and stacked into a wobbly tower. A rusty-wheeled excuse of a ladder leaned into it.

In front of him, a lantern's glow lit a profane halo above the bare-skinned skull of a third man, who stood with arms crossed. "You do not follow instructions very well, Mr. Payne. You disappoint Sombra. You disappoint me."

"Life's full of disappointments, Mister. . ." Nicholas drawled out the last word, fishing for the man's name. Unless the man lied, the name would be French, though the fellow had done an admirable job with a Southwark twang.

"Who I am is not important. Where is the money?"

"You think I can lug in five hundred pounds alone?" He rolled his shoulders and shot a pointed glare at his upraised arms. "I have a back condition, Mr. . . .Frenchie, for lack of a better name. And holding my hands up like this merely aggravates that condition, so if you don't mind. . ." He lowered his hands, measuring the calculation in Frenchie's stare. Though the movement brought him one step closer to disarming the fellow behind, he wasn't yet quite sure how he'd do it.

"Your back is the least of your concerns, Mr. Payne." The Frenchman widened his stance. "Where is the money?"

"Where is the girl? You think I'd hand over a small fortune to the likes of you without seeing her? I'd sooner trust ol' Prinny with my daughter." The question earned him more pressure from the muzzle. If the man pushed any harder, he'd die from a puncture wound instead of a bullet.

The Frenchman cocked his head like a vulture studying a carcass.

"You will have the girl when I have the money."

"How do I know she's still alive? I want proof."

A smile rippled at the corners of the man's mouth. "You English. So predictable." Without varying his gaze, he ordered the man with the lantern. "See to it, Weaver."

Nicholas filed away the name. Weaver set the light on a nearby crate, disappeared behind another, then reappeared with a newspaper in hand. He extended it to Nicholas then stepped back.

Nicholas's breath caught in his throat. Emily's signature, shaky but familiar, was near the top of the *Times* header, next to the date—today's. He slid his gaze from the paper to the Frenchman. "This shows me she was alive earlier today. Doesn't mean she is now."

"You'll have to take my word for it."

"The word of a criminal?"

Frenchie unfolded his arms and advanced. Though his hands fisted at his sides, the fellow would not use them. With his thumbs tucked in, he'd break his bones in one swing. This was a man used to having his dirty work carried out by others. What kind of sway did he hold?

"You are in no position to bargain, Mr. Payne. Supply the money, or the girl is dead, and you as well." He stopped six paces away, far enough that should a shot go off, Nicholas's blood wouldn't sully his shirt.

Fie. This was not going as he'd hoped. He nodded toward the alley-side wall. "Look out the window. Your chest is there."

With a single snap of the Frenchman's fingers, Weaver strode the length of the empty space, taking care to step over missing planks. He didn't come at the glass straight on, but edged in sideways, like the snake he was. Smart move, though, in case a sharpshooter waited to pull a trigger. He peered into the darkness then swiveled his head back to Frenchie. A single tilt of his chin was his only response.

The Frenchman laughed—the jagged-edged kind that rang of

doom instead of humor. "Did you really think leaving the money outside would assure you of your safety?"

"My man's been instructed that if I don't walk out that door with Emily, he's not to—"

"I'm afraid that's impossible. I said she was alive. I did not say she was here." The man's mouth curved upward like a scythe, his words every bit as sharp and cutting.

Nicholas sucked in a breath. "Where is she?"

"Barbados? America? Who can say?" He shrugged. "The captain did not apprise me of his route. I suppose that depends upon if he intends to keep her or sell her."

Every muscle in Nicholas's body hardened. He'd been duped, double-crossed—but not defeated. Not yet. Timing would be everything. He counted the steps needed to clear Frenchie, the inhales and exhales of the man behind him, and the pounding of his own heartbeat.

Then he smiled. "Thank you. Very helpful. Now, if you'll excuse me. . ."

He waited, watching for the ripple of disbelief across the Frenchman's face. There. The beginning of a sneer. Check. And the parting of the lips to issue a command to kill him.

Nicholas spun to the left, jerking up his arm. He snagged the gun muzzle under his armpit and thrust his other elbow forward with all the force he owned. Cartilage gave way. Bone cracked. So did a bullet. Fire burned the tender skin of his inner arm. Shouts echoed along with footsteps.

He shoved the man from him and wheeled about. Tearing past Frenchie, he sprinted for the back right corner of the warehouse.

Another bullet lifted the hair on the side of his head. Hope's information was the only barrier between him and his last breath— would to God that the girl was correct. Hard to tell when the lantern light didn't reach this far.

He leaped into the dark corner. Either he'd crash into the floorboards, making him nothing but target practice for the thugs on his heels, or he'd sail through a hole concealed by a burlap bag and disappear down a drainpipe.

Midair, the next shot bored into his flesh.

≈

Ten paces one way. Ten the other. Years ago, Emily had seen a lion at the Tower of London's menagerie. Now she understood the animal's bizarre pacing behavior. Locked in Captain Daggett's quarters, she was every bit as caged—yet deprived of the roar that begged for release. Still gagged. Still bound at the wrists. The only things free were her feet and her mind.

So back and forth, one foot after the other, she slowly wore away the thin leather of her shoes, worrying, wondering, waiting. What was to become of her? A month ago she'd had her entire life planned out. The perfect marriage. The perfect husband. A fresh trickle of tears leaked down her cheeks. The only thing perfect now was the mess she was in.

And this time Nicholas wouldn't be getting her out of it.

At the wall, she stopped and rested her forehead against the wood paneling. Nicholas. Just thinking his name brought a small measure of comfort. The short time she'd spent with him hadn't been enough. Would never be enough. Above, the footsteps of sailors preparing for a dawn departure beat a steady cadence. Would she ever see her guardian again?

A sob rose in her throat. The gag cut it off. She'd never felt so alone in her life. Not when her mother died. Not when her father ignored her. Not all the times she'd clung to her little pug, trying to ease the ache in her heart.

Whirling, she flounced to the single chair in the room and sank. Deprived even of speech, she closed her eyes. *God, why? Why? I have nothing left to hope in. Not my father's provision, not a prosperous marriage match. Not even Nicholas. How will I survive? All I have is the dress on my back and You. Is that enough to live through this? Are You enough?*

"I am!" The words rumbled like the crack of an unexpected thunderstorm tearing from one end of the sky to the other.

Her eyes snapped open. A jolt of heat shot through her. Prickles raised gooseflesh on her arms. Had God seriously just answered her?

"And if you think I am not the sole reason you live and breathe," the voice continued.

She slid off the chair to her knees. *Yes, Lord. Yes, God. You are. You are!*

"Then I'll give you some time to think on it in the brig. Is that understood, Mr. Snelling?"

The door crashed open—but it wasn't God who entered. It was Satan.

Captain Daggett.

Chapter 31

Nicholas fell through the jaws of hell. Spikey edges ripped through fabric and flesh alike as he plummeted through the hole in the warehouse floor. It was a great escape route—for a small child. Not for shoulders like his. Splinters lanced into the gunshot wound in his upper arm. Darkness swallowed him and then spit him onto the mucky bank of the Thames. Pain stole most of his breath. Low tide's stench took the rest.

How had things gone so wrong?

Panting, he rolled to his knees and pressed his hand against the torn muscle on his arm. Warmth oozed through his fingers. Dizziness swirled in like an eddy.

And another pair of boots *thwunked* into the muck behind him.

He doubled over, giving the impression he'd been hurt badly, though the added moan was real enough.

Footsteps neared. Closer. Louder. He waited for the telltale whoosh of air, signaling the lift of a pistol handle to crack against his skull.

Then he twisted and sprang.

The heel of his hand thrust into the soft flesh of Weaver's throat. The man's windpipe gave. His head snapped back. He dropped like a drunk on a binge. If he lived, he'd never again hit the high notes of a bawdy song.

Sucking in air, Nicholas forced away the blackness creeping in at the edge of his vision, then turned and ran. Staggered, really. Sludge yanked his boots with every step. The incline of the bank wasn't steep, but that didn't make it any less treacherous. Slipping, he caught himself and pressed on until the mire stopped at a wall of rotted timbers—the barrier marking the alley's end.

The place where Flannery should have been crouched and waiting.

Dread knocked the wind from him an instant before an explosion thundered through his bones. A red flash desecrated the black sky. Both happened within the space of a breath.

Neither boded well.

Nicholas threw himself against the wall and hoisted himself upward, not caring who heard his deep grunt each time he grabbed for a handhold with his wounded arm. Clearing the top, he rolled over the edge, the fire in his arm burning well past his injury.

Gritting his teeth, he forced himself to his feet. The reek of burnt flesh added to the nausea building in his gut.

God. . .no.

Swiping the back of his hand across his mouth, he straightened. Onlookers emerged at the opposite end of the alley, creeping out like life-size cockroaches. Two bodies—or what remained of them—lay on the far side of what had been the rigged chest. The body nearest him sprawled facedown. One of his arms stretched out. Reaching. As if he'd tried to swim the current of the blast to safety. Remorse ran red through Nicholas's veins. . .the same color as the hair on the man lying dead still.

He sprinted and slid to a stop on his knees next to Flannery. Grabbing him by the shoulders, he carefully eased the man over. "Here now, come on. Flannery? Come on, man!"

Sharp bits of gravel pitted Flannery's brow. His eyes didn't open. His lips didn't part. A sour taste pooled at the back of Nicholas's throat. He never should have given such a dangerous task to an untried man.

"Flannery!" His ragged voice bounced from wall to wall.

Somewhere deep inside Flannery's rib cage, a low rumble started. Or was that merely because Nicholas wanted to hear it? To believe it? To not have to live with Flannery's death on his conscience? He bent closer.

Flannery spasmed. His hands shot up, grabbing handfuls of

Nicholas's coat, and pulled him nose-to-nose. "Did we. . .did you. . ." His grasp slackened, thin as his voice. When his eyes rolled back, he let go completely.

Nicholas stared, horrified—until the rhythmic lift and fall of Flannery's grit-coated chest caught his eye. He was alive. For now. But how much longer?

Rising, Nicholas hated the choice set before him. He reeled to catch his footing. Should he hasten Flannery to a doctor and risk the possibility that Emily might set sail for God-knew-where? Or should he leave the man here and continue his search?

Rock. Hard place.

His decision was every bit as granite—cold and unyielding.

He cried out as he slung Flannery's limp form over his shoulder. Even so, the white-hot agony in his arm was nothing compared to the torture in his heart.

The instant the gag was cut from behind and pulled off, Emily whirled. Frightening as it was, facing danger head-on was better than a stab in the back. And with the captain's knuckles still wrapped around a knife hilt, that was a distinct possibility. Though doubtful, the way his eyes undressed her.

She retreated until her shoulder blades smacked against the farthest wall—not far, in this tiny cabin. Fear wrapped tight around her chest. Nonetheless, a crazy peace steadied her fingers as she ran them across her lips. God was here. She knew that now, not just in her head but in her heart. Slowly, she worked her jaw, surprised that it still moved at all.

Captain Daggett slipped the blade into a sheath at his waist and advanced. His body blocked the single escape route out the door. The only way around him was to hurdle the table laden with maps and measuring tools—or scramble across the bed.

His bed.

"You cur!" The words rubbed raw in her throat, sounding more like an animal's growl than a lady's. What he'd done to Wren, what Wren had done to her, the lick of his gaze fondling places that ought not be touched—all of it boiled up and spewed out. "You filthy cur!"

"Ugly words from such a pretty mouth." His words slurred together, and she felt a tremble to his touch as he ran his knuckle along her cheek. He stank of rum and salt and treachery.

She jerked her face aside. "Don't touch me."

"Ahh, but I've waited nearly a year for this."

His breath drifted over her skin, and she shivered. "Beast!"

"You have no idea."

"I have every idea!" She wrenched her gaze back to his. "You ruined my maid then turn your back on your child. You trade for me as if I'm nothing but a—"

"Child?" He staggered then braced a hand against the wall. "What are ye talking about? What child?"

"Your child!" She studied the tic at the corner of one eye. Was he daft as well as drunk and dangerous? "Wren carries your babe, Captain. She's an outcast because of it."

Her words whipped up a tempest. For one sober moment, emotions rippled across his face like waves on a storm-swept sea, too fast for her to navigate the thoughts running through his mind.

"A. . .a babe?" He staggered again, though he still held the wall.

Emily tensed. Was this some kind of ploy?

He lurched from the wall and shored himself against the table, his eyes searching her face. "Are ye certain?"

A fierce frown pulled at her sore mouth, completely unstoppable. The man was either a consummate actor—to what end she couldn't imagine—or he truly was clueless. "How can you be so surprised?"

"Impossible!" The denial draped years onto his frame. Deep lines creased his brow. He stomped to a cabinet door and retrieved an amber bottle.

As he pulled out the cork and tossed back his head for a drink, Emily edged sideways toward the door, careful with her light movement. Too fast and her chance for freedom might shatter, the opportunity thin as glass.

Five steps from freedom, his voice stopped her. "Where is she?"

Slowly, Emily rubbed the chafed skin at her wrists. Though Daggett hadn't been the one to tie her up, that didn't make him a saint. "Have you not done her enough harm?"

"Please." His voice bled like a bruise. By faith, he sounded as if he'd been the one wronged.

She kept her gaze locked on his while daring another step. "Perhaps you ought to explain yourself, Captain."

He lowered the bottle to his side, a long slow breath escaping his lips. His mouth barely moved when he spoke. "I was married once. 'Twas an abysmal match. I was young. Foolish. She was a real beauty, though. A widow. . ." His face hardened. "And a shrew."

He wrenched up his arm and threw the bottle. Glass exploded.

Emily flinched.

"The woman was a harpy! A hag!" Daggett's shout filled the small room. "She came with four extra mouths to feed. Four! Should that not have been enough? Should *I* not have been enough? Yet she wanted one more, one I couldn't afford. One I couldn't produce." His voice lowered until his last word was nothing but a whisper.

Emily watched transfixed as a shiny film covered his eyes. Did he even know she was still there? Maybe not, between his memories and the amount he'd drunk. She dared another step.

"She said the fault was in me. Me! That I wasn't man enough to sire. . ." He shook his head, and for a moment, his shoulders sagged.

When his face lifted to hers, she gasped. A shadow moved across his face. This was no charade. The captain's soul sailed in a sea of darkness. He knew what lay on the other side of pain so deep, so black that no amount of time could separate him from the hurt.

Her breathing hitched. Compassion was a strange friend, calling at the most inopportune time. But now was definitely not the moment to take tea with empathy. "I am sorry for what happened to you, Captain." She snuck another step closer to the open door, speaking as her skirt swished to cover the movement. "But that doesn't justify what you did to my maid."

His sigh could've filled the ocean. "I suppose it does not. But believe me when I say I had no idea there'd be lasting implications. I merely thought the one time, the one night—"

Emily's jaw dropped. "How can you think so lowly of a woman, to use her like that?"

"How can a woman think so lowly of a man, to scorn him in public, make him a laughingstock? Flaunt his impotence to the world!" He barreled toward her faster than she could flee. His fingers dug into her arms, pinning her in place. Anger sharpened the bones of his face. Grief mingled with the rum on his breath. "I never wanted to go a'sea, Miss Payne, but I didn't have a choice! Life on land was hell itself."

Her heart beat loud in her ears. His heavy breaths, all the louder. Everything hinged on this moment. Her future. Her freedom.

His salvation.

"You were wronged, sir," she began slowly, casting the words like a life preserver. "Wronged and damaged, through no fault of your own. So was Wren. And so am I. A wise man once told me no one escapes this life without scars. Not even God."

She paused, waiting for the slightest hint of a break in his stormy gaze. "Let me go, Captain. I am not the woman who hurt you."

His jaw tightened. Nothing more. His fingers still bit into her arms. Overhead, the thumping of sailors' feet readied to sail. She measured time by the vein pulsing on the captain's temple.

After an eternity, she tried again. "Don't add wrong to wrong. I'll see that you're paid back every penny you spent for me if you simply let me go."

A low laugh rumbled in his chest. Then he shoved her, wheeled about, and retrieved another bottle. While he uncorked it with his teeth, she resumed her slow trek to the door.

Daggett swilled half the contents on his way to the porthole, where he stooped and looked out at the inky darkness before dawn. The way the lamplight fell, he couldn't have seen anything other than his own reflection. Emily shuddered. Truly, was there anything more horrific than peering at one's own self?

The image of the broken Captain Daggett branded onto her heart. Even so, she took the opportunity to fly the remaining steps to the door. Would he notice if she slipped out?

Before she crossed the threshold, she turned back. An insane move, as were the words burning on her tongue, but altogether necessary. "I don't know if Wren will have you, Captain, but there's one thing I am certain of."

He didn't look at her. He didn't need to. She spoke as much to herself as to him. "A child needs a father's love. As long as you draw breath, it's not too late to make things right. Think on that."

He grunted then tipped the bottle one more time. Rum dripped down his chin, dampening his collar. Tilting back to drain it dry, he lost his balance and crashed backward. The captain sprawled out flat, his eyes rolled up.

Emily turned and ran into the narrow corridor then paused. Where exactly should she go? Portman Square? Nicholas's room? Neither was safe.

Undecided, she scurried ahead. First she'd have to clear the deck and the docks.

Chapter 32

Uncertainty—the only thing Nicholas despised more than waiting. He circled the doctor's small receiving chamber for the twentieth time in as many minutes, turning his back to the jeering clock on the wall. Why must life—and death—hang on the spindly arm of a timepiece? And honestly, how much death could one handle in the space of a day?

As soon as the door to the infirmary swung open, releasing the stinging odor of ammonia and vinegar, he pivoted. The fast action pumped a fresh flow of blood beneath the binding on his arm. The warmth, and pain, reminded him he ought be thankful his own body was not yet counted among the corpses of the past twenty-four hours.

He pinned his gaze and his hope on Dr. Kirby. "How's Flannery?"

Without his hat, tufts of white hair stood at attention above each of the doctor's ears, giving him a perpetually surprised look—and making it impossible to read the truth in the lines of his face. "Did I not tell you to remain seated, Mr. Brentwood?" His chin lifted, and he eyed the growing stain on Nicholas's sleeve. "Even from this distance I can see you disregarded that order the second I left the room. At least your man is a more compliant patient."

Nicholas sucked in a sharp breath. "So he lives?"

"Thus far." Kirby stepped aside, sweeping one arm toward the open door. "Which is more than I can say for you if you continue to stand there and bleed all over my floor. Let's get you patched up, shall we?"

He didn't need to be told twice. Nicholas strode past him, entered a familiar corridor, then turned right, crossing the threshold into a small surgery. Before Kirby's footsteps caught up to him, he tugged off what remained of his shirt and hopped up on the table at center, ignoring the discolored sawdust coating the floor. Practiced from warming this bench a time or two, he focused instead on a bottle-lined shelf.

Kirby snorted. "Someone's in a hurry."

He would have shrugged—but it would hurt. "Have at it."

Instruments rattled. A cork loosened. The fresh waft of alcohol competed with the mix of pungent odors permanently embedded in the pores of the walls.

Kirby's grip held Nicholas's injured arm aloft as he unwrapped the temporary bandage. Nicholas set his jaw against the fiery pain. The doctor's cold fingers did little to offset it.

"I assume you've made arrangements for your sister," Kirby mumbled as he worked.

Nicholas gasped, as much from the fresh reminder of Jenny's passing as from the insertion of a probe. The metal end dug around for a bullet, no less excruciating than the grief boring into his heart. He winced so hard, his eyes cinched tight, making it tough to form words. "Mistress Dawkins. . .is overseeing. . .the details."

"You have my condolences, Mr. Brentwood. Your sister was a rare one."

So was the new agony Kirby inflicted. The white-hot thrust and pull of the extractor blurred the individual bottles on the shelf into a smeared streak. This time, the bottles disappeared. Completely. A primeval growl roared out his mouth, and Nicholas gripped the table's edge with his free hand to keep from falling over. The doctor shored him up further with a steadying hand at his back.

"There now." Metal pinged against metal. "Care to see the beast that bit?"

"Just. Sew. Me up." Wheezes punctuated each word, but at least the glassware on the shelf reappeared.

"Your rough-and-tumble ways are going to catch up to you one day, Brentwood. Soon you'll be more scar than man." Kirby left his side to retrieve a silver tray from a counter.

Nicholas wobbled, missing the doctor's support—then recanted when Kirby returned. A needle dug into his arm. "Ahh!"

"Sorry. As I said, there's not much pristine skin here to work with, and tugging the suture through—"

"Don't explain. Just—" The needle stabbed again. Nicholas grunted. "Finish." His request traveled on a groan.

"Oh? Pressing engagement, have you?" The needle bit thrice more before Kirby's sigh and the snip of a scissor cut through the air.

After the doctor wrapped a fresh bandage over the site, Nicholas slid off the table. Two shelves materialized where the one had been, with double the amount of bottles. He threw a hand out for balance. Kirby was right. His lifestyle was catching up to him more quickly than he'd care to admit. Allowing the doctor to play valet, he eased his wounded arm into his ruined shirt and greatcoat.

Kirby did not miss his grimace. "I suggest you lay low for the day, Brentwood."

The doctor's counsel followed him into the corridor. He didn't have time to answer, let alone lay low.

Not until he upturned every dock from here to the North Sea.

Stepping out into the black before dawn, he set his feet toward the Wapping Dockyards. By the time he turned the corner of Newman Street, a faint sliver of gray lightened the eastern sky. When his boot heels left behind cobbles for wooden walkways, the promise of morning spread across the horizon.

He scowled, the stench of emptied bilge matching his foul mood. Already the vessel farthest down the line slipped its moorings and floated toward the sea—and this was only one of many wharves lining the busy riverway, representing a smattering of the ships already lost to him. If Emily were aboard one of those. . .no. Better to not even brook the thought.

Squaring his shoulders, he approached the first ship, noting any twitchy reactions from those aboard. He gauged the captain's responses to his questions through a filter of presumed guilt, all the while inhaling deeply. The slightest whiff of lily of the valley and he'd tear the vessel apart one-handed. He'd have to. The fire burning in his wounded arm rendered that limb useless.

But nothing seemed out of the ordinary, except for him. His battered appearance drew open stares. Undaunted, he moved on to the next ship—and the next—until he investigated each floating hulk, eyed every passing man, and stalked the length of the quay from one end to the other. Now fully unclothed in the sky, the sun taunted him. In a defiant move to prove it wrong, he fished around in his pocket and pulled out his pocket watch. Ten o'clock. Ten!

Terns screeched overhead, echoing the roar of frustration building in his throat. It would take him all day to scour the Greenland Docks then the East India's. There was no way he could do this alone.

His shoulders sank, the movement releasing a fresh burst of pain in his arm. He needed reinforcements, sleep, faith. . .a miracle. *God, please, just one.* Or more. He frowned. Once the magistrate heard of Flannery's fate, he'd be lucky were Ford to grant him even the lowliest grate cleaner to help him search for Emily. With the back of his hand, he scrubbed at the stubble on his face.

Better to not brook that thought, either.

Crossing to Newton Street, he hailed a hackney, and though he tried, a black cloud of malicious what-ifs and your-faults escorted him all the way across town. Admitting defeat never came easy—especially when it involved those he loved.

But at this point, he'd do anything, say anything, to get Emily back.

Sunlight warmed his face when his feet hit the cobbles in front of Number Four Bow Street. The shaggy blond-headed man leaning against the wall further lightened his spirits. Nicholas smiled for the first time in an eternity. Had anyone ever thought of Moore as a miracle? "You're a sight for sore eyes."

Officer Alexander Moore surveyed him from head to toe, frowning. "And you're a sight. About time you haul your lazy backside to the station. I do all the work for you, and then you've the nerve to keep me waiting."

Nicholas cocked his head, his gaze following Moore's hand as it disappeared inside his coat. He pulled out a leather wallet, and without a word, handed it over.

Shutting out the bustle of carriages and pedestrians, Nicholas honed all his attention onto the money case. A scrolled "P" was engraved on the front—the same crest adorning Payne's strongbox in his office. Judging by the thickness—or rather lack of it—he didn't bother opening the thing.

His gaze locked onto Moore's. "Where'd you find it?"

"Pried it out of the grip of a smuggler down Dover way. The money's long gone, but at least I know what happened to Mr. Payne... and it wasn't suicide." Moore shook his head. "Those that deal with brigands never meet with a good end."

"I expect you enacted justice?"

He flashed a grin. "Case closed."

Maybe for Payne, but not Emily. Nicholas's heart lurched. He tucked away the thought and the wallet. "Not quite. I need you to—"

"Tut, tut." Moore's hand shot up. "You should know by now, Brentwood, that I am always correct. I've got one more thing to deliver to you. Come along."

Before Nicholas could grab one of the many questions swirling in his head, Moore's broad shoulders vanished through the front door. By the time he entered the foyer, Moore was halfway up the stairwell, a question of his own spiraling down.

"Were you missing something? Or should I say...someone?"

The words stole his breath. His heart—dear God—was it even still beating? Nicholas took the stairs two at a time, nearly crashing into Moore's back at the landing.

Moore stopped in front of the magistrate's public receiving room and turned to him. "It's fortunate the lady encountered me before Ford. He doesn't know about your loose grip on your sleeping beauty, and with the humor he's in today, it might be better if he didn't."

"I owe you." Though Nicholas tried to conceal it, emotion thickened his voice.

Moore smirked. "That you do." Then he pivoted and called over his shoulder as he strode down the corridor. "And Brentwood, I've enough work of my own to care for. Don't lose her again."

"I don't intend to." He grasped the doorknob as firmly as his resolve. "Ever."

A deep voice hung in the thin space between waking and sleeping, balancing on the edge. One false move and the smooth tones might shatter into a thousand pieces. Too many to sweep. Too small to piece together. Emily shifted her head on the settee's pillow—carefully—unwilling that the slightest jostle might fully awaken her. Of all the fitful dreams she'd suffered throughout the last few hours, this one was by far the sweetest.

The jiggle of the doorknob ended that aspiration. Her eyes sprung open, and she pushed up to sit. Officer Moore had encouraged her to rest, but that didn't mean she ought be caught lounging like a slackard.

When the door swung wide, for the briefest of moments she wondered if a heart could explode. Hers pulsed in her temples, her wrists, her knees.

Her guardian stood framed in the doorway. Stillness surrounded him, or was that her breath that stopped? His hair was coated with a fine layer of gray ash. Soot and sweat and fear smeared across his brow. The heat of his gaze spread a wildfire of emotions through her veins.

He stepped forward, filling the room with his presence, banishing all the darkness and terror of the last month. "Emily."

She launched from the settee and ran into his arms. "Nicholas!"

He pulled her close, wrapping his strong arms around her, and pressed a kiss to the crown of her head. "Thank God."

She nuzzled into his chest, breathing deeply. He smelled a musky combination of blood and safety. Always the paradox, this man. Was it his wild unpredictability that drew her or the home her heart had found in his arms? She grabbed handfuls of his coat and held on, burrowing into him. For now she memorized the contour of the muscles beneath his shirt and the feel of his stubbly cheek rubbing against her hair.

"You'll be the death of me, you know?" His voice rumbled in her ear.

"I was so frightened." Tears garbled her words. She closed her eyes, surrendering to the relief leaking down her cheeks, dampening his shirt, washing them both.

"You're safe, now. Hear me?" He pulled back and tipped her face to his. The rough pad of his thumb traced along her chin. "Safe, now and always, for I'll not leave your side ever again."

Pulling back farther, he slid to one knee. His green eyes blazed with a passion so pure, so candid, she shivered.

"This is hardly the time or place, but the past twenty-four hours have taught me nothing is certain, not even the best-laid plans." His voice cracked, and he reached for her hand. He pressed a kiss into her palm before continuing. "You have stolen my heart, Emily Payne, a crime for which justice must be served. And so I ask. . .will you have me?"

Yes, without a doubt, was on the tip of her tongue, but "You're hurt!" flew past her lips. She dropped to his level, her heart breaking at the stained, torn fabric on his arm. Why had she not noticed that first? "Are you all right?"

"I might be." With a gentle nudge, he tilted her face back to his. "If you would but answer my question."

She lifted her hand to his cheek, smoothing back lines of worry etched from years of care. All her dreams and hopes and plans were here, wrapped in the guise of a tattered, scruffy lawman. "I would have no other."

His lips came down on hers, soft as moonlight, hotter than the sun. He tasted of cloves and mystery and sweet, sweet promise. She leaned into him, heedless now of his injury. A tremor shook through him—no. That quivery feeling was inside her. Deep. Low. She ran her hands up his back, feeling desire ripple along each smooth muscle. Unless he held her in place, she'd fall and never, ever be found again.

He groaned and pulled her closer, his lips forming her name against her mouth, her jaw, her neck. The warmth of his breath brushed a shiver along the curve of her collarbone. A crazy rushing sounded in her ears, heady, swirling, entirely intoxicating.

And a sobering voice boomed from the door. "This is not a brothel, Brentwood."

Chapter 33

Nicholas shot to his feet, pulling Emily up with him. The magistrate's face was granite. His mouth soured into a scowl that prickled over Nicholas's scalp and crept down his spine. Of all the inopportune moments for the man to enter, he had to choose this one?

Emily huddled at his back. Her trembling filtered through the fabric of his coat—and he didn't blame her one bit. He widened his stance. "I can explain, sir."

Ford's mouth flattened. Was he biting back words or too busy formulating a censure? The magistrate closed the door and advanced across the carpet, bypassing Nicholas without a glance. From the bank of windows, daylight collected atop his shoulders. He pulled it with him as he went, leaving a distinct chill in his wake.

"Pleased to meet you at long last, Miss Payne. I am Magistrate Ford." He bowed his head then offered his arm. "Allow me to escort you to a seat. Brentwood's explanations are entertaining and somewhat long-winded. And judging by the looks of him," he arched one brow at Nicholas, "this one promises to excel on both accounts."

Emily's wide eyes stared into his own, and he nodded his assurance—a confidence he searched for in every nook of his own soul. None was found. As Ford led Emily to one of the settees in an L-shaped arrangement near the hearth, Nicholas made haste to the other. The sooner this confrontation was over, the better.

Ford's "uh-uh-uh" stopped him. "Remain center stage, Mr. Brentwood. I promised the lady a show, and you will deliver." Flipping out his coattail, the magistrate sank next to Emily then pierced him with a glower. "Start talking."

Nicholas shored himself against the mantel, grateful for the solid brick against his back. His thoughts of how to begin were nothing but vapor. Perhaps the end would work best, leastwise for Emily's sake. "What you witnessed as you walked in, sir, is no stain against the lady's character. I intend our banns be read beginning this Sunday, and in three weeks' time, I would that you officiate at our marriage ceremony."

If the magistrate had been wearing his judicial wig, his brows would've lifted it a full inch from his scalp. "You've outdone yourself this time, Brentwood. Very entertaining!" He slanted a sideways glance at Emily. "Not that he isn't a noble enough prospect, but are you entirely certain about matrimony to this man, Miss Payne?"

A slow smile brightened her face, and though she spoke to the magistrate, she locked her gaze with his. Joy sparkled there—unabashed and sincere. "I'm afraid I have learned to think things through the hard way, Mr. Ford, and while I appreciate your concern, my conclusion is that my best, my dearest, my *only* choice is indeed Nicholas Brentwood."

His name on her lips was as sweet as her kiss, but as Ford turned his frown toward him, he shoved down the memory and stored it away for later. Careful to erase any emotion from his face, he straightened his shoulders.

Ford quirked a brow. "I don't believe charming the lady into oblivion was part of the original guardianship arrangement. Nothing to be done for that now, I suppose. There are a few loose ends, however, that ought be tied up before you two embark on the marital journey. What of Miss Payne's father?" He held up a hand, staying an answer, and turned toward Emily. "I know I promised you a show, my dear, but if you find the topic too sensitive, Brentwood and I can take this into my office."

She lifted her chin. "Thank you, but no. I wish to stay."

"A woman who knows her own mind, eh?" Ford cocked his head back at Nicholas. "She will suit you, I think. Go on with your tale—and this time start from the beginning instead of the end."

The old man didn't miss a trick. A good trait in one who warmed the judgment bench. Nicholas ran his hand through his hair. Ash and soot rained down. "The evening I began my employ at Portman Square, Mr. Payne departed to the Wapping Wharf, his wallet padded with what remained of his fortune and that of his partner, Mr. Reginald Sedgewick. Because of the passing of the recent ban on slavery, they were at odds as to which direction the business should go. Sedgewick favored tobacco and cotton. Payne, something a little more lucrative."

Ford leaned forward. "Such as?"

"Smuggling. Payne needed a large sum of money and fast. Unbeknownst to Sedgewick, he'd gambled their business into quite the precarious position. So Payne took all of what they had and cut a deal with a Spanish smuggling ring led by a man known only as Sombra."

"The Shadow. I've heard of him." Ford stroked his chin. "He's a villain, with quite the grudge against the East India Company. There are rumblings, according to Officer Moore, that the man's intent is to undercut then monopolize the saltpeter and opium trades."

Nicholas nodded. Like colored bits of glass in a kaleidoscope, all the details he'd collected over the past month rotated into a single stunning picture in his mind. He stepped from the hearth and began pacing the length of it, his steps matching the swiftness of his words. "Fearing Sedgewick's reaction to the theft, not to mention the American captain who wanted to be paid for his delivery of tobacco, Payne hired me to see to Emily's well-being until his return. He never guessed that other brigands might get to him first, steal his money, then hang him...yet that's exactly what happened."

He lengthened his stride, envisioning a dark-skinned Spaniard waiting for Payne. Lifting his good arm, Nicholas ran light fingers over a ridged scar on the back of his neck. He knew better than anyone what kind of a mistake Emily's father had inadvertently made. "Payne never made his appointed meeting with Sombra—and one should *never* keep a Spaniard waiting. In retaliation, Sombra sent out his watchdog, Ambrose de Villet, to collect the promised amount then kill Payne for standing him up."

"But de Villet had no idea Payne was already dead." Ford grunted. "Interesting."

At the mention of her father's death, Nicholas stopped in front of Emily, searching for a quivering lip or any other kind of reaction. This turn of conversation might be more than she bargained for, yet she remained expressionless, giving no hint she wished to flee.

Ford must've noticed his blunder, for he reached over and patted her hand. "Sorry, my dear. I'm afraid my blunt ways are somewhat ingrained."

"A Bow Street trait, I assume, for I have often noted Nicholas's directness." Her brown gaze lifted to his. "Have I not?"

"Frequently." The smile they shared burned through him from head to toe, so warm, so intimate, a flush rose on her cheeks, and he was glad for the stubble darkening his.

Ford cleared his throat.

Nicholas resumed his pacing—it was either that or a cold bath. "You are correct, sir, that neither Sombra nor de Villet had any inkling Payne had been murdered. Quite the contrary. Because I rarely left Emily's side, de Villet thought I was the man. But here's the twist."

He paused and faced the settee. Both the magistrate and Emily pinned their gaze on him. "All that explains Payne's connection to Sombra and de Villet, but I suspect that when Payne first contacted Sombra, he used his partner's name, Reginald Sedgewick."

Ford cocked his head. "Why the deuce would he do that?"

"With Payne's gambling debts so widely known, he wouldn't have risked Sombra finding out his net worth wasn't quite what he purported it to be. That would explain why de Villet first went to Sedgewick's home for collection. I believe Sedgewick and de Villet found out together about Payne's dubious dealings."

The magistrate shook his head. "That must have been quite the conversation."

"Yes, and de Villet couldn't let Sedgewick live with that much information, so he killed him." Once more he studied Emily's face for signs of grief or remaining horror from that terrible night. Her lips pressed tight, and he waited for her slight nod before he began again.

"When de Villet paid a visit to the Payne household, only Emily was home. He made his threat quite clear—and if nothing else, he is a man of his word. Or was, rather. At any rate, he abducted Emily, held her for ransom, then sold her off while waiting for me to bring his chest full of money, which would have doubled his profits. He'd pay off Sombra and keep the rest for himself. My payment, however, was a little more than he bargained for."

Ford lifted a hand. "Hence your appearance."

"About that." A ragged sigh rippled up from his lungs. The faded green walls of the room closed in on him, the exact color of the guilt squeezing his chest. He rolled his shoulders, wishing the words he had to say might as easily flow. "Flannery didn't fare so well, sir. I never should have given him such a dangerous task. If only I'd devised a better plan. Something safer. His life hangs in the balance because of me."

"Pish!" Ford's stern tone stopped him cold. "Stop flogging yourself, man. Flannery knew the risks involved. Such is the life of an officer. Better he know that up front than find out after a commissioning. I expect nothing more nor less than you see to him and keep me posted."

Of course Ford was right. Nicholas knew it in his head—but his heart would have none of it. Gritting his teeth, he methodically ground the remaining guilt into a thick paste and swallowed it. "Yes, sir."

"Very well. You rescued the fair maiden, and so I find you, a little worse for the wear, eh?"

"Not quite." Nicholas turned his gaze to Emily. "How did you end up here at the station?"

Two pairs of eyes focused on Emily. A bug beneath a magnifying glass couldn't have been more exposed. Shifting on the settee, she ran both hands along her skirt, hoping to coax out enough information without having to go into great detail. "I don't have Nicholas's flair for story telling." Ignoring his snort, she continued. "Suffice it to say de Villet sold me to a captain with whom I'd had previous dealings. After a lengthy conversation, he let me go."

"Let you go?" The magistrate's brows bounced upward. "You must be quite the conversationalist."

"Persuasiveness is one of Miss Payne's hallmarks." Nicholas crossed from the hearth to stand before her, offering both hands. When his fingers wrapped around hers, warmth shot up her arms.

He pulled her to her feet, the green of his eyes deepening to a storm-tossed sea. "Forgive me for not asking immediately, such was my relief at finding you here. Are you all right? The captain didn't hurt you, did he?"

"I am fine."

The worry puckering his brow hinted he wanted to know everything—and the thought of reliving the awful situation here and now added a whole new depth to her exhaustion. Her lips curved into a smile she didn't feel, and she gave his hands a light squeeze. "The captain was too far into his cups to have hurt me, so truly, I am fine, though I should like to go home now. It's been a long night."

For an unguarded moment, his shoulders sank, and an unexplained sadness pulled at the lines near his mouth. Then it was gone. Just like that. Leaving her to wonder if she'd seen the breach of emotion or not.

Dropping her hands, Nicholas turned to the magistrate. "The lady speaks truth. It has been a very long night indeed. If you are satisfied, sir, may we take our leave?"

Ford rose, tugging loose the neckcloth at his throat. "Your long night was nothing compared to that courtroom full of reprobates downstairs. But yes, I think we can officially say this case is closed, though I assume you'll help the future Mrs. Brentwood settle her father's estate?" Nicholas nodded. "Yes, sir."

"I suppose you'll be wanting some time off as well?"

Emily held her breath. How Nicholas answered might very well be a clue as to where she lined up in his queue of priorities. Would he choose his job over her?

He leveled his gaze at her yet spoke to Ford. "If you don't mind." "And if I do?"

Nicholas shrugged, and she breathed in all the love she read in the lines of his face.

"Bah." Ford shook his head and turned to her. "For all his rough edges, Nicholas Brentwood is a good man. If he cares for you half as much as his sister, you will be well tended indeed."

Behind him, Nicholas stiffened at the mention of his sister. An almost imperceptible movement in anyone else, but one she now recognized as a serious sign of something important. Something bad. A monster swam beneath his cool exterior, and her own stomach tightened in response.

"...wish you all the best, my dear."

She snapped her gaze back to the magistrate. How much of what he'd said had she missed? Playing it safe, she flashed him a smile and defaulted to a polite, "Thank you."

"Good day to you both." The magistrate strode from the room.

As soon as Ford's coattails disappeared out the door, she turned to Nicholas. "What's wrong? It's about Jenny, isn't it? I know it. What's happened?"

A halfhearted smirk lifted his lips. "Perhaps you ought think about becoming a Bow Street officer."

His attempt to lighten the heaviness filling the room fell flat. Dread of what he might be covering up squeezed her chest, making it hard to breathe. She reached for him, resting a light touch on his sleeve. "Nicholas, do not dodge the question."

He shook his head, looking older, worn, beaten. She could only imagine all the death he'd seen in his lifetime, more than any human should be asked to bear, but this. . . Her throat clogged.

Oh God, please, not his sister. Not Jenny.

"There was none sweeter than Jen." His voice broke on his sister's name, crushing her heart with the sound.

Tears pooled in her eyes. A few slipped free and slid down her cheeks, landing on her lips. The salt tasted like bitter loss. "I am so sorry."

"As am I." He pivoted and strode to the window, each step carrying him farther away, the space between them an eternity. How to reach him, to console, to comfort? All her years of mourning the lack of love from her father paled in comparison to the heavy weight bending Nicholas's head. She stood in place, clutching handfuls of her skirt, unable to grasp the full nature of his pain.

"I am an officer, Emily." He stared out the window, his voice husky. "There's no guarantee you won't have to shoulder a grief like the one I now bear should I meet as untimely a death as my sister." When at last he turned toward her, the intensity of his gaze weakened her knees. She grabbed the back of the settee for support.

"I won't hold it against you should you decide to change your mind." His face was a mask, as if the real Nicholas had departed and nothing but a shell remained. "I once advised you to think carefully before running headlong into a marriage, and so I do now. Are you certain I am the man for you?"

Was he? This demanding, rugged, by-no-means-wealthy man who'd barged into her life and taken over her world? She walked over to him, aware that her decision would mark them both to their dying day. Reaching for his hand, she lifted his knuckles, bruised and battered, to her lips. He flinched—or was that a tremor?

"My best." She moved her mouth to the next knuckle, speaking against his skin. "My dearest." She kissed another. "My only choice." She lifted his palm to her cheek, all callouses and strength, and leaned into it. "Is you."

Her name was a whisper, wrapping as tightly around her as his arms. It was a distinct possibility this man's days would be cut short on London's streets. But for now, she nuzzled into his chest. It had taken a long time for love to come her way, and she intended to memorize every beat of Nicholas Brentwood's heart.

Chapter 34

Descending from the hackney, Nicholas reached into his pocket and flipped the driver a coin before both his boots hit the cobbles. Then he fished around once more to retrieve his watch. Not that he needed to. The morning sun peeking over Dr. Kirby's rooftop said it all.

He was late.

The minute hand stood at attention, which should have indicted him all the more. Instead, a bittersweet smile curved his mouth. The golden needle on the watch face pointed straight up at Adelina's portrait—leastwise, what had been. Nothing but a ghostly collection of watery lines remained of her sweet face. He rubbed his thumb over her memory one last time, breathed out his final regrets, then released at last what could never be undone.

With his nail, he pried out the worn parchment. Holding it up to a gust of wind banking in from Bowler Street, he whispered, "Good-bye," and let her go. Adelina hovered for a moment, caught between earth and sky. He watched, mesmerized. How well he knew that feeling, the in-between and not yet. She spiraled once, twice, then rode a swift up-current toward heaven.

Nicholas turned from the sight. His own heaven on earth waited for him at Portman Square, packed and ready to go. The sooner he finished this errand, the better.

Ahead, Dr. Kirby emerged from his shop, bag in hand and hat on head. He pulled shut the door then stopped, wide-eyed. "Well, well, Brentwood. Aren't you the dapper fellow today."

"More like uncomfortable." Nicholas tugged at his cravat. He'd rather go hand-to-hand with a back-lane thief than choke and swelter in a suit. Thanks be to God, he'd only have to go through this once.

Kirby snorted. "I've seen you slit-eyed, bled out, and unconscious, and yet you always spring back. Surely a little culture won't hold you down."

"At least not for long, if I have anything to say about it." He nodded toward the doctor's bag. "I see you're leaving. Mind if I step in and check on Flannery?"

Kirby shook his head. "Too late, I'm afraid."

Nicholas sucked in a breath. The doctor's blunt statement rattled through him as chill as the next gust of wind. *Oh God, not Flannery.* He'd seen the Irishman only two days ago. Noticed the first sprouts of new eyebrows growing back. The angry burnt skin on his neck and cheek had cooled into a waxy red patch, and he'd claimed it didn't hurt so much. How could he be gone, just like that? So quickly?

He worked his jaw, forcing words past the tightness in his throat. "Was he. . .did he. . .suffer much?"

"Pah!" Kirby's mouth pulled downward. "The only one suffering around here was me. Ever since I unwrapped Flannery's face and freed his lips, it was all 'oh for the bonny green isle' and tales of his mother's cooking. I couldn't stomach it anymore, so I let him go home yesterday. I'm about to check on him, though. Care to come along— say. . .you feeling a'right?" The doctor paused, narrowing his eyes. "You look a bit pale, though admittedly I've never seen you without bruises or blood coloring your face."

"I'm fine, or rather I was until you scared the life out of me." He straightened his cuffs then nailed Kirby with a glower. "Your bedside manner, Doctor, is lacking."

"Yes, so you frequently tell me." The next windy draft knocked Kirby's hat to a rakish tilt. With a swipe of his free hand, he straightened it then stepped away from the shop. "I'm off. You coming?"

Nicholas shook his head. "Just give Flannery my regards, would you? I. . .uh. . .have a more pressing engagement that I ought not miss." He scrubbed his neck, hoping the doctor would not detect the rising heat burning a trail clear up to his ears.

"Oh? Yet another of your famous pressing engagements, eh?" Kirby's gaze assessed him. "Yet it appears this one is of another nature from your usual. Well, I shan't be back until this afternoon, though from the looks of it, I doubt this engagement involves any fisticuffs."

Nicholas grinned as he watched the doctor set his long legs into motion. Somehow, Kirby had guessed—or come close to a correct conclusion about—what Nicholas would be doing this day. Did love show on a man's face? Even one trained not to tip off his emotions?

But the good doctor was right. He wouldn't need Kirby for bandaging or stitches. Fatigue, maybe, for he intended to show Emily just how much he loved her—and that would take a very long time.

⌒

Nibbling on her fingernail, Emily narrowed her eyes at the image in the mirror, blurring her focus to see more clearly the outline of her shape. Mary had worked hard the past few weeks to refashion this gown into a wedding dress, but the maid was no skilled seamstress. White silk poofed out a little too much at the waist, and. . .wait a minute. Emily turned, cocked her head, and yes. Just as she suspected. The fabric behind billowed out in a most unbecoming way.

She spun to Mary, the quick movement attracting her pug. Alf scampered over with a yip, and she bent and wagged her finger. "Do not even consider it, little prince."

He parked his chubby little body at her feet and tilted his head at a sharp angle. One eyebrow rose then the other, back and forth until she couldn't help but smile. "Scamp!"

Straightening, she pointed to the dressing table, heaped with ribbons and lace. "Mary, could you bring over the blue satin? I think it will be just the thing."

Her maid retrieved the shimmery trimming and pursed her lips. "I like the idea of a splash of color, but where exactly would you like it?"

She pressed the poof against her rib cage, flattening the fabric into place. "Tie it as a sash, and make sure to catch up the extra bit of fabric behind me."

"Ahh, good idea, miss." Mary smoothed the ribbon into place then scooted behind her to tie a bow. "I'd like to thank you again for recommending me to Miss Grayson, though I daresay you'll miss having a maid."

"Did I not tell you?" She quirked a glance over her shoulder. "Mr. Brentwood has secured a wonderful new assistant for me."

"Oh?" The maid's tone pinched as tight as the ribbon she knotted.

"Chin up, Mary. You know I'd keep you if I were able, but an officer's salary doesn't stretch very far." In spite of herself, Emily smiled. Trifling over expenses would indeed be a challenge—one she'd forget about every night when Nicholas held her in his arms. "My new maid is nine years old, a sweet young thing he rescued off the streets. In time, Hope will become proficient, but until then, you're right. . .I shall feel your loss."

"You're very kind, miss."

A rap on the door and a yip from Alf ended the conversation. Mrs. Hunt peeked in, frightening the pug into the corner. "There's a gentleman downstairs to see you, miss."

Emily sprinted, heedless of the impropriety and Mary's complaints. Why care if a bow was looped to perfection when green eyes and broad shoulders waited for her in the sitting room? Shoving past Mrs. Hunt, she flew down the stairs and raced across the foyer, not slowing until she dashed through the door.

Then she froze.

Broad shoulders met her, all right, along with a barrel chest and cinder-grey eyes. Captain Daggett stood stiff as a ramrod, his hat clutched in front of him with white knuckles. "Good day, Miss Payne. I wasn't quite sure if you'd see me."

"Well, I—" she bit the inside of her cheek, holding back the *had*

I known it was you, I'd have turned you away. At the very least, she should call for John or Mrs. Hunt, for this rogue was not to be trusted. She opened her mouth, then paused. Where was her fear? Pounding heart? Why did his presence not instill any trepidation?

On second look, his shoulders sagged. The usual hard set to his mouth softened with humility. Even the haughty gleam in his gaze was gone. For the most part, the outside trappings of the man were the same, but something was different on the inside.

Taking a deep breath, she searched for the right words. "Good day, Captain. Excuse me if I seem a bit surprised at your visit."

He cleared his throat, looking for all the world like a man about to face the gallows. "Rightfully so. I merely came for. . .what I mean to say is. . ."

The bill of his hat crumpled into a tight wad beneath his fingers. Morning sun from the window highlighted a fine sheen on his brow. If she didn't know better, she'd swear the man was every bit as broken beyond repair as his hat.

A small ember of empathy sparked in a dark corner of her heart. "Go on."

His chest swelled and ebbed with a sigh. "What you said in my cabin, that it's never too late to make things right, well. . .I took that to heart. By God's grace, I am a changed man. I wish to make things right with Miss Hunt and. . ." His gaze darted from door to ceiling and finally to hers. "I acknowledge I have no right whatsoever, and in truth expect to be turned down on all accounts, yet I feel compelled to ask. May I speak with your maid, Miss Payne? Fully in your presence or anyone else's, of course. I should not like to frighten her, or hurt her any worse than I already have."

Emily pressed her lips tight to keep her jaw from dropping. Was he serious?

"Wren is no longer my maid, Captain. She lost her employment when it was found she was with child." She cast the words slowly, watching for his reaction as they sank in.

Emotions rippled across his face, one chasing another. His hat, or what remained of the mangled bit of banded felt, dropped to the carpet. "Please, I. . ." He fumbled inside his greatcoat and pulled out an envelope, offering it over to her. "I know I shall never be able to compensate for what I've done, yet I wish to make some kind of amends. If nothing else, I would like to support the child and its mother. Would you see that she gets this?"

The envelope weighed heavy in her hand, padded thickly with what felt like a small fortune. "I would be happy to, Captain."

"Thank you for your time, Miss Payne. You have been more than generous with me." He swept up his cap and strode past her. "Good day."

She stood there a moment, hardly believing what had just happened, then crossed to the curio desk to tuck away the envelope. What a strange and wonderful oddity. Wren would want for nothing, leastwise financially.

Out in the foyer, the click of the front door closed, then clicked open again. What more could the captain possibly have to say? When she turned, her heart caught in her throat. The long lines of Nicholas Brentwood's body filled the doorway. His dark hair was combed back, his face clean-shaven and smooth. Sunlight brushed along the strong cut of his jaw. His white silk cravat stood out in stark contrast to his midnight-blue tailcoat. Matching breeches rode the curve of his thighs.

"I came to escort my bride to her wedding." He lifted his chin, pinning her in place with his green gaze. The space between them charged with desire and promise. "Have you seen her?"

She crossed the room in a heartbeat and thumped her finger into his chest with each of her words. "You, sir, are a rogue."

"And you, miss"—his voice softened—"are beautiful."

She tilted her face toward his, and when his lips came down, she raised to her toes. Closing her eyes, she surrendered to the urgency of his kiss and the strength in his embrace. His mouth moved along the arch of her neck to the hollow of her throat. The sweet sensation radiated through her, stealing her breath, her thoughts, her heart. He tasted of distant horizons—altogether consuming and far too heady.

He groaned and loosened his hold, setting her at arm's length. "No more." His husky tone shivered through her. "Not until I can finish the job." His eyes glimmered with the knowledge of what lay beyond, after the ceremony, when vows were committed to action.

The heat in his gaze sent a tremor up her arms and down her back, settling in her legs and turning her knees to jelly. She swallowed, praying to keep her quivers from warbling her voice. "Then we'd best be about it."

A slow grin slid across his face. Capturing her hand, he tucked her fingers into the crook of his arm. Steely muscles moved beneath the fabric. "So, I was correct about your grand designs all along, was I not?"

Her nose scrunched up, and she was glad he reached for the door instead of noticing her likely resemblance to her pug. "Whatever do you mean?"

Pausing, he turned to her. "The first morning we took breakfast together, you all but admitted your goal for the season was to garner yourself a husband."

Fire spread across her face. Had she really been that shallow?

"Don't be embarrassed, my love." He bent and pressed a kiss against her brow. "For indeed, that is exactly what you have done."

Author's Note

Who Were the Bow Street Runners?

Traditionally, every male householder in London was expected to police the streets in their neighborhood, and every citizen was to report anyone they witnessed committing a crime. This changed in the eighteenth century because of increasing concerns about the threat of dangerous criminals who were attracted by the growing wealth of London's middle class.

Prompted by a postwar crime wave in 1749, Magistrate Henry Fielding (who himself was a playwright and novelist) hired a small group of men to locate and arrest serious offenders. He operated out of Number Four Bow Street, hence the name "Bow Street Runners."

Fielding petitioned the government and received funding, but even so, he soon ran out of money to pay these men a worthy salary. Still, the runners were committed to justice, so they took on odd jobs such as watchmen or detectives for hire or even—as in the case of Nicholas Brentwood—guarding people or treasures.

What attracted my interest as an author was an old newspaper advertisement put out by Fielding. It encouraged the public to send a note to Bow Street as soon as any serious crime occurred so that "*a set of brave fellows could immediately be dispatched in pursuit of the villains.*" I wondered about those "brave fellows" and what kind of villains they might come up against, and thus was born Nicholas Brentwood.

Despite Bow Street's efforts, most Londoners were opposed to the development of an organized police force. The English tradition of local government was deeply ingrained, and they feared the loss of individual liberty. So, as gallant as the runners were in tracking down criminals, the general public did not always view them in a positive light. Even the nickname given them by the public—Bow Street Runners—was considered derogatory and was a title the officers never used to refer to themselves.

Bow Street eventually gave way to the Metropolitan Police, and by 1839, the runners were completely disbanded.

Interested in further reading? Here are a few of my favorite resources:

Beattie, J. M. *The First English Detectives: The Bow Street Runners and the Policing of London, 1750–1840*. Oxford: Oxford University Press, 2012.

Cox, David J. *A Certain Share of Low Cunning: A History of the Bow Street Runners, 1792–1839*. New York, London: Routledge, 2012.

Hale, Don. *Legal History: Bow Street Runners, Scotland Yard & Victorian Crime*. Coast & Country, 2013. Kindle edition.

Discussion Questions

1. In chapter 3, **Emily Payne** is told by her guardian that she needed to begin building trust with him by keeping her word and being completely honest. Of course we should always speak the truth, but are "little white lies" permissible, especially those that would keep the hearer from becoming hurt?

- Read Ephesians 4:15, 25 and Zechariah 8:16
- When was the last time you were tempted to tell a little white lie?

2. In chapter 4, **Jenny Brentwood** tells her brother Nicholas that she's "dandy and grand," her trademark response when asked how she's feeling though she's dying of tuberculosis. What circumstances tempt you to give in to self-pity?

- Read Philippians 4:8 and Proverbs 17:22
- Do you know someone who has a great attitude despite life's challenges? Take the time to write them an encouraging note today.

3. In chapter 9, **Wren (Lauren) Hunt** tells Emily, "Only by losing everything could I gain the one thing I would've overlooked. Need." Why would she see need as a gain instead of a detriment?

- Read Psalm 34:18 and Romans 8:28
- What tragic circumstance has happened in your life that may be considered a blessing in disguise?

4. In chapter 11, when **Nicholas Brentwood** makes a visit to the morgue, he reflects that "God should so bless everyone with a visit to the dead house." Why in the world would looking at corpses be a blessing?

- Read Psalm 90:12 and Psalm 39:4–6
- When is the last time you took a moment to meditate on the brevity of life?

5. In chapter 24, **Mrs. Hunt** is credited with the sage advice that extraordinary situations call for extraordinary measures. What unexpected situation have you faced that called for drastic measures?

- Read Exodus 14:5–31
- What does this story say about the character of God?

6. Which character in *Brentwood's Ward* did you relate to the most and why?

7. Historically, the English people were skittish about having an organized police force. They felt it impinged upon their privacy. At what point does a government-run organization cross the line into privacy invasion?

About the Author

Michelle Griep has been writing since she first discovered blank wall space and Crayolas. She seeks to glorify God in all that she writes—except for that graffiti phase she went through as a teenager. She resides in the frozen tundra of Minnesota, where she teaches history and writing classes for a local high school co-op. An Anglophile at heart, she runs away to England every chance she gets, under the guise of research. Really, though, she's eating excessive amounts of scones while rambling around a castle. Michelle is a member of ACFW (American Christian Fiction Writers) and MCWG (Minnesota Christian Writers Guild). Keep up with her adventures at her blog "Writer off the Leash" or visit michellegriep.com.

Also Available from
Shiloh Run Press. . .

Brentwood's Ward

Unabridged Audiobook